THE
KING OF THE
CRAGS

THE
KING OF THE CRAGS

THE
MEMORY OF FLAMES,
BOOK II

STEPHEN DEAS

A ROC BOOK

ROC
Published by New American Library, a division of
Penguin Group (USA) Inc., 375 Hudson Street,
New York, New York 10014, USA
Penguin Group (Canada), 90 Eglinton Avenue East, Suite 700, Toronto,
Ontario M4P 2Y3, Canada (a division of Pearson Penguin Canada Inc.)
Penguin Books Ltd., 80 Strand, London WC2R 0RL, England
Penguin Ireland, 25 St. Stephen's Green, Dublin 2,
Ireland (a division of Penguin Books Ltd.)
Penguin Group (Australia), 250 Camberwell Road, Camberwell, Victoria 3124,
Australia (a division of Pearson Australia Group Pty. Ltd.)
Penguin Books India Pvt. Ltd., 11 Community Centre, Panchsheel Park,
New Delhi - 110 017, India
Penguin Group (NZ), 67 Apollo Drive, Rosedale, North Shore 0632,
New Zealand (a division of Pearson New Zealand Ltd.)
Penguin Books (South Africa) (Pty.) Ltd., 24 Sturdee Avenue,
Rosebank, Johannesburg 2196, South Africa

Penguin Books Ltd., Registered Offices:
80 Strand, London WC2R 0RL, England

Published by Roc, an imprint of New American Library, a division of Penguin Group (USA) Inc. Previously
published in a Gollancz hardcover edition. For information contact Gollancz, an imprint of the Orion Publishing
Group, Orion House, 5 Upper St. Martin's Lane, London WC2H 9EA

First Roc Hardcover Printing, February 2011
10 9 8 7 6 5 4 3 2 1

ROC REGISTERED TRADEMARK—MARCA REGISTRADA

Library of Congress Cataloging-in-Publication Data

Deas, Stephen, 1968–
    The king of the crags/Stephen Deas.
        p. cm.—(The memory of flames; bk. 2)
    ISBN 978-0-451-46376-0
    1. Dragons—Fiction.   I. Title.
    PR6104.E25K56   2011
    823'.92—dc22   2010039714

Set in Adobe Garamond
Designed by Ginger Legato

Printed in the United States of America

In memory of the Slayer of Strings

and the Bringer of Death to Small Furry Things

Rebel and Rasmus

The Kings and Queens of Sand and Stone and Salt

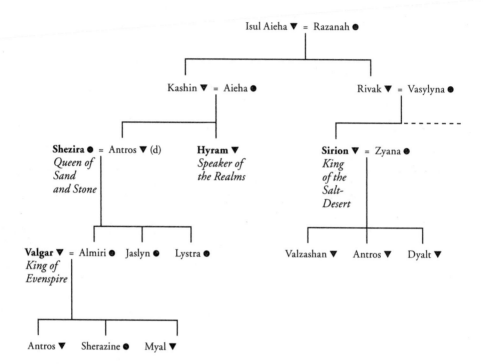

Isul Aieha ▼ = Razanah ●

Kashin ▼ = Aieha ●

Rivak ▼ = Vasylyna ●

Shezira ● = Antros ▼ (d)
*Queen of
Sand
and Stone*

Hyram ▼
*Speaker of
the Realms*

Sirion ▼ = Zyana ●
*King
of the
Salt-
Desert*

Valgar ▼ = Almiri ●   Jaslyn ●   Lystra ●
*King of
Evenspire*

Valzashan ▼   Antros ▼   Dyalt ▼

Antros ▼   Sherazine ●   Myal ▼

▼ Male

● Female

THE KINGS OF THE ENDLESS SEA

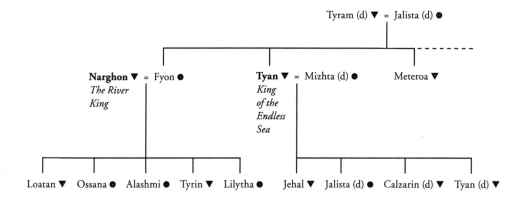

KINGS AND QUEENS OF THE PLAINS

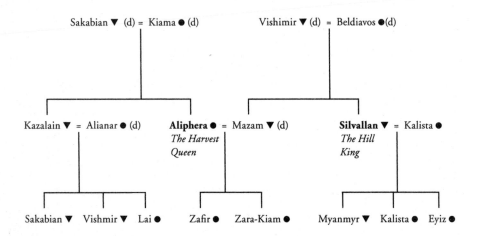

Sakabian ▼ (d) = Kiama ● (d)   Vishimir ▼ (d) = Beldiavos ●(d)

Kazalain ▼ = Alianar ● (d)   **Aliphera** ● = Mazam ▼ (d)   **Silvallan** ▼ = Kalista ●
                              The Harvest   *The Hill*
                              Queen   *King*

Sakabian ▼ Vishmir ▼ Lai ●   Zafir ● Zara-Kiam ●   Myanmyr ▼ Kalista ● Eyiz ●

THE KING OF THE WORLDSPINE

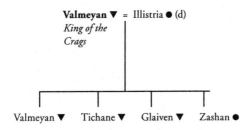

Valmeyan ▼ = Illistria ● (d)
King of the Crags

Valmeyan ▼   Tichane ▼   Glaiven ▼   Zashan ●

THE DRAGON REALMS

OORDISH MOORS

Bloodsalt Lake

Tipazhing Way

Bloodsalt

The Sapphire River

REALM of the SALT KING

Samir's Crossing

HUNG
Mour
PLA

Natta
Brid

PLAINS of ANCESTORS

The Emerald Cascade

The Sapphire Cascade

Lake of Ghosts

THE PURPLE SPUR

Hejel's Bridge

Lake Evenan

Ravenspire Road

REALM of SAND and STONE

Ishmar's Valley

Riverfishdale

Dragondale

The Silver Ringstone

Lake Laval

Sand

Oathwatch

Ravenspire

Dragonscliff

Deniasdale

Dragonsdale

Southwatch

Fardale

BLACK DALES

Ravendale

Ashdale

Blackwater

REALM of THE

THE WORLD D

REAL
HI

RE.

THE
KING OF THE CRAGS

PROLOGUE—THE DEAD

The Worldspine surrounded them. Mountains like immense teeth, jagged and huge and white, reared up all around their little valley. Monsters overshadowing the dense dark greens and blacks of the pine forest surrounding a lake of glacier water, the brightest, purest blue that Kemir had ever seen.

Very slowly, they were dying. Nadira couldn't see it yet and Kemir didn't have the heart to tell her, but it was true. He'd kept them alive for five days now, since Snow had vanished beneath the frozen waters of the lake, but it couldn't last. The weather had been kind to them, but wind and rain were always fickle in the Worldspine. One day he'd run out of arrows, or his bowstring would break. Or one of them would get hurt or fall ill. He wasn't catching enough food, and they didn't have the clothes or the shelter to stay properly warm. A hundred things could go wrong, and sooner or later one of them would.

They had to move. He tried to break it to Nadira, to make her understand that Snow wasn't coming back, that their only chance was to leave and head for lower ground. A boat, he thought. Or at least a raft. Water always found the quickest way down the mountains.

She screamed in his face. Shrieked at him that Snow *was* coming back. He backed away. One more day, he promised himself. One more day and then he'd leave, with or without her. He could force her to come, he knew that, but he'd let her choose. She could stay and die if she wanted. That was what Sollos would have done.

As that last day began to fade he made his weary way back to the lake, carrying with him what little food he'd been able to hunt and gather. The forests here were harsh and hostile and yielded little. He was hungry. They were both hungry. They'd eat and they'd still be hungry.

He reached what passed for their camp at the edge of the lake and the hairs on the back of his neck bristled. He couldn't see Nadira. The forest was silent except for the wind and the ever-present creaking and groaning of the glacier. He stared out across the lake. And suddenly he felt the fire and iron of the dragon's presence, a moment before the water began to churn.

Little One Kemir, I am hungry.

Kemir froze, rooted to the spot. The dragon was rising out of the lake as white as the glacier ice, clouds of steam billowing around her.

And she was hungry. *Five days lying at the bottom of a frozen lake would do that, I suppose.*

She was probably going to eat him, then. Somehow, he couldn't bring himself to be properly terrified. In some ways it would be a relief.

"Right. So you're not dead," he growled. It was just as well, he decided, that Nadira wasn't anywhere nearby. As last words went, those definitely weren't the best.

That was when her absence hit him right in the chest. Nadira. Where was she?

No.

"Alchemist's poisons didn't kill you, then. Freezing water did the trick, eh?" Why wasn't she there?

Yes. And no, I do not intend to eat you. I am . . . grateful . . . to you for showing me this place.

If dragons had expressions, Kemir hadn't learned to read them yet. The dragon's name was Snow, and as far as Kemir could tell, she always looked like she was about to eat him. *Come on, woman, where are you? You should be here. Your dragon's back.*

"Hurrah for me, then." He sat down. "So you're hungry. So go eat something." He couldn't keep it in anymore. "You didn't eat Nadira, did you?" He felt almost stupid asking. Of course she hadn't.

There was a long silence. *She was not your mate.*

"No! She's not my mate! She's my . . ." Yes, now that was a good question. She was his what, exactly? His friend? Don't be ridiculous. His companion? He grimaced. That made him sound like an old widow.

Your nest-sister.

Which made him laugh. Since he couldn't think of anything better, he nodded. "Yes. My nest-sister. So, *did* you eat her?"

Yes.

Kemir didn't move. Snow was joking. She had to be. Even though dragons had no sense of humor, even though Snow had never said anything funny about anything, this had to be a joke.

I was hungry. He could feel something in her, though. The same feeling as had been inside her when her Scales had disappeared. Shame, perhaps.

No, she wasn't joking.

The rage started in his face. At the end of his nose. A heat that washed slowly into his cheeks. "And that's what you do when you're hungry." Down his neck, growing hotter and stronger. He picked up a stone from the lakeside, jumped to his feet and threw it at the dragon in the water. It bounced off her scales.

Yes. And I am hungry still, Kemir.

Across his shoulders. "Whoever happens to be there. Whoever is closest. You couldn't wait. You couldn't hold it in. You couldn't go hungry. You just . . ." Through his arms. He hurled another stone at her and then threw up his hands in exasperation. "Bang. Gone. Whatever happens to be there. She was your . . ." She was what? What could you be to a dragon?

Food is food, Kemir.

There weren't any stones big enough to answer that. Or rather there were, but Kemir couldn't lift them. "What?" *Oh yes, that really told her.*

She was not your mate, Kemir.

The heat reached his hands, oozing down his fingers like lava until it reached the very tips. Then it all came rushing back. From everywhere. From his fingers, from his toes, from his arms and legs and chest and exploded all together in his head. He roared with rage and loss and sheer disbelief and hurled himself into the water, clutching his hatchet. "Why did you do that?" He stopped. He had to stop. He was already floundering in freezing water up to his waist. Snow was too deep to reach. He threw the axe at her as hard as he could and watched as it it too bounced off her scales and vanished into the water. He screamed at her again. "Why? Why did you do that?"

His words echoed off the mountainsides. Snow didn't move. Kemir pounded the water with his fists.

"Come here! Come here where I can reach you!"

If it is any help to you, she did not particularly mind.

"What? She didn't . . . ? She didn't what?" He clutched at his head and surged back to the shore, slipping, falling, lurching out of the water. There had to be something, somewhere. Anything. A weapon. Something to batter a dragon. He'd rip her apart with his bare hands if he had to.

She did not particularly mind.

He picked up another stone. Snow was coming toward him, very slowly, one careful step at a time. He threw the stone, then another and another, as fast as he could until Snow reached the shore. Then he let out a mad shriek and ran at her, hacking at her legs and claws with his knife. But no matter how hard he stabbed, her scales turned his blade. He beat on her with his fists and howled. "Why? Why did you do that?"

Because she was hungry. That was all. She didn't even have to say it. And now she was just letting him vent his anger.

Kemir backed away.

"Eat *me*!" he roared, and threw down the knife. He stood in front of her head. "Come on, then! Eat me!"

No.

"Why not? She was all I had left. My last. Come on, dragon, eat me too!" He picked up another stone and then put it down again and reached for an arrow. "Curse you, dragon. She didn't particularly mind being eaten?" He pulled back the bowstring. *Maybe if I aim for the eye . . .*

No, Kemir, she did not.

He looked down the length of the arrow to aim and met Snow, eyeball to eyeball, at the other end of it. *What am I doing?*

I was wondering that myself.

He took a deep breath. "You tell me, dragon—how do you know that she didn't *particularly* mind? Did you *ask* before you ate her?"

An arrow in the eye will hardly kill me, Kemir, but it would leave an unpleasant sting.

Slowly, Kemir lowered the bow. He could almost believe it. Nadira had been the one who'd made them wait while Snow lay deep in the lake. If it hadn't been for her he'd have left days ago. She'd made them stay because she couldn't let go . . . And he'd seen her, after they'd failed, after Snow had vanished into the lake. He'd seen her curled up when she thought he wasn't near, sobbing softly, talking to the children she no longer had as though they were still there, to the husband she'd seen murdered. The fight had gone out of her and with it all the light, all the life. Was that it? Were the memories too much? Was that why she wouldn't let go? *Were you just waiting to die?*

Waiting for her next cycle, Kemir.

He had tears in his eyes now. Now he thought about it, he could almost believe that Snow was right, that Nadira really didn't mind at all. "We don't get a next one, Snow. We're not like you."

And how is it that you are so sure, Kemir? She stretched her wings and looked up at the sky. She was thinking of leaving. Just like that.

"What if I don't want to come? Do I get eaten too?" The thought scared him. Not the thought of being eaten. The thought of being alone.

Would you mind?

"Yes, I'd fucking mind!" He put the arrow back in his quiver and then shuddered, shaking the dread and the emptiness away, back into the bottle he carried deep inside him. Anger was better, much better. He threw another stone at Snow instead, then another and another. "Why, dragon? Why did you kill her? Why did you do that? She wasn't much, maybe, but she was all I had. She was the closest thing I had to a friend. Shit!" The worst of the rage was gone, though, and he couldn't find the will to rekindle it. What was left behind was only sadness.

Why?

"She was *your* friend. Holy sun! That could have been me! What?"

Why? Why would you mind, Kemir?

"What?" He shook himself and then held his head in his hands. "Are you soft in the head, dragon? What sort of question is that? Why would I mind? Why would I mind if you ate me?"

Yes. Why would you mind, Kemir?

"Because it would fucking *hurt*!"

It can be very quick.

"Well, then because I'd like to be alive, thank you."

And why do you wish to be alive, Kemir? What will you do with this existence?

"I don't know!" He turned away and stamped his foot. "Get shit-faced, fuck whores and kill dragon-knights, that's what. Just as soon as I'm shot of you."

I know where your alchemists live, Kemir. I know how they make us weak. I will go now and I will consider how things should best be done. When I return, I will make a proper end of it. You will come with me. Your knowledge will be of use.

"Uh-uh. You go, dragon. I can't stop you but I'm not helping you. Not now." Kemir pursed his lips. He looked around the lake, at the thick walls of snow-speckled trees, at the frozen glacier, at the whiteness of the peaks above. "I think I'd rather stay here and slowly die of cold while I mourn. Tagging along, waiting for the day when it's my turn to be food? No, that's not my choice." *Really though? Could I bear that? To be left out here? Alone?*

Do not pretend, Kemir. Remember that I see inside you. I see fear. I see horror and surprise and a great deal of vengeance. Mostly I see loneliness. That is something I understand, Kemir, for I too am alone. I do not see much regret. You will not mourn for long.

Kemir sat down, shook his head and unstrung his bow. "That's because I still don't quite believe you did it," he said quietly, as much to himself as to Snow. He sighed. "*Do* I have a choice, dragon?"

There is always choice, Kemir. The Embers have shown you that.

He spat out a bitter laugh. "Yeah. Right. I can help you burn dragon-knights or I can die." He sighed again. "Well I'm not one for dying. So I'll come with you. As soon as we're out of the mountains, you do whatever you do and you leave me alone. Finished. Done. We go our separate ways. Find someone else."

As you wish.

He took a deep breath. "Snow?"

Kemir?

"If you ever eat someone I call a friend again, I *will* find a way and I *will* kill you. I don't care how much they don't mind. I don't care if they're positively trying to claw their way down your throat. Never again. Am I clear?"

You are clear, Kemir.

She was laughing at him. He could tell.

ONE

THE RED RIDERS

———— ⟡ ————

Out of the sun there shall come a white dragon, and with the white dragon a red rider. Thieves and liars shall quiver and weep, for the rider's name shall be Justice, and the dragon shall be Vengeance.

I

❦

THE PROPHET

He was running through a forest, between trees beside a river, wearing nothing more than a shirt. He was soaking wet and the water was icy. Here and there patches of snow lay on the ground but he didn't feel the cold. He was much more afraid of the heat. In the skies above the treetops, two dragons laced the world with fire. They were past rage, past fury. They were dying. He'd killed them and they knew it. They knew where he was too.

He'd tried to hide deep amid the darkness, beneath layer upon layer of leaf-shadow and branches, but they always found him. He'd tried to run, but the fire always followed him and the forest turned to flames and ash behind him. He'd tried the freezing waters of the river and the dragons had simply boiled it dry. Somehow they never quite caught him. He knew exactly why. They were slowly dying and so was he. When the trees ran out, they would all burn together. Was he afraid? He wasn't sure. Angry? Yes. Desperate? Yes. Willing to do almost anything to stay alive? Yes. But afraid? No. He'd done what needed to be done. Jaslyn would survive. The princess had been saved from the dragon. The knight had done his duty. Now the trees were running out and the end was coming, but no, he wasn't afraid.

"Stop!"

He felt the voice more than he heard it. It wasn't a real voice, not even a human voice. It boomed like a thunderclap, shaking mountains and felling trees. The air filled with ash shaken up from the ground and the dragons fell from the sky and were still. The forest and the river were suddenly gone. Where they'd been, only bare stone remained. Bare stone and a man, standing waiting for him not more than twenty paces away.

Semian stopped. He looked the man up and down. Long robes the color of blood. A craggy face. Long white hair and a long white beard, braided, that reached almost to his waist. Every inch a dragon-priest. Except for his skin, as pale as ice, and his hands, which were black and cracked, his fingers burned to stumps. And his eyes, which blazed with bloody fire.

"Stop!" said the priest again. This time the world didn't shake. Semian looked behind him. The old dragons were gone now. There was no sign of them or of the river or the trees, or even the smoking ruins of the alchemists' stronghold. Only the mountains were the same. Rising among them, taller than even the highest peak, a single massive crimson dragon filled half the sky. It lifted its head and stared lazily at him with eyes the size of lakes. Semian fell to one knee and bowed his head. The priest and the dragon were somehow the same. He didn't know how he knew, didn't know how that could be, but he knew it as surely as he knew the feel of his own sword in the palm of his hand.

"Rise, rider."

Semian didn't move. "I am dead, am I not?"

The priest said nothing.

"You taught us that we would join the great dragon whose fire is the sun. That we would be taken into that fire and our souls would be forged anew."

"You are not dead," said the priest.

"I followed with the other Embers with dragon-poison in my blood, and in our dying we did what we left our caves to do. The dragons are slain."

"No, they are not, and nor are you," said the priest again. "You drank the dragon-poison and you survived. You are one of us now. One dragon too survived. One and one, balanced against one another. A harmony of fire."

"I . . ." Joyful tears filled Semian's eyes. He felt the heat of passion explode inside him, filling him until there was no space for anything else and then growing still greater.

"You have always been a loyal servant of the church," said the priest. "You have always stayed true. Your heart is pure. Now you shall have your reward. Kneel. And remember. Remember the stories. Remember the myths. Remember the legends. Remember what only we priests and our faithful care to preserve. Remember the beginning and remember the end."

The beginning and the end.

Before there was time there was the void. Into the void there came the sun and the moon and the earth and the stars.

"And each created life."

The shifting stone-creatures of the earth. The moon-children made of liquid silver. The ghost-forms of the star spirits. And us. The children of the sun.

"Of the Great Flame."

The Great Flame.

"And each claimed to be the foremost of the gods."

And war and strife and sorcery shattered the land.

"And in the cracks of creation the dragons were born."

They tore the magic from the land. They scourged the earth with fire. They sought to return all things to the void from which they had come.

"For only then could they too return."

And yet through blood-magic, the children of the sun cheated the end of the world. Through alchemy they called to them the Silver King, who chained the dragons and stilled the restless void.

"Thus spoke the prophet with the voice of the wind."

Semian was already kneeling. He bowed his head again. The priest ran one ruined hand through the braids of his beard. It came out dripping red with blood. "Your reward for your faith." The bloody hand waved over Semian, spattering him, and then pressed against his forehead. Semian could feel the blood running slowly down his face. "For then the prophet's face became terrible to behold and he spoke with the voice of the desert. All chains break. Fire will sweep the bones of the world. Out of flames there shall come a white dragon, and with the dragon a red rider. Thieves and liars shall quiver and weep, for the rider's name shall be Justice and the dragon shall be Vengeance." The hand pressed harder against his brow. "Arise, rider. The end-times are coming. You have been chosen. You have taken the poison and you have lived. The white dragon flies free. The flames of destruction have come, and out of the flames the red rider shall be born. Be Justice, Rider Semian. Be the red rider and find the dragon whose name is Vengeance. Cleanse the world of its wickedness. Burn it away. Justice and Vengeance, Rider Semian, Justice and Vengeance. For I am the Silver King and I have set you free." The priest and the mountains slipped away into dust. Only the priest's hand remained, still there against his skin, and the voice.

Justice and Vengeance. Justice and Vengeance . . .

The priest's words echoed for an eternity, yet even they decayed. Other voices, other words rose up, drowning the priest in mindless chatter. Familiar voices. People.

Friends?

Semian listened to them as best he could, but his mind was adrift and nothing made any sense. Nothing until three words pierced him like a lance.

The Red Riders.

2

TORCHLIGHT

A rider without a dragon is a like a one-armed swordsman." Jostan was drunk. He was slumped in the darkest corner he could find of the worst drinking hole within walking distance of Southwatch. His words were slurred. He glowered at the table in front of him. The wood was stained and on the stains there were more stains. Where there weren't stains there were letters or, more often, crude pictograms badly hacked into the wood by a hundred years of drunken knights determined to leave their mark. "No. It's worse. It's like a no-armed swordsman. With no legs."

Beside him a rider was weeping. He didn't even know her name. She'd found him there, glaring in the gloom, and simply sat beside him. She obviously knew the place well since she barely had to lift her eyes toward the tavern-keeper to summon another flagon of ale. She was already drunk when she'd sat down beside him and she showed no signs of slowing down.

"I've got a dragon," she said suddenly. "I didn't use to have a dragon, but I've got one now."

"I *used* to have one." Jostan sighed. "Then the Embers poisoned it. Now I haven't got one anymore. Princess Jaslyn was supposed to give me another one. But she's gone away." Gone away having virtually dismissed Semian from her service. And, Jostan discovered, him as well, almost as an afterthought. Whatever Semian had said, apparently, had been spoken for them both.

Stupid little girl. That was what she was, after all. Almost a girl. To think he'd held a torch for her not long ago. And there was another thing. What was he thinking? A rider from a nothing family and a dragon-princess? *I must have been wearing my stupid-cap.*

"She used to look at me, though," he mumbled. Little looks that made him wonder; and then Knight-Marshal Nastria had sent him with her to the alchemists and the dragons had come and burned everything and he'd held her in his arms, stopping her from running into the flames, and she'd liked it. For a moment at least, she'd liked it.

Or that was what he'd thought. Maybe he was fooling himself. Deluded. She was made of the same heartless flint as her mother. "No dragon. Thrown away. Semian's no better. Spent days sitting with him trying to make him not die and now that he's come back, he's gone crazy. Had some stupid vision while he was in his coma and now all he talks about is the Great Flame and the Red Riders."

The rider beside him lifted her head and turned toward him. "Red Riders? You know where they are?"

Jostan shook his head. "No. No idea."

The other rider slumped and promptly lost interest in him again.

"Semian says we have to find them and join them. Says that's where he's meant to be. Not that he's got a dragon either. Fat lot of use either of us would be. Justice and Vengeance without any dragons." He spat on the floor. "I suppose we could tend the campfires while the *real* riders fly. I've done that before."

"Hyrkallan leads the Red Riders," slurred the other rider. "He's the greatest there is. Was there too. He was." Her head lolled sideways and she looked at him. "Who flies with the Red Riders?"

Jostan shrugged. "I don't know their names. The riders who fought their way out of the Adamantine Palace on the Night of the Knives. Knights who served Hyram or Queen Shezira. Who see through the speaker's lies. Her and Jehal. We could have . . . We could . . ." The thought petered out in disarray. *We could have what? Stopped Lady Nastria from trying to kill Queen Zafir? Stopped Queen Shezira from pushing Hyram off a balcony?*

The other rider slowly slid sideways, slumping against him like a sack of potatoes. Her head lolled on his shoulder. Jostan sighed. *That's all I need.*

"Can I come too?" She sounded ready to pass out. Jostan pushed her away. She grumbled and groaned but managed to stay upright.

"Leave me alone."

"But I want to come with you."

"I don't even know you." Jostan started to get up, but now the other rider grabbed hold of him and pulled him back down with all the fierce strength of the very drunk.

"Nthandra of the Vale."

Jostan sat slowly back down. He looked the woman carefully up and down, wondering if she was lying. *Nthandra of the Vale.* Everyone in Southwatch knew the name. Nthandra of the Vale, whose father was King Valgar's knight-marshal, whose brothers and sisters were his honor guard, whose betrothed was his adjutant. Nthandra of the Vale, whose entire family had died at King Valgar's side on the Night of the Knives. Nthandra of the Vale, who was said to roam Southwatch like a ghost.

"Nthandra . . . ?"

She fell across the table and then turned her head to leer at him. "You know what they say about me?"

"Your brothers . . . your father . . . your husband . . . They all died."

"All dead, all dead, all dead. So what else do they say about me?" She reached out a languid arm and stroked his cheek. Jostan swallowed hard.

"I don't . . . I don't know."

"Don't they say that I gave myself to the man I was to marry before we were wed?"

"I . . ."

"Don't they say that I'm carrying his child inside me?"

"Um . . ."

"Don't they say I'm a drunk who'll give herself to any man who takes her fancy as freely as the autumn wind plucks leaves from the trees?"

A strange feeling crept over Jostan, starting from his feet and rising slowly. A numb sort of paralysis. "I haven't heard such things . . ." He couldn't take his eyes off her. That was the drunk inside him, throwing care and caution to the wind.

"Don't they say that I lay with three riders in one night on the day that I learned my betrothed was dead?"

"I . . ." Jostan didn't know what to say, but that didn't seem to matter. Nthandra's face screwed up and she started to sob.

"When I'm alone, all I think of are the dead." The hand on his cheek moved to his shoulder and gripped his shirt. "Don't leave me alone. I can't be alone. Use me like a whore or hold me like a baby, I don't mind, but please, *please* don't let me be alone."

Jostan's tongue seemed to have swollen so it didn't fit in his mouth anymore. He had to work hard to make words come out. He took hold of her hand. "There's a place we can go."

The sobs went away and her eyes gleamed. "There are lots of places we can go."

"No. There's a place for forgetting." He staggered to his feet and pulled her up after him. She could barely walk so he put one of her arms around his shoulders and half dragged her away to the door. Eyes watched him go. Other riders. He didn't care what they thought. All the time he'd spent serving one mistress and then another. He'd nearly died, back in the caves with Jaslyn. Yes, could easily have died. *And what does she do? She throws me away. Whatever Semian said or did, I didn't do anything. I just held her when she needed to be held. When that mask of stone cracked for a moment. And the thanks I get?*

He looked at Nthandra of the Vale, glassy-eyed, head flopping from side to side, barely even conscious. She didn't look much like a princess, but somehow he saw Jaslyn's face anyway.

"I'm not just going to hold you," he muttered.

"I don't care."

You should. So should I. But he didn't. He took her to the door of another place. A place where drunkards lay sprawled in the street and two heavy men in thick leather coats lounged by the door. A place where he knew, from the smell of the air, that they could both forget.

One of the men stepped away from the wall and blocked his path.

"Rider." He nodded. Jostan nodded back, not knowing what he was supposed to say. The other one was standing straighter now, only pretending to be bored.

"Got gold?" asked the first. Jostan nodded. He leaned forward and fumbled in his boot, where he kept a few gold dragons. Nthandra slipped off his shoulder and fell gracelessly into the dirt. The men in the leather coats both laughed.

"You sure you need to go in?" asked the second one. Jostan shot him a filthy look and gave the first one a coin. That wasn't enough, so he felt around and fished out a second one.

"Gold," he said. The man nodded again and went back to propping up his wall. Jostan hauled Nthandra to her feet. She was gone now, completely gone. He took her in anyway. As soon as he walked through the door, the smell of Souldust hit him like a brick in the face. Souldust fresh from Evenspire where men freely offered it in the streets. Semian would never speak to him again if he found out, but as much as anything that was why Jostan was doing this. *You can all screw yourselves. I don't have to do anything for any of you anymore.*

Inside, he could barely see a thing. A single dim candle lit each room. Bodies lay strewn about, some of them sleeping, some of them sitting, eyes glittering in the candle flame, openmouthed and motionless. Some of them seemed to be naked, but in the darkness he couldn't be sure. From a few rooms deeper in came the grunts and moans of some couple. Here and there, as he stepped over legs and arms, faces glanced up at him. They were all empty. Empty, yes, and he wanted to be exactly like them.

He eventually found a room that was a bit less crowded than the rest, where there was space to sit down. This was where the sounds of the man and the woman were coming from, growing louder as they slowly approached their climax. The air smelled of sweat and musk. Only, as he realized after a few minutes, it wasn't a man and a woman but a man and another man. They ignored him, lost in their own world, and Jostan did the same. He propped Nthandra up beside him and held her tight, sucking in deep breaths of the dust-laden air. It didn't take long before the drug and the gallon of ale he had inside him took him away, far away.

Sometime in the night he became aware of something moving, and then a sensation of exquisite pleasure. He wasn't sure when he opened his eyes, for the candles had long gone out and the room was as black as pitch. Filled with snores too. Something soft brushed his lips. His skin was tingling, his heart thumping. He was intensely, painfully aroused. As he shifted, he realized that someone had their hand in his trousers.

He jumped, thinking of the two men who'd been there when they'd come in earlier.

"Shhh."

Nthandra pressed her lips to his, while her hand continued to work. Jostan moaned.

"Did you mean what you said?" she whispered. "About the Red Riders?"

His hand reached out and touched skin. As he explored her, he found she was almost naked, her clothes hanging loosely, every button and fastening open. He reached between her legs, but she batted him away.

"Did you mean what you said?"

"Yes," he said. "But I don't have a dragon."

"But you can find them."

"Yes." He had no idea how, but it was the answer she wanted and that was enough.

"*I* have a dragon," she breathed.

3

WHAT A DRAGON COSTS

Deep among the dry pine valleys that edged up to the Worldspine north of the Purple Spur, Hyrkallan watched two dragons land. One of them he knew because it was his own: B'thannan, an immense war-dragon who could make the earth shake merely by looking at it. The other one was a stranger, a long slender hunter. An unexpected stranger at that. Hyrkallan watched from a distance, always cautious until he was sure there was no trick. He sniffed the air, sweet with resin and fallen needles. Then he crept cautiously out from the undergrowth. As he came closer, his back straightened, his strides grew longer and he lowered the heavy crossbow he had gripped to his chest.

"Knight-Marshal!" One of the riders on the back of B'thannan had spotted him. Hyrkallan squinted. There were two up on B'thannan's back, one tall, one short, and it was the short one who was waving at him. Shanzir. She always had sharp eyes.

He waved back. "Shan! Did the queen give us everything we need?" B'thannan was loaded up with sacks and barrels that hadn't been there when he'd flown off the afternoon before. Obviously Queen Almiri had agreed to his offer. He wasn't surprised. She had little to lose and a great deal to gain.

"Food. Weapons. Blankets. Everything," shouted the other rider. Deremis, his brother.

Hyrkallan peered up. Even though B'thannan was crouched on all fours, Deremis was still twenty feet up in the air. "I don't see any alchemists."

"Oh, *they* won't help us." Deremis slid down from B'thannan's back and ran over to embrace Hyrkallan. "Not their business, they say. In fact they wish us naught but ill and would have nothing to do with us." He grinned. "Good to see you, brother. I know it's only been a day, but it seemed it might be a very long one."

Hyrkallan let his little brother go. "These dragons have been more than a week away from any eyrie." He tried to smile. "I swear B'thannan has started talking in his sleep. Much longer and we have to go back. Almiri must know that. If we cannot shelter in any eyrie and we have no alchemists of our own . . ." As if on cue, B'thannan lowered his head and swung it toward them. His head alone was as big as a horse, with teeth the size of shortswords. The dragon gave them a baleful look and then stared at its feet. The war-dragon's claws had already sunk a good foot into the soft earth. If it carelessly flicked its tail, trees would come crashing down.

Deremis punched Hyrkallan in the arm. "And the gracious Queen Almiri does indeed know this, and so behold!" He waved at the crates and barrels. "Enough of their potions to calm a dozen dragons for a month, taken in secret from the eyries of Evenspire!"

Smiling came easier now. Hyrkallan embraced his brother again. Then he looked at the other dragon and the three riders on her back. "And these?"

"Nthandra of the Vale and her mount. She lost many of her family on the Night of the Knives."

Hyrkallan nodded. "She's too young, but I won't say no to another dragon. The other two?"

"You know them. Rider Jostan and Rider Semian. They were in Southwatch until about a week ago, and then they seem to have decided they should come here. I found them prowling the eyries of Evenspire. They were with Princess Jaslyn at the battle of the alchemists' redoubt."

"Yes." Hyrkallan cocked his head. "I thought Semian was dead. What are they doing here?"

"Been cast out." Deremis chuckled. "Said something they shouldn't to Princess Jaslyn and she threw them out."

"Riders without dragons and one of them a stiff prick to boot. Still, I suppose they can make themselves useful. Right." Hyrkallan hauled himself up onto B'thannan. "I'll take us to today's camp then."

"Is it far?"

Hyrkallan grinned. "You'll have to wait and see . . ." His words fell into silence. Shanzir was pointing up at the sky. Hyrkallan couldn't see what she was pointing at, but it could only be other dragons. "How many?"

"One, I think."

"Then we'll take it." A lone dragon out here meant one thing. The Usurper, sending out her scouts. *And still stupid enough to think she can send them out one at a time. Well I'll thank you later for the opportunity to bloody your nose.* "Are you sure there's only one."

Shanzir shrugged. "No. It's coming toward us though."

"Right." Hyrkallan nodded. "Deremis, get the scorpion ready as soon as we're in the air. Shan, watch in case there are others. Hey!" he shouted across to the other dragon. Underneath all their dragon-scale armor, he had no idea which rider was which. Presumably the one sitting at the front was Nthandra of the Vale, if the dragon was truly hers.

The riders turned. They didn't seem to have much with them. Certainly no scorpion. Hyrkallan didn't bother shouting at them, but made a series of sweeping gestures, signs that any dragon-knight would understand. *Up. Fight. You follow, we lead.*

The rider at the front signed back. *Understood.* They must have seen the interloper too. *Am I the only one who can't? Am I going blind?* Best not to think about things like that or all the other fears of age, though, lest he start worrying about how long it would be before he couldn't climb onto B'thannan's back without taking his armor off first and having it handed up to him, piece by piece. He shouted at the war-dragon instead. B'thannan turned on surly feet and lumbered into a run, rattling the trees with each step until he launched himself into the reluctant air.

There! He could see it now. A war-dragon. A big one, still coming toward him. Someone either brave enough and stupid enough to fight outnumbered, or else someone with a friend lurking. He wondered if he should have let the hunter make its own choices, let it fly low beneath him and take the enemy from a different angle.

No. I haven't seen their faces. I don't even know who they are. It might be Nthandra of the Vale under that helm or it might be one of the Usurper's spies. No no, you stay close where I can see you. He shouted to Deremis: "Keep an eye on Nthandra's hunter too." B'thannan was in his prime, though, one of the best dragons in the realms. Hyrkallan was one of the best riders and Deremis was one of the best scorpioneers. He shouldn't worry. The Usurper's riders, *they* were the ones who should be afraid.

They came closer and closer. Abruptly, the unknown war-dragon turned and started to climb. Hyrkallan made as if to follow it up. B'thannan's nose came up . . .

"Hunter!" shouted Shanzir. Hyrkallan still didn't see it but he wasn't surprised. The Usurper's war-dragon *did* have a friend after all.

. . . and dived down again. Shanzir was wrong; there wasn't just one hunter with the war-dragon, there were two, both shooting up from the trees. An ambush, exactly as Prince Lai laid out in his *Principles of War.* Except Hyrkallan was supposed to be flying up right now, blissfully unaware of what was coming from below, instead of down, straight toward the ambushers.

"Go for the one on the left!" he roared at Deremis and veered B'thannan toward the hunter on the right. Hunters were faster and more agile, but not when struggling to climb against a war-dragon diving toward them. A war-dragon more than twice their size . . . Hyrkallan grinned. He could almost feel their surprise and their fear. The hunters both turned and started to dive back toward the ground but they were too late. All they managed to do was to expose their riders even more. He felt the saddle and harness shudder as Deremis fired the scorpion, and then B'thannan, all fifty tons of him, slammed into the back of the nearest hunter. Both dragons shrieked and then pulled apart. Except now the hunter's riders were in B'thannan's jaws.

And that's the end of you. Hyrkallan spared a glance for the riderless dragon as it spiraled down, looking forlornly for its riders and a place to land. Then he looked for the war-dragon. It was above and behind him, wings tucked in, hurtling toward him. Trying to do to him what he'd done to the hunters.

Except that doesn't work when my dragon's bigger than yours. Doubtless whoever was on the war-dragon expected B'thannan to dive and run and for the fight to turn into a chase, but Hyrkallan was having none of that. He turned B'thannan sharply in the air, facing his enemy head-on. He didn't have time to pick up much speed, but even war-dragons had some sense of self-preservation. They both swerved and passed each other close enough to touch, belly to belly; claws and jaws and tails reached around each other, trying and failing to get at the other's riders.

They flew apart. Hyrkallan glanced over his shoulder. *First I ruin your ambush, then I even the odds and now I have the heights. You must be wondering who it is you're facing. I am Hyrkallan, dragon-master of the north! Winner of the tournament a decade ago when Hyram took the Speaker's Ring. And a decade before that as well, when it was Iyanza.* He felt his harness shudder again as Deremis loosed another scorpion. B'thannan turned and Hyrkallan saw Nthandra of the Vale swoop past the enemy dragon. She raked it with fire, and then her hunter managed to wrap its tail around one of the war-dragon's riders and pull, and its whole harness fell apart. For a moment everything that had been on the back of the war-dragon hung in the air, one end still held fast, the other hanging from the hunting-dragon's tail. Riders, scorpions, saddle, everything, all of it stretched out in a line, dangling in the air.

For a moment. Then the dragons pulled apart, the line went taut and snapped, and everything fell in a lazy cloud of pieces toward the ground.

That's that then. The last of the enemy dragons, the second hunter, was already skimming away. B'thannan would never catch it and he wasn't about to risk Nthandra. Not after a victory like this. Let the Usurper hear all about it. Let her send out ever more scouts to look for him.

The war-dragon was heading for the ground now. Nthandra was following it down. She had every right, since she'd made the kill. Hyrkallan tipped B'thannan skyward once more. Let her pick up the grounded dragons while he flew circles overhead, watching in case the hunter came back.

"It's a good day!" he bellowed back to Deremis. "Three new riders and now three new dragons. That's twenty wings we have now. We'll have to start our own eyrie soon!" He laughed. Deremis and Shanzir didn't answer, but that was probably because they hadn't heard him over the noise of the wind. Or else they *had*, and *he* hadn't heard *them*. He let his eyes scan the skies one last time, then turned back to them.

Not the wind. Deremis was sprawled away from the scorpion, speared by a shaft half the length of a man. It had gone right through him and nicked at Shanzir as well, caught her in the top of the thigh. Blood was everywhere. Hyrkallan blinked, as if that might somehow make the blood and the scorpion bolt go away. *Deremis? My brother?* He couldn't see properly. For a moment he didn't know why. Then he understood. His brother was dead. He couldn't see because his eyes had filled with tears.

"Shanzir!" He put a hand on her shoulder and shook.

He didn't hear her, but she moved an arm, made a jerky gesture to tell him that she was hurt, and badly, but that she wasn't about to die. He promptly forgot about her and stretched out past her for his brother.

"Deremis!" Their harnesses held them both too tightly for him to reach. He couldn't even see his brother's face, hidden behind his helm.

He hadn't seen the enemy riders fire their scorpion. Couldn't even think when it had happened. He shook his head. They must have fired as the two dragons passed and pulled apart. He'd felt the shudder as Deremis had fired. They must have fired back.

He shivered. A foot to the left and Deremis would have been alive and Shanzir dead. A foot the other way and perhaps he himself would have been hit. Two or three feet and they'd all be alive. Two dragons passing at speed, in such a way . . . A desperate piece of luck to hit a rider like that, and yet there was his brother, right in front of him. Dead.

Below, Nthandra of the Vale circled over the riderless war-dragon. Someone was going to have to bring that one home without a harness. Most riders tried that once, when they were young and stupid and thought they were immortal. Most of them didn't try it again.

I'd do it. Hyrkallan reached out for his brother again. *I'd do it for you.* But Shanzir was hurt and someone had to fly B'thannan. As he watched, Nthandra looped her hunter through the air, dived and almost landed on the war-dragon's back. She pulled up at the last possible moment, and as she did, one of the riders with her jumped. He landed on the war-dragon's back and somehow managed to stay there. Nthandra made one more pass and then flew on, chasing the fallen hunter.

You'd do that, would you, old man? He could almost hear Deremis laughing at him. *You'd do that? I seem to remember you tried the same thing twenty-five years ago, before you went fat and half blind. You slid off, broke one arm and three ribs and almost got trampled if I remember it right. We were all very impressed. After we'd finished laughing at you.*

"I didn't see any of the rest of you try." Hyrkallan swallowed hard. Up here, where no one could see, he could afford to shed a tear and whisper words to the dead. Up here, but not on the ground. *There will be a pyre, my brother. We'll send you on your way as though you were a king. We'll sing your name and send you to the ancestors, and then I swear to you, one way or the other, I'll bring this Usurper to her knees.*

Later, back among the rest of the Red Riders, Hyrkallan took his brother's armor. They burned his body and sang old songs of battle and victory and loss. After that, Hyrkallan gave them leave to celebrate what they'd gained. Three dragons, three riders, an alliance with Almiri's eyries and a bloody nose for Zafir. Enough to make any young rider drunk with excitement.

He left them to it and slipped away. Without Deremis, their victories felt hollow. Others might have drunk themselves into a stupor or lost themselves in Souldust, but Hyrkallan had no use for such things. Instead he sat alone in his tent, still and straight, and recited the names of all the riders who had died on the Night of the Knives, all the riders killed by the Adamantine Men on the Usurper's order. He added his brother's name to the list, and then did what he did every night. Planned Speaker Zafir's downfall in fierce detail, step by step by step by bloody step.

4

THE BLOOD-MAGE

Jostan hadn't brought a tent with him. He hadn't brought a bedroll or any blankets either, or indeed anything that might have been useful. Semian was no better off. Nthandra had some blankets but no tent. They ended up, all three of them, in the tent that had belonged to Hyrkallan's brother simply because it was there, and because Deremis didn't need it anymore. They watched Deremis burn. Hyrkallan and some of the other riders sang songs and Jostan sang with them. Nthandra stared at the fire. On and off she wept. Thinking of Deremis perhaps, but more likely of all the menfolk she'd lost. From time to time Jostan wondered where he was. He had almost no idea. They'd crossed the Great Cliff and the Silver River valley and then veered west and then south again. Somewhere near the merging of the Purple Spur and the Worldspine. That was about as close as he could guess. Somewhere in the mountains.

Semian stared at the fire as well. Jostan had no idea what *he* was thinking at all.

When the first flash of the burning was done, Hyrkallan stood up and with a simple gesture he silenced them all. He raised a drinking horn. "To Deremis, my brother. Another brave and noble and honest rider slain." He emptied his horn. "I will mourn him as a kinsman should, but *you* should not. We are at war, and in war the noble and the brave die. We will be the spark that ignites the realms. We have a victory today. Three dragons gained and three new riders too. That is how my brother should be remembered. So I give you another toast, one to celebrate. I give you Queen Shezira and King Valgar, freed from the dungeons of the Adamantine Palace. I give you Speaker Zafir's headless corpse rotting on a rope!" He raised his horn a second time. "So warm yourselves at my brother's pyre. Know that he died a fine death and that he would be proud of what we have done, of what we will do tomorrow, and of what we will do every day after that."

Hyrkallan threw his drinking horn into the fire, turned his back and vanished into the darkness. Nthandra started to sob. Semian stared at the flames.

"It's a strange day," Jostan muttered.

"He doesn't believe," whispered Semian. Jostan didn't know what to say to that. *Doesn't believe what?* It was hard to feel much of anything except bewildered, and perhaps a little pleased that he found himself with a dragon again.

Nthandra reached out a hand and rested it on Semian's shoulders. "*I* believe," she said.

"Oh, believe what?" complained Jostan. When Semian turned to look at him, Jostan wished he'd kept his mouth shut. In the flickering firelight, Semian looked demonic.

"Rider Hyrkallan does not believe in the name he has given to the men who follow him," said another voice, standing behind them. Jostan twisted around and found himself looking up at a nondescript man leaning on a staff. About the only thing Jostan really noticed was that the man's hands were scarred and burned and that some of his fingers seemed to be missing. The man with the staff was looking at Semian, and Semian's face had changed. The expression on his face was suddenly one of shock, and even awe. Jostan frowned.

"You do though, don't you?" said the man with the staff to Semian. Semian nodded. "The problem," the man went on, "is that Hyrkallan has no faith." He crouched between Semian and Jostan. Now the man's face was closer, it seemed familiar.

"I've seen you before," said Jostan.

"Yes. We both served the same mistress. I am Kithyr. I served Lady Nastria. I was her blood-mage."

Jostan felt himself turn rigid with a mixture of distaste and fear and anger. *Blood-mage. Abomination.* He half expected Semian to jump to his feet and reach for a sword, but Semian didn't even blink.

"Rider Hyrkallan chose to call these men his Red Riders because it's a common enough piece of folklore. Everyone knows the stories, little parts of the prophecies, handed from village to village, from generation to generation, a little more broken and warped with each telling. The red rider and the pale dragon. Justice and Vengeance. Mostly they forget the vengeance part. Yes, the red rider, who flies from town to town, bringing the wicked to justice for their crimes. Everyone knows *that* story."

"But that's not the true story," whispered Semian, "is it?"

"Names have a power of their own, don't they, Rider Semian." The blood-mage smiled thinly. "In the original revelations the red rider is the herald of the end of the world. The burning of everything. I don't think Rider Hyrkallan has quite such apocalyptic intent."

Jostan jumped to his feet. "Semian, why are you even *talking* to this . . . this creature? You *know* what he is! He *told* you!"

"We saw some blood-magic once," said Semian mildly. "Do you remember, Jostan? It was an alchemist who did it."

"The queen outlawed its practice! On pain of death!"

"And yet this man worked for her knight-marshal." Semian shifted closer to the blood-mage and gripped the man's knee. "I drank dragon-venom and I survived."

Kithyr nodded. "Most people do, actually."

"I had a vision!"

"Also common, I understand."

"I saw a priest. And a dragon." Semian seemed to see Kithyr's hands for the first time. "His hands were burned. Like yours, but worse! He told me what I had to do!"

"And what was that?" asked the magician.

Jostan had had enough. He was already half drunk and the last thing he needed was to listen to Semian going on about his vision again. "He thinks he's the red rider." Jostan spat. He expected the magician and Nthandra to both fall about laughing, but neither of them did. If anything, they both looked at Semian with even greater interest. "Did you hear me? He believes it. Prophecies, end of the world, he believes the lot. He thinks it's him." There. "He's crazy. And if you don't think he's crazy, then you're both crazy too." He walked away and left them to it. Not just crazy crazy, either. Dangerous crazy. Cracked. Mad as a bag of spiders. That sort of crazy. He looked back over his shoulder at the tiny circle of light surrounded by a near-infinite darkness. The three of them were huddled together as if they hadn't even noticed him go. Nthandra had draped both arms over Semian's shoulders now. She'd had her eye on him since they'd arrived, but Semian seemed oblivious. Close by, other riders sat and stared at the fire; around them, looming mountain shapes reached up to gouge dead black holes from the starlit sky. Some drank, others sang softly to themselves. Jostan knew a few of them, recognized more. Several caught his eye and gave him a nod. One or two waved him over to sit with them and share their drink or their sorrow. They'd all known Deremis. He was the first of the Red Riders to fall, and none of them, it seemed, knew quite how to take the news that he was dead. Jostan went and sat among them for a while, but somehow they were still apart. The Night of the Knives had brought these riders together and he'd missed it. While the Night Watchman and his Adamantine Men had put their brothers and their fathers to the sword, while Queen Shezira and King Valgar had been taken to be tried for treason, Hyrkallan and these few had fought their way out of the speaker's palace. With them, somehow, they'd taken Queen Almiri—Shezira's eldest, Valgar's queen, mistress of Evenspire and now, because of these few riders, the fulcrum to end Speaker Zafir's rule if only the right lever could be found. And Jostan had missed it. Missed it because he was with Semian and Princess Jaslyn at the alchemists' redoubt, facing something far worse, but he could hardly say that, could he? Hyrkallan's riders had all lost friends or family or both, and what did he lose? Nothing. Nothing and everything. They knew, of course. They knew he and Semian had faced the rogue dragons. They knew about the caves and the smoke and fire and the alchemists and the Embers. They knew that he'd shielded Princess Jaslyn and that Semian had taken dragon-venom so that, in being eaten, he might kill one of the dragons. They knew, they just didn't . . . understand.

They didn't care. There. That was the truth of it. They only cared about Zafir and that she had tried to murder them. Them and their queen.

When he looked again, Semian and Nthandra and the blood-mage were all gone. He stayed with the others for as long as he could bear it and then slipped away, back to their tent. Deremis' tent. He approached it slowly, quietly, not wanting to disturb anyone inside. If Nthandra was with Semian, well, then he didn't much care either way, as long as she gave him some warmth as well once she was done. He was beginning to understand how she felt. Anything, *anything* not to be alone.

Sure enough, as he crept close, he heard whispered voices from inside.

"I can feel it. I know it's there."

"Yes."

"I need to know. I need to know if I'm right."

"Yes." Jostan slipped closer. The first voice was certainly Nthandra. The second didn't sound much like Semian.

"It is true." Jostan had almost reached the flap of the tent. He froze. She was with the blood-mage. The thought made him want to be sick. He could almost see her, naked, straddling him while he pawed at her with his ruined fingers.

"Let me touch you." *No! Don't let him touch you!* "Yes. It is true. You carry a child within you. You carry a boy, Nthandra of the Vale. You carry your dead husband's heir."

"What do I tell the child when it's born? That it has no father?"

"Have a few years of joy with him and then see if perhaps the alchemists would take him."

"They won't. He has a bloodline. Even if he doesn't know it."

"You could give him to the Adamantine Guard. No one will care whether he has one father or ten."

"No! I'd rather cut his throat when he comes out of me than give him to Zafir."

"The speaker will be long gone by then."

"I said no!"

"Then tell him whatever you wish. You tell him that he carries all that is left of his father within him. Make him his father's son. Sit him on whatever throne is his."

"No one will believe me."

"No."

Jostan couldn't move. He ought to slip away, come back later, but he couldn't. He couldn't move forward either. He needed to see and yet was too afraid to look.

"Because behind your back they call you a whore, Nthandra of the Vale."

"He'll be a bastard. It's not fair." Suddenly she was shrieking. "We were to be wed as soon as he came back! I was unbroken! I never lay with another man."

The magician's voice softened. "It is unfair, but think of this son as a gift. Men such as he are often born to be great. Destiny has fingered your son, Nthandra of the Vale. Do you want him to be great?"

"Yes!"

"I can help with the hole inside too. With the helplessness, the hopelessness, the uselessness. I can help you make all that go away. If you want me to."

"Yes." Her voice was quiet now, sobbing. "Please."

"Which one, Nthandra of the Vale? I can do only one."

"The child then," she said, her voice so broken that Jostan could barely understand her. "I owe it to him."

"Greatness and happiness are rarely the same thing. You know that."

Jostan didn't hear what Nthandra said next. He wasn't sure if she even said anything at all. Then he heard the magician again.

"So be it. Will you give yourself to me, Nthandra of the Vale? Your body and your soul must be mine."

A real rider, he knew, would have heard enough. A rider like Hyrkallan or Deremis would burst in on them right now. He knew that. They'd kick the magician out of the tent and send him packing, either with a boot or with a sword. Nthandra might curse and wail and spit at them, but they'd do it anyway because it was right. Not because it was wanted, but because it was right.

And I am not like them. He silently turned and moved a little way away. Too far to hear their whispers but close enough in case they turned to screams. They didn't. After twenty minutes the blood-mage came out. He straightened his clothes, brushed himself down. He paused for a few seconds and looked straight at where Jostan was sitting, invisible, buried in shadows. Then he went away. Jostan stayed where he was—long enough, he thought, for the magician to be far away—but before he could bring himself to move, Kithyr was back and now he had Semian with him. They walked right past him.

". . . with this," said the magician.

"If I must."

"You must. Unless you are a charlatan like Hyrkallan."

"It seems wrong."

"Needs must, Rider Semian. Hyrkallan wears the legend. You must live it. Once you have her, others will follow. I can see to that . . ."

They parted at the entrance to the tent. The magician walked away for a second time and Semian went inside. The noises that began soon after were easy enough to understand. Jostan waited for them to finish, and then waited a little more before he got up and slipped inside. The air was hot and stale and smelled of Nthandra. She was lying tight against Semian's back. From the snores, they were both already asleep. Jostan curled up beside her, close to her because close felt better. When he woke later on in the small hours of the morning to find her pawing at him, he didn't even think of turning her away.

5

DROTAN'S TOP

We need a harness for the war-dragon." Hyrkallan's face was a mask of stone. Semian watched him carefully. The other riders had been up late, celebrating or mourning or both. He couldn't blame them for that; they'd all lost friends, brothers, fathers or lovers. Some of them were barely awake. Some had wept when they'd burned Hyrkallan's brother, but as for Hyrkallan himself, his eyes had stayed dry then and they stayed dry now. That deserved respect, Semian thought, to lose a brother and still stay true to your purpose. In a way, Semian was glad that someone had died. Not that he had anything against Deremis; he barely knew the man's name. But yesterday had mixed triumph and tragedy and spared him from more attention. He didn't want that. Not yet.

"We need ammunition for our scorpions and food for us. And potions," Hyrkallan continued.

Semian glanced at the piles of barrels and crates that he'd brought from Almiri's eyrie. Good for a week or two, perhaps, but they needed to fend for themselves.

We need to fend for *our*selves, he reminded himself. He was one of them now. For better or for worse, he wasn't sure. But he had to start somewhere. He was already slowly turning Nthandra. Others would follow.

"Since none of these things are going to make themselves, we're going to steal them. The Usurper owns a tiny eyrie on the edge of the Spur.

Drotan's Top. Understand this, though. There's to be no burning, no slaughter unless there has to be."

Semian pursed his lips and clenched his toes at that. *No burning?*

"We take what we want and we leave everyone alive when we go. We take their dragons, their weapons, their food, their potions, everything we can possibly use, but we do not take lives. Let the Usurper's servants live to tell of us. Let them spread fear."

That, at least, Semian could agree with. The Great Flame was coming. *Let them tell of us indeed.*

Hyrkallan had already turned his back, heading toward the monster B'thannan. Semian knew of Hyrkallan's beast—every rider in the north had probably heard of it—but he'd never seen it until they'd reached King Valgar's eyrie; then Deremis had come for his secret meeting with the queen, pledging Hyrkallan's support to her if she would pledge hers to him, and B'thannan's landing had shaken Evenspire to its roots. B'thannan was enormous, by far and away the biggest war-dragon Semian had ever seen, almost as long as a hunter but three times as massive. He felt small enough as it was, surrounded by a score of dragons that could crush him with a careless step.

A pity it's not white. The war-dragon he'd stolen from Speaker Zafir's riders wasn't white either. There weren't any white dragons. Queen Shezira had managed to breed one as a present for the viper Jehal but somehow it had broken free. Eventually the Embers had killed it by poisoning themselves and then being eaten. Or at least that was what people believed. *The white dragon flies free. The flames of destruction have come, and out of the flame, the red rider shall be born. It will come to me, somehow. Vengeance. And I will ride it.*

Any dragon was better than no dragon for now. He and Jostan had left Valgar's eyrie without mounts of their own and fate or destiny or perhaps sheer blind luck had provided for them. Fate would provide again, when it was ready. He mounted his stolen dragon and launched into the air with the rest of the Red Riders. This one would be called Vengeance too.

Hyrkallan led them straight to Drotan's Top. They shot between the white-capped mountains of the Worldspine, among sharp narrow valleys filled with trees until they reached the Silver River, a dozen dazzling threads of water knotted and twisted together and gleaming in the sun. Hyrkallan led them low, the wind wet with spray thrown up by the sheer force of B'thannan's wings, screaming past Semian's face. As the valley grew wider and the mountains on either side shrank to hills, they began to climb again. In the distance to his right, Semian saw the faint outline of the Great Cliff, the sheer walls of stone that marked the start of the Purple Spur. Hyrkallan changed course now, leaving the river behind to rush on to its doom in the caves of the Silver King's Tomb. They turned south, straight at the Great Cliff, climbing ever higher until they were a full mile above the ground and the hills of the Blackwind Dales stretched out below like the wrinkled old skin of some ancient desert mystic. Then the Great Cliff rushed to meet them. It ripped away the space below and suddenly they were shooting between jagged peaks of white-capped stone again. Through the neck of the Spur for an hour or more, skimming over thick carpets of trees and racing rushing water until the mountains fell away and so did the rivers, and they emerged on the other side into the Maze. Here they flew lower still, sinking among the narrow pillars and canyons carved from dry barren stone. No trees grew here in the warrens of the Maze, and as they followed the helter-skelter waters from the Spur downward, the air grew dusty and warm. Walls and columns of stone flashed by in streaks of yellows and oranges and reds, punctured now and then by black pits of shadow. Piece by piece, the stone walls fell away, first one layer, then another, then faster and faster in a blur until the whole landscape collapsed away and spat them and the waters below into the abyss that was the Gliding Dragon Gorge, the great rent in the land torn by the mighty Fury River below. They crossed the gorge, using it as cover, climbing steadily, creeping up to the cliffs on the other side so low that the tails and talons of their dragons scraped the stone. When they emerged on the other side, there it was. Drotan's Top, perched on a long flat hilltop overlooking the fringes of the gorge. Half a day of flight and then to war with no warning. That was the dragon-rider's way and it filled Semian with joy.

True to his word, Hyrkallan didn't burn it. Instead he brought the riders in to land. A small company of Adamantine Guardsmen saw what was coming and fled the landing fields for the sanctuary of Hyram's Tor, and that was that. No blood shed. Not even a sword drawn. Semian was disappointed and vaguely disgusted. The Adamantine Guard was supposed to fight to the last man to defend the speaker and the realms. The last ones he'd met, the Embers in the alchemists' redoubt, had understood that. They'd understood that even throwing yourself naked into a dragon's maw could be a victory.

He was still standing at the edge of the landing fields, scowling to himself, when a hand slapped him on the shoulder.

"Drotan's Top is ours. Not bad for your first day, eh?" Semian turned around. The hand belonged to an older rider. One with a very slightly familiar face, but no name to go with it.

"I know you," said Semian slowly.

"GarHannas." The rider bowed. "I served Speaker Hyram before he died. I know you too. Semian. You were at Princess Jaslyn's side at the alchemists' redoubt. You missed the Night of the Knives, but they say you nearly died anyway."

"But not quite. I was reborn."

"Lucky for you!" GarHannas grinned. He obviously had no idea what Semian was talking about. "There are a couple of riders and a score of the Adamantine Guard who've locked themselves in Hyram's Tor. They're trapped and they know it. The alchemist is in there as well. Everyone else is busy taking everything we can carry from the landing fields, but Hyrkallan's gone to get the guard out of the Tor. We need the alchemist, or at least his help, and Hyrkallan doesn't want to burn them." He grinned again. "They don't know that, of course. We'll threaten them with fire and offer them their lives if they surrender. Want to hear the old man? He's good for this sort of thing."

Semian shook his head, absently staring up at the tower. Slowly he dropped to one knee. "Praise to the Great Flame." He closed his eyes and murmured a short prayer. He felt GarHannas shift uncomfortably beside him. "Let the riders standing watch over our captives hear Hyrkallan speak. I will take their duty."

GarHannas nodded. He started to move away, but Semian shot back to his feet and put a warning hand on the other knight's shoulder.

"I'll give you some words for the soldiers you've trapped, though," he said. "You can tell them that those who are *devout* will be spared. Tell them that those who aren't will be given the choice: turn their backs on the Usurper and serve the Great Flame or they burn."

"That's not what—"

Semian ignored him and left GarHannas standing there. He waved to Jostan and Nthandra, calling them over. He walked to where the Scales and the other men who were now their prisoners sat, sullen, scared or simply bemused. "This lot!" He pointed at the Scales. "These ones serve the Order and the Order serves the Great Flame. They have nothing to do with our fight. Let them go. As for the rest . . ." He scanned the prisoners. They were all little people. Huntsmen and craftsmen and laborers and the like. No one of any consequence.

But that was no excuse. He glanced around. The other riders were gone away now, off to the tower to hear Hyrkallan storm and bluster. These souls were his.

"As for the rest! You served the Usurper. You are sentenced to die." He drew out his sword and counted them as he spoke. Eighteen men and women. Him and Jostan and Nthandra watching over them. Three riders. If they ran, some of them would escape. *That's what you should do then, isn't it? Why do you stay?*

"Hyrkallan said that we should let them go," said Jostan.

Semian ignored him. "Or you may choose a different master. Fall to your knees and pray to the Great Flame. Give yourselves to the fire and you may be reborn. You may live again. Refuse the fire and die now."

Nthandra hadn't moved. Her hand was resting on her sword. He took another look around to be sure. No other rider was close enough to pay them any attention. They were all busy with whatever Hyrkallan had set them to do.

"Justice and Vengeance!" Semian roared. "Fire or death!"

They didn't run. They begged and pleaded and cried and one by one fell to their knees, praying as Semian had told them to do. They were liars though. Semian walked among them, and as he passed each one, he laid a hand on their head and saw into their heart. One he found, only one who truly believed. The rest of them were liars, all liars. He wrenched the one soul worth saving to his feet, pulling him up by his hair, and pushed him toward Jostan.

"Take this one away. We'll deal with him later."

Nthandra still didn't move. She didn't turn away either. She was here for revenge. They all were. *And the Flame is with me. Masked as a blood-mage, but I know who you are really are, and you promised Nthandra would be the first. So we will see . . .*

He went back to walking among his prisoners, waiting until Jostan was out of sight. *Two of us now.* The rest of them thought they were saved. He could feel it. *Liars. All liars.* As soon as Jostan was gone, he lifted his sword. *And now, truly, we will see . . .*

"Liars!" he screamed as his blade chopped down. "You're all liars! Burn in the truth of the Great Flame!" For a split second, as Nthandra drew her own sword, he didn't know whether she meant it for him or for them. Then she stabbed a man as he started to his feet and chopped the legs out from another, screaming at them something that even Semian couldn't understand. The others ran, but not far. The rest of the Red Riders nearby saw to that with bows and swords, mistaking the rush of men for an attack. When they were all butchered, Semian dragged their bodies into a pile. The other riders watched now, faces mixed with curiosity, awe and horror. As much as anything, Semian knew, this was a lesson for them. They were young, most of them, the ones that Hyrkallan hadn't taken with him to the tower. Young and scared and angry. Perfect for his purpose. Some of them had just cut a man down for the first time. Now they were realizing what they'd done. Justice, that was what it was. Hard, cold justice. They needed to learn that now, needed to learn what it would mean to follow the Great Flame.

When the pile was done, he called Vengeance. He climbed onto the dragon's back. From up there, he could see right across the eyrie. The bodies below seemed small and distant, not really human anymore. Semian closed his visor and Vengeance set the bodies ablaze. "The Great Flame reclaims its own," he shouted out. He closed his eyes and let the sound of the fire wash over him.

"What in the name of Vishmir's cock are you doing?"

Semian lifted his visor and looked down from his saddle. Hyrkallan was back, puffed and out of breath. GarHannas was with him, and two other older riders that Semian didn't know.

"What happened?" GarHannas looked sickened. "What did you do? They were common folk. They had no part in this."

Semian could only laugh. "We are all the same before the Flame. Did you take my words to the tower?"

"Are you mad? The alchemist, the servants and one of the riders have come out. The rest of them saw what you did and chose to stay inside."

"Then you should kill the alchemist for serving the Usurper, and the rider too! The servants from the tower can have the same choice as those we caught outside!"

"And what choice was that? Get down here, Rider! If you claim to serve Princess Jaslyn then I am your lord and you will *beg* me for mercy." Hyrkallan looked ready to climb up and rip Semian out of the saddle with his bare hands.

Semian spared him the trouble. He slid to the ground and spat at the old dragon-knight's feet. "We are the Red Riders, not some gang of bandits. You should know since you chose the name. If you don't have the stomach for holy work then step aside for someone who does. I'll lead them myself."

"You will not." Hyrkallan's fist landed on Semian's jaw, knocking him down. The other riders bowed their heads as Hyrkallan glared at them, one by one. Inside, Semian smiled. He'd seen their faces light up, if only for a moment. Here and there, embers smoldered inside them. Kithyr was right. He would have them. Today, tomorrow, the next day, the when didn't matter; he would have them.

He looked at Hyrkallan as the old knight walked away. *And he knows too.*

The common folk from the tower were as devious and insincere as the ones outside had been. Semian couldn't see even one worth saving, but Hyrkallan let them all go anyway. He let the alchemist go too. The rider though was one of Zafir's. One that Semian knew. One with nothing worth saving. Even Hyrkallan had to see that. Yet he was merely stripped and whipped and sent running naked away.

"We are the Red Riders," Hyrkallan shouted at the tower. "Take those words to the Usurper you serve! We will not rest until justice is served."

"Justice and Vengeance!" shouted someone else.

"Justice and Vengeance!" came another. Hyrkallan spun around, and the riders fell silent. Slowly he nodded.

"Aye," he said, too quietly for the men in the tower to hear, but the words carried to Semian well enough. "And vengeance, if justice alone will not serve."

They finished looting the eyrie, taking everything they could carry and use and destroying what they couldn't. When they left, the tower was still intact. *Let them live*, Hyrkallan had said. *Let them carry my words to where they need to be heard.*

Semian smiled to himself. *Yours. And mine.*

Hyrkallan led them back to their camp in the Spur, never straying far from Semian as they flew. As soon as they landed, he and GarHannas took Semian away out of sight of the others. Semian didn't try to resist.

"We've taken another three dragons." Hyrkallan's voice was a low growl. "Three more for the Red Riders, three fewer for the Usurper. Another victory. I will not mar it by a hanging. I know you, Rider Semian. I know you served Queen Shezira faithfully and well. I know what you did at the redoubt. So you will merely be flogged, in front of these riders who serve our cause, and we will cut you down in the morning and you will never disobey me again. If you do, you *will* hang. I'll tie the noose around your neck myself. Do you hear me?"

Semian met his stare. "Justice and Vengeance, My Lord. For the Great Flame never rests and neither shall its servants." Hyrkallan shook his head in disbelief and walked away. GarHannas and the two riders who flew at Hyrkallan's side took hold of Semian. He let them strip him and then lead him to a tree and bind him to it. He could feel the Flame, burning triumphant in his heart. The flogging, when it came, was only pain after all, and he was a man who'd been consumed by fire.

Late in the night when everyone was asleep, when it might only have been a dream, a voice whispered in his ear. A woman's voice. Nthandra of the Vale.

"I am with you, Rider Semian. I found the alchemist again, as we were leaving." A bloodstained knife flashed in the starlight to cut his bonds. "Justice and Vengeance, Rider Semian. I hear the words. Justice and Vengeance."

6

◦❈◦

THE UNBELIEVER

G ood things never last. Never did, never would. After Drotan's Top, the speaker had to answer. And answer she did. With dragons in the skies and . . .

The last of the soldiers was on his knees, gasping. He had an arrow sticking out of his back. Hyrkallan snarled and casually kicked him over. Before the soldier could move, Hyrkallan drove the point of his sword down into the man's belly. The soldier gasped and rolled over. It would take him a good few minutes and a lot of pain to finish dying, but Hyrkallan didn't care too much about that. Sell-swords were scum. The realms would be better without them. At least that was something he could be sure of. As for everything else . . .

Three weeks had passed since the heady victory of Drotan's Top. Three weeks of playing cat and mouse with the speaker's dragons. Three weeks of hiding among the mountains, achieving nothing, watching everything he'd aspired to slip away. Three weeks to wonder if he was wasting his time. To think that if he'd stayed in Southwatch, Deremis would still be alive. Three weeks and he'd lost three dragons back to Zafir's patrols and not one single rider had come over to his cause. *Three good dragons too.* Three weeks to wish the Red Riders had never been born. Three weeks to watch Semian's madness spread a little further every day. Nthandra, Shanzir, Jostan, Riok and the rest. The young ones who thought they could set the world on fire. He closed his eyes. Shanzir hurt the most. She was almost a daughter to him. She flew with him on B'thannan. She was his spotter. She was his scorpioneer now that Deremis was gone.

Best not to think about that. He kicked the dying man in the ribs and then left him to get on with it. Over on the far side of the clearing, Rider Hahzyan and the Picker had another pair of sell-swords and were stringing them up to one of the trees. As he drew closer, he could clearly see that the sell-swords were dead. One of them had had his belly slit open and his guts were trailing all over the ground, dirt and pine needles sticking to them. The other had had his head hacked half off. Hyrkallan was about to ask Hahzyan what he thought he was doing when another figure emerged from the nearby trees. Kithyr. The blood-mage. Hyrkallan stopped. He gave the mage a long hard look and a chill ran through him. *Evil. We're driven to this.* No wonder they were turning away from him. Now he turned away too. Best to let the mage get on with his business. Best not to watch.

Hahzyan clearly thought the same. Only the Picker stayed. The Picker was another strange one. Not a rider, like the rest of them, but he'd shown his mettle on the Night of the Knives. Hyrkallan had seen him kill two Adamantine Men. No mean feat for a man who didn't even have a sword.

He shuddered. The Picker was one of Knight-Marshal Nastria's curiosities. So was the blood-mage, and now the old knight-marshal was gone and *he* was left to pick up the pieces. Both the good and the bad.

They'd all fought and fled together. The Picker was a killer and the blood-mage was an abomination, but they were *his* killer, *his* abomination, and he was in no position to be choosy, no position at all. Except . . . except, did it matter anymore? The last news from Evenspire warned that the Usurper had called a council of kings. Zafir was putting King Valgar and Queen Shezira on trial. Hyrkallan had done what he'd done and changed nothing. He'd already failed, hadn't he?

The blood-mage set to work. Hyrkallan turned away and looked for a more comfortable face.

"Jostan!" Rider Jostan looked on the outside the way Hyrkallan felt on the inside. Disturbed. That came from spending too much time around Semian.

Jostan hurried over and gave a cursory bow. "Knight-Marshal."

"Take three dragons and search the area. There might be more of these shit-eaters. Take Semian and Nthandra up with you and keep your eyes peeled." There. That would make life a little more pleasant for the next few hours. A few months ago, Semian had been one of those riders who had his head stuffed so far up his arse that he could see out of his own mouth. And how Hyrkallan missed that Semian. The last thing they needed on top of everything else was a madman. On the surface Semian had been quiet in the weeks since Drotan's Top and his flogging. Done as he was told and not spoken out of turn, but he still had the insane fire in his eyes. He had his converts now too. They gathered around when they thought Hyrkallan wasn't watching.

The Red Riders weren't doing any good. That was the long and the short of it. After the Night of the Knives they'd been heady with amazement at being still alive, flushed with the success of spiriting Queen Almiri out of the palace and back to the safety of her own eyrie. There was rage too, rage at the Usurper who wore the Speaker's Ring, her and her scheming lover, Jehal. Justice needed to be done and they'd sworn, as riders of the realms, to do it. And what had they done? Nothing. Burned a few soldiers, stolen a few wagons and spent most of the time hiding. Drotan's Top, was that really such a victory? They weren't even worth the trouble of hunting down properly. Did Zafir the Usurper send riders? Did she dispatch the Adamantine Guard? No, she sent shit-eaters, and poor ones at that. That's what Hyrkallan's riders were worth. Nothing. *Because that's what we've done. Nothing.*

Nothing. Not because they were impotent, but because he didn't dare. Because Shezira was still alive, and he was too afraid to tip the balance of her fate.

He watched Jostan and the other two jog out of the trees toward their dragons. Semian was limping, almost hobbling. Someone had stabbed him in the leg. Quite a wound by the looks of it. He had been the only one hurt, but then, when they'd engaged the shit-eaters, he'd led the charge.

Hyrkallan sighed. The sell-swords hadn't had a chance. If it had been otherwise, he wouldn't have fought them on the ground. If they'd been at all dangerous then he'd have burned them from the air. They hadn't been anything more than sport. He clenched his fists. Maybe he should have burned them anyway. It would be no more than they deserved. But he'd needed something to fight and burning them from the air would have been too distant, too cold. He'd wanted to feel his steel crunch on the bones of his enemies for once. *Because you sold your swords to the murdering bitch who calls herself the Speaker of the Realms and I wanted to see your faces before you died. Because I'm mad. Table-pounding, chair-smashing, see-red mad, and Drotan's Top was three weeks ago and now Zafir's winning and I need to do something, anything, to feel like we have a purpose.*

They'd have to move their camp again. A nuisance but hardly a chore. With dragons to ride, they could find another place to hide that might be a hundred miles away. The Maze was huge, the Worldspine endless, and after a while all the mountains looked the same. No one would ever find them. They'd still be every bit as useless, though.

When the blood-mage was finished, Hyrkallan pretended he was too busy with his other riders and sent Hahzyan back to see what the mage had to say. In truth, he didn't know what to do with the abomination. Most likely what he ought to do was kill him out here in the woods. That would be the right thing to do with one like him, and most likely he was going to regret that he hadn't. The magician had been with them on the Night of the Knives but did that really give them anything in common? Likely as not he'd take the Usurper's gold if he knew what she was offering.

"What's the blood-mage got to say for himself?" he asked when Hahzyan returned. The rider looked pale. *Was it bad then? Glad I sent someone else.*

"The speaker has increased the price on our heads. Enough to draw in every sell-sword across the realms. She now offers her own weight in gold for every one of us. These are only the first. The Maze will be swarming with them before long."

Hyrkallan nodded, frowning. He wasn't really interested. "That's a lot of gold. Too much to be true." But then this was Speaker Zafir. Going back on her word to a shit-eater was hardly likely to trouble her.

"They have to find us first."

We should give it up. Go home, go back to our eyries. However much he tried to hide it, he'd lost his heart for this the moment Almiri had told him about the trial. Or perhaps it had gone when he'd lit the pyre to burn his brother. He could only see one future now. The Usurper would have her way. His queen would die and there would be war. He didn't belong here anymore. None of them did.

Hahzyan seemed to read his mind. "We're not wasting our time, Knight-Marshal. Every day, word of the Red Riders spreads further."

"And so what if it does?" *Red Riders. How I regret wearing that name.*

"Others have already come to us: Semian, Jostan, Nthandra . . ."

"Three riders, Hahzyan." *Two of them mad, the third fast heading toward it.* Still, Hyrkallan had to smile, if only at the blind enthusiasm. He too had been young and bright-eyed once. A long time ago, before he'd come to see the full measure of spite in the lords and ladies that he served.

"Three is more than none, Knight-Marshal."

"Semian and Jostan should have been with us in the first place. Semian has also quite possibly lost his mind."

"But he is a leader. Like you." And it was true. The more weary and cynical Hyrkallan became, the more Semian burned. When the time came, and it would be soon, he would tell the other riders what they wanted to hear. They would listen to him. That, if nothing else, was a good enough reason to end it while he still could.

They don't need me anymore.

"There is GarHannas."

"Aye." That there was. GarHannas, who'd served Speaker Hyram. GarHannas was, when it came down to it, Hyrkallan's one cause for hope. An experienced rider, well known, well respected and well liked. There was always the dream that others would follow, that GarHannas was the first, that the trickle would become a flood and riders from across the realms would flock to the Purple Spur to bring Zafir down. Not much of a hope, but it had given him something to cling to. For a while.

Who am I fooling? Kings and queens tear down speakers, not riders. I should fly home. Give up on this charade. Deremis haunted him. His own brother. *Killed because of this folly. My folly.*

He wouldn't fly home though. They were all too young, these riders. They needed wisdom. If he left them and Zafir wiped them out, they'd be nothing except more souls on his conscience. So instead he watched them pack up their meager belongings and mount their dragons and then he led them as he should, between the mountains. He took them north this time, away from the majestic dead canyons of the Maze. That's where the sell-swords would assume he was: on the south side where he could easily reach Drotan's Top and the edges of Zafir's realm. A dragon-knight would know better, but the sell-swords would think only of feet and boots and wagons and wheels, not of wings. Maybe that would buy him another week or two of peace and quiet. Long enough for the Usurper to have her council of kings and its aftermath. Long enough to see if anyone else would follow GarHannas. And when they didn't, long enough to talk Hahzyan and the others into going home.

So he took them away, a dozen dragons streaming in a line behind B'thannan, up into the high valleys where the pines grew thicker, higher still toward the snow line, skimming the treetops, keeping low to avoid the eyes of Zafir's scouts; then the dive over the Great Cliff, the mile-high sheer walls of stone that made the northern edge of the Spur, down into the valley of the Silver River below. Hyrkallan had been flying dragons for thirty years. He'd been to every part of the realms. He'd spent half his life soaring high above the endless Desert of Stone and among the dead peaks of the far north of the Worldspine. Even so, crossing the Great Cliff still took his breath away. The sudden *absence* of the world below gave him vertigo and in the dive that came after, the wind roared so fast it seemed it would tear him out of his saddle. Even behind his visor, he couldn't open his eyes but had to trust to B'thannan not to simply plow into the ground. B'thannan loved to dive, loved the speed. All dragons did.

He almost blacked out as B'thannan pulled out of his dive and arrowed above the water of the Silver River leaving a shock of spray in his wake. And then the moment was gone, the magic and the wonder, and he was left as he'd been before. Old and bitter. He led the way down the valley, back to a place they'd been before Drotan's Top, hardly even noticing the hills turn to mountains as they drifted past. He took them to the far end of the

Purple Spur, to where it merged with the immensity of the Worldspine. Far enough away that the Adamantine Palace was a full day's flight away. That was enough. So distant that they were hardly a danger to anyone but themselves. Then he watched them make their camps there, walked among them, helping them where he could. He'd keep them here, he decided. Waiting, watching, listening until they got bored. It was all in the hands of kings and queens now. Another week or so and he could put an end to this mistake and they could all go home.

He hadn't even put his tent up, hadn't even washed the sell-sword blood off his gloves, when the revolt began.

"Marshal." Hyrkallan closed his eyes and wished for strength. Rider Semian.

"Rider." He didn't turn around. He didn't want to even *see* Semian.

"Marshal, I think it's time you went home."

Now Hyrkallan did turn around. His lips curled and he laughed bitterly. "Really, Semian? You might be right, but you're the last person I expected to say such a thing. So what do you propose? Should we wait a little while until the others see the light, or has your little coven discussed this amongst yourselves already? Shall we all pack up and leave right now?"

Semian shook his head. "No, Marshal. *You* should go home. The riders who followed you here hunger for justice and vengeance. That is what you promised them. Yet you have not led them against the speaker. We have done nothing except flap our wings. The speaker barely knows we exist. Drotan's Top should have been a beginning and you have made it an end. Since then we've done nothing but wither."

"And you propose?" Why was he asking? Semian was as transparent as glass.

"Princess Jaslyn needs you. She needs a knight-marshal who will guide her with caution and wisdom. These men need fire and glory and death." His face was solemn. He believed every word.

Hyrkallan laughed and shook his head. "And do *you* mean to give it to them?"

Semian nodded. "Yes, Knight-Marshal. I will lead them to glory. I will lead them to the Adamantine Palace itself."

"No." Hyrkallan wanted to slap Semian for being so stupid. "You won't even get close. You will lead them to their deaths."

"Then they will be glorious deaths, Hyrkallan. Better than this."

"No, they will not, Rider Semian; they will be ignoble and barely remembered. You will all be gone and then you will be forgotten." And maybe the realms would be all the better for it. He turned away from Semian and tried to put the man out of his mind. Madness. Madness and death. That should be his mantra, not justice and vengeance. That was the way of the dragon-priests. If someone set them on fire, they'd probably rejoice.

For a moment he smiled. Now *there* was a thought.

7

THE PRICE OF ASKING

Jostan helped Semian out of his armor. Inside, his left leg was bloody down to his foot.

"It doesn't look too bad." Jostan scratched his chin. The cut was ragged but didn't seem too deep and the bleeding had already stopped. Jostan pressed a wad of cloth over the wound and started to strap it to Semian's leg. "It shouldn't give you any trouble when it heals. Not like the arrow that sell-sword left for you."

That spawned a moment of tense silence. Semian still limped from that and Jostan knew it pained him sometimes too. Maybe that's why he'd been so keen for a taste of sell-sword blood.

Semian spat. "This is absurd." He clenched and unclenched his fists. He'd be pacing as soon as Jostan was finished. "We should have burned those sell-swords. We could have burned them from the air or from the ground. Why did we have to fight them?"

"It felt good to do something at last."

"Maybe so, but we should have been fighting Zafir's riders, not shit-eaters. We should have been fighting them weeks ago." Jostan tied off the bandage and sure enough, Semian shot to his feet and started to pace. "We have a calling, Jostan. We must answer it."

"You know there's going to be a council of kings and queens. You know he's waiting for that."

"Which is *wrong.*" Semian stamped his foot and then winced. "We should be burning the speaker's eyries. All of them. We should be showing the kings and queens of the realms who we are. They should *fear* us. Hyrkallan has to go."

Jostan looked down. "Even the Syuss have more dragons than we do," he said quietly. "What's to fear?"

"Hyrkallan needs to go," said Semian again. He pulled on a light riding shirt. "Princess Jaslyn will need him for the war. I told him that. I need to find Kithyr. Wait here for me."

Semian didn't wait for Jostan to say anything. He pushed his way out of their tent and limped into the twilight. Jostan watched him go. *Hyrkallan won't listen to you. He knows you're mad. He knows you don't give a fig about what happens to Queen Shezira anymore. This is something else for you now. You and all the others who've forgotten why we fly together.* He could have said it too, and it wouldn't have made a jot of difference.

Nthandra ducked into the tent. At least Jostan could understand why *she* followed Semian. He'd given her a new family, something to fill the hole.

"Where's Semian?"

"Gone looking for the blood-mage." Even the word left a sour taste in his mouth.

"He was hurt."

"Nothing serious. The wound's already closed." Shanzir and Riok followed her in, and then Leistar and Mallizan and Joen. Semian's coven. No, they were the blood-mage's coven. Semian just gave him a voice.

"Is he here? Is he all right?"

"Yes, yes," Jostan mumbled and watched them sit down. They were all here for Semian, not for him. *But why? What do you see in him? Why do you believe in him so?* Shanzir still looked pale from the wound she'd taken when Deremis had died. She was lucky. If a scorpion hit you, you were dead, and that was that. Almost no one ever got *injured* by a scorpion. Jostan had seen the wound in her leg, and it was huge, even though Deremis had taken the worst of the impact for her.

The Picker and Kithyr came in last. They were at the heart of this, but Jostan didn't have time to think about that before Semian followed them in.

Kithyr cocked his head. "So?"

"I told him we should be burning the speaker's palace instead of her filthy hirelings. He said we wouldn't get close. *You will lead them to their deaths, ignoble and barely remembered.* That's what he said." Semian spat. "He's too old and too cautious. He doesn't belong here anymore."

"Is that what you would do, Semian, if you led us?" asked Shanzir. "Would you lead us against the palace itself?"

"Yes!" Semian's eyes flared for a moment. "Yes! Yes, we'd burn her on her own throne."

"The palace is defended by the Adamantine Guard," Jostan heard himself say. "With so few dragons we'd never get close enough. They would shoot us down."

The blood-mage closed his eyes. "Not if they didn't see you."

"And how could they . . ." *How could they not see us?* But no one was listening to Jostan. He wasn't one of them and they all knew it. They were all looking at the mage.

"How?"

"Is it possible?"

"Could it be done?"

Ripples of wonder spread among them.

Kithyr pursed his lips. Jostan felt a sickening smugness radiate out from the magician, but none of the others seemed to notice. "Do you know," he asked, "how the dragons were tamed?"

"By potions brewed by the alchemists," snapped Semian. "Could it be done or not?"

"You are wrong about that," said Kithyr softly. "The alchemists came later. When the dragons were tamed, there was only blood-magic. In the stories I was taught there were other magics once, but they went when the dragons came. After that there was blood or there was nothing. There were no cities of men, no great armies, not even towns. All that existed among what we called the realms were frightened bands of wild men who were little more than animals, hiding in the fringes of the world, in the caves and the hills and the mountains and the forests where the dragons didn't find them. And there were lost places, places left behind by the sorcerers who had once taught us our craft before they abandoned the world. The greatest among them were the three fortresses of the Pinnacles. And that is where the dragons were tamed."

"The Pinnacles?" Kithyr had their rapt attention now. The Pinnacles were Zafir's palace now.

"That was the greatest of our strongholds. Encased within the stone, the dragons could not reach us. We labored always, day and night, to find a way to tame them. For as long as we could remember, we had failed, and yet we labored anyway and always to no avail. Until the white sorcerer came to us, that is. He had no name that we could understand, for he was the last of his kind. He wore armor of quicksilver. He carried the Adamantine Spear. Where he walked, the dragons obeyed him. He did not ask our consent to rule us. He simply did. His commands were few, but if they were not carried out above all other things, he would turn a hundred men to dust with a flick of his finger. We called him the Silver King. It was the Silver King, not any mortal human, who tamed the dragons."

Kithyr paused. He fixed his gaze on Rider Semian. "There is always a way. In time, the Silver King took us to a place, to what has become the alchemists' redoubt. To the caves there." He smiled. "What do you know of the alchemists' secrets? There are certain molds and mosses and lichens that grow in the caves there, yes. The sorcerer showed us how to make potions from those that would tame the dragons. But there was more to it than that. It needed a sacrifice, you see. Blood. Death. A soul." He smiled again, this time at Jostan. "You've been there, Rider. Perhaps you know. The alchemists don't need blood anymore. Do you know why?"

Jostan, despite himself, shook his head.

"No. Because that is where the Silver King taught us his greatest secret, that anything and everything was possible if the sacrifice was right. Because we blood-mages learned that lesson well and there and then made a pact. We all gave of our blood and we bound the demon-sorcerer to our will and took his blood instead. We held him down and split open his skull and took out his spirit, which was like a luminous silver snake. I imagine he's still there, still bound by our blood-magic, still pouring his life energies into the potions the alchemists make to keep the likes of you in the skies. It was hard, the hardest thing we ever did. It cost us a great deal of our power, all of us. Look at us. Reviled and hated while our little brothers the alchemists, who were once our apprentices, rule over everything." He grinned. "I suppose you think that it is the speaker who wields the power . . ."

Semian stood up and loomed over the mage. "Can. It. Be. Done?"

Kithyr didn't flinch. He met Semian's eye with a lazy gaze. "My point, Rider Semian, if you must have it so soon, is this: If blood-magic can be made to tame dragons and to enslave gods, why, then yes, it can do a little thing such as make men blind. Yes, it can be done. But there would have to be a . . ." Kithyr pursed his lips. "There would have to be a sacrifice."

And here it comes. Jostan sat back to see what would happen. *How many of you are actually ready to die for whatever this is? Because it's certainly not going to be me.*

Semian gave a decisive nod. "Whatever it takes." He looked at Nthandra, who nodded, and then the others. They nodded as well. Then he clasped Kithyr's hand. "Whatever it takes, Kithyr, we will do. We will bring the speaker to her knees and burn her on her throne."

One by one they got up and left for their beds. Jostan watched them go in disbelief. Maybe the ease of today's victory had gone to their heads. Maybe that was it. Maybe that's why they weren't thinking. The speaker's palace was guarded by two hundred dragons and ten thousand Adamantine Men. In times of war, the walls and towers could be be lined with five score scorpions on every side, exactly according to the rules of Prince Lai's *Principles.* Even a hundred dragons wouldn't be enough, and the Red Riders had what? Twenty?

"Jostan, walk with me." Semian was offering Jostan his hand. Jostan stood up. He glanced uneasily at Nthandra and Kithyr, the last left in the tent. He never felt comfortable leaving them alone. The blood-mage had had a sickening interest in Nthandra from the very day they'd arrived.

Semian was tugging him away. "Leave them, Jostan. I know you mean well but she doesn't need your protection."

"She's not even old enough to be called a rider, not really." But he didn't resist. He let Semian push him gently outside.

"That's war for you."

"Are we at war?"

"Yes." Semian put an arm around Jostan's shoulder, something the old Semian would never have done. "We all loved Queen Shezira, but there's nothing we can do for her. We have to look past that. Zafir will execute her and nothing we do will change that."

As if you cared. "Rider Hyrkallan doesn't agree."

"Hyrkallan should go home. Jaslyn will need riders like him for the war. She needs riders like you too. And there *will* be a war, Jostan. The Great Flame has shown it to me."

Jostan felt something inside him break. "Are you sending me away, Semian? Are you telling me you don't want me here with you?"

Semian shrugged. "You only came because Jaslyn sent us both away. I know how you used to look at her. I felt the same way for a while. And yes, she's a princess, soon to be a queen, but in war who knows what could happen? The Red Riders don't mean anything to you, Jostan. You came because you had no dragon and nowhere else to go. Well now you have a dragon, and if you go with Hyrkallan then I'm sure Jaslyn will have you back. She will need every rider she can get. Please understand: I don't want you to go if your heart is here, but it isn't, and I don't want you to stay while your heart is elsewhere."

Jostan looked back. Semian was walking them steadily away from the tent.

"Don't tell me you want to be with Nthandra." Semian shook his head. "She's not right for you, Jostan. She's one of us. She's given herself to the Great Flame. She embraces the fire and the fire brings her joy. Have you given yourself to the Flame?"

Jostan shook his head. "I don't even begin to understand it."

"You see. You belong with Hyrkallan and Princess Jaslyn and the riders of the north. What we're doing here is . . ." He frowned, reaching for something. "It's something special. You were a good friend, Jostan, almost a brother to me, but do you see how our paths must move apart? And Nthandra has chosen too. I'm sorry for you that she didn't choose you."

Jostan closed his eyes. "She's a girl, Semian." Even more than Princess Jaslyn was. He wasn't sure which one he feared for the most.

"Yes. And I *will* look after her."

"That's not what I mean. I mean that's not why I'm going to stay, Semian. I'm not going back to the north, and I doubt you'll rid yourself of Hyrkallan so easily either. But even if you do, I'm staying with you because I remember who you are and because of what we endured together. Because you *are* almost a brother. Because I don't trust your new friend the blood-mage and I think someone should stay to look after *you.* Besides, who knows, maybe the Great Flame will touch even me given time, eh?"

Semian stopped. He shook his head and looked Jostan up and down, and for a moment Jostan thought he was going to get a rebuke, but then Semian smiled. "Then you're as good a friend as I'm likely to find and I shall be proud to fly with you. There may come a time when you wish to change your mind. You know you can leave whenever you want. We'll give you everything you need to get back to one of our queen's eyries. I'll even give you a dragon."

Jostan laughed too. He couldn't help himself. "You realize you're talking as though the Red Riders are already yours."

"Oh, they are." Semian was still smiling. "Hyrkallan just doesn't know it yet. He and the others who haven't been touched by the fire, they'll leave soon enough. But you can stay. I still have hope for you. Come." He tugged Jostan into motion again. "Whatever Kithyr and Nthandra had to say to each other, I'm sure it's said."

He was right: the blood-mage was gone when they returned. Nthandra was almost asleep, and as Jostan and Semian lay down one either side of her, she made no move to go to either of them. Jostan felt the weight of his arms and his legs and his head pressing him into the ground. A good fight was always a guarantee of a good night's sleep. The last thing he remembered was Nthandra's hand, snaking between the blankets, reaching out and holding his own, squeezing tight. She almost seemed happy. And then the darkness engulfed him and sucked him down into a place so dark and so deep that he thought he might never escape; and as he sank he dreamed, and in his dreams he saw his friend Semian, crying out against the tyrannies of the speaker. He saw riders rally around him, a few at first, then dozens, then thousands, and among those faces were riders he knew were his friends. He saw the riders rise as one and descend upon the Adamantine Palace from all sides, an irresistible tide of fire and scales. He saw the speaker and her lover caught naked and whipped; he saw Queen Shezira freed and given the Speaker's Ring. He saw the realms rejoice and sleep in peace. And amid the teeming happy crowds, through the endless celebration, he saw Princess Jaslyn, smiling at him, reaching out her hand. He saw everything that he wanted to see and he felt a presence at his shoulder, an old and wise and respected mentor whose name he couldn't quite remember, whispering softly in his ear.

Do you see? This is how the world should be . . .

The dream stayed with him, more real than the waking world, when Semian shook his shoulder an hour before dawn and told him to get dressed and put on his armor.

"I had a dream," he said. "I dreamed that we set the realms to rights."

In the moonlight he saw Semian smile, no trace of surprise on his face, as if he'd seen it all too. "Yes. And that is how it shall be."

Jostan dressed and then reached out to wake Nthandra but Semian stopped him.

"No, Jostan. Let her lie. Let her sleep. Come. It's time to wake the others."

In a daze he followed Semian from tent to tent. Everywhere riders awoke with a happy puzzlement in their eyes and spoke of dreams. They dressed as Semian asked and followed him until they all stood outside Hyrkallan's tent, waiting patiently. *I know what this is,* Jostan thought, and yet it was a dreamy thought, and one that didn't seem to have much weight. He half noticed Kithyr sidle in among the crowd, the last of them, pale and shaking and yet with a hungry gleam in his eyes. His head felt full of clouds. *Am I drunk?*

As Hyrkallan emerged, the riders watched him in silence. Twenty pairs of eyes followed him as he moved among them. Semian was in the middle, standing awkwardly, tipped slightly to one side from the wound that Zafir's mercenaries had given him.

"What?" Hyrkallan shouted, when he couldn't bear their stares anymore. "What?"

They were looking at him, not at Rider Semian, but somehow he was their heart. Jostan could feel it, even in himself. And the blood-mage, standing next to Semian now. Shanzir, Hahzyan, even GarHannas, who really ought to have known better. Hyrkallan was looking at them all, sizing them up. Jostan could almost read his thoughts. *Why did I do this? Why did I even start this stupid, doomed crusade?*

For Queen Shezira, Jostan wanted to say, to him, but his mouth stayed firmly closed. *For the queen you served for all your life, the queen you love more than anyone can know. Except me. I know.*

Hyrkallan threw his helm to the ground. "You want glory?" he screamed at them all. "Then do what riders have done since time began and serve your queen. You!" He pointed at one of King Valgar's men. "Go home. Serve your queen. When Speaker Zafir turns her eyes to the north, Almiri will need every dragon Valgar had. You!" He was pointing straight at Jostan. "Go home and serve yours. Serve Queen Jaslyn." Jostan blinked and tried to listen, and yet the words seemed to slide over him like water over a stone, never sticking in his mind, never quite heard. Hyrkallan clenched his teeth and a shiver of fury ran through him. "You!" He stabbed at GarHannas. "Why are you even here?"

GarHannas turned a dangerous shade of red, but he didn't move. Didn't speak.

Jostan bowed his head. Hyrkallan had gone too far. Even he knew it. Screaming and shouting at young blades like Jostan and Shanzir was one thing. Screaming at someone like GarHannas only made him look stupid. He'd lost them.

"Lead us, Rider Hyrkallan." It was GarHannas who spoke. None of the rest wanted him.

Hyrkallan shook his head. "No. I'm leaving you. I'm going back where I belong. Where we all belong. I'm going home, and I'm going to serve my queen by making the north so bloody dangerous that Zafir won't dare lift a finger against a single hair on Queen Shezira's holy head. You should join me." He looked straight at GarHannas now. "You can piss about in the mountains all you like, but twenty dragons aimlessly burning peasants in the Spur won't even get Zafir's attention. I'm going, and if I ever have to come back, I'll have the whole fucking horde of the north with me, five hundred dragons and fifty thousand men. That's where I should be and so should all of you."

Jostan was barely listening now. Hyrkallan shook his head in disgust.

Semian spoke so softly that it seemed he was whispering, yet his voice was clear. "Jaslyn heeds a knight-marshal. Shezira needed a knight-marshal, a proper one, not one who could barely hold a sword. A marshal who would lead and conquer, not one filled with so much guile that she was strangled by her own schemes. Lady Nastria is dead, and now you're going to have what should have been yours a long time ago. You would never have let this happen."

Hyrkallan's brow furrowed and for a moment he looked lost and confused. Then he shook it off. "Sell-swords. Shit-eaters. That's what we're worth to Zafir. She probably doesn't even know we exist." He grinned then and laughed. "If you really want to sting her, burn her eyries." He spat. "Yes, Rider Semian. Go burn her palace. If you can." They were all still looking at him in silence. "A pox on all of you."

They watched as Hyrkallan left them, great in his day yet now old and worn. No one said a word. Or maybe GarHannas had said something. Jostan wasn't sure. They all watched B'thannan fly away into the dawn sky and vanish, and then they stared, lost in thought perhaps, or lost in wonder, or simply lost.

"Riders!" The crack of Semian's voice jerked Jostan awake. He felt as though he'd been sleeping and someone had tipped a bucket of water over him. He shook himself and looked around.

Next to him, Shanzir almost fell over.

"What happened?" she whispered. She looked confused.

A dozen yards away, GarHannas held his head in his hands.

"What have we done?"

"Riders!" shouted Semian again, "Red Riders! Hyrkallan is gone. He has left us, but we remain. We are the Red Riders! We were forged together and we will follow our purpose to our death if that is what the fates demand. I say again, we alone remain! I will lead those who will have me, and we will take the fight to where it belongs. We will fly our dragons to the walls of the speaker's palace and we will make her burn! Stay or go, but do it now."

Most of them stayed. All except GarHannas and a couple of others, who milled around aimlessly, confused and desolate, only to be herded toward their dragons and sent on their way with rude haste. Semian couldn't hide his glee once they were gone. He stood with the blood-mage beside him and smiled, nodding. It made Jostan feel sick. *And yet I stay. Why?*

He couldn't listen to another of Semian's speeches so he stumbled back toward their tent to find Nthandra, only to be met by a scream. As he drew near, she staggered out, wearing only a shirt, her hands pressed between her legs. There was blood running down her thighs. Jostan froze; his stomach turned to lead. His face and his hands went numb. He felt distant tears roll down his cheeks. In a flash, he knew exactly what this was. *This was the sacrifice Kithyr had demanded.*

"Oh . . ." He couldn't speak. His lips were made of wood and his tongue tasted of ash. He reached for her and she recoiled, shrieking and wailing like an animal. Then she looked at him as though he was mad. He wasn't sure, through her grief, that she even knew who he was.

"The blood-mage. He did this." He shook his head. Any moment now he was going to be sick. *She's just a girl.* "I am so sorry. I knew . . ." He was shaking, horror and rage flooding together. *She's too young to be a rider.* "I should have . . ." *He was after her right from the start, from the moment we came . . .* "I'm sorry, Nthandra of the Vale. It's too late, I know, but I'll stop him, Nthandra. Whatever it is, I'll stop him." He sighed and held his head in his hands, then screwed up his face and screamed at the sky.

"No, you won't," said a voice behind him. An edge burned across his throat. His mouth filled with something hot and salty and he started to choke. He staggered and coughed and blood gushed out of his mouth. He turned and then fell over. He could hear singing. The Picker was standing over him, holding a knife so thin that you could see right through it. Or you could have, if it hadn't had Jostan's blood all over it.

"Suppose you should have gone with the others." The Picker shrugged and walked away, and all Jostan could see was the sky, fierce and bright. The singing was getting louder. He heard Semian somewhere far away, bellowing promises of blood and fire and victory, and then the singing swallowed everything.

And then it stopped and there was nothing.

TWO

OF PRINCES AND QUEENS

8

THE LOVERS

C an I kill your bride yet?" Speaker Zafir curled her arm around Prince Jehal and stretched her long neck, tilting back her head, inviting Jehal to sink his teeth into her throat. He duly obliged, nibbling gently at her skin. A few feet to one side of him was a bed. *Their* bed, high up in the topmost room of the Tower of Air, scattered with silk sheets from the silkworm farms on Tyan's Peninsula. *His* farms.

"That would hardly be wise, my love." A few feet the other way was a gaping open arch. More silk fluttered in the breeze. Beyond that, a tiny balcony; then nothing but air and the hard ground of the Speaker's Yard a hundred feet below. He liked it up here. For the view across the palace and the City of Dragons beyond and then the sheer dark cliffs of the Purple Spur and the glittering rain from the Diamond Cascade.

And yes, for the bed too. Although sometimes, when push came to shove as it always did when they were alone, he wondered what would happen if he pushed for the window instead. *Two speakers falling to their death in such quick succession would show such a lack of imagination though . . .*

"I was wondering whether to have her poisoned, or whether I should simply slit her throat."

Tedious, tedious. Jehal put on his best smile. How many times had they talked about this? He gave a petulant little sigh and stepped away from her, a little closer to the arch and the empty air. "Must we go over this again? Lystra is Queen Shezira's daughter. Her other two daughters are already riled enough. They have well over three hundred dragons between them and they want your head. The speaker is supposed to weld the realms into a unity of peace and harmony, not start a war. You should let Shezira and King Valgar go."

Zafir snorted and turned away from him. "Let them go, let them go—that's all you ever say. I'm beginning to think you're far too attached to this new family of yours. Let them go? Why? So Shezira can wage war on me? I'd rather face the skinny little rag of a daughter that rests so uncomfortably on her throne. So Valgar can stir trouble on my borders? Let his feeble-minded wife be the thorn in my side."

She was flaunting herself, letting him see the slit of her undergown, the long gash of naked skin beneath, all the way to the small of her back. She knew exactly what she was doing, of course. He felt himself stir. "Not so feeble, my love. She is undoubtedly supporting the Red Riders."

Zafir threw back her head and laughed and brushed her fingers over the silk sheets on the bed. "The Red Riders? Twenty dragons loose on my borders, and so far all they've done is burn a few peasants. If that's the best she can do then I've no fear of her. No, they're just loose ends that our idiot Night Watchman failed to clean up when Shezira murdered my husband. Let them brood in the Worldspine for a few weeks. They'll go home soon enough."

"They stole five of your dragons and they burned Drotan's Top."

"And I've already taken three of them back. They tickled my feet, Jehal, that's all. Drotan's Top was some huts on a hill. And they didn't *burn* it. They didn't dare."

"I remember your face when you first heard the news, my love. Dark and stormy as the Endless Sea."

She pouted at him. "They won't be allowed to do it again. The Red Riders are barely even a nuisance now. I'm inclined to let them be for a while. We can make some sport with them after I kill their queen."

Jehal shifted on his feet. "They make me nervous." *If I were you, I'd stamp on them. But I'm not, and sometimes it amuses me to watch you falter.* He smiled at her. "Hyrkallan leads them and he's no fool."

Now she yawned. "Then he'll know to give up and go home."

"Don't be so sure, my love. He might just burn something that matters first." He moved behind her and ran his fingers along the skin of her spine. "Show some grace. Let Shezira go. Let the cloud of suspicion hang over her for the rest of her reign. Let everyone wonder whether Hyram fell or whether he was pushed. The longer you hold her, the more your enemies will rally under her banner. Let her go and some will start to question her. Your Red Riders will quietly fade and disperse."

Zafir waved him away. "The world thinks Valgar tried to have me killed. I'd look laughably weak if I let *him* go."

Here we go again. "Fine, fine. Hang Valgar if you have to hang some-one. But let Shezira go."

"She pushed my husband off a balcony."

"No, she didn't. He was drunk and he fell, and you were glad to be rid of him. Not only is that something that most of the kings and queens will believe, it happens to be true." *Not quite true, actually, but that's one little secret I'll keep to myself.*

"I want Lystra gone, Jehal. Before she gives birth to your heir. Other-wise I'll have to get rid of both of them, and that means two assassins and paying twice as much money. Better to get them both together, eh?"

On some days the window called more loudly than on others. He growled, a mixture of frustration and desire, pushing the thought away. *Not yet.* "I am here, my love. Lystra is far away, pining for me no doubt, as any woman would, but not actually having me. I am here, I am yours and only yours. I haven't even touched another woman since you took the Ad-amantine Spear in the Glass Cathedral and became mistress of the realms." *Although the ancestors know how I've been tempted. More and more of late. I might start with your vapid little sister.*

She turned back to him and smiled. It always worked, appealing to her vanity. A hand reached out and stroked his cheek. "O Jehal, I find that very hard to believe. Is it really true?"

"You know it is, my love." He wrapped an arm around her waist and pulled her close again. "I have eyes only for you, no matter how far away you are."

"Mmm. Don't I know it." She had a lecherous look on now. *Almost done.*

"If Lystra dies, her sisters will see your hand in it, guilty or not. You've taken their mother, whom they feared. They grumble and moan and rattle their swords, but that's all. Take the sister they love and they'll fly straight for your throat."

"My throat or yours?" Zafir tipped her head back again. She shivered as Jehal wrapped his fingers around her neck.

"Both." He pushed her back, hard and fast enough to startle her, until she was pressed against the bedroom wall. *An arch to either side. See, that's how easy it could have been.* His other hand felt for her knee and then started upward, pushing its way between the silken layers of her gown. She gave a little gasp and pushed herself into him as he found the heat between her legs.

"I know how much you like to talk of murder."

"No. This is just the only way I know to shut you up." He tugged at the drawstrings of his trousers. Her hands moved to his, eager to help.

"Then I'm sure we'll talk of murdering your starling-bride again," she murmured. After that she didn't say much for quite a while. Not unless the squeals and moans carried some veiled meaning beyond the obvious.

Afterward, when Zafir fell asleep in his arms, Jehal lay awake. He stared at the ceiling of the great open chamber at the top of the Tower of Air. The walls around them were little more than a ring of huge arches opening out onto the balcony that encircled the upper level of the tower. He got up and went to stand in one, naked, teased by the wispy gauze of silk that hung rippling in the warm breaths of wind that puffed off the plains. Spread below lay the Adamantine Palace, the heart of the speaker's power. Four huge open yards, each large enough to assemble two thousand men, and overlooking each yard was a massive tower. The Gatehouse first, the oldest, the strongest and the largest tower in the palace, where the alchemists and the Night Watchman and the other senior servants made their beds. Then the vast space of the Gateyard, lined with stables and barracks. After that, the elegant Towers of Dusk and Dawn, black granite and white marble, the Fountain Court and the squat bulk of the Speaker's Tower, the place where the speaker and his or her servants traditionally made their home. Then the largest space of all, the Speaker's Yard, wrapped around the hulking misshapen tumor of glassy stone that was the

Glass Cathedral. After that, the palace became a little smaller. The Tower of Air was the tallest tower in the palace, but it was slender and lacking in space, a fitting monument to the vanity of the speakers. Finally there was the Circle Court, the azure Tower of Water and the City Tower. Proper towers again, fit for visiting kings and queens.

Around them all lay the palace walls. Not particularly tall, but they were wide enough to drive a horse and cart right around them. In fact there were several ramps to allow the Adamantine Men to do just that when they were putting their scorpions up. More than anything else, that was what the walls were for: to mount the hundreds upon hundreds of scorpions that would defend the speaker from the dragons of her enemies. The walls, as of now, were empty. Zafir hadn't seen fit to deploy her arsenal. *That would show the realms that I am afraid, Jehal . . .*

Jehal stood in the wind and chuckled to himself while his gaze wandered and explored the world outside the palace. Below the low slopes of the Palace Hill, the City of Dragons fed and decorated itself with the wealth and power that oozed from the speaker's presence. Somewhere down there too were the barracks of the ten thousand men of the Adamantine Guard. Past the city, the Diamond Cascade falls poured out from the peaks of the Purple Spur, the water falling so far that it never quite reached the ground but instead filled the city with a perpetual misty haze. The bottomless Mirror Lakes glittered and gleamed and rippled in the breeze. Beside them, the Adamantine Eyrie was currently filled to bursting with riders and dragons from the realms to the south. Very empty of dragons from the north. Through a different arch, the Hungry Mountain Plain stretched away to the south, to the chasm of the Fury River and Gliding Dragon Gorge. Beyond that, far away, lay the warm hills and valleys and meadows of Zafir's home, and then his own, Furymouth, and the sea, and beyond that, perhaps, the lands of the Taiytakei sailors and other places Jehal had never seen. To the east, the plains rolled and twisted into the foothills of the Worldspine, the dominion of the King of the Crags. To the west, they grew slowly more broken and wooded until they reached the Sapphire River and then rose sharply to meet the moors and bogs of King Silvallan's realm. To the north, beyond the wall of the Purple

Spur, the plains became the great deserts of sand and stone and salt that wrapped the northern realms.

He looked back at Zafir. *I stood here naked once, at the windows, when Hyram was about to make you a queen. Looking down at all that was going to be mine. If anyone had seen me here they would have known we were lovers, you and I, and all would have been lost. But they didn't.* He tried to look away but it was hard. Too hard. For all her flaws, she was still beautiful. *I watched you so many times, through the eyes of the Taiytakei dragon. I watched you writhing and moaning under Hyram, drawing him in to you, and I watched you make yourself sick each time he left. And I watched you writhing and moaning alone, just for me, knowing my eyes were there.*

So many fond memories. Below them was the room where he'd watched Zafir poison Hyram and then destroy him as cruelly as she could. Where he'd finished what she'd started and broken Hyram's mind. Where he'd struggled with himself not to throw Hyram off one of the balconies when he was done. Here, from this arch, was where he'd watched, that same night, as Hyram had thrown himself off another one right in front of Queen Shezira, spouting gibberish about kings and queens who'd been dead for decades.

And now . . .

And now he was slowly getting bored. He sighed and his eyes fell away from Zafir's skin. The Night of the Knives, they called it behind Zafir's back and to her face too. The night Valgar tried to have her assassinated and Shezira pushed Hyram off his tower, if you were inclined to believe Zafir's version of events. The night that Zafir imprisoned a king and a queen, the first time that a speaker had done such a thing in nearly a hundred years. The night that the riders of the north had fought with the Adamantine Guard and left more than a hundred corpses strewn across the palace. The night that the Red Riders had been born.

That had been a month ago. The next day, High Priest Aruch had placed the flawless shaft of the Adamantine Spear into Zafir's hands and her reign had begun. And then . . .

And then? And then nothing, that's what. More than a month of kicking my heels around the palace when I should be back in Furymouth, watching over my realm. A month of listening to Zafir bellyache about Lystra. A whole month of nothing to do except . . .

Jehal looked at Zafir's naked shape, sprawled out before him. *Well it could be a lot worse, and one must confess to having found a few diversions, I suppose.*

Above the bed, two pairs of ruby eyes looked down at him from the rafters. Jehal stared back at them. Two golden mechanical dragons, wedding gifts of the Taiytakei, imbued with magics that let him look through their eyes. Perfect spies and yet now he had no one to spy on. He had to wonder, sometimes, why they'd given him such precious things, and why he'd given one of them to Zafir.

No, that wasn't right. He knew exactly why he'd given one to the Speaker of the Realms.

He took another step forward, out onto the balcony until his toes curled over the edge. This time, if anyone saw him, what would it matter? The whole palace knew they were lovers.

This isn't what I wanted. I thought I did, but I was wrong. He glanced back at Zafir, watching her chest slowly rise and fall. *If I was speaker, what would I do? Bathe in the power, in the glory, in the knowledge that there was no higher place to be? Yet I see now that the view from up here was far better when it was forbidden.*

Shit.

Of all the things that might have happened, of all the things he'd planned for, of all the fates that might have befallen him on his path to this place, here was an outcome he'd never foreseen. He was bored.

Jehal walked back to the bed. He let his eyes linger on Zafir for one last time and listened to her breathing, slow and untroubled. *You understand, don't you? That's why you can't simply let Shezira go. Because then it would be over.* He leaned down and gently kissed her hair. "Have a care, my lover," he whispered. "Listen to your advisers, for they're no fools. And please let us not become enemies."

He picked up his clothes, quietly dressed, and slipped away.

9

A QUESTION OF PRIORITIES

Vale Tassan, Night Watchman, commander of the Adamantine Men, most feared soldier in the realms, bowed his head and waited.

"What do you mean, he's *gone?*" For a moment Speaker Zafir went rigid. Vale thought she might be about to throw something at him. Speakers came and went and Queen Zafir was the fourth that Vale Tassan had lived to see. If he'd been permitted an opinion, it might have been that the others had been immeasurably better. Since he wasn't, he did exactly as tradition and the law demanded. He bowed precisely as low as was required, ready for whatever orders would come his way.

"He has left the palace, Your Holiness," he said calmly and quietly.

"Idiot. Where did he *go?*"

Vale bowed again. The action was mechanical, a reflex honed over years. He didn't have to think about it anymore. "To the eyrie, Your Holiness. He went with most of his riders to the eyrie, woke up Eyrie-Master Copas, demanded his dragons be roused and they all flew away, Your Holiness. I believe they flew west, toward the Worldspine and Drotan's Top. What's left of it." Which put him heading toward the Red Riders, but Vale saw no need to mention something so obvious.

If anything, the speaker's anger grew. Vale watched, calmly indifferent. Adamantine Men were chosen almost before they could talk. Usually they were orphans or unwanted children of poor folk who couldn't afford another mouth to feed. Some were bastard by-blows of higher-born men, conveniently pushed away to a place where they wouldn't cause any trouble. In the Guard, blood didn't matter. Everyone was the same. Vale might have been the son of a king or a fool, but in his own mind he was a son of the Guard, nothing more and nothing less. He'd stood in shield walls with his brothers, the ones who managed to stay alive, for more than twenty years. Together they defied the strength and fire of the dragons. He might have been alone before the speaker's throne but he always felt his brothers at their posts and at their work, not far away. Queen Zafir's anger meant nothing to him. He waited, silent and still, for her to send him away.

"In the middle of the night." Zafir shook her head.

"At dawn, Your Holiness. They flew at dawn. As soon as there was enough light for the dragons to fly."

"He hasn't gone west, Tassan. He's gone south. Back to his home and his starling . . ." She hesitated. Vale saw it. Other words had been lining themselves up to come out and she'd bitten them back. Vale stood motionless and thought about Speaker Hyram. Hyram the clever and wise. Hyram, who had presided over a decade of peace and prosperity throughout the realms. Hyram, who for reasons Vale would never know had named Zafir, the least worthy candidate by far, to succeed him. And who'd been pushed off a balcony for his trouble. *He should have named the King of the Crags. That would have stirred up these fat, soft kings we have nowadays. A proper speaker.*

He pursed his lips. That was a thought he should not have had. Zafir wasn't looking at him though, so presumably she hadn't noticed. She was looking at Prince Tyrin instead. Tyrin was the fourth or fifth son of King Narghon and Queen Fyon, which made him a cousin of some sort to Jehal. So much had changed in the last month that Vale found himself alarmingly vague about who was who. Princes and princesses seemed to come and go and he was starting to lose track. He supposed he ought to care but somehow he didn't.

The speaker cocked her head. "And do *you* know anything about this, Tyrin?" Tyrin was a decade younger than Jehal and clearly wanted to follow him in every possible way. He was looking at Zafir right now; his eyes were stripping her naked and he was wondering how long it would be, with Jehal gone, before she came looking for another lover.

A muscle twitched in Vale's cheek. *Were they always so transparent?*

Tyrin licked his lips. "I went to the eyrie with him. He offered to let me ride with him back to the south but I declined. My place is here, Your Holiness, to serve you in any way I can." He half-smiled, half-leered. If Zafir couldn't see what was on his mind then she was surely the only one in the room.

"Why, Prince Tyrin, did he go?" Her face changed. An almost imperceptible smile, perhaps. A slight change of posture, a slight widening of the eyes, the raising of an eyebrow. Vale couldn't say exactly what had changed but the effect was electric. *Yes*, she seemed to say. *You might yet have me.* Even Vale felt it, though the look wasn't meant for him. Tyrin's jaw hung open. If Tyrin hadn't been sitting down, Vale was sure he would have fallen over. Instantly, Speaker Zafir had made him her slave.

He felt a grudging admiration. *That* was what a speaker did. A speaker ruled. *This is why we don't think*, he reminded himself. *We are the speaker's swords and spears, her shield and armor. Nothing less and nothing more.*

"He may, ah, be gone for some time, I think, Your Holiness." Which wasn't the question Zafir had asked at all but Tyrin's mind was too firmly set on one thing to be working properly anymore.

Zafir's face didn't change. No twitch of anger or impatience, despite her rage of only a few minutes ago. "Why, Prince Tyrin? What do you think will be keeping him in Furymouth?"

"He said he'd had a premonition, Your Holiness. Someone was going to die, someone very close to him, he said. He needed to go back, he said. To see if they could be saved."

"And who was this *someone*, Prince Tyrin? Did he say?" Vale heard the slightest change in Zafir's voice. A brittleness beneath the seductive softness. To Vale the danger seemed obvious. Zafir had set a bear trap right in front of Tyrin's feet. He wondered if the prince would manage to spot it.

"His father, King Tyan, I assume. They say he's been getting steadily worse ever since he returned home." Vale kept his face still. *Well done, little boy. But was that deftness or blind luck?*

Zafir pursed her lips. She sat back into her throne, lounging there with the same affected boredom as Prince Jehal would have done. And Tyrin too, if he hadn't been so on edge. "Very well. Let us begin then. Away, Night Watchman. Jeiros, dazzle us with news from the Order."

Acting Grand Master Jeiros, acting head of the Order of the Scales and chief alchemist of the realms, stepped nervously out in front of the throne. He'd taken a long time to adjust to his position, Vale thought, but was just now starting to act the part. His predecessor, Bellepheros, who should have lasted a good few years more, had simply vanished one day nearly six months ago. Coincidentally, on his way back from Furymouth. Vale supposed that Grand Master Jeiros had spent most of the first few months expecting his former master to reappear.

"Your Holiness," he began. He sounded confident these days. "We are continuing to audit eyries in an attempt to ascertain whether—"

"Yes, yes, yes. You're *still* counting dragons, trying to work out whether the one that got away died or survived." Zafir straightened and stamped her foot. "When you have an answer, I'll be delighted to hear it. Until then, I do not wish to hear daily complaints about how difficult it is."

"Your Holiness, if you would order a search of the Worldspine—"

"And give Jaslyn and Almiri an excuse to fly their dragons right up to my doors? They might *say* they were searching, Grand Master, but that would not be what they were *doing*. If the white dragon is dead then it has been reborn to an eyrie. If it isn't, it hasn't. As you are so fond of reminding us, the number of dragons in the world never changes, so if the white died of your poisons, you can answer your question by counting them. Counting, Grand Master, is surely not too great a challenge, is it? Even Prince Tyrin can count. So when you can tell me that one of them *is* still missing then I shall listen with more open ears. Until then, no more excuses, alchemist. Now bring me other news."

Jeiros paused for a moment. He was angry, Vale saw. That's how far his confidence had grown. A month ago he would have been quivering. The speaker and her master alchemist were at odds. In their own different ways they were the two most powerful figures in the realms. Things like that made Vale uneasy. As Jeiros talked about the rebuilding of the alchemists' redoubt, Vale carefully catalogued all the other things that made him uneasy. The Red Riders. Queen Shezira locked in the Tower of Dusk. Anything about Prince Jehal. The Speaker's Council—the council had long ago become a farce, that was worst of all. Three of the dragon-realms didn't even have a voice and Speaker Zafir was plainly bored by them. Now that Jehal was no longer present to entertain them with his wit, who would be first to abandon it? Prince Tichane, who spoke for the King of the Crags? Lord Eisal, who listened for King Sirion? Prince Sakabian, Zafir's own cousin? One of the others? The alchemists, perhaps? Or would the speaker herself be the first to go?

Vale, however, was the commander of the Night Watch, and so he would come as he was called and he would listen, even if it was to the empty walls. Today what he heard was the master alchemist of the realms explain how they were still rebuilding the redoubt where the Order made the potions that kept the dragons in check. He heard Jeiros describe in terse detail the damage that had been done by the smoke that the white dragon had blown into the caves, the current poor quality of the whatever it was that they harvested in there, their shortages of men and resources. In a very roundabout way, what he thought he heard was that the potions that kept the realms alive might soon run short. That a wise man would begin planning now for a cull of dragons. No one else though seemed to quite hear the same thing. When Jeiros was done, Zafir batted him away with some scalding remark. No more men would be forthcoming. The same answer as she'd given him day after day after day for weeks now. Vale, who had ten thousand soldiers sitting idle in their barracks, couldn't help but wonder why.

Other men came and went, most of them with little to say of any interest. Vale listened anyway. A war was coming. It was obvious, and yet no one seemed concerned. The council was split, Vale decided, into two equal halves. Those who were too stupid to see and those who simply didn't care.

And then there was him, who would likely be expected to fight it. Presumably none of the rest of them were that bothered if the odd city full of their own people burned, as long as they kept their precious eyries. *A cull.* His heart beat faster at the thought. *Would that not be for the best? At the very least it would make them pause and think.*

At last the one man who might have something interesting to say got to his feet. Zaster, the old palace spymaster. "Your Holiness, there have been movements among the dragon-knights of the north." Even Zafir straightened very slightly. Now she was only pretending to be bored.

"Go on."

"Princess Jaslyn has left Outwatch and returned to Sand. Several dragons have been seen heading for the Desert of Salt. She may remain reluctant, but she is negotiating her marriage with King Sirion's son, Prince Dyalt."

Zafir glanced at Lord Eisal, who shrugged. "Shezira promised her to my lord in exchange for his support."

"And then murdered Hyram, my husband and your lord, when that wasn't enough." Zafir wrinkled her nose and turned back to Zaster. "And what about Almiri and Evenspire?"

"My spies have seen several dragons flying from the Spur to Almiri's eyrie. And a war-dragon flying back again, heavily laden."

"Is that it? You've seen a dragon? I could have told you that myself. My riders have eyes too, Zaster."

"Yes. The war-dragon your riders saw, Your Holiness." Zaster bowed low. "B'thannan. Rider Hyrkallan's mount. It confirms that he is leading the rebellion, Your Holiness."

"Pshaw!" Vale winced. The speaker had half a goblet of wine dangling from her fingers. She'd been known to throw it at councillors who annoyed her. "What else? Will you dazzle us with the revelation that the sun rises in the morning and sets at night? Of course Hyrkallan leads this insurrection. And Almiri? How much is she helping them? What about Sirion? Does he send aid to them too? Tell me something useful or be silent. I want proof of these treasons, not hearsay!"

Zaster had always been too quick to take offense. His lips drew tight together. He started to sit down; as he did, Vale found himself rising. It was such a surprise that he didn't quite understand what was happening at first, and then had to wonder whether some sorcery was at work. But no, his own legs, nothing more. He looked from face to face, suddenly uncertain. He wasn't supposed to have opinions, so what in the realms could he be needing to say?

His legs seemed to know what they were doing though, so he extended the same trust to his mouth.

"Hyrkallan won the Speaker's Tournament a decade ago when Hyram took the Speaker's Ring, Your Holiness. And a decade before that as well, when it was Iyanza."

Zafir gave him a scornful look. "Since when do Guardsmen speak in the Speaker's Council?"

He bowed and fell silent, but he'd done enough. The spymaster nodded. "When the talk is of warriors, Your Holiness," he murmured. "Hyrkallan is a clever man, a good rider, strong, brave, with all the best qualities. Most of all he has experience and respect. The other riders of the north will follow him. They are much more dangerous with him than without, Your Holiness. As they have already shown." A thundercloud passed across Zafir's face. No one spoke about Drotan's Top, but it hung in the air throughout the palace. Hyrkallan had bloodied her nose there and it still stung, even if she'd bloodied him back since.

"Give me dragons!" shouted Prince Sakabian. "Let me smash them!"

Zafir glared him into silence.

He's right though. Any other speaker would have summoned a hundred dragons, sent out the Guard and crushed this nonsense. Zafir does nothing. Why?

Vale felt he ought to have been sitting down but somehow he wasn't. Instead, there were more words coming out. "Why is he doing this, Lord Zaster? Why did he not go north all along? He has the whole of the north as his weapon if he chooses to use it, for they would follow him. He could force Jaslyn off her throne and come at you with ten times the dragons that follow him now. Why does he not?"

Zafir glared at him. "If you'd done what was asked of you, Guardsman, then Hyrkallan and his Red Riders wouldn't even exist, would they?" She spat the words out. The fingers holding her goblet were twitching. "If you'd taken all of Shezira's riders. If you hadn't let *Almiri*, of all people, escape. I should have removed you from your post there and then."

Vale bowed. He sat down.

"They need to be dealt with, Your Holiness," snapped Zaster. "You should send Watchman Tassan—" He didn't get any further. Zafir's goblet caught him on the side of his head. Hard. Zaster staggered and put his fingers to his temple. They came away bloody.

"You *presume* to *tell* me what I should do?" She waved a hand at Vale. "Send this idiot to finish cleaning up the mess he should never have allowed in the first place? Now that they have their dragons? And how many of the Adamantine Guard shall I throw away into the Maze?" She snorted. "Very well, Lord Zaster, if they *must* be dealt with, and if my dragon patrols are not enough to satisfy you, *you* deal with them. Hire more sellswords. Put a bigger reward on Rider Hyrkallan's head. On all of them. My weight in gold for every one of them. And while you're at it, they must be getting their potions from somewhere. Get me *proof* that Almiri is sending them supplies and I will reduce Evenspire to ash. Let their dragons turn rogue and eat them!"

Jeiros jumped to his feet. "Your Holiness, Evenspire is a city of thousands! As large as the City of Dragons itself! Your dispute—" He bit his lip. "*Our* dispute is with Queen Almiri, not her subjects."

Zafir snarled: "Then why don't you find some way to lure her away from her defenses, eh, alchemist? But *after* you have finished learning to count." She turned back to Zaster. Her face softened a little. "Spymaster, you have not answered the Watchman's question. Why *is* Hyrkallan pursuing this foolishness?"

Zaster licked his fingers and shook his head. The look he gave Zafir was venomous. "Oh I dare say he'll tire of this soon enough. Without him, I'm sure the rest will disperse." That would have earned him the goblet again, if Zafir hadn't already thrown it at him. The speaker bared her teeth.

"Sell-swords, Zaster. More sell-swords. They are cheap and expendable."

"Wasn't Rider GarHannas among them?" asked Prince Tyrin suddenly.

"GarHannas of Bloodsalt?" He was looking at Lord Eisal. Eisal pretended he hadn't heard but the damage was done. The council slipped back to doing what it did best, sniping at one another and making sure that nothing useful ever got done. Vale closed his eyes for a moment. Ten thousand men and two hundred riders sat idle at the palace. If he'd been permitted an opinion, it might have been that they should be doing *something*.

10

JASLYN

I s there news, Your Holiness?"

Jaslyn sighed and slid off her dragon. Her *new* dragon with his glittering silvery black scales. A real prize. Morning Sun, Isentine had named him, but Jaslyn still thought of her old dragon, Silence, every time she flew. In her head, this new one had a different name. Not morning, but mourning. It felt much closer to her heart. They sounded the same too, which kept everybody happy. Her little secret.

She took off her helmet and dropped it on the packed, scorched earth of the landing field. One of the Scales would pick it up later. "I wish you wouldn't call me that, Eyrie-Master." She didn't even glance back at the dragon behind her. The sun was low and its bulk cast them both into shadow.

Eyrie-Master Isentine bowed as best his age and stiff back would let him. "A thousand apologies, Your . . . Your Highness."

"That's all I am, Eyrie-Master. For as long as my mother . . . for as long as Queen Shezira is alive. Even imprisoned within the Adamantine Palace, *she* is your mistress. You should call me student and I should call you master." That had been one of her mother's last commands. Isentine was getting old and they'd need a new eyrie-master before long. A master or perhaps a mistress.

She tried to smile but it seemed she didn't know how anymore. Isentine stared at his feet.

"Not much," she said after they'd stood in awkward silence for far too long. "Hyrkallan has plundered Drotan's Top. The speaker's dragons have taken a couple of his riders but so far he evades her grasp. Everyone demands that I call him back and make him knight-marshal in Nastria's place." She shook her head. "We don't even know that Nastria is dead. Almiri begs and pleads for us to go to war. My husband-to-be is alive and still hasn't found his way to Sand. His father, King Sirion, continues to shout for revenge for Hyram's death but can't decide whether it's Zafir or Shezira who should feel his wrath. And I, I just feel that my time is running out. I want to climb onto Silence and fly away. Far, far away and never come back. Except Silence is gone."

Isentine screwed up his face in horror. "Holiness!"

"Highness!" Jaslyn scowled.

"Highness! You cannot—"

"Cannot speak like that, Eyrie-Master? If not to you then to whom? Our knight-marshal is dead and our queen is imprisoned for treason. I'm surrounded by men and women I barely know who wear long stern faces and expect me to be my mother when I'm not. My elder sister only wants my dragons and my younger sister Lystra is far away, married and a hostage to that monster Jehal." She clenched her jaw. Sometimes when she thought of Lystra she wanted to cry, but that wasn't allowed, not even where only Isentine would see. "I miss her most of all, Eyrie-Master. In her letters *she*, at least, sounds happy."

"Perhaps, Your Highness, she will persuade . . ."

"My—Queen Shezira and King Valgar have been in the speaker's dungeons for more than a month. Our knight-marshal plotted with King Valgar to murder Speaker Zafir, and our queen apparently pushed Lord Hyram off a balcony."

"Lies, Your Highness. All lies."

"Really? I want to believe you, Eyrie-Master. But their accusers are not Zafir's servants or Jehal's. They are Adamantine Men. Perhaps they might be bribed to lie about Nastria, but about Hyram? They were his own Guardsmen. He died under their watch. They failed. Why would they lie? I cannot believe they would conspire against their own lord."

"But surely you cannot believe—"

"What? Can't believe that my mother would have pushed Hyram to his death? After the way he betrayed her? I remind you, Isentine, of whom we are talking."

Jaslyn tore herself away from Morning Sun, walking briskly toward the looming tower of Outwatch. Isentine struggled to match her pace. Walking meant he couldn't see her face. She wasn't like her mother. She couldn't hide it all away. She couldn't be strong all the time on the outside no matter what she felt on the inside.

She took a deep breath. "That's not why I came here, Eyrie-Master, nor why you called me." Although any excuse would do. She liked the bleakness of Outwatch, sitting on the top of its cliff, presiding over miles and miles of tunnels and caves where the dragons were kept. Liked the flight over endless miles of barren, featureless burning sand and rust-colored stone that brought her here. Liked this isolated and inexplicable oasis of green that just happened to be the greatest eyrie in the north. Now that Isentine knew better than to turn out the guard for her whenever she arrived, it was the windy, lonely, lost place it had always been meant to be, and it drew her in whenever it could.

"It feels empty here," she murmured, as much to herself as to Isentine.

"Most of your dragons are at Southwatch," huffed Isentine. Of course they were. She'd sent them there, after all, to stand guard over Almiri in case the speaker brought war across the Spur.

"Yes." And the few she'd left here spent most of their time in the Worldspine. Wasting their time searching for the remains of the white dragon that had nearly killed her.

"I might have found the dragon you're looking for."

The words grabbed hold of her as surely as a strong pair of hands. She froze. For a moment she thought he meant the white.

"What?"

"There's been another hatchling, Your Highness. A male. A hunter."

Jaslyn's heart climbed into her mouth. "What color?"

"Deep blues and greens, Your Highness."

Jaslyn started walking again. An overwhelming disappointment settled around her. Not the dragon she was looking for. Not her Silence.

"But he's a vicious one, Your Highness. He won't eat or drink anything we bring him. He attacks the Scales. He'll die before the end of the week. I've never met anything quite like it. We've always had hatchlings that wouldn't take and there *have* been a lot of them lately, but this . . . this is exceptional. I might even have put him down if it wasn't for your order."

"Does he speak?"

Isentine didn't reply. As far as the eyrie-master was concerned, it seemed that anyone who thought dragons could talk probably believed in ghosts and gods and all manner of other foolishness. It didn't help that the one time Silence had spoken to Jaslyn, as he lay dying, he hadn't *spoken* as such; rather, his thoughts had mingled with hers.

Or maybe she was going mad.

Silence had been ash-gray. He was dead now, but in his last thoughts he'd told her that he would be reborn. He'd told her that dragons lived in an eternal cycle of birth and death. No one had ever thought to mention this to Jaslyn before, but Isentine had confirmed, when she'd pushed him, that the alchemists believed this was true. It was a secret passed down among them, shared only with kings and queens. She was as good as a queen, he'd said, so now she could know. She'd nearly hit him for that.

They don't remember, though. They don't speak. He'd told her that too. Jaslyn didn't know whether she believed him or not but she didn't want to, and so she was looking, hoping that out of all the eyries across the realms, Silence would be reborn to one of hers.

One of my mother's . . .

"I'm looking for a sooty gray, Eyrie-Master." It sounded like madness, but when she'd spoken to the alchemists, they'd looked at her with shifty eyes as though she'd uncovered some secret that she wasn't meant to know. Several secrets, in fact. They wouldn't tell her, and when her demands grew more threatening, they haughtily reminded her that, for now at least, she was a mere princess, and that the alchemists of the realms answered only to kings and queens. Only Isentine would answer her questions and she no longer trusted even him.

She walked past the yawning doors that led into the cavernous halls of Outwatch, on to the edge of the scarp slope. The wind was strong there, tugging at her hair. At the bottom of the slope was a lake. Above it, caves studded the cliffs, dark holes leading into the tunnels of the eyrie. She couldn't look at a cave now without a shudder of fear, without smelling smoke, without starting to cough and choke, but if she closed her eyes she could imagine herself at Clifftop, Jehal's eyrie in the southernmost corner of the realms. A place almost as far away from Outwatch as it was possible to be, but another eyrie built over underground caves and tunnels at the top of a cliff looking out over water. If she tried, she could bring back the smell and the sound of the sea, of the waves breaking at the foot of the cliff. Of Lystra, standing next to her, looking around at her new home with wonder in her eyes and laughter on her lips.

If you were here, I could do this. I miss you, little sister.

She opened her eyes again, dispelling the sound of the Sea of Storms and bringing back the hot dry desert winds that filled her mother's realm.

"You will take me to this hatchling, Eyrie-Master." She had to see, after all, even if it wasn't her Silence. Probably he'd been born in another eyrie, far away. If he'd been reborn at all. If it wasn't a myth.

"He will try to eat you, Your Highness."

Through the gloom-laden hall of Outwatch, Isentine led the way to an immense pit lit by hundreds of alchemical lamps, a hole in the earth fifty feet across with a spiraling staircase clinging to its side. They went down. He walked slowly, clutching at the guardrail bolted into the stone. Jaslyn had lost count of the number of times she'd come here, yet she'd never been all the way to the bottom. They reached the hatchling caves, but the stairs and the pit went on. She always found herself wondering how many people had slipped and plunged down into the inky blackness, and whether they were still there, still falling. When she asked Isentine what was down there, he only shrugged and told her it was flooded, that no one went down there anymore.

He led her off the staircase toward one of the higher caves. Jaslyn clenched her fists until her knuckles went white and her fingernails gouged her palms. This used to feel like home. She'd pause and take a deep breath and fill her lungs with the smell of dragons. Now what she remembered was being trapped underground with dragons trying to kill her and all she ever smelled was the memory of choking in the smoke.

"The hatchery isn't far, Your Highness." As if she didn't know. She'd told Isentine everything because Lystra wasn't here and she had to tell *some-one*. She couldn't tell anyone else. If she closed her eyes that made things ten times worse; the stench of smoke in her mind grew so strong that she was almost sick. She tried thinking of cold mountains and running water but that didn't help either. Nothing helped. Nothing would. Except maybe if she found the reincarnation of one of the dragons that had nearly killed her. Maybe then. Maybe when she understood *why*.

"Here." The eyrie-master stopped at the entrance to a cavern gouged out of the side of the cliff. The end of the cave was open to the sky. Jaslyn wanted to run to it, to embrace the sky and the freshness of the air, but Isentine had a hand on her shoulder. He was offering her something.

"What is this?"

"Against the Hatchling Disease, Your Highness."

Which she should have known without having to ask. Cross with herself, she took the ointment from him and rubbed it over her hands and face. It was brown and smelled of mud. Then she went over to the opening. With the wind whistling around her, the claustrophobia and the smoke eased away.

A hatchling dragon was chained to one wall. It couldn't have been more than a few days old, skinny and sickly, but it must have been ten feet long already from the tip of its nose to the end of its whip of a tail. They came out like that, all scales and bones, usually dark-colored. They uncoiled from their eggs like a flower opening from a bud, painfully and slowly. Sometimes it took them days to stretch themselves out. They'd lie there dozing as their skin dried and shrank. And then, usually, they'd wake up and eat everything in sight. Unless they were one of the difficult ones, like this one.

Jaslyn knew at once that this wasn't the dragon she was looking for.

"It refuses to eat and attacks any who come close to it," said Isentine. "The usual for a hatchling that fails, though more aggressive than most."

"It attacks them because it's hungry." Jaslyn looked at the dragon curiously. It was curled up with its eyes closed, pretending to be asleep. She wasn't quite sure how she knew, but secretly it was watching them.

"No doubt. But we've had hatchlings like this much more often these last months. Since . . ." Isentine trailed off, but Jaslyn knew what he would have said. Since the white dragon attacked the alchemists. *Since Silence died.* He clasped his hands and looked at the floor. "They won't eat unless they've made the kill themselves."

"This isn't Silence." Jaslyn stepped closer, cautious but curious. The dragon knew she was there, she was sure of it. And she'd left her helmet up above. The rest of her was still covered in dragon-scale armor, but if the hatchling spat fire at her face—

She didn't have time to finish the thought. The dragon lunged and snapped its jaws. Fire burst out between its teeth, aimed straight at her eyes. She ducked and raised her hands to shield herself, but the fire didn't even reach her and all she felt was a waft of hot air. The hatchling must have been desperately weak. Then the chain around its neck jerked tight and it collapsed on the floor, seemingly too drained to move.

"Did you read my mind, little one?" she asked, absently. "Is that how you knew to strike at my head? Or was it simply obvious?" She turned to Isentine. "This one's going to be dead in a few hours if it doesn't feed."

The eyrie-master nodded sadly. Jaslyn looked back at the baby dragon. She wanted to stroke it and nurse it, but even as weak as it was, it was quite capable of biting her arm off. She crouched down and looked it in the eye, careful to keep her distance.

"Can you hear me in there? Can you understand? Do you remember?" What had Silence said to her as he was dying? *I remember the flames.* "Do you remember the flames?"

The dragon cocked its head and gave her a quizzical look, surprise mixed with hatred. A look that said *Yes*. She waited to hear it speak inside her head, but nothing came. They stared at each other for a few seconds, and then the dragon closed its eyes and laid its head down on the floor. Maybe she'd imagined it. Just seen what she so desperately wanted to see.

She turned away, away from the dragon and away from Isentine as well. She didn't want either of them to know of the despair that was welling up inside her. Instead she stared out of the cave, at the sky and the distant fields.

You delude yourself, little one. You do not understand.

Jaslyn almost jumped out of her skin. She whirled around, but the dragon hadn't moved. Isentine was looking at her curiously. "Did you . . ." *Did you hear?* But she could see the answer to that straightaway. No.

"Did I?" He peered at her.

Did I imagine it? "Bring it something, Eyrie-Master," she said. "Something alive that it can kill for itself."

"We already have, Your Highness." She sensed the reproach in his words. Of course they'd tried. They tried with every dragon, as hard as they could. "Every—"

"I know, I know. Every hatchling is precious. Do it again. This time, don't let the alchemists near whatever you bring."

She still couldn't bring herself to look at him. The tone of the silence was enough to tell her how much he disapproved of her order.

"They won't allow it," he said at last.

"Then don't tell them." The alchemists would forbid it, she realized. They'd tell her, again, that she wasn't the queen of this realm and that they answered only to kings and queens. She didn't even rule her own eyrie. The thought didn't help her, but at least it gave her a little anger, anger that she could harness into motion. She swept out of the cave, past Isentine and back toward the pit, heading out to the fresh air and the open skies as fast as she could. The look the hatchling had given her would haunt her, she knew. Was it the look of a spirit that knew what was waiting for it, one prepared to die and die and die again, over and over, rather than become a slave to the eyrie alchemists? Or maybe she was imagining all that, and the look was simply one of hunger and desperation. She'd never know. Isentine would never defy the Order. By tomorrow, the hatchling would be dead.

When she reached the surface again, a messenger was waiting for her. "Your Holiness." He bowed, and this time she couldn't be bothered to correct him. "Rider Hyrkallan has returned to Southwatch."

11

LITTLE SISTER

Lystra stood at the window. This was her window, high in King Tyan's palace, at the top of one of the towers, in a solar where her husband had once bedded his lovers. The place where he'd brought her, on their wedding night. The room didn't have much to offer except a luxurious bed and an extravagant view. Most of the windows in the palace looked south toward the sea, but here Lystra had found a view that reached out over the walls of the city, over the sweeping breadth of the Fury River flood plain, and out toward the distant and invisible north. Sometimes she squinted, imagining that if she tried hard enough she might see all the way to the Adamantine Palace, to her lover, her husband, her lord, her prince. To the father of the child growing inside her. He'd been away for a long time. Too long. She was pining.

Sometimes when she'd had enough of thinking and wondering about Jehal, she'd think about her sisters instead. Almiri, who was strong and clever. Almiri, who would always find a way, somehow, to make everyone happy again. And Jaslyn. She thought about Jaslyn most of all. Thin, hollow, mean Jaslyn, who burned on the inside with passions clenched tight and buried deep within her. Starved middle sisters.

Jaslyn whom she missed more than anyone else.

She had ladies to keep her company and they amused her well enough.

But when she came to this window she sent them away. Even Lord Meteroa, Jehal's strange uncle, the eyrie-master who ruled far more than an eyrie, knew better than to bother her when she was at her window.

She was surprised then when she heard footsteps shuffling slowly up the stairs. The tread was unfamiliar. Not Meteroa, who walked briskly and usually viewed a staircase as a challenge to be overcome as rapidly as possible. Not one of her ladies either; they would have coughed to warn her they were coming.

She let her eyes wander for a last few seconds, dreaming that she would see a speck in the sky that would be Wraithwing, Prince Jehal's dragon, bringing him home. Then she turned, facing the door.

The shuffling stopped outside. The world fell suddenly silent. All at once, Lystra was afraid.

"Who's there?"

Silence.

With a fluttering heart, Lystra took a step toward the door and then stopped. She could hear breathing, low and rasping.

"Who is it?"

"Princess Lystra," whispered a voice, "do you love your husband?"

"Who are you?"

"Do you love him, Princess Lystra?"

"Yes, of course." She took another step toward the door. Lord Meteroa was forever forbidding her this and that, warning her of the constant dangers of assassins sent by the speaker, although *why* the speaker would want her dead was something he could never quite explain. She'd never paid his warnings much heed. Not until now.

"No," growled the voice. "Not the right answer. Do you *love* him? Does your heart yearn for him? Would you give yourself away for him, body and soul? Would you die for him?"

"Yes." She bit her lip. She knew at once what Jehal would have said: *Yes, but do I really have to?* Or: *Of course, but only when I'm very old,* or something like that. He would have made her laugh. At that moment she wished he was there with her more than ever.

"And he for you." A figure stepped into the doorway. He threw back his hood and Lystra squealed and wept for joy.

"Jehal!" She threw herself into his arms, staggering him.

"Careful, careful!" She couldn't see him properly for happy tears. He held her tight, just the way she wanted him to. "Ancestors! Next time I make a surprise return, I shall make sure I stand a little further from the top of a long and steep and winding stair before I reveal myself!"

"You've been gone for such a long time!"

"Now that is just *so* typical of your sex," he chided. "A prince has to work, you know. Weeks away without you, far from home, alone and friendless, toiling away for the good of my kin. Work, work, work, and when I finally limp home, exhausted and saddlesore, all I get are complaints about how *long* I've been *gone*." His grip on her didn't loosen though, so she knew he was joking.

"I wasn't complaining."

"No, well, Lord Meteroa got to me before I could find you hidden away up here, and he most certainly was. After that, I dare say you could have thrown daggers and chamber pots and screamed abuse at me and I would barely have noticed." He pushed her back into the room, still crushing her to him. "Oh look, a bed." His voice turned sly. "Or did you somehow *know* that I was coming back?"

She didn't bother to reply: she was too busy kissing him. And she couldn't have said whether she was pulling him or he was pulling her or whether the bed was somehow pulling both of them. She stopped him though, when they were nearly naked, and put his hand on the side of her belly.

"Feel!" she said, and watched his face. The baby inside was kicking, feeding from her own excitement perhaps. She watched his eyes light up, watched his mind working, frantically searching for words and for once failing. Watched an amazed little smile creep across his lips.

"Your son," she whispered.

12

❦

DIPLOMACY IN ALL ITS FORMS

I'm grateful you came. This used to be Hyram's favorite place." Zafir stood high above the City of Dragons, perched on a tiny shelf of rock overlooking the top of the Diamond Cascade Valley. Hyram had brought her here, before she'd become the speaker. Afterward she'd come here with Prince Jehal. Today, she had a king beside her, watching the water rush by, hundreds of yards beneath their feet. Set back from the edge behind her was a tiny lodge, a single room squashed under an overhang. From the bottom of the cliff it was invisible; even from above it was almost impossible to spot unless you knew it was there. It had become a secret place passed down from one speaker to the next. One of several, tucked away up here among the silent crags of the Spur.

"I know. We came here often in the earlier days of his rule. Before the shaking sickness took him." King Sirion, Hyram's cousin, stood beside and slightly behind her. Zafir made sure that she was right at the edge. The wind pulled at her. If Sirion wanted to push her over, it would hardly be any effort at all.

"Shezira came up here with Hyram a few days before she killed him. This is where he told her that we were to be wed. She must have stood here, beside him, like we are now. She must have known at that moment he would not name her to follow him. I wonder why she didn't push him over the edge there and then."

"Perhaps because she is a true queen, born and bred, forged of steel and honor." Sirion's words were stony. "I do not easily believe these stories of murder."

Zafir ignored him. "Before I came here, I thought the Purple Spur was just another cluster of mountains, like the Worldspine only a bit smaller. It starts that way, over by the Spine. If you fly across the end of the Spur into the realms of the north, that's what it looks like. But here . . ." She gestured around her. "It's as though some god reached down and pulled this part of the world up by the roots. There's nowhere else in the realms like it. No gentle foothills and valleys, just a sheer cliff all the way around. And then on the top . . . These aren't mountains. Anywhere else and we'd say they were hills. Canyons. Caves. Snow and waterfalls and gushing rivers. The Diamond Cascade here, the Emerald Cascade and the Sapphire Cascade. Cold forests. It's like a tiny realm all of its own, torn up out of the Hungry Mountain Plain. But not mountains, King Sirion. Sometimes, when you see something from a distance, you do not see it for what it truly is." She leaned back, fractionally closer to Sirion. "I would never have thought Shezira capable of such a murder either. That she might go to war, yes. I feared that, I admit it. But that she would kill Hyram with her own hands?" She tried to sound a little mournful, a faint tinge of wistful regret, but Sirion was having none of it.

"And very convenient for you that he should fall, eh? And I have known both the Purple Spur and Queen Shezira for many years and have found them both to be *exactly* what they seemed from a distance."

"You are cruel, King Sirion."

Sirion snorted. "Don't pretend that your heart is broken, Speaker. You may have fooled Hyram but it is clear enough to me that you and Jehal were lovers before and are lovers still. I will not believe in illusions of any affection between you and my cousin. Say your piece, Speaker. Tell me why you have asked me here, alone and far away from prying eyes. I can think of only two things, so which is it to be? Do you plan to seduce me as you seduced my cousin? Or do you mean to murder me? Although I warn you, you will find neither easy."

Zafir half turned, glancing over her shoulder, and met his eyes for a moment. "Perhaps I mean to do both."

"Then you will fail twice."

"Very well, King Sirion. I will not trouble you with sentiment, but with cold pragmatism. Hyram and I had a simple trade." She turned to face him. "Am I young, King Sirion?"

"Very."

"How many children have I carried?"

He took a step back. A frown shadowed his face. He peered at her. "None that are known. Why do you ask such a thing?"

"Do you suppose I am fertile?"

He looked distinctly uncomfortable now. Which, as far as Zafir was concerned, was perfectly fine. "I do not know, Your Holiness."

"Then guess."

"I . . . I suppose there is no reason to think otherwise."

She took a step toward him, closing the distance between them. "Am I deformed?"

"I would not say so." He stepped back, and so Zafir stepped forward again.

"Am I beautiful?"

"Of course." He tried to step away, but as he did, Zafir caught his hand and pressed it against her breast.

"Am I desirable?"

He pulled his hand away, but for an instant he'd hesitated. Her heart was beating strong and fast. She knew he'd felt it. His face colored. "I am not to be had, harlot."

Zafir brushed the insult aside. She smiled. "I would not presume such a thing, King Sirion, not from you. But look at me. Look at me with Hyram's eyes. Imagine for a moment that you are him. Am I desirable?"

"You may well be, Your Holiness. Although I can't imagine why you would ask such a thing."

"Hyram made me speaker. In return I shared his bed. I would have made him heirs if he'd lived. He would have kept much of the power that he had. That was the nature of our arrangement. A simple contract, bound by a marriage. Are not all weddings for the same reasons? Heirs and power?" She laughed. "You think I brought you here to bend your ear about Queen

Shezira? No. The Adamantine Men have accused her. I've heard their evidence and to me it's strong enough to make her hang, but you can all make up your own minds about that. The kings and queens of the realms will hear the case against her and each of you will make your own decision. I do not care, King Sirion, what fate awaits her. Frankly, I will have as little part of it as my duty allows. I care only that a decision is reached, and that whatever is decided is decided by the rulers of the nine realms and not by me. What I care about, King Sirion, is making sure there is no dragon-war. I care about peace."

"Peace?" Sirion snorted. "You?"

"A happy coincidence of duty and self-interest, Your Holiness. You may make your own judgment as to how securely I sit on the speaker's throne now that Hyram is gone."

Sirion was frowning. Obviously he hadn't expected such bluntness. "Then why . . . ?"

"Why did I bring you here? To ask you a question, Your Holiness. To ask your *advice* as a great king of a great realm. I am a queen and I am the speaker. I have carried no children. I am, as you have agreed, young, fertile and desirable." She took another step close to him. "My husband is dead. I should have the pick of all the princes across the realms. There is certainly no shortage of them, and more and more arrive at my court with every week that passes. You see that for yourself and doubtless find many of them as tedious as I do. But they are all southern princes, from the courts of King Narghon or King Silvallan or King Tyan. The peace of the realms requires that I marry to the north, not the south. I do not seek a war with Shezira's daughters, but nor can I marry them."

Sirion frowned again. He shook his head. "I cannot offer you any advice. If Queen Shezira had a son, that would be your answer. There are others who carry her blood."

"Plenty of them. But I cannot marry into her line if she murdered Hyram. If she were to be found innocent then perhaps so, but not if she's guilty."

"Valgar has a son."

"He's two years old."

"He has brothers."

Zafir looked down the sheer drop to the river below. "That is true. Valgar's realm is small though." *And now, Sirion, the seed is planted. Although you might be too vain and think yourself too wise to answer me now, the seed is in there nonetheless. For if I cannot marry into Shezira's realm, and will not choose Valgar's, then only yours remains. But only if Shezira is found to be guilty . . .*

"There is—" She held up a hand and he stopped. She glanced inside. There wasn't much to the lodge, only a single airy room with open arches instead of windows. At the back were two wide alcoves, both piled with luxurious furs and soft cushions. It wasn't hard to guess what the visiting speakers had used *those* for. She'd lain in them, naked, with both Hyram and Jehal; flying here again with Sirion she'd wondered if she might lie there naked again. He reminded her of Hyram though, which was unfortunate.

No. She'd done as much as she could with him. As much as she'd hoped. Now all she could do was trust time and greed and doubt and pride.

He followed her eyes and must have guessed her thoughts, for his face went hard.

"I—"

She struck first, before he could finish. "*Don't* flatter yourself, Sirion. You have an unmarried son, Dyalt."

"Promised to Princess Jaslyn."

"Promised but not yet given. And promises, as we have seen, can be broken."

Sirion flushed with anger, but before he could say anything else, dragon shrieks ripped through the air—first one, then another, then several more, answering the first. Cries of warning.

He jumped away from her and half drew out a knife. "What trickery is this?"

Zafir barely heard him. Her skin prickled with an acid mix of fear and fury. The cries were coming from her own dragons, circling overhead, but what they'd seen was flying down the valley, skimming the waters of the Diamond Cascade River. Three dragons were heading almost straight at them. They were hard to see at all against the backdrop of trees and water and broken stone, but they weren't hers. She squinted, paralyzed with dread. Her lookouts were too high. These new dragons would get to her first, before any of her riders could stop them. If they were here to kill her, she was as good as dead . . .

As they rushed toward her, she recognized them. Two of them at least. Dragons that she'd lost to the Red Riders only weeks ago. They could only be here for her. As they flew closer, she closed her eyes. They were huge. She was going to die in agony and fire . . . *No! No no no!*

The fire didn't come. When she opened her eyes again, the dragons were flying past right in front of her, nose to tail, their necks straining forward, their immense wings so wide and so close that they almost touched the stone at her feet. She still couldn't move, but then Sirion grabbed her and hurled her to the ground away from the edge an instant before the wind of the dragons' passing picked them both up and flung them around like a pair of dolls. The dragons dived over the falls toward the City of Dragons and the palace below. Zafir rose shakily to her feet and watched them go. She still could hardly move. She touched a finger to her brow where the skin was beginning to sting. She was bleeding. A scratch, that was all. *If they'd seen me. If they'd known I was here . . .*

"You're shaking, Your Holiness. You're very pale." King Sirion touched her shoulder lightly, awkwardly. She flinched away, ignored him, frantically waving her arms at her own riders already swooping out of the sky. Within seconds, a hunter thundered awkwardly in to land nearby. Zafir ran, screamed at the rider to move aside and hauled herself up onto the dragon's back. Sirion was forgotten. Never mind that he might have saved her life only a moment ago—for all she knew or cared, the hunter might have crushed him or swept him over the cliff and into the river below. Before she'd even strapped herself into the rider's harness, she commanded the dragon to fly. What mattered was her palace.

The dragon felt her need and threw itself over the edge of the Diamond Cascade, soaring out into the immensity of the void below, into the skies above the City of Dragons.

Streaks of flame flashed across the ground far below. What mattered was her palace, and her palace was burning.

13

JUSTICE AND VENGEANCE

Rider Semian shot out of the mouth of the Diamond Cascade and into the void beyond. Vengeance, the dragon he'd stolen from the Usurper, tucked in his wings and fell out of the sky like a stone toward the city below. The wind roared and screamed in Semian's ears and tore at his clothes. The wound in his leg hurt; there was a fever in his blood and when he closed his eyes all he saw was fire and endless burning plains. He whispered a prayer to the Great Flame. Drotan's Top and three other eyries ringed the speaker's domain and a fifth stood close to her palace gates. Today they would all burn. *Let the kings and queens of the realms answer the speaker's call and find only ash and embers.* The Red Riders, *his* riders, had dispersed. They'd flown north and south and east to strike at all the speaker's eyries at once. *And while they do, I will find the heart and cut it out. Hyrkallan, when you hear of our deed, I wish you could know how I pitied you as I sent you away.*

He opened his eyes. The City of Dragons had grown enormous. Vengeance stretched his wings and opened his mouth wide. Scorching winds blasted Semian's face even through his visor; the glorious smell of scorched air filled his nose and the city burned. He could feel the raw strength and power of Vengeance ripple through him and he knew the dragon felt the same. They were as one, burning bright with righteous fury. *See how your ruler protects you. See how powerless she is?* Three or four dragons were in pursuit of him now, guardians loitering up on the edge of the Purple Spur, but they were behind him. Too far away to reach him before he himself reached the palace. Fate and destiny had flown here with him and slipped him between the Usurper's patrols. They were his shield and his armor and they would protect him from the scorpions of the Adamantine Men too, he was sure. As the walls of the palace came up to meet them, Shanzir and Nthandra peeled away to either side, striking at the eyrie and the barracks around it. He alone would have the glory. Vengeance smashed at the walls with his tail as they crossed, lashed a scar of cracked stone into the greens and blues of the Tower of Water and then let loose, spraying fire in all directions, cleansing the walls, the earth, the towers, everything within his reach. Men and women and horses all screamed and burned; servants and beasts, kings and lords, all were the same when they were made into ash.

Something hit Vengeance and the dragon shuddered and gave an angry snort. From the walls, soldiers were firing at him, shooting their handful of scorpions. In front of him, a company of Adamantine Men had formed up with their shields, turning the fire away. Vengeance lashed them with his tail as he flew overhead, but as Semian raced toward the Tower of Air and the Speaker's Tower beyond, more and more Guardsmen emerged. A second scorpion bolt hit Vengeance, and then a third. The dragon shrieked and veered, straining to turn and strike back. Only Semian's iron desire held him in check.

There! There in front of him were the open doors to the great Chamber of Audience. If the speaker was anywhere, she should be there. Guards were closing in on them though, and now hundreds of soldiers were spilling onto the walls and into the yards, raising their shields, dragging their scorpions.

It wasn't to be. Another scorpion struck Vengeance in the back of the shoulders, barely a yard away from where Semian sat, and this time the dragon would not be denied. Flames washed across the soldiers closing the door and then Vengeance pivoted his head and sprayed the walls, veering toward them. A few scorpion bolts would never take a dragon out of the air but they still hurt, and by the time Semian had Vengeance under control again, the moment was gone. The doors flashed past, still half open, inviting him in, mocking him. With a howl of rage he urged Vengeance onward, upward. He pulled away from the palace, jaw clenched with frustration, and finally glanced over his shoulder to see how many of the speaker's dragons were chasing him.

And saw something wonderful. A miracle of the Great Flame. No dragons were after him; they were all converging on another. For a moment he thought it might be Shanzir, but no. Nthandra. Nthandra of the Vale had set fire to the speaker's eyrie as he'd told her, but now, instead of flying away, she'd turned back into the palace. Semian felt a strange pang of jealousy and joy. He saw her dragon almost crash into the doors he'd so narrowly missed, landing among the soldiers, crushing and scattering them. He saw its head lunge through the doors, smashing them to splinters, and then he saw fire fill the tower, exploding out of every door and window.

And he saw her die, shattered in her harness by three scorpion bolts at once and burned by her own fire, erupting back out of the tower. He closed his eyes and prayed for her, offering her soul to the oblivion of the Great Flame. The first martyr in two hundred years. *Saint* Nthandra of the Vale.

He flew south and then west along the Fury Gorge. No one came after him. Kithyr had promised him that he would be invisible, and so it seemed he was.

His head sang for the rest of that day, even as the other Red Riders returned with failure after failure. Samir's Crossing north of the Purple Spur was filled with the speaker's dragons and they'd turned away. Drotan's Top—they'd found to their cost—had been much the same, and four riders and their dragons were lost. But none of that mattered, and when he told them what Nthandra of the Vale had done, the other riders all seemed to understand. So they should. The riders not fit to follow the Flame had returned to the north, or else, like poor Jostan, gone some other way, willing or not. The ones that were left were the ones that would serve the Flame to their deaths.

The speaker is dead! The Usurper is slain, and by my command! Was that too much to think, too much to hope? When he turned to his tent as the sun sank below the hills, he lay in his bed and stared into the emptiness and prayed. *Let her be gone. Let the victory be mine. Let the standard of the Great Flame burn across the realms!* He closed his eyes and tried to think of the world as he would make it. Where the dragon-priests wielded the power that had once been theirs, with Semian at their head, the Knight of Fire of myth and legend. Justice and Vengeance. The visions filled his head as he drifted away.

You cannot rest, whispered the Flame as he slept. *You cannot rest. All of it must burn.* He tossed and turned in restless dreams and the sun was already high in the sky when he awoke. He'd missed dawn by hours. In his tent beside him sat the blood-mage, Kithyr.

"You did well, prophet," said the mage solemnly. He laid cool fingers on Semian's brow.

Semian gripped Kithyr's hand. "It's just the start. Just the beginning. We have to . . ." He tried to rise but Kithyr forced him to be still.

"You have a fever again. I have told the others to rest for today and so will you."

Semian lay back on his bed. "You were right. Everything happened as you promised us it would. No one saw us until we reached the palace. The Adamantine Men were slow and half asleep. It was as though they didn't see us until we were already past them."

Kithyr nodded. "Blood has power."

Blood-magic was wrong. Wicked and evil. Or at least so he'd always thought. Before the Great Flame had spoken to him, Semian wouldn't have suffered a blood-mage to live. Queen Shezira had outlawed them, as had many other kings. He'd even seen blood-magic once, wielded by an alchemist. Watching had made him queasy and uncomfortable. Yet that alchemist had been a servant of the Order, and the Order in its own way served the Great Flame. He knew better now. Kithyr had *shown* him. The men who'd first tamed the dragons, the very first alchemists, *they* had been blood-mages too. Blood and fire ran together.

"Let me dress your wound again." Kithyr helped him to sit up and started to unwrap the bandages on Semian's leg. Semian almost pushed him away but relented at the last moment. The magician, it seemed, knew a great deal about dressing wounds.

"It's painful this morning."

The mage nodded. "It is festering and needs to bleed. I will suck out the corruption and dress it again."

Semian rubbed his eyes. He felt weary and lethargic. "It's getting worse. I don't even remember how I got it."

"It is not a deep wound but it is long and ragged and the flesh is torn. It was a sell-sword's blade that cut you—a fool, coming to a fight with a dull edge on his blade."

"I don't remember it."

"You fought with fury. We won. They died. Yours was the only wound we took. What else is there to remember?"

Semian stretched his shoulders and fought against the growing fuzz in his head. Kithyr had the dressings open now. His leg throbbed and the air smelled rotten. "A man should remember every wound and the person who gives it to him. You never know which one might kill you."

Kithyr snorted. "The sell-swords are all dead and I doubt this wound will be your last."

"Are you sure? I can smell the air. The wound has gone bad."

"It's been going bad for some time, Rider, but it will not kill you. While I am with you, no wound will kill you. Now hold your tongue. I have to cut the corruption away. This is going to hurt."

"I know. I am not afraid of the pain, Blood-Mage." He closed his eyes. His belly filled with anticipation; the pain, when it came, transcended all his expectations. The world he knew fell away and he found himself engulfed in ice so cold that it burned. He was back in the valley of ash-covered stone, with the crimson dragon that dwarfed even the Worldspine. With the dragon-priest with his pale skin and his white hair and his long bloody robes, holding out the blackened stumps of his hands.

Yes, said the priest. *Yes. It is a start, a beginning, nothing more, but it is good. You have done well.*

He tried to talk to the priest, to ask him what he meant, but even as he opened his mouth the great crimson dragon lifted a wing and slowly blocked out the sun. The sky went dark, the moon turned black and the world followed and Semian's head filled with the roar of rushing water.

When he opened his eyes again he was lying on his back, looking up at the roof of his tent. His leg was in agony. Kithyr was bandaging it up.

"I had a vision," Semian said.

"I'm not surprised." The mage sounded as though he didn't much care for visions. "You were right. The wound *is* getting worse. I had to drain a lot a pus out of it. I've done the best I can. It will heal now, but you'll be weak and tired for a while."

"The Great Flame will fill me with its strength."

"Yes." Kithyr stood up and nodded. "It will. It will fill us all. You may need to lean on someone to walk for a while. You can still ride though, so all is well."

Semian tried to get up, but the pain in his leg simply wouldn't allow it. "Yes." He winced. "All is well."

"The last of your Red Riders came back in the early light of the morning. They brought better news."

"Yes?" The riders he'd sent to the further eyries. "Did they burn?"

"Yes. They burned. The speaker's eastern eyries are reduced to ash. Narammed's Bridge as well."

"Great Flame be praised!" Semian sank back to the ground. Those eyries weren't much more than fields and huts—there probably weren't even any soldiers there—but none of that mattered. His vision had been true. The kings of the east and the south would come to the speaker's call. Where they stopped to rest their limbs and feed their mounts they would find nothing but destruction. They would see her weakness.

He felt dizzy. He closed his eyes again and reached out. The mage took his hand and held it tight.

"I must leave you soon. You know that, don't you? The Great Flame calls me to a different destiny."

"I understand."

"We all serve the Flame in our own ways. I have done what I can for you. Semian, you must listen to the words of the Great Flame. It will speak to you in fire, but also in blood. When blood comes to you, you must heed it."

Semian screwed up his face. "I don't understand."

"But you will. I'll have to bleed you again," the magician said.

"If you must, but I cannot stay here. We have struck a blow, Kithyr, and many more must follow. It is a start, a beginning, nothing more."

The world was getting hazy and starting to spin. The mage squeezed his hand. "Yes it is. But it is good. You have done well."

As Rider Semian slipped away into unconsciousness once more, the blood-mage let his hand fall. He smiled. "You did not light the fires," he whispered, "but you will fan their flames into an inferno that cannot be extinguished."

14

A PRINCE HAS TO DO WHAT A PRINCE HAS TO DO

Jehal took a deep breath, sighed, and sat down in the middle of the floor to see whether anyone would even notice. He'd been in Furymouth for two weeks and he was pacing his palace like an animal in a cage.

Why can't I be content? The coffers in his treasury were full. His city prospered and his dragons were strong. Cousin Iskan was steering himself comfortably toward a marriage alliance with one of King Silvallan's brood. Furymouth was easy. A king could put his feet up here, indulge himself and watch the realm largely rule itself. If that wasn't enough, Lystra was carrying his heir inside her and yet was still as eager and soft to touch as ever. *So why can't I be content? Why can't I be happy?*

Approaching footsteps stopped behind him. Even from the sound of them, Jehal knew exactly whose they were. His uncle. Meteroa.

"Are you unwell, Your Highness? Or simply meditating? Please don't tell me you've gone mad. This family has had quite enough of that sort of thing."

"No, Eyrie-Master, I am trying not to be restless."

"And have traded that for disturbing your subjects with odd behavior?"

"Zafir is hurling us all toward a war. I've been trying not to think about it but it's not really working. She wasn't listening to me. I thought it might be better if I wasn't there to see it happening anymore. No more hammering my head against the stone walls of stupidity that most of the Speaker's

Council seemed to have erected around themselves." Jeiros was far too clever not to see what was coming but he was powerless to do anything about it. Jehal was fairly sure that the Night Watchman, Tassan, could see it too. The man was shrewd for a commander of the Adamantine Guard. But the rest of them . . . The rest of them simply refused to see it. He smirked to himself. *Maybe that's because the rest of them haven't met Princess Jaslyn for long enough.* He lazily stood up and turned around. "Not being there, I have discovered, is considerably worse. I lie awake at night and think of a hundred and one things that Zafir might do, and none of them are ever good. I find myself convinced that Zafir will turn everything we achieved to ruin. I ought to go back." *Why, though? Can't I leave them be? Can't I let Zafir drown in her own stupidity?* He took a deep breath and growled, "I am bored here, Uncle. This realm runs itself too well."

Meteroa gave a little bow. "I shall take that as a compliment. But were you not bored when you left the speaker's palace? Was that not why you came?" He raised an eyebrow but didn't wait for an answer. "No matter; if you're bored then this should please you. I have news."

Jehal shook himself. Meteroa had a gleam in his eye, one that always meant trouble. "You never bring good news, Eyrie-Master. I'm not sure I should listen to you. Lystra, I'm sure, will have sweeter words than yours."

Meteroa sounded bored too, but then he *always* sounded bored. "Oh, I'd like nothing more than for you to go and spend a few more days closeted away with your queen. Running this realm is so much easier when you're not around to interfere."

"You're supposed to run my eyries, not my realm, Meteroa. Still, if you wish me to scurry away then by all means tell me I have yet another ambassador from the Taiytakei pleading to speak with me."

"They *have* been a little busy of late."

"Haven't they just."

"Always scheming." Meteroa yawned. "Should I assume now, as a matter of course, that the Taiytakei are to be dealt with by the lord chamberlain or some such minor functionary?"

Jehal almost laughed. The lord chamberlain was supposed to be the eyes and ears and voice of the king. Strictly, even Jehal had to defer to the chamberlain's orders, although the last chamberlain to try that had retired from his office in something of a hurry some years back. "What a fine suggestion. I sometimes wonder if we *should* give them a hatchling. Or an egg or two. Let them live with the consequences."

"My Prince! As you have so pointedly observed, I am your eyrie-master, and that is the worst treason to escape even your lips for a good long time. I should be fleeing as fast as I could to send word to the speaker and the grand master of the alchemists." He shook his head. "That you should even *speak* it. Jeiros would shriek for your head at the mere whiff of such a thing."

"Oh pish-tosh! I wasn't advocating we should give them any potions. Only a hatchling." Meteroa was still glowering. Jehal sighed. "Well *I* thought the idea of one of their ships drifting back into port with nothing left alive except an awake and very hungry dragon was rather amusing."

Meteroa's look was acidic. "A veritable earthquake of hilarity, I'm sure. But no, Your Highness. It is not the Taiytakei. This is news that concerns your bride and it will not wait."

"Oh well, now I am suddenly *quite* convinced that I shall not like whatever you're so eager to say. I should warn you that I have been considering breathing new life into certain ancient traditions regarding the bearers of bad news."

"Then I shall dress it up otherwise. Wondrous news, Your Highness. The speaker has called a council of kings and queens. Oh joyous, joyous times."

Meteroa's voice was so dry it could have swallowed the sea. Whatever good humor Jehal had been nursing left him right then. "She's putting Queen Shezira on trial, isn't she?"

"Yes. And King Valgar too."

"Oh screw Valgar. Inconsequential king with an inconsequential voice."

"But with a not inconsequential queen, Your Highness."

"Yes, yes, married to Lystra's big sister. You didn't suppose such a thing would slip my mind, did you? But still inconsequential beside Shezira." He clasped his hands tightly together. "Zafir will demand Shezira's head and she'll probably get it. Jaslyn will take Shezira's throne and Almiri already speaks for Valgar's realm. Put the two of them together and they're as strong as the King of the Crags. Put Sirion with them and they'll split the realms clean in two. War, fire, death, destruction. Everything burns."

"Perhaps." The eyrie-master raised an eyebrow. "However, I cannot help but observe that it will likely all happen very far away from Furymouth."

"Furymouth may be far enough removed, Eyrie-Master, but *I* am not. *I* am precisely in the middle."

"And very adroitly done, Your Highness. I bow to your talent for blending strategy and mischief. A lover on one side and a bride on the other. You may jump to one or the other as it pleases you. As the tides of their fortune wax and wane and they quietly rip each other to pieces."

Jehal could have slapped him. "You are naive and shortsighted sometimes, uncle. If they rip each other to pieces, it *may* be of little consequence to us, but it will *not* be quiet. It may be a surprise to you, but I would prefer not to see the realms torn to shreds, and that is most certainly what such a war would do. You might as well give the Taiytakei that hatchling and the potions to go with it. That might be all that's left." He paced. "Since I intend to follow Zafir to the speaker's throne, I would prefer to rule more than a desert of ash. No, I shall stand between them."

"Not choose between them, My Lord?" Meteroa raised an eyebrow.

"I have made one speaker, Eyrie-Master. When I make another, it will be me. No." Jehal pursed his lips. "No choosing. Not yet. I shall answer the speaker's summons and attend her council. I shall argue with passion and conviction that the realms will be safer if Queen Shezira lives. And then we shall see."

"I'm afraid to say, Your Highness, that you are quite pointedly not invited to the council. Your father may attend and his voice will be heard. Not that anyone, even if he is able to speak on that particular day, will understand a word of what comes out. You, however, are courteously advised to stay home and keep feeding the starlings. Whatever *that* is supposed to mean."

Jehal hissed. "Oh! Believe me, Eyrie-Master, the speaker could not have made her meaning more clear. Nevertheless." He looked at Meteroa long and hard. "Zafir can do what she likes with King Valgar, but if she executes Shezira, both of Lystra's sisters will go to war. That must be stopped."

Meteroa raised an eyebrow. "I trust that Princess Lystra and I will no longer be hearing complaints of boredom?"

Jehal suddenly grinned. "That depends on how long it takes me to change Zafir's mind. You may go, Eyrie-Master."

Alone, Jehal's grin fell away. He stared blankly into space. He'd put Zafir on the throne. He'd always known he might not control her but he'd never given it much thought.

And now it's time that I did. He turned and walked briskly toward his father's apartments. Something else was long overdue, something to which he'd given a great deal more thought over the years. Something best done quickly while he had the will to do it. When he reached his father's rooms, he sent all the servants away with orders to find Lord Meteroa and bring him. He waited until they were all gone and then stepped inside, through the antechambers and into his father's sickroom. A long dark room, lit only by the embers of the hearth and thin curtains of sunlight that squeezed through the cracks in the shuttered window. A room he'd come to less and less over the years. *I used to come here every day, in the beginning. I'd hold your hand and look for any signs that you were getting better, filled with a strange melange of fear and hope in case there would be a miracle. But you weren't and there wasn't. You were always getting worse and miracles, it turns out, are for fools.*

Prince Jehal sat by his father's bed and took his father's hand. He leaned toward the old man's ear.

"I know you can hear me," he whispered, soft as silk. "I know your mind is still alive in there, even while your body wastes away. Even though you can't speak, can't feed yourself, can't do anything much but lie there and stare, I know you can hear me. If there's anything you have to say, this is your last chance to say it. Spare me the complaints that I never come to see you though. I know I've not been a good son, but then a better son might have come from a better father, eh. I have to go away again now.

Queen Zafir is waiting for me. I made her want me, Father, and now I might have to destroy her. I did the same to her mother, Aliphera. Does that make you sad, Father? I know you liked Aliphera. I think you'd like Zafir better though. She squeals like a pig. Oh, I'm sorry." Jehal gently wiped his father's brow. "I suppose I shouldn't speak of such things. Do the women I send to your bed still give you any pleasure? I hope so. I picked them myself."

He paused and squeezed his father's hand, stretching his senses for any response. He thought he felt a twitch, but that could simply have been his father's condition. It could have been anything. Most likely it was nothing.

He whispered again. "I don't know if you've been keeping track of things in there, but if you have, you must know that Speaker Hyram's time as master of the Adamantine Palace has been and gone. He's dead now. Did anyone tell you that? He went mad with grief and despair, with the help of a little cocktail of poisons that I made for him, and then he threw himself off a balcony. You were my key to him, Father. You and Zafir. I couldn't have done it without you. Pathetic, drooling, shaking, empty shell of a man that you are. You let him see what time had in store for him, until the dread of it gnawed at his bones. Until the terror of age and impotence and helplessness ate his heart. Well he's gone now, your old enemy. You survived him and you had a good part in killing him. I thought you'd want to know that. I thought you deserved to know why I let you linger like this for so long."

Jehal rose. He had tears in his eyes. "I've killed one queen and one speaker and made another of each. Because of me yet another king and queen are marked to die. I'm sorry, Father, I really am, but I had to. I know you understand. But I am not sorry for this, for what I'm about to do. I should have done it a long time ago. I should never have let you suffer so."

He looked into his father's blank eyes, searching for something, for any little spark. They were dull and dead. The only sign of life was the slow rise and fall of his chest. With deliberate slowness Jehal picked up a pillow and pressed it hard into his father's face, until the breathing stopped. He held it there for a very long time. There was no struggle. *A mercy. For both of us.*

Finally, Jehal lifted the pillow away. He looked at his father's dead face for one last time. "I do wish you could have told me, just once, that you were proud of what I've done. That I'm not a monster like Calzarin." He stroked his father's cheek, cold as glass even when he'd been alive. "But you didn't and now you can't anymore. Go and be with your ancestors. Maybe now you're dead you can watch over me as you never did while you were alive."

Jehal took a deep breath, and when that wasn't enough to stop his head spinning he took another. He put the pillow carefully back on the bed and laid his father's hands across his chest. As an afterthought, as something to do while he waited for his heart to stop racing, he threw open the shutters and let daylight flood the room. In the sunlight his father's skin was so pale that it seemed to glow.

"Sent away, summoned back, sent away, summoned back. I do wish you'd make up your mind, Your Highness . . . Oh."

Jehal spun around. Meteroa was in the doorway. He had the *audacity* to disturb him here instead of waiting outside. Jehal put a trembling finger to his lips. "Not a word, Eyrie-Master, not another word. In this moment and this place, you're a sneer away from losing your head to the sharpness of your own tongue."

Meteroa's face was a mask hidden under a mask. For a long time he stood stock still, staring at the dead king. Then he bowed. "You're going north?"

Jehal nodded. "Lystra stays here, under your protection. Whatever happens to her happens to you. As before."

"He was my brother, Your Holiness." Meteroa's face was still blank. Jehal barely heard him.

"I'm leaving right now. From this room I will get my white horse. I will ride to Clifftop as fast as it will carry me and I will fly tonight, in the dark, whether Wraithwing agrees with me or not."

"And what shall I tell your queen?"

"Tell her what she needs to know. Tell her that I am sorry, but that sometimes a prince has to do what a prince has to do. Now get out! When I'm gone, see to my father."

Meteroa backed away, vanishing into the shadows outside the door. Jehal spared his father one last look, and then followed as fast as he could. *All the way to the palace, and I will not look back, for now I am a king and my voice will be heard.*

15

THE DUTY OF KINGS

Jeiros, acting grand master alchemist, cracked open his door, peered into the empty passageway beyond and slipped out like a schoolboy. A little voice in his head mocked him for his stupidity. This wasn't going to achieve anything. Someone was going to see him sneaking around in the dark like this and get suspicious. If he'd just gone where he was going in broad daylight, no one would bat an eyelid.

The little voice didn't stop him though. It only made him even more careful. *You forget,* he told himself, *that I've done things like this before.*

When you were ten years old, snapped the voice. *When you were a little boy and it was what all little boys did.*

He reached the end of the passage where it opened out into a stairwell. The Gatehouse was actually two towers, one on either side of a pair of wooden doors called the Dragon Gates. The gates themselves were bigger than some castles. They were close to fifty feet high, which made them twice as tall as the walls around most of the palace. They were bound with iron, and when closed and locked it took a hundred men about an hour to open them. When they were fully open, they were large enough for any dragon in the realms to walk through.

He chided himself. *That's an exaggeration.* He peered into the blackness of the stairs and opened his ears, listening for any footsteps. When he didn't hear any, he tiptoed down. The alchemists lived on the upper levels of the east stair. Where he wanted to be required that he go all the way down to the bottom, across the gates, and then all the way up the west stair. And all of it without being seen.

Back to the gates. The gates gave him something else to think about. They were, in their own quiet way, a miracle. They weren't hinged because no one had ever made a hinge remotely big enough or strong enough. Instead, they pivoted on a bearing, with huge iron and lead counterweights balancing the mass of the doors. Except even that wasn't enough, because no one could make a bearing that would take such a weight without collapsing, so most of the weight of the doors and the counterweights was held up by a series of steel ropes that then rested on a pair of massive stone pilings on either side of the pivot. It was said that when the palace was built, some three hundred years ago, the gates took as long to build as the rest of it put together. The Gatehouse towers were as large as they were because they had to be to support the gates. Sometimes the alchemists joked that the maze of rooms and passages and staircases the towers contained were just something to fill all the spare space.

There. He was at the bottom of the stairs and no one had seen him. So far. He unlocked the door into the Gateyard, opened it, locked it again and slipped into the warm night air. No one was watching, but still, this was where one of those mythical potions of invisibility would have come in handy.

He hurried across from the east tower to the west. There was no avoiding the guards who stood by the gates—the gates within the gates that allowed people and horses and even carts and wagons to come and go without ever having to open the Dragon Gates themselves. But in the darkness, with his hood pulled up, they wouldn't know who he was. He steered a wide course around them and no one challenged him. *Pitiful*, sneered the little voice. *As if any of this mattered.*

Except it did matter. It mattered a lot. He opened the door to the west stair. That was one door that was never locked, for it led into the quarters of the officers and senior staff of the Adamantine Men, and no one would be daft enough to go into a place like that unless they had a very good reason to be there. Jeiros ran up the stairs as fast as he could, almost to the top, and banged on a door. He was afraid that he might have to bang several times, given the hour, but the door swung open of its own volition. It wasn't even shut.

"Grand Master." The Night Watchman was sitting in a hard-backed chair, tilting back with two bare feet up on a little table, squinting at a book that he was holding at arm's length from his face.

"I thought you'd be asleep."

"We never sleep, remember?" Vale Tassan slowly leaned forward, took his feet off the table and replaced them with the book. Jeiros wasn't sure whether he meant it as a joke or whether he was serious.

"You need a Taiytakei eyepiece," he said, to change the subject.

"No, I don't." A slight smile played across Vale's face. "I need books to be scribed with bigger letters. The Night Watchman cannot wear an eyepiece."

"He can in the privacy of his own chambers." Jeiros stepped in and closed the door behind him. When he turned back, Vale was giving him a very pointed look.

"And what, exactly, is this privacy to which you refer, Grand Master? As you see, my door is always open to my men and my friends."

"Well it's shut now." Jeiros looked for a bolt or a lock but there wasn't one. "I require a moment or two of your attention, Night Watchman." His scowl softened and he bit absently on a knuckle. "I need an ear, perhaps."

"Then go and see Aruch." Vale shook his head and made to settle back down with his book.

"No. I need *your* ear, Night Watchman. Who do you serve?"

"What an odd question." Vale cocked his head and then rose slowly to his feet. "I serve the speaker, Grand Master. I am her sword and her shield. I execute her will and her enemies. That is my whole and only purpose. Would you like a drink? I don't myself, but I sometimes have visitors who do. I have a collection of fruit wines that I'm told is very good, and it seems a shame for them to go to waste."

"No!" Jeiros took a few quick steps into the room and looked around for a place to sit down. All he could see was a chair by a table covered in maps. He took another step toward it and felt a hand on his arm, turning him, pulling him away.

"That table is for Adamantine Men," said Vale quietly. "Have my chair. I will squat on the floor. I'm quite used to it."

"Do they teach you history when they make you a soldier? I don't suppose they do."

"They teach you how to fight and how to die for your comrades," said Vale mildly. Then he looked up at his walls, covered in bookshelves, books and scrolls, and made a gesture with his arm. "However, I have undertaken extra study over the years."

"Do you know how the Order of the Scales came to be?"

Now Vale smiled. "No. I know at least half a dozen different stories which *claim* to be of how the Order of the Scales came to be. All of which disagree, and all of which are provably false, at least in part. Do *you* know, Grand Master? Which story have you come to sell me tonight? Is it the one where the alchemists are nothing more or less than blood-mages with a different name? Is it the one where you slew them or the one where you chased them away? What are you today? Are you noble heroes or dark villains?"

Jeiros clenched his fists. "Let me tell you who we are. We are the ones who keep the dragons at bay. Not you, not the speaker, not the kings and queens of the nine realms. Us. Without us, none of the rest of you matter a whit. You'd all be dead in a flash. Yes, we are descended from blood-mages. Our power has its root in theirs. We are descended from those who sided with the men who became the kings and queens of the realms when the blood-mages were broken."

Vale smiled amiably. "All the stories I have read say that the blood-mages demanded sacrifices to appease the dragons. That their binding of the monsters required blood and plenty of it. A hundred slaughtered each and every week. I found that number in some story or other. And now you do it with potions. No blood at all?"

"Become an alchemist and find out," snapped Jeiros. "We keep the dragons in check. That is what we do and all you need to know. Above all else. Above *everything* else. Do your stories tell you how Narammed came to be the first speaker?"

"They agree rather better on that."

"The nine realms were falling to war. We chose Narammed. Us. The alchemists. We put ourselves behind him and we pushed him to power. He was wise enough to understand what we were doing and why. The speaker keeps the kings and queens of the nine realms in check so that we alchemists can do what we must without impediment. That is the purpose of the speaker. They are arbiters, that's all. Most who have come since have not understood it and none save Narammed himself would acknowledge it, but we do not serve the speaker. The speaker serves us."

Vale chuckled. "I don't think so, Grand Master, but you could try that on at the next council and see how far you get."

"The speaker serves the realms, Vale. So do I. So do you. We all have the same master. You know, strictly, according to all the laws of the Order, we serve Aruch. Both of us."

Vale was quiet for a moment. When he spoke, he spoke very softly, almost whispered. "Some of what you say I grant is true. The first Adamantine Men gave themselves to Narammed because they understood his cause. He had forsaken his dragons and the power that came with them so that he could mediate the disputes of other kings. The story that everyone thinks they know is that Narammed slew a dragon with his bare hands." He cocked his head and gave Jeiros a glance, begging to be contradicted.

"With the Adamantine Spear, Night Watchman. That's the legend. Except it's not true."

"No." Vale smiled and shifted on his haunches. "Because it wasn't Narammed; it was some other warrior. The nameless hero. All these other warlords we call kings and queens were nothing more than thugs, brutal ones at that. Even those who were clever enough to understand Narammed's wisdom wouldn't have wanted it. So we showed them his strength instead. Us. The Adamantine Men. Even we don't know the name of the man who slew the dragon, but we revere him. He was the greatest hero of all. He gave the power of his name and his deeds to Narammed. We showed them that we could kill their dragons and *that* is why they bent their knees to Narammed. We went from one eyrie to the next carrying his message. The dragon-slayer." Vale rocked back on his heels. He wasn't looking at Jeiros anymore, but somewhere distant, off into the past.

"Don't get all misty-eyed on me, Night Watchman." Jeiros took a deep breath and paused. The Adamantine Men almost worshipped their story. The Order had a different story, one with a lot more dragon-poison in it, but with much the same outcome in the end. He'd been thinking of sharing it with the Night Watchman, but the look in Vale's eyes changed his mind. He settled for something else instead. "It's a fine legend you have. But think. Your stories speak of lone men with swords and axes slaying dragons. How possible is that? One man on his own cannot kill a grown dragon. Even the best of your soldiers could never, ever do that. Not by the strength of his arm. He must have been quite a clever fellow, don't you think?"

"It was a unique feat. One never to be repeated." Vale snapped back to the present. "What is your point, Grand Master? I would happily make a habit of talking history with you, but I suspect you have a point you wish to make. The trouble with you lot is that you're so used to coming at things askance that you've forgotten how to ask a direct question."

"I am leading you to a certain way of thinking."

"Then let me spare you the embarrassment of being any more ham-fisted about it than you already have. I will agree with you, within these four walls and never beyond them, that Speaker Zafir leaves a great deal to be desired. Nevertheless, were any man to come to my room late at night and intimate that I should enter into some sort of conspiracy with regard to ridding ourselves of her, I should be obliged to inform her, and she would doubtless have them killed or something equally unpleasant. I serve the speaker, Grand Master. Orders. The Guard obeys orders. From birth to death. Nothing more, nothing less." He smiled, and there wasn't anything friendly about it this time. "That's our creed."

Jeiros sat very still and quiet for a few seconds. Then he took a deep breath and let it out very slowly. "But whose orders, Night Watchman?"

"The speaker's orders, Grand Master."

That's me told then. He didn't get up though. "I know how Adamantine Men are made. Do you know how to make an alchemist?"

Vale sighed and his face hardened. Jeiros had outstayed his welcome now, that much was clear. "Every year I watch as thousands of the desperate and the poor come to the City of Dragons to try and sell their children to the Order. I know that some of the ones who don't get taken are left on our doorstep. I know there are men who will, for a fee, take a child from its parents and bring it here. I know that a few such men are even honest. I also know that a good few are not. I know that the Taiytakei slavers profit handsomely." He smirked. "What do you want me to say, alchemist?"

"That there are secrets no one else should know, Night Watchman. Not even a speaker. Not even you."

"I don't like secrets, Jeiros. The blood-mages built their power on secrets. You alchemists broke them by breaking their secrets first, but you have forgotten that and now you follow the same path. So now I am left to wonder, what can you know that the speaker should not?"

Jeiros stood up. "I should go. But I can think of two things. The first is that we alchemists are not so far removed from the blood-mages we overthrew as to leave any of you comfortable, if you knew the truth of it. The second is a secret that you know too, if only you'd cast your mind back to think of it. I know what Narammed said when he gave you your name, Night Watchman. Do you remember?" *When night comes it falls to the Adamantine Men to keep watch over the nine realms.* No need to spell it out though. Vale would know the words inside and out. "How dark does it have to be, Vale?"

"Let me ask you this, master alchemist. If there is to be a war, can you not stop it? Can you not simply take away their dragons? How many cities will burn before you do that? If our land is burned by dragons who happen to have riders on their backs, why is that so different from dragons that do not? If it all burns anyway, what exactly was the point of you being here?"

Jeiros' voice dropped to a dry whisper. "When the dragons have riders, there is at least still some hope," he breathed. "That is the point." The words sounded hollow though.

Vale hadn't moved as Jeiros went to the door; now the Night Watchman had his back to the alchemist. Vale didn't move. "Well then," he said very softly. "Here's your answer. Pitch-black, master alchemist. It has to be pitch-black."

Jeiros let himself out. He didn't bother trying to hide himself on the way back. All things considered, it seemed rather futile.

16

THE SPEAKER ZAFIR

She was at her best when she was angry, and the more her fury waxed the more magnificent she became. Jehal watched her in silent admiration. He was thoroughly enjoying himself. Today's entertainment was watching acting Grand Master of the Order of the Scales Jeiros being metaphorically flayed alive. Yesterday it had been Tassan. The Night Watchman, it seemed, was now a routine victim of the speaker's ire. *And so he should be. I would have him hanging from a gibbet. Ten thousand invincible warriors guard the palace, and look at the state of it! You should have taken your own life and spared everyone the embarrassment of looking at you.*

"Unacceptable!" Zafir was already on her feet, but now she picked up the empty wine goblet from the arm of her throne and hurled it at the grand master. It was a good throw, and would have hit Jeiros squarely in the face if he hadn't ducked. It clanged across the floor behind him and lay still. None of the servants who usually rushed to clear away errant goblets and the like moved a muscle.

There was a moment of silence. Jeiros was red-faced and trembling, although out of fear or fury was hard to tell. Probably a rather delicious mixture of both, since Zafir's temper was both fierce and unpredictable. Jehal kept his face stern, but inside he was beaming. *Goblet throwing, the sport of kings. How I've missed this . . .* Both Jeiros and the speaker looked like they'd had plenty of practice at this sort of thing while he was away. They might even have rehearsed it.

The silence continued. He could feel the tension between the speaker and her grand master rising and rising, until even the air between them seemed to be trying to get out of the way. With a sigh, he stood up. As soon as he did, he could feel the wave of relief through the hall. *Thank the ancestors for Prince Jehal.* He'd been doing a lot of this lately, almost from the moment he'd landed in the wreckage of the Adamantine Eyrie. The Red Riders' attack had been no more than a scratch, superficial and quickly healed, but the wound to Zafir's pride had been savage.

See what happens when you don't listen to me? But that doesn't help either. Although I'd rather enjoy saying it. He bowed to Speaker Zafir. "Your Holiness." It took her longer than usual to give him a grudging nod and sit back down on her throne. She folded her arms angrily. Jehal set his eyes on the grand master. Jeiros was looking at him with a mixture of pleading and defiance.

"The council of kings recognizes Prince Jehal!" boomed the court herald. Jehal winced. Calling this farce a council of kings was absurd, but that was Zafir for you. Calling it that had at least forced King Sirion out of his tower and into the chamber.

"Grand Master Jeiros." Jehal favored him with a smile. "Let us be reasonable. No one holds the Order responsible for the Red Riders, whoever they are . . ."

"I should hope not! They've burned—"

"Several of the Order. I know. We *all* know." Jehal let his smile slip. "Please don't interrupt me while I'm speaking. It does nothing for my disposition. If you do it again, I shall simply leave you to resolve your dispute with the speaker on your own. Doubtless you've always wanted to make a close inspection of the dungeons under the Glass Cathedral."

Jeiros went from being red in the face to purple. "How dare you threaten me, *Prince.* Only a council of kings can—"

He didn't get to finish before Zafir was on her feet again. "This *is* a council of kings, you old fool," she shouted. Jehal could see her hand looking for something else to throw. *A knife, perhaps?*

Jeiros took a step forward. "Then where are the *kings?*" he shouted back.

Zafir came down from her throne, step by step toward him. "Would you have me drag Queen Shezira and King Valgar out of their prisons? Prince Tichane is here for King Valmeyan. King Tyan is dead and Prince Jehal is not yet crowned. King Silvallan hasn't yet deigned to answer my summons, and King Narghon is content to let us resolve this matter without his advice. What would you have me do?"

Jeiros snorted. "Prisoners and princes. I say again, where are the kings? Where are the queens?"

"King Sirion is here," thundered Zafir, "and *I* am a queen!"

There was another moment of silence. Jehal broke it, clapping his hands slowly. *Before either of you do anything irrevocably stupid.*

"Bravo, Grand Master, bravo. A cheap point bravely won. Yes, Speaker Zafir has still yet to appoint an heir to her own throne and pass on her crown." He shot Zafir a glance that told her to keep quiet. He could hardly count on her doing what he asked these days, but on this occasion she did. "I applaud your courage."

Grand Master Jeiros took a step forward. "Until she does—"

"But not your wisdom!" barked Jehal. "Where do the Red Riders strike? South of the Purple Spur. In Queen Zafir's lands, in the speaker's lands, in the border between them. It is a well known principle of war, written in the first chapter of Prince Lai's *Principles*, that an effective campaign requires a single absolute leader. Speaker Zafir is wise to keep her crown until these renegades have been crushed. I'm sure, as soon as that has been done, she will be delighted to name her heir." He shot Zafir another glance. *And you better had.*

"Prince Jehal—" Jeiros began.

"The Red Riders fly on the backs of dragons, Grand Master. What would happen if those dragons did not receive your potions, Grand Master?"

Jeiros rolled his eyes. "As we all *very* well know, they would become wild. They would turn on their own riders." Which was barely scratching the surface of the truth, but was as much as the grand master or any other alchemist would admit to, except perhaps to a council of kings that actually had some kings in it.

"Since that has clearly not happened, one must assume that they *are* receiving your potions, Grand Master. Who makes these potions?"

"The Order of course."

"Anyone else? Perhaps you would care to speculate, Grand Master? Who is supplying your potions to these outlaws?"

The alchemist snorted and his lip curled. "I cannot begin to imagine. They have stolen a goodly quantity from the speaker's eyries. As for the rest, ask amongst yourselves. Ask the kings and queens of your illustrious council." He sounded a little uncertain; he was quite clever enough to see where Jehal was going with this.

"They are *your* potions, Grand Master, and I am asking *you*. We will most certainly inquire of the kings and queens of the realms, but is it not possible that these riders have friends within your Order? For all their treason, they are doubtless powerful men, with powerful families." *Not that their families will know what they're doing, since the penalty for this will most certainly run deep into all their bloodlines.*

"Preposterous."

"Really?" Jehal raised an eyebrow. "You don't sound entirely sure."

"The Order would never . . ." Jehal could see the grand master thinking. Thinking that he was *almost* certainly right. That there was *almost* certainly no treachery from within the Order itself. That he had *almost* nothing to fear. And then too he was thinking about the consequences, if one of those *almosts* turned out to be wrong. Catastrophic for him at least, with no *almost* about it. And he was thinking about Jehal, and of what he knew about the prince that Hyram had called the Viper, who twisted and turned and knew secrets about people that they didn't even know themselves. Jehal let him stew for a second or two, before putting on his most reasonable voice.

"All the council of kings is asking, Grand Master, is that you audit your potion supplies."

"Counting, Grand Master," muttered Zafir acidly.

Jeiros stamped a foot. "Do you think we are not already *doing* that? I have spent months, *months*, merely trying to count all the dragons in the realms to determine whether Queen Shezira's renegade"—he glared at Jehal—"is dead or alive. Do you have any conception of how *difficult* it is to count even dragons? And yet you ask me to count *potions*? And frankly, as this council should be very aware, nearly all of my alchemists are fully occupied *making* them."

Jehal smiled. "The Red Riders are not some local insurrection, Grand Master. They are attacking the speaker; they are attacking everything she stands for, and by inference everything that *you* stand for. All I am asking, Grand Master, is that you tell us who is requesting more of your potions than usual. Because you must know that. If you didn't, you would not be doing your duty, and I know that cannot be the case. When you give us this answer, we shall know where they are getting their supplies." *As if we didn't know already.*

"They are stealing them from the speaker's eyries!"

"All of them, Grand Master? Then you can show us by what records you know this."

Jeiros stood there for a second, quivering. Then he bowed his head. "It shall be done."

"And soon, Grand Master," snapped Zafir. "Very soon."

The council moved on to other things: to the repairs to the eyries, to preparations to receive the remaining kings and queens of the realms, to the impending trial. Jehal watched behind half-closed eyes. In particular he watched King Sirion, who looked as comfortable as a man sitting on a hill full of stinging ants. *She's got to you, hasn't she? Whatever she offered you, it must have been good. So which way will you jump, when someone comes to kick you off your fence?* Most probably King Sirion was thinking the same thing about him. *Except that I don't look like a man riven by indecision. Or do I?*

The council slowly dispersed. Sirion hurried away back to his tower. Usually Zafir did the same, spurning Jehal's company, but today she lingered. Jehal counted the glances that turned to watch her. Tyrin, her cousin Sakabian, even Prince Tichane. *I was hardly even away, and they're all sniffing after her like she's a bitch in heat.*

"Walk with me," she said and offered him her arm. She led him outside into the open air. Scorpions and Adamantine Guardsmen packed the palace walls and towers, and a dozen dragons circled overhead on permanent overwatch. Most of the damage from the Red Riders' attack had been cleared away but the Speaker's Tower still bore the scars; the lower floors, including the Chamber of Audience, were still being gutted. Zafir had drafted in almost every craftsman from the City of Dragons in an attempt to repair it in time for the trial.

"No more hirelings, eh? I warned you that these Red Riders might grow into something you couldn't control," said Jehal.

"They're no great threat now. They made a terrible noise and a mess, but they have become rash. This must have cost them a third of their number and I have all my dragons back and more. But it's true that they've made me look foolish in front of the council. I've had enough of them. I want them gone." She turned to look at him. "And on the subject of my council, I don't recall inviting you, *Prince* Jehal. I seem to remember inviting kings and queens."

"You sound like Jeiros."

"And you should have stayed at home, playing with your starling. How is she? Still showing off her pretty plumage?"

"Not as pretty as yours, Zafir."

She slipped him an arch look. "Oh, is *that* why you came back?"

"Of course. Why else?"

"Then I can't help but wonder why you left in the first place. Although I did hear a rumor that someone died."

"I might have mentioned it, yes. I seem to have become a king since last we met."

Zafir laughed, a pretty tinkle of breaking crystal. "You're not a king until I say you are."

Jehal pointed over to the Glass Cathedral. "Then say I am."

She smiled. "I thought you'd return. I was expecting to hear that someone had died too. In fact I had a quite particular expectation in that regard. I am sad and disappointed to learn of your father's passing. Very sadly disappointed. Were there any witnesses? Should I put you on trial as well? Or were you extremely careful?"

Sometimes, Jehal thought, life would be much simpler if he gave in to the urge to wrap his hands around her delicate little throat and squeeze until she shut up. "King Tyan passed away peacefully, I think you will find. Now Furymouth requires a king, and thus I require a crown."

"After the council, Jehal. Not before."

Jehal pursed his lips. He nodded slowly. "You're going to call for Shezira's head then."

"And you're going to try to stop me from getting it."

"Why yes, Your Holiness. Having no particular desire to see the realms ripped to pieces by war, I do think I might. Since I will doubtless succeed, you might be inclined to show some of that magnanimity I was mentioning and avoid making a fool of yourself in front of your kings and queens. Of all people, I should be your ally, Zafir. Furymouth and the Pinnacles have always stood side by side. Even in the War of Thorns, there were as many knights from the Harvest Realm who fought with Vishmir as fought against him. Besides, what are all these northerners except blood-mage spawn?"

Zafir pursed her lips. "History, Jehal? Here is some history for you. The Pinnacles are the heart of the realms. The Silver King came to us there. He tamed the dragons there. The blood-mages ruled from there. The Order of the Scales ruled from there. Even after Narammed built the Adamantine Palace and the City of Dragons, we were the heart of everything. For most of those centuries, Furymouth was mud and huts."

Jehal shrugged. "And yet look at us now. You keep your history and I'll keep my wealth. We both have plenty enough dragons though."

She sniffed. "You want me to let Shezira go?"

"Yes."

"Let suspicion hang over her? Leave the world to wonder? Did Hyram fall or was he pushed?"

"I see you remember."

"My answer is no."

Jehal grinned and bared his teeth. "Then I look forward to humbling you at your council."

"You will not be there, *Prince*."

"Nevertheless."

Zafir stopped. She turned to face him, looking up with wide earnest eyes. "Are you going to be my enemy now, Jehal?"

Jehal put the palm of one hand against the side of her neck, the age-old gesture of brotherhood. "I am your best and truest friend, my lover. You will know your enemies at your council, for they will be the ones who shout and bellow their support when you call on them to hang Queen Shezira."

She took a step away, withdrawing from his hand, and slowly shook her head. "No. My enemies will be the ones who oppose my will. And I will not forgive, Prince Jehal. Whoever they turn out to be."

17

UNWANTED ATTENTION

Vale Tassan watched as the last scorpion was hoisted into place. The Adamantine Palace bristled with them now. He sighed the long satisfied sigh of someone who'd got exactly what he wanted. The Red Riders were enemies of the realms and now at last the speaker had set her mind to crushing them. Dragons were moving up from the eyries in the south and combing the Purple Spur. The Adamantine Men had been unleashed from their barracks. Some had been dispatched to join the dragon-riders in their search, but the large part remained to guard the City of Dragons and the speaker's palace. He'd got all the weapons he'd asked for. No dragon would get close enough to burn the Speaker's Tower for a second time. If they did, that would mean his head.

Seventy-four days since Head Priest Aruch had handed Zafir the Adamantine Spear. Seventy-four days gone in a flash. The last Night Watchman to go to war had served mad old Anzuine in the War of Thorns and died fighting Vishmir's dragons. Dying didn't bother Vale though. What bothered him was that three dragons had flown straight through his defenses, meager as they were, and burned the speaker's palace. He couldn't blame that on Zafir, not all of it. There had been fifty scorpions on the walls when the Red Riders had come. Now fifty Adamantine Men had been executed and fed to the speaker's dragons. One for each crew that had missed. Good men all. How could they all have failed? *How could we have been so lax when it is our duty to be vigilant?*

Not being ready. That was what kept Vale awake at nights.

"Satisfied with your handiwork?" asked a voice behind him.

"Prince Jehal." Vale turned around, dropped to his knees and bowed. "Yes, Your Highness. Most satisfied." He kept his head down, eyes to the ground. The Adamantine Men, even their commanders, were mere servants after all. Servants to the dragon kings and queens, princes and lords. Sometimes being lowly and small could have its advantages.

"You can get up, you know. I'm not Zafir."

"As you command, Your Highness." He rose slowly, his eyes fixed on Jehal's feet. *What does he want?* Nothing good. Nothing good ever came from the Viper.

"Tell me, Night Watchman, what did you think of the council this morning?"

Vale slowly shook his head. "I have no opinion to offer, Your Highness. I exist only to serve."

"You might try that on Zafir and get away with it, but not with me. Speaker Hyram, unless I am misinformed, once valued your advice."

Vale stayed silent. Silence was always the safest defense. Words only made trouble. Especially with this one.

"Well? Did he or did he not?"

Vale shrugged. "I cannot say, Your Highness. Only our late lord may say as to the value he found in what few words I had to offer. And he is dead." *Dead because of me. My fault.*

"So he is. You served him for a long time. Why do you suppose he turned his back on Shezira?"

"Again I have no opinion to offer, Your Highness." *Because of you. You and your potions and your sick father. Because of Zafir and because, in the end, he was weak like all men are weak when they grow old. He will not be making such a mistake again.* He frowned. He would have to watch those thoughts lest they turned from thoughts into words and then to actions, and before you knew where you were, it would be him throwing people off balconies. He knew exactly where he'd start too. He bit his tongue.

Jehal's smile was bland and false. "He was a good speaker, I think, until the end. He wanted too much to live, perhaps? Is that how Speaker Zafir turned him? Was she just too pretty to refuse, do you think?"

"You might be a better judge of that than I, Your Highness." Inside, Vale winced at his own words. *Silence! Remember, silence is your defense.*

Jehal's eyes glittered. "Really?"

"Love of women and a long life are two things that we of the Guard have long forsaken."

Jehal laughed. "Oh, then I could never be an Adamantine Man. Although you do confuse me. There are whorehouses around your barracks, and I can tell you from exhaustive personal endeavor that some of them are really quite good."

"*Love* of women, Prince Jehal. We have forsaken *love*, not lust. We are swords. We sate ourselves in flesh as the need comes upon us and then we move on."

"Cold words, Night Watchman!"

"Forgive me, Your Highness." Vale bowed. "They are not my words, nor those of any Guardsman before me. That is how Prince Lai described us."

"In *Principles*? I don't think so. I would have remembered that."

"Prince Lai wrote other works, less well read or well received, Your Highness. I have a small library of my own." *There, now why did you say that, Vale? That sounded like a boast, and Adamantine Men have no need to boast.*

Jehal cocked his head. "You *are* a fascinating fellow. Especially for someone who has no opinions of his own. I've always admired *Principles*. We used to have all his other works in our own library and then we had a fire. I didn't know any copies had survived."

"The monastery in Sand has the most complete collection, Your Highness. I have but a few, but I would be honored to offer them to you." *There. Is that enough? Will you go away and leave me alone now?*

"I will take you up on that, Night Watchman, but not as a gift. I couldn't take such treasures from anyone, least of all a man who has forsaken love. War is all you have left."

Jehal turned away but Vale didn't allow himself to relax. *Hyram called him Viper because poison came out of his mouth, but there's some scorpion sting in him as well, I think.*

Sure enough, Jehal took one step and then stopped. "Night Watchman, may I ask you a question on which your opinion is most certainly relevant? How many dragons do you think your scorpions and your legions can stop? More than three, I hope."

I will not rise to that. "I cannot stop the dragons, Your Highness. Only their riders."

"Then how many riders, Night Watchman?"

"The answer to that is in *Principles*, Your Highness, as I'm sure you know. A legion may face ten mounted dragons at best before it breaks. I have twenty legions. In the field, therefore, two hundred riders at best. Here, behind these walls and towers, maybe twice that number."

"Are you sure?"

"No one can be sure of such a thing, Your Highness. No one has ever tried."

"It would be a slaughter."

"The palace and the city would burn and most of us would die. Perhaps all. But that's what we are for."

Jehal laughed, although he didn't seem to find anything funny. "Then get yourself ready, Night Watchman, for when Zafir puts Shezira to the sword, the north will come to war with you. The flower of their manhood will be pierced by your bolts, while these walls and towers are smashed and burned and your legions with them. There will be nothing left of any of you. Everything Hyram preserved will go up in flames. If the realms survive at all, he will be remembered as the Great Fool."

Vale bowed his head. "If the speaker commands us to fall on our spears, that is what we will do." *One might ask where you will be, Prince, when this war comes. Here with us, defending the heart that holds the nine realms together? Or will you watch from a distance and pick off the survivors? Shall we see if I can guess?*

"You do that, Night Watchman. You do that." Jehal still had a smirk on his face as he turned away again. Vale kept very still, holding back the urge to wipe the smirk away with his fist. At least Jehal didn't turn back a second time.

He put the Viper out of his mind and immersed himself in inspecting the defenses. His soldiers had placed over three hundred scorpions on the walls in less than three days and all of them needed to be perfect—he would accept nothing less. He watched as horsemen raced around the palace flying target kites from their saddles. By the end of the day, every scorpion had been fired. Each and every one of them worked. He knew which crews had hit their target with the first shot, which ones had hit it with their second, and which ones had failed and would have to be replaced. They would practice every day now until the council of kings and queens was done and the lords of the realms had dispersed back to their own lands. Long after dark he sat awake in his little room, burning lanterns, poring over rotas and lists, staring at his maps, shuffling crews around, placing his best at the points of the palace most likely to be attacked. Being certain that he was ready.

He was about to admit defeat and accept that some decisions would have to wait until after he'd had some sleep when his door slowly swung open. He glanced up, half expecting to see Jeiros come for another try at changing his mind, but no. The Viper again. Instantly, Vale was on guard.

"I saw the light under your door, so I knew you were still awake." Jehal pushed past Vale and sat himself down. With casual rudeness he looked at the maps and starting picking through them. "Trying to decide where and when Jaslyn and Almiri will strike?"

Vale clenched his toes. *Why are you here and what will it take to make you go away?* "I am more concerned, Your Highness, that the Red Riders will try to disrupt the council."

"And condemn their queen to an even more certain death? Why would they do that?"

"They have struck at us once, Your Highness." *The books. That's what he's here for. Prince Lai's books. A shame to let them go, but needs must as the devil drives.* He started to look among his shelves.

"Yes, they have, haven't they? Last I heard, Rider Hyrkallan was leading them. I wonder what madness possessed him to burn the palace. He always struck me as a very sensible sort of fellow. Pity about his sense of humor. I wonder sometimes if they do something to their children in the north. Do they cut out some part to make them like that? Queen Shezira was as bad and as for her daughters . . ." He smiled and shook his head. "*Don't* get me started on her daughters."

Vale pulled three old books down. "I hear rumor that Hyrkallan abandoned the Red Riders some weeks ago and that he has been seen in the north. I am inclined to believe this is true. Their actions made sense to me when Hyrkallan led them. Now I don't understand them at all. They are destroying themselves. They will not last long."

"An enemy is at his most dangerous when you don't understand his reasons." Jehal smiled. "*Principles*, Night Watchman. Perhaps it is a trick."

Vale shrugged. "Here, Your Highness." He put the three books on the table. "I will wager you these that when the Red Riders fall you will not find Rider Hyrkallan among them. These are what you came for, are they not?"

Jehal gave him a lazy look. "No, Night Watchman, no they are not."

They stared at each other. Vale said nothing. *Silence, remember.*

For a long time they both watched each other in silence. Finally Jehal spoke: "Do I have to spell it out for you in simple words?"

"Forgive me, Your Highness, but I am a soldier. We are men of direct action, not guile. We do not deal well with innuendo and insinuation. If not the books, I have no idea what you want from me, Your Highness. Yes, simple words would be best."

Jehal frowned as if confused. "Hyram hated me and I had no love for him. I wonder why it should trouble me to see everything fall to ruin." He sighed and shook his head. "Are you really so stupid, Night Watchman? No, I don't think you are."

Vale stood very still. He didn't speak, only waited. The Viper would either go away now or he'd say what he wanted. *Then* he would go away.

Jehal clucked his tongue. "In fact, I'd say you are one of the more astute minds on the Speaker's Council, Night Watchman, although I will accept that is somewhat of a barbed compliment. Very well." He frowned again. "I am here to ask you for your help."

"I exist to serve, Your Highness."

"And therein lies the problem, Night Watchman, because the help I want from you is a small matter of *not* serving, and it will cost you your head if you are discovered."

Silent and still. Let him speak and say nothing.

"So. If the council of kings and queens takes Queen Shezira's head, there will be a war. The Red Riders are only a start. Would you agree?"

Vale said nothing. He kept his face blank and still, with the pleasing result that a twitch of irritation flashed around Jehal's lips.

"Simple words. Yes, yes, very well. Shezira has three daughters. Queen Almiri now sits on the throne of Evenspire and is certainly helping the Red Riders. Zafir will have proof of that soon enough. Soon-to-be-Queen Jaslyn sits on Shezira's throne and she is betrothed to the fool son of King Sirion. Two queens and one king. Three realms and many dragons, and they are already furious with Zafir. And with me, for that matter, but I doubt that is of any consequence here."

There was that flicker of annoyance again. Or was it something else? Was it . . . ? Vale felt an unexpected thrill blossom inside him. Jehal was nervous. He might even be scared.

Jehal tapped his foot irritably. "You know all of this. If killing Shezira isn't enough to send the north to war against her then Zafir will demand Almiri's head next. Do you think Almiri's own sisters will abandon her?" He shook his head. "Queen Shezira sitting on her rightful throne would stop that from happening. She would not allow a war to tear the realms apart, no matter how she'd been wronged. The rest of them . . ." He shrugged. "Who knows, eh? So here's a choice for you, Night Watchman. You can sit idly by while the speaker wrecks everything you're sworn to defend. Or you can do something about it."

The inside of Vale's mouth had gone very dry. He felt light-headed. *Jeiros I could understand, but you? What makes you think I would even countenance such a thing when you are surely thinking of nothing but yourself? And yet I find I am still listening. Why? Why am I not calling my own men to arrest this traitor?*

He shook the questions away. "And exactly what, Prince Jehal, do you suggest I do?" *There. Even for asking that question I should have myself hanged.*

Jehal wrinkled his nose. "All I require of you is that you do what the Adamantine Men always do." He bared his teeth. "Be vigilant. Don't lose another speaker, Night Watchman. Watch her and watch her well. Perhaps to the exclusion of others." His grimace finally managed to turn into a grin. "I think you are quite clever enough to understand me." He held up his hands as if to cut off Vale's reply. A wasted gesture, since there was none forthcoming. "Oh, and don't get too excited, Night Watchman. Whatever happens, you can be sure I'll be nowhere near to be touched by it. The worst you can do is kill a few men who want nothing more than for the realms to be at peace." He nodded curtly and swept back out of the door. Vale stood very still and watched him go.

There goes a prince, he thought with a certain amused wonder, *who thinks he is far cleverer than he actually is.*

He let Jehal's words roll around his head for a few seconds until he knew what he was going to do with them. Then he set to correcting the disarray inflicted upon his maps.

18

THE KING OF THE CRAGS

One by one they arrived. Six of the Syuss on the back of a pair of jet-black hunting dragons. King Narghon and twenty of his riders. King Silvallan and six of his Golden Guardsmen. Rumors raced back and forth through the palace that Princess Jaslyn had left her eyries in the far north and was coming with a hundred dragons. On the next day she was coming with two hundred, then three; then she was coming alone and in disguise. The speaker's eyries around the palace were overflowing with Jehal's dragons and Sirion's and those of the other kings, but mostly with Zafir's. Many of her riders were here now and nearly all of her adult dragons, all scouring the Purple Spur. There were always at least a dozen dragons in the skies above the Adamantine Palace, watching in case Hyrkallan's traitors crawled out of their caves once again. From his perch up on the Gatehouse Jehal watched them all come and go. He spent more and more of his time up there, looking down over the eyries. He was waiting for the Night Watchman. Putting himself in Vale's way. Looking for an answer.

An answer I'm not going to get. He was there again on the evening before the council that would decide the future of the realms. He looked down along the palace walls, thick with scorpions. *If I was Vale, I would stay silent. I'd leave me to get on with it and then make my decision as it suited me.*

He sighed. It didn't really matter which way the Night Watchman jumped. Well, unless you were worried about the small matter of the thousands and thousands of people who would burn in a dragon-war, and the tens of thousands who'd probably starve afterward. But as long as it stayed in the north, nothing that particularly *mattered* would get damaged. The easy route, of course, was to make sure the council made the right decision in the first place. Narghon would do as he was told: specifically he would do as Queen Fyon told him, and now that Tyan was dead, Fyon was left as the eldest of Jehal's family. Silvallan wasn't stupid and had nothing to gain from taking Shezira's head. Sirion though . . . *Which way will you jump? I can see Zafir's touched you, but I can't see how. What did she offer? And how easily are you taken in?* He'd spent a lot of his time on Sirion, making sure that little whispers reached him. The right little whispers. He was the key, but all he had to do was stay silent. Inaction would suffice. *Should I just tell you that your cousin wasn't pushed, that he simply fell? I could tell you how it all went. I could tell you that I pushed him right up to the edge, until he was teetering on the brink, but that the last step was his own. I could tell you that I saw him. I could even show you how. Is there a punishment for any of that? I suppose when you consider everything else, there probably would be. What with all the poisoning and so forth.*

That, in many ways, would be the best thing for the realms. To stand up in front of the council and tell them exactly how he'd driven Hyram mad. Tell them everything he'd done. Leaving Zafir carefully out of it. Shezira would be spared. The north would be appeased. Zafir would be blameless, her position secure. At the very worst they'd exile him. He'd be forced to spend his time in Furymouth with his queen. Wasn't that what he wanted anyway?

No. That's only half of what I want and so it's not going to happen.

Jehal watched the Night Watchman pacing his walls, and knew that he wouldn't get an answer. Finally he retired to his bed in the Speaker's Tower. Hyram's bed, not many months ago. When he slept there though, Hyram's ghost couldn't be bothered to haunt him. Instead he always dreamed of home. Of years long ago when King Tyan had been strong and well. Of Lystra in his arms. Of the Taiytakei and their strange and magnificent gifts. Of the last thing he'd done before he'd left Furymouth. Night after night he saw himself poised over his father's bed, the pillow in his hands, watching the last light in his father's eyes finally die.

Except tonight his father wasn't his father but Lystra, and the pillow wasn't a pillow but a knife, and the bed was covered in blood, and her mouth and eyes were wide with terror and she spasmed and writhed, and however much his heart filled with horror at what he'd done, he couldn't leave her like that, and he would lift the knife to finish her, blinded by his own weeping, except that no matter how hard he tried, she wouldn't die, and the screaming only got louder . . .

The nightmare woke him up. He lay in the darkness of his room, staring at the ceiling above his bed, listening to Kazah, his pot-boy, snoring. His heart slowly stopped its pounding. Outside, the palace was quiet.

He got up and walked to his windows, opened them and stepped through to the balcony outside. Hyram's rooms, Hyram's balcony, where Hyram and Shezira had stood that fateful night. Hyram had had three different poisons in him by then. He shouldn't have been able to move and yet he'd dragged himself outside. Where Shezira had found him, rambling and not making any sense.

Jehal stood where Hyram had stood. He peered down. He'd watched it all unfold through the eyes of the little mechanical dragon, his wedding gift from the Taiytakei. Shezira had never touched the former speaker. He could say that, if he wanted to. But then he'd have to admit that Hyram only fell because he'd flown the Taiytakei dragon straight at Hyram's face. He'd thought he was being so damn clever, but all he'd done was make a mess of a perfect plan.

Zafir had married Hyram. Hyram had made her speaker. All the hard work was done. Hyram would have lost his mind over the months that followed. No one would have been surprised when he fell off his own balcony once he couldn't even wipe his own arse anymore. Lystra would die in childbirth. He and Zafir would rule the realms together for two decades. Longer, if they could find a way. Their enemies might have their suspicions, but suspicions were all they could ever be.

Down below the stones were dark. Too dark to see if Hyram's blood still stained them. It could still have been perfect. But Shezira was there when

Hyram fell, and now Zafir was intent on casting what might have been a tragic accident as a murder. *Because, if Shezira is gone, I really have no reason left not to slit Lystra's throat. We both know that I have to choose and choose soon. Ah, Zafir, impatience will always be your undoing. So now I have to decide what I want. Do I want you? Do I want Lystra? Do I want your throne?*

He sighed. Shezira wasn't going to die. Sirion would dither and abstain. Narghon and Silvallan would call for her to live. Zafir would stand alone and lose. And she would blame him. Now was no time to be uncertain. Before the council and whatever consequences it brought, he would have to decide between his lover and his queen, otherwise it would all go on and on and on, and before you knew where you were, he'd have to avert *another* dragon-war. No, one of them would have to die, and soon. No room for kindness, no room for mercy.

He wandered back inside. There was another hour before dawn but the air was still and stiflingly hot and the nightmares had destroyed any possibility of sleep. He kicked Kazah awake.

Bring me light! he snapped in brusque gestures. Words were lost on Kazah, who was as deaf as a wall. They spoke in signs, in a bastard language of their own devising. Kazah hurried away and was soon back with a candle.

Clothes! Jehal took the candle to a table by the balcony and rooted around until he found a quill and some ink and some writing paper. Behind him, Kazah was holding a tunic and trousers. Jehal dressed himself. Then he sent Kazah away. He sat down and stared at the empty page in front of him.

Lord Meteroa,
   My previous instructions regarding Princess Lystra are withdrawn.
   Jehal

He looked in horror at the words he'd written. So simple, so pure, so innocent in their way, yet they would tell Meteroa everything he needed to know. Anything more would be superfluous. The eyrie-master would understand exactly what was required of him.

He shook his head. *I can't send this. The words may hide their meaning from others, but I'll always know what I've done. I'm commanding Lystra's murder.*

The words sat on the page as words were wont to do. Still, unmoving, accusing. He bit his lip. *And that's exactly what I have to do. She's in the way and she has to go. That was always how it was going to be, and if you weren't prepared for it, you should never have married her in the first place. You could have turned her down when the white dragon you were promised was never given. Face it, you were just being greedy. Just being you, who can never say no when it's served up on a plate for you. Well you've had her every which way you know and so now you can move on. Let her go. Marry Zafir. Follow her as speaker. It's not as if you'll have to wield the knife yourself, not if you don't want to. Say the word and Meteroa will do it for you. You can be a thousand miles away, hands as clean as Zafir's silken sheets.*

I think I might love her though. There. That was an admission, wasn't it?

Pah! Kings have no room for feelings, remember? Who said that, Jehal? Was it you? Yes, I rather think it was. Zafir's much better in bed. Take that and be grateful.

Lystra is carrying my heir. My first-born. A son, perhaps. A son who could one day wear my father's crown. There. Wriggle out of that one.

But was that anything so special? First-born? He must have sired at least a dozen bastards by now. Zafir freely admitted that she might have conceived at least twice because of him and that both times she'd drunk a dose of Dawn Torpor and bled it out. Was this so different? If Lystra knew what was at stake, she'd probably even accept her fate. *My life to save my mother? Yes, my love.*

Without even thinking about it, he'd dropped a blot of molten wax onto the page. It sat there, waiting for him, waiting for the press of his ring to turn his words into a royal command and seal Lystra's fate. The trouble was, his hand wouldn't move.

This is stupid. In a minute the wax is going to go hard and I'm going to have to scrape it off and start again.

He closed his eyes. He didn't have much time for any of the many possible gods that the realms had to offer. Most people saved their prayers for their ancestors, but when it came to that, all Jehal could think about was his father, drooling and useless. And even if dying had restored Tyan's senses, Jehal wasn't at all sure he ought to be praying to someone he'd murdered, especially when it came to murdering someone else. *Conscience troubling you, son? You never prayed to anyone about finishing me off, did you? Got a little trouble with some guilt there? And you thought for some reason that I might want to help you with it?*

Still, he couldn't think of anyone more useful to ask for forgiveness.

Somewhere over the palace, in the first light of the breaking dawn, a dragon shrieked. Two short calls and then a long one; and with the last one it must have swooped straight over the palace, and low too. The whole tower shook with the thunder of its passing.

Jehal froze and then rushed to the window. No one in their right mind would do that, not now, not with the Night Watchman's scorpions lining the walls. There were shouts down below, but they weren't shouts of alarm, and when Jehal swiveled his gaze, he saw that the dragon hadn't flown across the palace, but had actually landed within the Gateyard walls. Men with torches were running toward it. A rider was dismounting and he wasn't waiting for a Scales or anything like that. He was racing straight for the Tower of Air. To Zafir.

Jehal left the letter where it was. He pulled on his boots and ran out of his rooms, out of the Speaker's Tower, and went to find Zafir as well. As he reached the Tower of Air, soldiers raced past him, heading away. He was halfway up the stairs when a bell began to toll. An alarm. More dragons. He ran faster and soon found Zafir, hurriedly dressed, coming the other way.

"Oh, trust you to be the first," she snapped. She swept past him, not quite running but not quite walking either. Jehal reversed and fell in behind her.

"The first to what?"

"We're going to war—what does it look like?"

"What? Are we under attack?"

"You're still not a king, Jehal. You have no voice in this, but if you must know, there are dragons pouring out of the Worldspine. Hundreds of them. Almiri's and Jaslyn's."

Jehal snorted. "That can't be right." *No, no, no, they weren't supposed to do that.*

"Why not? Slipped in and out of the Worldspine, where no one would see them. They mean to attack the palace."

"That *can't* be right." *Could it? Could they really be so bold? If it was true . . .*

"Jehal, listen to me carefully while I say it again slowly. Hundreds of dragons are flying out of the Worldspine. They are coming here. They have gone to war."

Jehal grinned. "If they have then I take off my hat to them. Can we stop them?" *They're insane. They can't possibly have enough dragons. Not with so many of Zafir's already here . . .*

"Of course *I* can stop them."

They were nearly at the bottom of the tower. Jehal's mind raced on. If the Night Watchman was right then Hyrkallan was probably leading the attack. But that couldn't be, could it? Hyrkallan was too canny. He'd never let Jaslyn do something like this. It was suicide. "I know Hyrkallan. He's one to wait and wait and wait and strike when the time is exactly right. Which isn't now. He's devoted to Shezira and an attack now would make her death certain. He'd wait."

"While Jaslyn is impatient and has little love for her mother. Your point?"

"My point?" Jehal laughed, but before he could say any more, a second messenger threw himself to the ground in front of them.

"Your Holiness!" he gasped. "It's not the north. It's the King of the Crags! The King of the Crags is coming!"

19

SILENCE

For all practical purposes, Jaslyn was a prisoner. She'd heard the new speaker's summons and she'd flown south without an inch of doubt inside her. She wasn't sure whether she wanted her mother freed or hanged, but in many ways that was a question that missed the point. Her mother would prevail. She would win because she always won, and Jaslyn would be tossed in her wake like a leaf in a storm.

She'd flown to Southwatch and then to Evenspire and then, quite to her surprise, all her dragons had been taken away. By her own sister. As jailers went, Almiri was as kind as they came, but a prison was a prison, and Jaslyn chafed at the invisible chains that held her to the ground. They might as well have cut off her legs.

"You're mad," Almiri said when Jaslyn had told her where she was going. "Speaker Zafir will throw you in a tower and have your head too."

"And *you're* afraid," was Jaslyn's reply. It hadn't been a good conversation after that. Maybe Almiri was right and Zafir was a monster. Did it matter? Not to go was to concede defeat, wasn't it? Jehal, who most certainly *was* a monster, who surely had his hand up Zafir as far as it would go, would waggle his fingers and make the speaker issue whatever decrees pleased him. Not to go meant no one would be there to challenge him, yet here she was, trapped by her own big sister as if they were both ten years younger and Almiri had been left in charge for the afternoon so their mother could go hunting. After days of frantic preparation, she suddenly found herself with nothing to do except to sit with Isentine and watch Almiri's Scales at their work while her riders kicked their heels in the vastness of the Palace of Paths.

"This is as close as I can get to them," she sighed. "*My* dragons. Just because she's my big sister, why does she think she can get away with this?"

Isentine had a faraway look in his eyes. "Your Highness, this is the first time I've been away from Outwatch in five years. Should I be honest with you?"

"Always. Someone has to be." They walked together among the buildings of the inner eyrie. Jaslyn knew they wouldn't be allowed out onto the landing fields, that Almiri's soldiers had orders to stop her. They were watching her now, a company of them, never too far away.

"I thought, when you asked me to fly with you, that I would never see Outwatch again. I thought that we would fly to the Adamantine Palace and that we would both die on the speaker's command. I thought you were foolish and reckless. I thought you should have come here to see your sister. That you should have come to plan a war together."

Jaslyn growled: "If that's what you thought then why didn't you say anything?" Even here within the outer walls of the Palace of Paths and its eyrie, most of the buildings were guarded. A few of them carried the sign of the alchemists on the doors. Somewhere not far away was the hatchery; the guards were unlikely to let her near Almiri's precious eggs though. *I might smash a few in my impatience to be away.*

Isentine ignored her. "That's what Queen Almiri really wants and you know it. You do yourself no favors spurning her and sulking out here, Your Highness."

"I'm not her little sister anymore, Eyrie-Master. I have almost three times her dragons at my beck and call."

"You should listen to Hyrkallan now that he's back . . ." Isentine kept on talking, but Jaslyn suddenly wasn't listening anymore. Or rather she wasn't listening to *him*. She was listening to someone else. Or something else. A voice, inside her head, so faint she could barely even hear it, and yet so loud it filled the world.

Who are you?

She froze. Two and a half months had passed since she'd last heard that voice in her head. The same voice. Except then it had come from a dragon half dead from poison, who'd breathed its last that same day.

A chill ran through her, down her spine and right to her toes, freezing them to the spot. Her jaw fell open. Her heart began to race.

"Silence?"

I remember you. A venom came with the thoughts, a snarling anger.

Isentine was looking at her, concern on his face.

We will break free of you. One day. One day. I told you that. The thought seemed to fade into the distance. She could almost feel something being wrenched out of her. Whatever it was, her heart went with it.

"Where are you? Silence!"

"Your Highness?" Isentine had an unforgivable hand on her shoulder. "Your Highness!"

She closed her eyes. All she wanted now was to fall to her knees and weep. With a heave and a shudder, she shook Isentine off and looked around. At least a dozen of Almiri's soldiers and servants were watching them.

"You forget yourself, old man." She slapped him. *Mother would have taken your hand and cut it off, even though you were her dearest friend. That's why I'm not ready to be her. I'm not ready to be anything. All I want is Silence. I want my dragon back. That's all.*

Isentine staggered away, bowing as best he could, apologizing and yet still asking whether anything was wrong. Jaslyn didn't know how to answer. The voice in her head had seemed more real than anything, a pinpoint brilliance of color in a world of hazy grays. Now she wasn't sure. *Did I imagine it? I can't ask if anyone heard a voice because there was no voice to be heard.* She took a deep breath and clutched at her head.

"Your Highness! Please!"

"I heard a voice, Isentine." Her face went very hard as she looked at him, willing him to simply listen, to be silent and to believe her. "I heard a dragon. It spoke to me in my thoughts. It was Silence. He remembered me, Eyrie-Master. He remembered everything. He remembered *me.*"

Isentine didn't say anything. Jaslyn could see the disbelief in his eyes, the refusal to even try to understand, but he didn't speak, didn't even shake his head. *He thinks I'm mad. Maybe I am. Mad with grief, mad with loss, but I know what I heard.*

"Your Highness," he said at last, "if he is here, where is he?"

Jaslyn shrugged. "Close, I would think. I don't know. But I have to find him. I have to know that it's true, that they come back and they re-member!"

"Then let us find him. He was yours after all, and if Her Holiness Queen Almiri has a dragon in her eyrie of the colors of smoke and ash and coal, she will not keep it secret for long." He didn't believe her. He'd never believed her. He'd spent forty years and more working with dragons. They'd never spoken to him in his head; they'd never died and been re-born and remembered anything. As far as Isentine was concerned, they'd never done anything except hatch, eat, breed and eventually die like any other animal. Yes, when one died, another was born and their numbers were always the same, but to Isentine that didn't mean anything. They were still animals. As long as they had their potions.

None of that mattered. If he helped her, then she would show him and he would have no choice but to believe her. She stamped her foot and glared at the soldiers. "They won't let us roam around among my sister's dragons."

"No, Your Highness." Isentine shook his head sadly. "Unless . . . Your Highness, I've badgered and cajoled Queen Almiri's eyrie-master and been steadfastly refused. The order comes from the queen herself. But if you promised you would join Almiri in her plans for war . . ."

"I do not *want* a war." Then Jaslyn almost smiled. She wagged a finger at her eyrie-master. "I see. You would have me join her council but not her war." She walked quickly now, forcing Isentine to hobble along as best he could in her wake. "Very well. She can have me at her table, but I will not throw my dragons into some foolishness." She took a turn, out of impulse, down a narrow alley between two low stone storehouses with long win-dowless walls.

"Hey! Your Highness! Stop!" The voice came from behind her. It sounded like one of Almiri's soldiers, so Jaslyn ignored it. "By the command of the queen, you are not permitted to enter . . ."

She reached the end of the alley. Several soldiers were in pursuit, but the passage was narrow, the soldiers were armed and armored, and Isentine was a frail old man, hobbling slowly and in the way.

"Move aside, sir!"

"I am Queen Shezira's eyrie-master, you insolent fellow! And I'm going as fast as I can."

Jaslyn watched them for a second, smiled, and walked briskly into the eyrie. Not because she particularly wanted to but simply because she could. She wouldn't get very far. There would be other soldiers to get in her way. She wasn't sure what they would do if she refused to stop, if she physically tried to push them out of the way. They surely wouldn't dare to lay a hand on her, not even on the queen's order.

She did stop though. Her path led her to a huge stone barn. Its immense black doors were ajar and a warm wind blew out at her from inside. The air reeked of hatchling and heat and death. Several soldiers stood between her and the door, but the smell would have stopped her anyway. Her face tightened. The smell was one that every eyrie knew. A hatchling had died.

As she stood there, she heard Isentine, still shouting at Almiri's soldiers, and then the soldiers arriving behind her.

"Your Highness, by order of the queen, you are not permitted—"

She spun around and slapped the speaker across his face, then turned straight back again. She didn't move, only watched as the great black doors swung open.

"One of your queen's dragons has died," she said, very quietly. Anyone who worked in an eyrie, even the guards, ought to know better than to do anything except be still and to watch until the alchemists and the Scales had done their work.

Four Scales dressed in heavy leather gauntlets and overalls emerged, dragging behind them a heavy stone sled. The dead hatchling lay on the sled, curled up. Not covered by anything in case it caught fire. Two alchemists followed behind. They carried silver bowls hanging from chains in their hands and they swung them back and forth, gently sprinkling water and their potions over the hatchling's sizzling scales. All six men wore masks. The alchemists made potions that mitigated the worst effects of Hatchling Disease, but the strain of the disease from a dead hatchling was the most virulent of them all. Even the Scales were not immune.

Jaslyn stood very still, watching as they dragged the dragon away. She felt the heat of its death fade as the body was pulled out of sight. When they were gone she moved very slowly, surrendering herself to the soldiers behind her, letting them walk her to the edge of the eyrie and into the inner walls of the Palace of Paths, toward Almiri and her council. None of that seemed to matter now. She was lost, swallowed by a delirious kaleidoscope of glorious hope and crushing despair. Never mind that the colors had been all wrong; she knew with a certainty that she couldn't understand that the dead hatchling had been her Silence.

Reborn.

Remembering.

Which made it all true. Every bit of it.

20

THE COUNCIL OF KINGS AND QUEENS

Vale stood on the walls as the skies darkened with dragons. After thirty years in the Adamantine Guard, the sight of so many still made his heart trip. He'd never seen them in such numbers before, even when all the kings and queens had come together at the passing of Iyanza to name Hyram as the next speaker. They flew in from the west and circled over the palace and then began to land around the edges of the Mirror Lakes. The speaker's eyrie was already full, but that didn't seem to trouble them. They'd brought their own, he slowly realized. Everything they needed. The excitement inside him felt strange and he wondered what was stirring him so. Later, as the skies cleared and the first riders walked their dragons to the palace gates, he understood. Thirty years in the Guard. He'd seen kings and queens and speakers come and go, but in all that time the King of the Crags had never come out of his mountains to the palace. It made you wonder why this time was so special.

"Apparently we nearly went to war this morning. All very exciting. I do hope there weren't any accidents."

Vale jumped and gritted his teeth. Prince Jehal had somehow crept up behind him.

"Mind you, I suppose we're still not quite sure, eh? My father used to tell stories about the King of the Crags. Back when he could still string a sentence together of course. Back when I was a little boy."

Vale bowed and said nothing. *Why are you telling me these things? Do you think that we shall somehow pretend that we are friends?*

Jehal was still talking and it didn't seem to matter to him whether Vale was listening. "All sorts of stories. They say the Mountain King has more dragons than any two kings or queens together. Is it true, Night Watchman. Did you count them?"

"I did not, Your Highness, but it will be done. I would say some three hundred and fifty beasts, but there are men in the Guard with better eyes than mine."

"Three hundred and fifty! Ancestors! My father wasn't making it up then."

What do you want from me? Again Vale held his tongue. The answer was obvious—Jehal wanted to know whether he would betray the speaker. *Well you'll get nothing from me now. We'll see about that soon enough.*

"I wonder if that means that the rest of it's true too." A procession of dragons was walking up from the Mirror Lakes. Twenty war-dragons each with four riders on their backs. Three scorpions mounted on each saddle. Vale frowned at that. It was unusual to see three. *Most eyrie-masters don't mount a scorpion on the nape of the neck like that. Too many accidents when a rider tries to shoot at an enemy straight ahead of him.*

Jehal seemed oblivious. "My father used to tell tales of mischief," he said. "He used to say that there was another race of people who lived in the mountains. Little people, short, who stood no higher than the pit of your arm. With mean spirits filled with wickedness. Said they served the King of the Crags and that he would send them out to sow the seeds of discontent and rebellion among the good men and women of the realms."

And why bother when there are teeth and claws and fire that serve the same purpose with a great deal more effect? Or when we have the likes of you among us? Vale said nothing.

"He said they moved among us, unseen but there nonetheless."

For a moment Vale couldn't resist. "The first Valmeyan fought against Vishmir in the War of Thorns. It is said among the Guard that he ran circles around even your Prince Lai. After Anzuine executed Speaker Voian,

Valmeyan abandoned him and flew to the mountains, taking half the dragons from the Pinnacles with him. He took his own alchemists. No one knew where he was."

Jehal chuckled. "The Great Dragon Hunt. Yes, I know all about that. Though I don't think he had much love for his speakers. No, I'd say what he did had a lot more to do with Anzuine and you Adamantine Men sacking the Silver City. Not a clever thing to do, burning the home of your foremost dragon-marshal. But I take your meaning. It is true that we of the south have little love for the mountain men. My father would say that all bad things have their birth within the caves and tunnels of the Worldspine."

"The potions that control your dragons have their origins there, Your Highness," murmured Vale.

"You have me again, Night Watchman. Good things have their birth there as well, I dare say."

"The Great Flame tells us two things: all that brought order to the world came from the Worldspine long ago; and all that will render the world unto ash will come from there also."

The prince made a face. "Don't tell me you listen to that priestly rubbish."

"I may have forsaken love and a long life, Prince Jehal, but I have not forsaken faith. The Flame burns brightly among the Adamantine Men." He spoke mildly, hiding the disgust he felt. *Were you not a prince I would reach out and with one hand I would crush your throat and snap your spine.* He had a flashing vision of ramming his fist right down Jehal's throat and tearing his tongue out by the roots. It was deeply satisfying.

"I didn't know that," said the Viper softly. "I will remember in future. I'm sorry if I offended you, Night Watchman."

Vale kept his face blank. "There is no offense, Your Highness." *You indolent, faithless piece of shit.*

"Good. Then shall we see what the Worldspine has vomited up for us this time?" Jehal laughed. "The King of the Crags draws near. And amid the pleasure of our conversation I seem to have quite forgotten my errand. The speaker has called for you at once. You are to greet the king on her behalf and escort him to the council of kings and queens. He is late, after all, and they're all waiting for him. You might mention that to him."

For a moment the iron control that held Vale Tassan together creaked and shifted. His face blanched. "*I* am to greet the King of the Crags?"

"The speaker is the speaker, and Valmeyan, for all his airs, is still a mere king and must bend his knee to her. *She* could not possibly come to *him*." Jehal smiled a happy smile. "Of course, if you are daunted, I will be happy to take your place."

Oh I don't think so, slippery one. "I am honored, Your Highness, and flattered. I will do as I am commanded, as all Adamantine Men have always done. You may tell the speaker and the council if you wish."

Jehal's smile didn't change. "I think the idea is that you do this with a few thousand of your Adamantine Men lined up at your back. A show of the speaker's strength, if you like, to counter Valmeyan's predictably portentous arrival." He glanced down. "I would say you have a few minutes yet before his dragons reach the gates. I do hope that's enough."

Here came that flashing vision again, except this time Vale simply saw himself smashing every last one of the Viper's teeth as well. *Oh, how I look forward to the day when I can cut that condescending grin off your lips.* His eyes narrowed in concentration. *A few minutes to call four legions or more of men down from the walls and into formation. We can only thank the Flame that the Dragon Gates are already manned and prepared . . .* Jehal didn't even move. Just stood, hands clasped behind his back, watching and smiling. *Grinning like a snake. Fine. Then see why we are feared as we are.* He whistled. Loudly. Loudly enough to see Jehal flinch, which was at least some small consolation. Across the walls, his soldiers turned to look, waiting for his orders. He made three clear gestures. *All legions. Guard of honor. Immediately.* Then he pointed down at the gates. The soldiers with him on the walls didn't need any telling. They were already sprinting to the nearest legion commanders in case they hadn't seen the signal. *Stupid, stripping the walls for a mere ceremony with so many dragons camped around the palace. Surely a single legion would have done?* He wondered then whether Jehal had exaggerated, or even made up the speaker's order on some whim of his own. He didn't think so. It had all the usual thoughtlessness he'd come to expect from Speaker Zafir.

It's not my place to question such things. All across the palace walls he could see his order take effect. Soldiers were leaving their posts and streaming down ladders and stairs.

"It's very impressive." Jehal was still grinning. "They're very attentive to you, Night Watchman."

"We obey without hesitation or question, Your Highness. That is our way. All of us. Such obedience is necessary to survive when the enemy breathes fire." Jehal was in the way. Vale almost had to push past him to get off the tower and down the steps into the vast space of the Gateyard. By the time he got there, hundreds of soldiers were already massing into orderly ranks, each man knowing exactly his place within his own legion. With a few curt snaps of his hands he made small adjustments to the legion positions as they continued to form. He almost didn't notice that Jehal had followed him.

"It's like watching a master puppeteer at his work. Or a wizard. Does it not leave a mark on you, Night Watchman, to wield such power with a simple wave of your hands?"

If I was a wizard then I would wave my hands and flick you away as if brushing a fleck of shit from my sleeve. Vale bowed. "This is the power of the speaker, Your Highness. Not mine." *And I don't have the time to have some mongrel prince dancing at my heels.* "All is well in hand. Please do not allow me to deter you from your business. If it pleases you, you may tell the speaker that the honor guard will be ready. I will have the gates opened for King Valmeyan as he approaches."

Prince Jehal pursed his lips and took a sharp breath. "Pithy, Night Watchman. You mean surely there is something more useful I should be doing, and please could I get out of your way."

"Not at all, Your Highness." *Although if you're in an obliging frame of mind, perhaps you could cut yourself on your own tongue and choke to death on your own blood. It would be an inconvenience to clear up such a mess but I daresay it could be done in time.* Vale marched briskly toward the gates. Still Jehal stayed with him, raising an eyebrow in his wake.

"Well, if I'm truly not distracting you from your duties, the truth is that I have none of my own and my curiosity compels me to remain. I would see the face of this King of the Crags for myself."

"It will be the same face in the council of kings and queens, I don't doubt." Vale clenched his teeth. *There, see. Now you've made me show my impatience with you. Is that what you wanted? Can you take your little victory and go away now?*

"Doubtless it will. But as I'm sure you are aware, Night Watchman, I am not yet a king, and thus my presence is not required. I am not sure I shall go."

"My own opinions are worthless and insignificant but I have noted that Speaker Zafir seems to value yours, Your Highness." Vale waved his hands again, shifting the front legions apart. They would need more space to allow Valmeyan's dragons to pass between them. Then he snapped a hand toward the immense gates, which immediately began to open. Outside, King Valmeyan's dragons were less than a hundred yards from the palace. He fought back the urge to look over his shoulder, to make sure that his legions were perfect. Of course they were perfect.

Inch by inch the gates ground open, a hundred men pulling on each of them. Vale walked forward and stopped inside their shadow. The first of the dragons stepped into the space in front of him, seeming to squeeze itself down to fit beneath the colossal Gatehouse arch. It stopped, its head a few feet away from his own. He smelled its breath, hot and rank. The creature had golden eyes as large as his head, teeth as long as his leg, a head the size of a horse and a body as big as a barn. A true monster, as large a wardragon as he'd ever seen. The sort of creature that could smash down even the mighty Gatehouse towers simply by crashing into them. It made him tiny, and as it lowered its head to look at him, it sniffed and its lips twitched, as if to remind him that a dragon this size was always, *always* hungry.

And here, Vale knew, was his strength, the strength of every man behind him. For where any normal man would be shaking and quaking and pissing his pants, he stood still, solid and unmoved. He looked for the fear that any normal man should feel in the presence of such a monster and found nothing. Nothing at all.

The rider mounted on the war-dragon's neck took off his helm. Prince Tichane. Valmeyan's second son and ambassador to the palace.

"King Valmeyan," roared Tichane. "The King of the Crags answers the speaker's call."

You should be begging to enter, as every other king begged to enter. And it was not a call but a summons. Vale bowed. Jehal was *still* beside him. And he wasn't shaking and quaking and pissing his pants either. "The speaker welcomes you and bids you and yours to enter, under the ancient laws of hospitality," Vale cried. He was about to move aside to let Tichane and his monster pass into the Gateyard, but suddenly Jehal had a hand on his shoulder.

"You may pass, Prince Tichane," shouted Jehal. "You and all those behind you. But no dragons save those of the speaker may enter the grounds of the Adamantine Palace. You should know that."

There was a very long silence.

"You did bring enough riders with you to walk all those poor beasts back to wherever they came from, I hope?"

Vale kept his face still. It was as well, he decided, that he'd had such extensive practice.

"You're also late," said Jehal, loudly enough to carry well past Tichane to the riders behind him. "The council convened at dawn. If you're lucky, they'll have waited. It would be a shame for such a grand entrance to be so utterly wasted."

For long seconds, Prince Tichane didn't move. Then the dragon lowered its head even more, so that it touched the ground. Tichane opened the buckles on his harness and slid down to the ground. He ignored Vale and walked up to Jehal. Back outside the palace, other riders were dismounting.

"You're a rude nasty fellow this morning," he said. Jehal gave him a florid bow.

"Be careful what you say, Tichane. You'll be calling me Your Holiness before you leave."

"So I hear. So you are the speaker's mouthpiece today, Jehal. I suppose

I should not be surprised. My father will be disappointed that she isn't here to greet him."

Jehal replied with a sad shake of his head. "If King Valmeyan wishes to set himself up as Zafir's equal, I'm afraid this disappointment will be the first of many. You may find yourself wishing you hadn't come."

Tichane snorted. "Then I will not be alone. Are we to run, then, since we are late?"

"Oh, I dare say a brisk walk will suffice."

They walked away together, in between the perfect legions of the Adamantine Men and toward the Chamber of Audience. On the outside, the damage from the Red Riders' attack had been made good. On the inside though, the chamber still bore the scars. Vale watched them go and waited. He wasn't here for princes, he was here for a king. He had to wait for the rest of the riders outside the palace to arrange themselves. One by one the dragons were turned and walked away, Tichane's was the last. When it left, two columns of riders marched through the gates. Vale studied them closely as they advanced. The rider at their head wore the same armor as the rest of them but he had an aura that Vale knew well. He was old for a rider too.

As they drew up in front of him, Vale bowed low, exactly as he would bow for any other king or queen. "Your Holiness. The speaker welcomes you and bids you and yours to enter, under the ancient laws of hospitality . . ."

They swept past him without a glance. Vale stayed exactly where he was until all the riders had gone. Then, with a gesture, he ordered the gates closed. As Valmeyan and his riders marched into the Chamber of Audience, he signaled his legions to return to the walls and their duties. Back where they should have been in the first place.

Most of them. A few he beckoned toward him. A dozen, that would be enough. They followed Valmeyan and quietly entered the chamber. The air inside smelled new, rich with fresh wood and paint. At the far end, Speaker Zafir sat with her kings. Valmeyan was standing before them. Further away stood riders from all the kings and queens assembled here, bearing witness to the words of the council, a company of them from every realm, even a few from the north. Jeiros and Aruch too, alchemists and priests clustered around them. Vale strode briskly among them, all the way to the speaker's table. All the way to the seat where Prince Jehal lounged insolently, sneering as the speaker and the King of the Crags exchanged their first ritual greeting in thirty years. Vale stood behind him. He gave himself a moment to savor what he was about to do.

"Prince Jehal."

Jehal looked up. He didn't look troubled so he obviously had no idea what was coming. "Night Watchman."

There weren't many moments of pure joy in the brief life of a Night Watchman. That was something Vale had come to understand a long time ago, and so he took his time with this one. "Prince Jehal," he said again, lingering on every word, "you are charged with conspiring to aid and abet the enemies of the realms. By order of the speaker, you are stripped of all titles and authorities."

"What?" Jehal half rose out of his chair. Vale put a heavy hand on his shoulder, forcing him back down again. *You can't begin to imagine how satisfying this is.*

"You will be taken to the Tower of Dusk. There you will stay for the remainder of your days, awaiting the speaker's sentence." At a gesture, four of Vale's soldiers seized Jehal and dragged him out of his chair.

"Zafir!" he shouted, but the speaker's face was cold. She didn't even glance at him. "Night Watchman, unhand me! I am quite capable of walking. I am hardly likely to escape."

Vale didn't look at him. He lowered his voice so that only Jehal would hear. "True enough. And I will admit to being impressed that you didn't even flinch in front of Prince Tichane's monster. But still, all things considered, I think I prefer to have you dragged, Your Highness."

The Gateyard outside was clear. His legions were already back on the walls and the towers. Vale took a moment to look around him.

A good day's work and we've hardly even started. He already had a heavy sword sharpened up for Queen Shezira's head. It could easily take another. One could always hope.

21

THE QUEEN IN THE TOWER

They opened the door, threw him inside and shut it behind him. Jehal sat up and rubbed his bruises. A pair of servants stared at him, wide-eyed like startled rabbits, then scurried away. As the door slammed closed, twilight enveloped him. The air was hazy with smoke despite the height of the room. Shafts of sunlight pierced the walls and lit patches of fire on the floor; everywhere else danced in flickering shadow.

"Hello, Prince Jehal. Please don't get up. I'll shoot you if you do."

Jehal froze. The voice came from off to one side. Shezira. He turned his head, and there she was, sitting half hidden by one of the massive columns that vanished into the vaulted gloom above. She was holding a crossbow, a large one, calmly, steadily pointing it at him.

His heart began to pound. *How much does she know?*

"The trouble with the condemned," he said, slowly and softly, "is that they have very little to lose. You appear to have been expecting me, Your Holiness."

"Did you think I was *entirely* powerless in here? The Night Watchman let slip that you would be joining me this morning. He also let slip a crossbow and a single bolt. Very careless of him, don't you think?"

"Very." An acidic smile settled on Jehal's face. "I appear to have been well and truly . . . expected."

"He must hate you very much, Jehal. I know he hates me. He thinks I killed Hyram. I don't imagine he much cares which one of us dies. He probably hopes for both of us."

"Did he tell you that I was conspiring with him to help you escape?" Jehal frowned. "*Trying* to conspire with him, at any rate. I wonder how long he pondered my proposal before he ran to Zafir."

"I've heard that you conspired a good deal. I'm left to wonder how much of it is true."

"Quite a lot of it, I don't doubt." Jehal shrugged. "I do so *enjoy* a good conspiring."

"As I would enjoy hearing about them."

Jehal snorted. "What, so we can pass the time with some civilized conversation and *then* you kill me? Why not do us both a favor and get it over with quickly."

"Killing you is clearly what I'm supposed to do, but I am not inclined to be cooperative. If at all possible, I mean to shoot you somewhere painful and leave you to live as a cripple. That would be much more satisfying."

"Pity you wouldn't be here to watch though, eh. But kill me now and three of the nine realms will be controlled by your daughters, all baying for war and revenge. I doubt Zafir would survive for long. I'm surprised you didn't get straight on and do it."

"I'm not much interested in a war, Jehal."

Jehal couldn't help but laugh. "That's what I keep telling them. Although . . ." He shrugged and sighed. "Not being interested in a war doesn't seem to have done me much good." *Keep talking.* Talking was good. Talking wasn't shooting.

Shezira almost smiled at him, although the crossbow didn't flinch. "I was under the impression that you being here to have this conversation had rather more to do with Princess Lystra. It is a little difficult to decide whether she'll live longer with you dead or with you alive. You understand, I hope, that she is my only consideration in how I deal with you."

"Ah." Jehal let that sink in along with all the implications that came with it. "Yes. Unfortunate thing that. I suppose you realize that Zafir had a certain amount of help getting to where she is. I didn't need to help her seduce Hyram, but I certainly let her steal the potions she gave him. I al-lied myself with you and made sure Hyram knew about it. Hyram would have had an accident around now. Lystra would have followed a year later. I would have married Zafir and in time I would have succeeded her. That was what we planned, as I'm sure you've already grasped. But Zafir got impatient and I found something in Lystra that I didn't expect, and so here I find myself. That is the extent of my conspiracy, Your Holiness. You can get on with shooting me now if you wish. I should warn you though that you may miss. If you do, why, then I think we shall have some fun." He shifted onto his knees, trying to get more comfortable, at the same time readying himself to spring to his feet. Shezira gave a slight shake of her head.

"You stay sitting exactly where you are. Keep your legs flat on the floor."

Jehal rolled his eyes. "If you prefer, Your Holiness, I will lie on my belly. Or on my back, with my feet in the air."

"As you are will be perfectly adequate." Shezira rose out of her chair and came slowly toward him, but kept a wary distance, circling around him. "I didn't push Hyram off his balcony, you know."

"Yes, I know. I saw."

"Really?"

"He fell. I've been trying quite hard to convince others of your in-nocence."

"Have you now?" Her voice was cold. She didn't believe him, probably didn't believe him about Lystra either. She was prowling around him now. Her hands on the crossbow were as steady as stone, and her eyes . . . Her eyes showed no forgiveness, no mercy. In the north they called her the Queen of Stone, the Queen of Flint. Jehal had called her that too, behind her back, but now he understood what they *really* meant. His heart skipped. He bit his lip.

"Were you poisoning him, Jehal?" she asked. Jehal hesitated. If he lied, and she already knew . . . but he'd undone himself anyway by not answer-ing straightaway.

"Yes," he said.

"And your father?"

This time he was ready. His face twisted into a sneer. "Everyone seems to think so. Why should I disappoint you all?"

The look she gave him was a queer one, as if he'd somehow answered another question, one that she hadn't asked but one that mattered a great deal more. "And me, Jehal? Why were you trying to poison me?"

He snorted, surprised. "You? Why would I poison you? You were no threat to me."

"I am now."

"Sadly, my powers of foresight did not predict this little awkwardness. Zafir having me thrown in a dungeon while she had you put to death, yes, I suppose I half expected that. It being *this* dungeon and my good friend the Night Watchman having left you so wickedly dangerous, that possibility I'm afraid had entirely escaped me."

"Again, Jehal, why were you trying to poison me? I cannot fathom what you would gain from it, yet I cannot see who else it could be."

Jehal furrowed his brow and shook his head. *What are you talking about, woman?* "Your Holiness, I never have tried to poison you. In actual fact, despite all Hyram's little fantasies, I've murdered remarkably few people. Your daughter, for example. Notably not murdered, however politically useful it might have been. You. Also not murdered. And I can promise you, Queen Shezira, that when I aim to make someone dead, they die. I helped Zafir steal the Speaker's Ring from you, but poison you? No. I would have been quite happy for you to go back to Outwatch and fester. I've never tried to have you harmed in any way; in fact, since Hyram stupidly fell off his own balcony, I've done everything I can to keep you alive. Not out of any love for you, you understand, but, believe it or not, for love of the realms. Of everything. Of life. Zafir doesn't just want *your* head. She's going to execute King Valgar as well, and then she's going to move on to all three of your daughters. I'm *trying* to stop her." He looked ruefully around the Tower of Dusk. "Not with as much success as I'd hoped, it would seem."

Shezira snorted and shook her head. "Why should I believe a word you say? Hyram called you a viper, and he wasn't wrong. We all should have listened to him."

"Your daughter Jaslyn sits on your throne. Almiri rules in Evenspire. With Zafir they will take all the realms into flames. You don't need *me* to tell you that."

"Jaslyn has Hyrkallan to guide her." For a moment, Jehal wondered how the queen could possibly know that Hyrkallan had abandoned the Red Riders and returned north. Then he realized that she probably didn't know that the Red Riders even existed. "Besides, she cares more for her dragons than she does for me." A touch of bitterness tinged Shezira's voice now. "She won't go to war, not for me. The only person she truly cares about is her little sister, your Lystra. Keep her alive and safe and Jaslyn will stay in her eyries."

"Lystra is carrying my heir."

"So I've heard. Another reason to keep her alive."

"I'm trying very hard to do so."

Shezira nodded her head. "Good. Unfortunately, I rather fear for my daughter after she's given you what you want. So let me give you something that is both help and encouragement." And with that, Shezira pointed the crossbow between Jehal's legs and fired.

The force knocked him back across the polished marble floor; and then came the pain, unbearable, burning, blinding, shrieking pain that seemed to run like liquid fire along every nerve and bone.

"Zafir will have to find another lover now," said Shezira, although Jehal could hardly hear her over the roaring in his head. He couldn't see anything either. "We are truly tied together now, blood to blood, Prince Jehal. If my bloodline dies, so does yours."

The roaring sounds, Jehal realized, were his own screams.

22

THE EXECUTION OF HIS DUTIES

V ale stood, still as a statue, as the Herald of Titles announced each and every sitting member of the council of kings and queens. Only the monarchs had any real say in what would be decided, but they'd brought a good few lords and ladies and a smattering of princes and princesses with them. Vale wondered if it made them feel more important. The other possibility was that it made them feel safe, a thought which he took as a personal affront.

He, of course, was not sitting and was not announced. His soldiers stood quietly, scattered around the Chamber of Audience, some more obvious than others, deceptive in their numbers. A casual glance might say he'd brought only a dozen men to guard the speaker and her guests. The truth was closer to ten times that number. Some of them were also witnesses. Witnesses who would say that they'd seen Queen Shezira enter the speaker's rooms, invited in by the speaker's wordmaster. That they'd heard the speaker call out, shouting for something that they hadn't been able to understand. That they'd gone into his rooms and found Queen Shezira standing on his balcony with the speaker already lying dead below.

But none of them actually saw the push. None of them saw him fall. He hadn't given it too much thought until the kings from the south and the east had started to arrive. Then they'd all started asking. Did you *see* it? Did anyone actually see Shezira murder Speaker Hyram? Narghon's queen,

Fyon, she was the worst. By the time she was finished, even the wordmaster, who'd been adamant that Shezira was guilty, was having his doubts.

I am the Night Watchman of the dragon-soldiers. We do not have doubt. The Guard are always certain of their cause. From birth to death. Nothing more, nothing less. Hyram fell. Shezira pushed. End. There is no other explanation that makes sense.

Eventually they finished and Speaker Zafir summoned him to the Table of Judges to speak what he knew. He did exactly as he was asked. He had gone to the Tower of Dusk to confine Queen Shezira and her men. The queen was not present in the tower. He had sent other men to stand watch over Speaker Hyram. When he heard of Speaker Hyram's death, he had ordered the Tower of Dusk to be stormed. Yes, he'd lost a good few men. Yes, the defenders had thrown back his first assault, and were only turned to flight by the arrival of the remainder of the legion. Yes, he had been impatient and possibly foolish, and yes, several of Shezira's riders had escaped. Including, as it had happened, Queen Almiri.

As soon as they had no more use for him, he bowed and walked away. Others would follow. His men. Good men. If there were any omissions or any falsehoods in what Vale had said, none of them knew it. They would tell the truth because they had no reason to do otherwise, but they would just as easily lie if he told them to. *Orders. The Guard obeys orders. From birth to death. Nothing more, nothing less. Why do they always forget that?*

For most of the morning the questions went on. The speaker grew visibly impatient. King Sirion sat and twisted his fingers in his beard. The King of the Crags looked as if he'd fallen asleep. Only the two eastern kings, Narghon and Silvallan, seemed to care about what anyone had to say. *They all made up their minds before they came here. All of them except Hyram's cousin.*

He'd made up his own mind too. Made it up long ago. As he listened, he wondered whether he should consider again, question his belief and be sure. But that sort of thinking wasn't going to get him anywhere. No one had ever asked him for an opinion and he'd never offered one. The kings and queens of the realms would make their judgment and he would execute it. That was all.

So why are my knuckles clenched white? Why is the inside of my head burning?

"Enough!" Zafir stood up and slammed the point of the Adamantine Spear into the marble floor. The blade drove at least three inches into the stone. Vale wasn't sure that Zafir even noticed. She glared out from the Table of Judges at all the standing members of the council. "The kings and queens of the dragon-realms will pass their judgment. I say Queen Shezira murdered Speaker Hyram. We have a hundred witnesses to say they were alone and that no one else could have been with them. My husband was old. He was sick and drunk and hardly able to defend himself, but not so sick and drunk that he'd simply fall off a balcony. Shezira was desperate and had every reason to want revenge. Further, I say that King Valgar and Knight-Marshal Lady Nastria were her pawns. I say that their efforts to murder me were at her command." She turned her glare onto the sitting council. "What say you? King Sirion, your judgment, please."

Sirion didn't move. He was shaking his head and couldn't have looked less comfortable. "I'll not condemn another king on such flimsy evidence," he said. "If Shezira's knight-marshal was truly set on murder that night, she would not have taken her orders from anyone but Shezira herself. I say Valgar has committed no crime. Shezira . . ." He took a deep breath and shook his head even more. "I don't know. Hyram was my cousin. My heart calls for justice and vengeance. But I cannot, despite the evidence, believe that Queen Shezira would murder him with her own hand. I simply cannot. I have nothing to say. I do not pass judgment."

Zafir's face darkened with fury. "He was your cousin! Who else was there to push him?"

"I have given my verdict," snapped Sirion. He didn't look at Zafir when he said it though. He looked like a man who'd be wondering whether he'd done the right thing for a very long time.

The speaker sneered. "And we all know that Shezira offered her daughter to Prince Dyalt. Has little Jaslyn not thought better of marrying a fool?"

"You have my answer." Sirion stood up. "I will not be the one to start a war, Speaker, and if *you* mean to do so, I suggest you consider who are your allies and who are your enemies very carefully. You'd not be the first speaker who failed to see out their first year." With that, Sirion walked away from the Table of Judges. The lords and princes of his entourage got up to follow him.

Vale flinched. His hand moved to rest on his sword and he almost took a step forward, he was so sure that Zafir would command Sirion's arrest. What he'd said was nothing short of a threat. Yet Zafir watched him go in silence. She only spoke when he and his were gone from the Chamber of Audience.

"It seems King Sirion does not share my opinion." She was all smiles now. "King Silvallan, what say you?"

"You can have Valgar if you must. I venture no opinion on his guilt or otherwise. But you may not have Shezira. She did not murder Speaker Hyram."

Zafir nodded slowly. "Are those your words or Jehal's?"

"They are mine, Speaker."

"And you, Narghon? I imagine your words will be exactly the same, almost as though someone had written them down for you both. Although they are *your* words, I am sure."

"I share King Silvallan's views. Shezira cannot be condemned without a witness who saw Hyram fall. Accept your defeat with some grace, Your Holiness, and accept that it is for the good of the realms that Shezira goes free."

"Then it seems I am alone. They sent an assassin after me and then, when she failed, they killed my husband. Yet none of you will condemn them." Vale bit his lip. *This is how Jehal said it would be. Shezira will go free. There will be no war between the north and the south, and the legions I command will not be hurled into battle against a sky filled with dragons.* He wasn't sure how he felt about that. The Adamantine Men were made for battle. Forged for it from the day they could walk and talk. They had no other purpose to their existence. The thought of war made Vale's heart race and his blood run hot. His head filled with visions of glory, of slaughtering riders and scattering their dragons. Any of the Adamantine Men would think themselves lucky and honored to be called to war. After all, that's what they were told from the day they took up their first training spears.

On the other hand, he was the Night Watchman. They were *his* men, and his second duty, after his devotion to the speaker, was to them. To their strength and to their lives and to their health, not to honor and glory. The Viper was right about one thing. Wars were bloody. Very many would die and few would be dragon-lords.

"King Valmeyan. Since you have graced my palace with your presence, what say you? Do you have an opinion to offer, or do you intend to doze until all the matters of this council have been closed?"

The King of the Crags barely opened his eyes. "I've heard one voice either way for King Valgar, am I right? I've never met him and probably never will. If I remember the law, the speaker casts the final judgment if the council is tied, so I will offer no opinion. King Valgar's fate rests entirely in your hands, Speaker. As for Queen Shezira, she I *have* met. She came to my eyries a decade and more ago, seeking my support to ensure Hyram sat where you sit now. I say she is quite capable of murdering a man. Perhaps she did, perhaps she didn't. I leave her fate in your hands too, Speaker Zafir. Shezira is guilty." He uncoiled himself from his slouch, slowly stretched and turned to look Zafir in the eye. "You hold a very sharp spear in your hand, Speaker. Who will you cut with it?"

The smile that curled across Speaker Zafir's mouth made even Vale's stomach turn. The feeling was strange and new, until he realized what it was. Not fear, that was too strong a word. Anxiety. Yes, he was anxious.

She was looking at *him* now. "Then they are both guilty. Yes. Since it is the duty of the speaker to cast sentence, they are both guilty and they are to be beheaded. Their remains will hang in cages by the gates of the Adamantine Palace, one on either side, until they have been picked clean by the crows. They will serve to warn all others who would overthrow the laws of the realms."

King Silvallan hammered the table with his fists. "You cannot do this!"

"I can and I will. Today, Night Watchman. As soon as possible. Valgar first. Let Shezira see! Go! Do it now!"

The Table of Judges was in uproar. Silvallan and Narghon were on their feet. Jeiros and Aruch were shouting at each other. Only the King of the Crags seemed unmoved. He'd slumped back into his seat and if anything looked as though he'd fallen asleep again. Vale hesitated. All his instincts said he ought to stay, that there was every sign of the council coming to blows. But he'd been given an order, clear and unambiguous. Reluctantly he bowed toward the chaos, turned and walked away. The Adamantine Men who served as his officers were all quite capable of taking his place. When it came to war, they had to be.

Outside, he set about the execution of his duties. Orders were given. The Guard had quietly prepared for this for days, just as they'd prepared for Shezira to be released. They all knew what to do. One company of men would bring out the headsman's block and sword and throw plenty of sand down into the Gateyard to soak up the blood. Another company would drag Valgar out of the tower where Zafir had imprisoned him. He'd get Shezira himself. *The cages were a little unexpected. They'll need some quick work to get ready but at least we have a little more time with those. She never said what she wanted us to do with the heads. Mounted on spikes would be usual.*

At the doors to the Tower of Dusk, Vale stopped. His head was filled with all the little details; underneath, something much bigger was stirring. He was old enough and wise enough to know what that meant. Doubts. He had doubts about what he was doing. And since Adamantine Men never had doubts, he was trying to hide them.

Come on then, doubts. Speak your piece and be done. There will be war, is that it? Shezira's daughters will fly out of the north on wings of fire. And out of the south too, perhaps. What of it? Many will die, but what of it? Is it my doing? Have I gone to their eyries and commanded their riders to fly against the speaker, who is their law? No, I have not. Or do I doubt that we will win? Well, doubts, if that's the case, I've seen enough of these kings and queens over the years to know that Zafir is safe. If any of them truly have the spine to take up arms against us, as likely as not they will be stabbed in the back by their own sons and daughters, hungry for a throne of their own. So be gone, doubts. My conscience is clear.

His doubts didn't seem convinced but they knew their place. They slid beneath the surface of his thoughts to lurk in the depths of his dreams. He ordered the door to the Tower of Dusk to be opened and entered with a dozen men behind him. He went in with care because Queen Shezira did have a crossbow, after all, and there was just a chance she hadn't done what he'd hoped and used it on Jehal. But he soon saw that he needn't have worried. The floor was stained by a big pool of blood, still sticky to the touch. Jehal, assuming that's from whom the blood had come, had obviously survived for long enough to drag himself away.

Not very far though. Thick brown streaks led away from the blood to a second pool. Jehal looked dead at first, curled up, both hands pressed between his legs. The Viper was still breathing, though. The breaths might have been ragged and shallow, but if he'd lived this long then he probably wasn't going to bleed to death.

Pity. This was meant to wound. If Shezira had meant to finish him, she had ample means. He stooped to look closer. The crossbow bolt he'd given Shezira was gone. Shezira was still dangerous then. Then a huge grin spread across Vale's face as he understood what the Queen of Stone had done to the Viper. He glanced around him, the sudden thought of finishing Jehal off running wild in his head, but there was no way to do it without being seen. Too many of his own men.

His grin faded. He kicked Jehal in the face and moved on. Shezira was waiting for him, calm and peaceful, holding the crossbow he'd given her, casually pointing it in his direction.

"What's it to be?" she asked. Vale didn't answer, didn't break stride. He saw the tension in her face, saw her finger on the trigger straining. He saw the moment she understood that he'd come to take her to her death. He saw her pull the trigger and stepped sideways exactly at the same moment. The bolt struck one of the men behind him, who grunted. He saw the fright in her face, a momentary fleeting thing, and then he reached her. He tore the crossbow out of her hands with a casual force and threw it away. Doubtless she held some idea of walking with calm dignity to her death, but Vale was having none of that. *You murdered Hyram. Murdered a speaker.* For that he had her dragged out of the tower by her hair. By the time he got back to the executioner's block, Valgar was already there, pushed down, held over the basket that would hold his head after his body no longer had any need of it. A few dozen of the Adamantine Guard stood around. Several dozen more were running into the Chamber of Audience. The council of kings and queens, it seemed, had spiraled out of hand. As expected.

Do it now! That's what the speaker had said, and so Vale didn't wait. He lifted the headsman's sword, a strange weapon with its weight and balance all wrong for fighting, but perfect for this one specific duty.

"Hold her head and make her watch," he said of Shezira. "Those were the speaker's orders. She has to watch." At least Shezira wasn't begging or pleading or shouting. She was as calm as anyone could reasonably be. She was afraid though, badly afraid, and that made her less than the men holding her. She kept trying to tell Vale something about Hyram and the night he'd died, but he wasn't listening. Whatever she had to say, he had no wish to hear it.

He turned back to Valgar and lifted the sword. "Whatever you have to say, there's little point. No one is here to hear it and no one will remember it. No one has come to witness your end, either of you."

The sword sang as it swung through the air. It cut through King Valgar's flesh as though his neck was made of cheese—a slight resistance but nothing more. Soldiers dragged the body away. Vale left the head and the basket where they were. Let the last thing Shezira saw be the severed head of her greatest ally.

In a blink she was on the block, held still, ready for him. He lifted the sword.

"I didn't push Hyram, Night Watchman." That's what she'd been telling him for weeks. Months. He wasn't interested. Her voice was ragged. *I ought to be silent. Whatever she says, it changes nothing.*

"That is not my concern. The council has spoken."

"He would have died without me, Night Watchman."

"But he didn't, Your Holiness. He died *with* you."

Her voice broke. Was she sobbing? Whatever her last words were, Vale didn't hear them. Something about alchemists and Jeiros and Hyram and poison, all spilling out of her mouth in a garbled mess.

He brought down the sword, and after that Shezira had nothing more to say.

23

※

WATCHING THINGS BURN

They slipped between the mountains of the Purple Spur in twilight. They were safe then, Semian thought, in the few short hours either side of darkness. In the daylight hours they hid from Zafir's dragons flying overhead, losing themselves among the cavernous valley forests, between trees that made even their dragons seem small. Mostly they slept. At night they loitered near streams, drinking and feeding, never staying in one place for long. They could move about at night. The speaker's riders would be in their cups, their dragons safely tucked up in their eyries when the sun went down. Only the day belonged to the enemy.

When they were close to the eastern end of the Spur, the palace end, they slipped out only in the dark, flying down through the valleys, skimming the earth, a few miles every day, no more. The dragons hated it, flying low in the dark. Their restless anxiety suffused their riders but Semian drove them on. They forayed out to the plains and left the Picker and the blood-mage a day's walk from the City of Dragons. They could do that now, for the blood-mage had served his purpose. Then they slipped away again, back into the safety of the peaks. The speaker never knew how close they were.

And there they waited. Semian sat quietly while his new acolytes fretted around him. The Great Flame had brought him here, he knew that. He could feel it. Taking the Picker and Kithyr to the city to be their spies was an excuse, a cloak of shadows obscuring something greater. In truth, he was sorry to be rid of the blood-mage. A strange understanding had grown between them as the magician had worked to save his leg. The man served the Flame with a deep and strange passion, and Semian felt stronger when he was around.

The Flame had called him though. Called him here. His leg was far from healed, would probably never heal, but there was no poison in the wound anymore. The magician had done what was needed, and so, with regrets, Semian had let him go. *We both have a greater purpose.* That's what the mage had said, and Semian understood him perfectly. In his dreams, the priest with the burned hands came to him night after night, always the same. *Wait. Be strong. There is a thing you have to do.*

On the day their food ran out, a mosquito landed on Semian's arm. Semian raised his hand to squash it and then paused. The mosquito was already bloated.

When blood comes to you, you must heed it . . .

He let it settle and bite him. Knowledge flowed into his veins. *Shezira and Valgar are dead . . .*

There was more, much more. King Tyan, Jehal, Valmeyan. All good. All speaking of chaos, of the realms bleeding and begging to be saved. When he knew it all, Semian slapped his arm, crushing the mosquito in a smear of blood. Not his blood. Kithyr's blood. Mage's blood. He thought it might burn his skin but it didn't.

He savored what he knew, picking and choosing what he would share with the other Red Riders. They'd sworn themselves to Hyrkallan to avenge Hyram's death and free Shezira. They'd failed, but that wasn't really the point anymore. They served the Great Flame now. They were his. Sixteen dragons, twenty riders.

They would have to do something, he decided. He wanted to hurt Zafir again but that was getting difficult. She was becoming cautious. Her dragons were everywhere and so were the Adamantine Men. Drotan's Top, maybe. That was always a weak point. If he threw everything he had against it, perhaps . . .

No. He smiled to himself as he realized what he must do, what he now knew he had come here to do. He ordered his riders into the air at dawn, but he didn't take them west and back toward the sanctuary of the World-spine. He took them north, out over the Great Cliff at the Emerald Cascade and high over the arid plains beyond, into the Stone Desert and Queen Almiri's lands and to the Evenspire Road. They flew all day, closer to the sky than the earth, or so it seemed. The Great Flame watched over them and none of Zafir's riders happened their way. As the sun sank, he dipped low, so the tiny dots and lines on the land below grew into monstrous outcrops of dark red stone in the dusty earth and the shadows that stretched for miles behind them. And there, on the Evenspire Road, he saw what he was looking for. A great column of soldiers and wagons. Lots and lots of wagons.

He led his riders in with the sun at their backs against a full legion of the Adamantine Men. Enough, if Prince Lai was right, to defeat more dragons than he had; but then Prince Lai had been talking about a pitched battle, a fight to take and hold ground where one side either fled or was destroyed. Semian had no interest in land. He didn't want the wagons or their precious cargo. All he wanted was to watch them burn.

No, that wasn't right either. As he skimmed the flat and lifeless earth, as the beating of Vengeance's wings threw up great clouds of dust behind him, as the soldiers bellowed their alarms and ran to form their shield walls, he no longer cared. The wagons could burn unwatched as long as they burned. What he wanted was to fly, to fight, to rain fire from the sky. Nothing, *nothing* felt like this, to sit on the back of a monster whose wings reached out a hundred feet on either side yet who could turn like a swallow. Whose claws and teeth could crush men like eggs, whose tail could smash castles and swat horses as though they were flies. And yet who could pick up their shattered riders when they fell and then guard them with gentle patience.

A scorpion bolt hissed over Vengeance's shoulder. A second hit the dragon in the chest, and Semian felt a surge of anger, anger that bloomed into exultation as he closed on his enemy. More bolts arrowed past him. Another pierced Vengeance's wing, more struck the riders behind him, but none came for him. He was charmed. Blessed. Shielded by the Great Flame.

Teeth and claws and tail, but above and beyond all that . . .

He flicked down the visor on his helm at the last second. He felt Vengeance tremble and heard the roar of fire. He tasted the air turn hot and scorched and he breathed deeply, sucking in the smell of war, of charred wood and seared flesh. He pressed himself flat on Vengeance's neck, closed his eyes and savored it while Vengeance passed close over the heads of the soldiers, lashing them with his tail. As the dragon rose, Semian lifted his visor again. Vengeance wanted more, wanted to turn and strike and burn and strike and burn until everything was crushed, but Semian checked him. *No.*

He looked over his shoulder as they flew away. At least four of his riders were dead, their dragons pulled to the ground by the weight of the training they were given as hatchlings, conditioned to defend their fallen riders no matter how broken they became. He had no idea how many Adamantine Men he'd slain. Not many, probably. But most of the wagons were smashed and ablaze, that was what mattered. The wagons carried potions. He knew that from the way they were guarded, knew that from his days at the alchemists' redoubt, the place where he'd been reborn.

No more potions for the speaker. That would do very nicely. He led his dragons away.

But it wasn't perfect. He hadn't counted the wagons. There had been perhaps as many as a dozen. A few had likely survived. Even one, it suddenly struck him, was too many.

So after half an hour had passed, as the sun drooped across the horizon, he led his dragons back across the desert and they did it all again. As things turned out, he did want to watch things burn after all.

THREE

THE WHITE DRAGON

24

THE WORLDSPINE AND THE HILLS BEYOND

The deeper they flew into the Worldspine, the taller the mountains became. Jagged spikes and streaks of rock stuck out, black and brutal, from the monotony of snow below. The trees fell away, then the lakes, and then everything except the glacial ice and stone. They had nothing to eat and only melted snow and ice to drink. Each day they flew higher, until the air grew so thin that Kemir could barely lift an arm before he was out of breath. If he hadn't had Snow to keep him warm, the cold would have frozen him hard in an hour. After the first day, the wind of Snow's flight was so biting that he could hardly raise his face to see where they were going; when he did, even through the dragon-rider's visor he wore, he felt as though the skin was being flayed from his flesh by a thousand razors dipped in acid. After the first day he had cramps from clenching his muscles, from hugging Snow so tightly. By the end of the second he could barely move. And then there were the nights. If the days were cold, what were the nights?

"Dragon, do you even know where are you going?" he slurred, when he decided for the hundredth time that he'd had enough. The roar of the wind whipped his words away but the dragon heard him. He wasn't sure quite how it worked, but as far as Kemir could tell, Snow could hear him think.

To the other side, Kemir. Snow's thoughts were far away, lost in distant memories that she kept carefully to herself. She wasn't really paying attention and Kemir was slowly starting to recognize the difference.

"I know the realms backward and forward, top to bottom. I've never heard of an other side to the Worldspine."

Whatever you have heard, Kemir, that is where we are going. Everywhere has an other side.

"And what if it doesn't, eh?" he grumbled. "What if it goes on like this forever, getting taller and taller?"

Then you will die of hunger and I will eventually follow. But nothing goes on forever, Kemir.

That made him laugh. "Except you. *You* go on forever. And it's all very well you talking about dying. Even when you die, don't you just come back again?"

That is true.

"Well I don't. You might live forever, but I've just got what I've got, and I'd quite like to make the most of it."

How are you so sure, Kemir? He could feel Snow's thoughts moving back to him, growing warmer and closer. When she tried, she could almost pretend that she wasn't a monster.

We are different, that is all. And we are not eternal. We were made, long ago, by sorcerers as old as the world. When that world ends, we will end with it, just as everything else.

"It doesn't look like it's ending anytime soon to me."

Between our lives in flesh and bone we walk the realms of the dead. I have seen things there. Things that should not be. They have broken loose of the sorcery that held them still. There is a hole where one of the four pillars of creation once stood. Tell me, Kemir, would you know the end of the world if you saw it?

"I don't know, but all I see right now is white down and blue up, with some more white and blue coming up in the middle distance, and far, far away, probably a hundred miles from here, guess what I can see? Can you guess? Yes! More of exactly the same. How far have we flown since that lake, eh?" He had to hiss the words out between clenched teeth, not daring to breathe too deep lest the cold strip the flesh from his lungs.

Not far enough to have reached the other side.

Kemir gave a frustrated groan and shifted to press himself face down onto the dragon's scales, trying to keep warm. "That's a dragon answer, not a real answer. Whether there's another side or not, *I* definitely won't go on forever if we keep going like this much further." There was no getting off though. He was stuck here, for better or for worse. *Which means there's really not much left to do but grumble and gripe about it, is there?*

You are right, I am *getting hungry again.*

There was a pause, and then Kemir snarled, "Was that a joke, dragon? Was that humor? Because if it was, it was a long way from being funny." It had only been two days, but the ever-present driving freezing wind had almost pushed Nadira from his mind.

It is the answer as you would have given it.

"Yes." Now Kemir chuckled. "I suppose it is. Well that's me told then." His anger faded. "I hope you're right, dragon. I hope there is an end to this. It would really piss me off to have saved you only to have you starve to death." *And Nadira deserves better than that too. That would make her death about as pointless as it's possible to be.*

You did not save me, Kemir.

"No? So everything would have been just dandy if you'd done what *you* wanted to do and stayed to watch Ash and the others burn from the inside? You, for some reason, would have been spared?" For a brief moment he risked a glance down. The wind tore at his face and froze his tears to his cheeks and all he could see was an endless featureless white.

No. But you *did not save me, Kemir. The ice water of the lake did that.*

"And who dragged you to the lake, dragon?"

I have said I am grateful for your advice, Kemir.

"You don't sound it." Every conversation eventually came to this, mainly because Kemir couldn't stay away from it. He'd saved the dragon's life. He knew it; the dragon knew it; Nadira knew it—*had* known it; probably even the alchemists knew it, but the dragon was damned if she was going to admit it. Even gratitude came with grudging reluctance. The whole idea that she might have been even a bit helped by a mere "little one" seemed to be a severe embarrassment. Did dragons feel embarrassed?

Did dragons feel anything? He didn't know, but this one certainly acted like she did. Stupid, really. *What am I going to do? Run to all the other dragons, point my finger at her and laugh?*

Very hungry indeed, Kemir.

Oh. Yes. Reading thoughts. *Well then you know I'm still terrified of you, dragon. In my own strange little way. And I still despise you for what you did.*

Snow, Kemir. The name your kind gave me is Snow. It is not my true name, but it will suffice.

"Just don't waste me, Snow. You need me. Don't waste me like you wasted Nadira. You need what I know." *Yes, and I'll keep telling myself that. Eventually at least one of us might believe it. Ancestors! What am I doing here?*

Staying alive. That's what he was doing, even if he had to remind himself from time to time. Not taking his choice of either freezing or starving beside a glacier lake somewhere in the depths of the Worldspine, that's what he was doing. Living and breathing. Desperately existing. Just like he'd always done. Waiting for his first chance to get off and run away.

You know I cannot let you go.

He had no idea how far they flew. They might have been in the air for three days and nights, or else he might have missed one in the general numbness of cold and hunger and it might have been four. He was dizzy with fatigue by the time he noticed that the air was warmer again. When he next bothered to look, he saw that the mountains were shrinking. There were lakes and rivers below them again, dark little lines in the shadows of their valleys, bright flashes of light where they caught the sun. As the dragon let herself glide ever lower, gleaming white snowfields rose up to either side of them. They flew between tufts of cloud snagged on jagged black peaks that fell away into gray stone slopes and black valleys filled with trees. Snow flew on and the mountains shrank still more, fading into crumpled hills and then into an endless sea of rolling forest. Kemir, too exhausted and ravenous to think, felt the dragon's hunger mingling with his own. As the trees spread out further below them, he felt an irritation growing inside him, too. Snow again.

Do you see anything for me to eat, Kemir?

Kemir peered down over Snow's shoulder. "All I see is trees." His eyes were too tired to focus, so all he saw most of the time was a great big dark blob that was the ground.

I do not like trees. It is hard to find prey.

Kemir digested that. "That's why we outsiders build our villages deep in the valley forests," he told her. "So you and your dragon-riders won't find us. And up on stilts so that the snappers won't eat us while we're sleeping."

They found a river. Snow dropped to follow it, still far above the tree-tops but close enough that Kemir could make out the individual trees. He looked wistfully to either side, out across the misty green expanse. Not just trees but a great forest like the Raksheh Forest of the realms. He saw deer too, coming out to drink at the edge of the water. Too small for Snow, but perfect for a man with a bow. He closed his eyes. *I could live here. I could hunt and build a shelter and stay out in the wilderness. Just let me off here and leave me be. I don't mind being alone. Just let me rest and sleep and have something to eat. Leave me be with my ghosts.*

No. Snow flew on until the green hills petered away and the river drained into a lake.

Look.

Kemir leaned forward and peered down at the water. He could see the ripples of a tiny boat and, as Snow dropped closer, he made out a single person sitting in it. Excitement gripped him. "Land!"

Why? There is only one of them and they are small and skinny. Barely a mouthful.

"It's a boat, dragon. And a person. Where there is one of us there will be more, and where you find people you'll find cattle."

Is that so? Your kind have changed then, for that is not how I remember the world.

Without warning, Snow tucked in her wings. They plunged out of the sky and Kemir was suddenly too busy holding on to see what she was doing. He might have been strapped into a dragon-knight's saddle, but he still couldn't quite bring himself to trust the thing. He gripped Snow's scales, fingers rigid as they leveled out and skimmed across the lake. He caught a glimpse of the boat again, straight in front of them, then Snow suddenly started to climb. Kemir pitched forward, smacking his face into the dragon's back. He thought he heard a scream, but he couldn't be sure.

Ah! Useless! Your kind are too fragile. Snow tossed something up into the air in front of them. Kemir was sure he saw flailing arms and legs before she snatched it into her jaws.

"That was the person from the boat, wasn't it?" *No, no. I don't want to know. I don't want to think about it.*

I did not mean to break him.

"You didn't have to eat him!"

I am hungry, *Kemir. I have barely eaten in close to ten passings of the sun. Ahh . . .*

The taste of Snow's thoughts changed. Kemir felt a satisfaction, an anticipation. She changed her course, arrowing across the lake. Kemir tried to see what she'd spotted.

A house. He saw a house at the edge of the lake. More of a hut than a house. With people, standing and staring at them . . .

He saw them for an instant, saw their faces, their mouths open, their eyes wide, their feet frozen to the spot in terror, too stupefied to run away; and then Snow opened her mouth and spat fire. A wall of burning air erupted in front of them. Snow slammed through it. Kemir screamed. Snow screamed. There might have been other screams too, but if there were then Kemir didn't hear them. He covered his face with his hands and wrapped his arms around his head, all far too late. He could smell scorched hair. *His* hair.

The next moment Snow crashed into the ground. Wood split and splintered. Kemir pitched forward, thrown helplessly back and forth and only kept on Snow's back by the saddle. Her head and neck lunged forward and she spat fire again. Kemir cowered, pressing himself into her, covering his face as best he could, but there was no burning wall of air this time. She lunged a second time and then a third, and then she stopped.

"What have you done?" he whispered. His hands and arms and face were agony. His clothes were still hot to the touch and smelled burned. Snow, he realized, was eating. Behind the hut had been a tiny fenced field with perhaps half a dozen pigs in it. They were all burned now. The smell of them made his mouth water, made him remember how long he too had been without food. The dragon was picking them off the ground with her claws, tossing them into the air and catching them in her mouth. The way his cousin Sollos used to eat grapes.

I am still hungry. This is not enough.

He didn't want to think about the people he'd seen. Maybe Snow had eaten them already. Maybe she was saving them for later. They were certainly dead. Burned to a crisp.

"I'd like to get down."

Are you sure? You are far safer where you are.

He ignored her. Slowly and painfully, he undid the straps and harnesses that held him in the saddle. He half slid, half fell to the ground. When he looked at his hands they were bright red. They were sore and getting worse. Burnt. Add that to the fact that every joint and muscle already hurt from their flight across the mountains and there was nothing left.

"Was that necessary, dragon?"

When he didn't get an answer, he moved gingerly through the smoldering wreckage to the shore of the lake. He lay down on the edge of the land with his face half in the water, his arms stretched out in front of him. The water was deliciously cool. The pain eased. He drank a little. It tasted good.

Behind him he heard the dragon shift, scattering more wreckage, and then a thin wailing shriek. When he looked around, Snow was holding a boy in her claws. She was going to eat him.

"No!" Kemir jumped to his feet waving his arms. "No, Snow! Don't! Don't you dare!"

Her mouth was already open. She looked at him and cocked her head. *But I am hungry, Kemir. Why should I not eat?*

"Why? Why? Because that's a person, that's why! A boy! Like me!"

It is food, Kemir.

"It's a boy, you stupid dragon. Half grown. Hardly even worth eating. You can't . . ." How did you reason with a dragon? "Am I food? Is that all I am?"

Snow's expression didn't change. He *was* food. Now he had time to think about it, yes, that *was* what she thought of him. Nadira had been food.

You have also been useful, Kemir. Perhaps you will be useful again.

"Useful food." He sat down and started to laugh, or to cry, or perhaps a bit of both. He wasn't sure and he certainly didn't care. "Useful food. Is that what I am?"

Yes.

"Useful didn't save Nadira, did it, dragon?"

Snow almost shrugged. *But, Kemir, she was not useful at all. She knew nothing. She had no other value.*

"Because you had me to tell you about the world?" He could have cried.

Yes. I see this troubles you, but it is the natural order of things.

"*Troubles* me? You could say that, yes." *I'm shouting. Shouting at a dragon. Not good.* He tried to gather his thoughts. "When I stop being useful, Snow. What happens then?"

Then we part, Kemir. Or before, if that is what you wish.

"And if you happen to be hungry when we part, I get eaten?" He looked away. "No. Don't answer that. I don't think I want to know."

I will not eat you just because I am hungry. I will eat you so that you cannot speak of me to others of your kind. Or mine.

The boy was still dangling from Snow's claw. He seemed to have fainted. Kemir picked up a stone and hefted it in his hand. "Then you let him go. Either that or you eat us both right now. Snow didn't move. She looked at him for a long time. Silent, eyes blank, alien and impenetrable. As he met her gaze, Kemir discovered something that he didn't expect. He meant it. Really, really meant it. They were both outsiders, him and this boy. They'd both seen their homes destroyed by dragons, their families, their entire worlds. "He's like us, Snow," he said, more softly this time. "He's a nest-mate too. You're alone, I'm alone and now so is he." He shook his head. "You have to be different, Snow. If you can't be different then leave us be. Leave us here. I want no part of you."

Gently, Snow lowered the boy to the ground at Kemir's feet. He must have been about ten, Kemir decided. Still a boy but not far away from being a man. Old enough to be useful.

Old enough to be useful, repeated Snow. *I think I understand.*

"He's older than you, dragon. And we're all useful. All of us. In our different ways."

Yes. Snow picked up the charred remains of what was probably one of the boy's parents and gobbled it down. *That is true.*

25

STRANGE LANDS

The boy ran away the first chance he got. Kemir didn't bother to look for him. Either he knew how to survive in the forests around the lake or he didn't. If he did, good luck to him; if he didn't then he'd be back and Kemir had quite enough other things to worry about.

Burns, for a start. When Snow had breathed fire his hands had taken the worst of it. The skin blistered and peeled over the days that followed; the damage wasn't deep and eventually they'd heal, but until they did he couldn't hunt, couldn't even string his bow, and that put paid to any idea of running away. All he could do was ease the pain in the cold water of the lake and hope that the healing would be clean and the wounds wouldn't go bad. That and shout at the dragon, telling her what to do.

Snow spent the next morning smashing down trees, pulling them out of the ground and hurling them into the lake. She was at it for hours, and Kemir couldn't understand what she was doing until she finally stopped, stood at one end and started to run. Each pounding step made the ground shudder. When she reached the end of the space she'd made, she stretched out her wings and launched herself out over the lake. Her back claws and her tail slashed the water, sending a tower of spray into the air, and then she was up and gone. She went hunting on her own every day after that, for longer and longer each day, until some nights she didn't come back at all. Kemir didn't ask where she went or what she found, but sometimes she told him anyway. *There are others of your kind. They are far away, along the river. There are homes like this one and then villages and then towns. I do not know if they are useful or if they are yet more of your nest-mates, so I did not eat them. There are cows and horses too. They are more filling but not as much fun.*

She brought the boat back to the shore, which meant he could go fishing once his hands started to heal. Then he found some mushrooms but they only gave him cramps. Finally, after Kemir lost his temper and shouted at Snow about how he was slowly starving to death, the dragon came back in the twilight with a cow. She gathered a mound of smashed-up wood and set it on fire. As the stars rose, she ripped the cow into pieces and tossed them onto the flames. Kemir had to laugh.

"I used to have nights like this with Sollos. We spent enough of our lives sleeping under the stars. We had fires like this all the time. Strips of meat were a bit smaller though . . ." His voice trailed away into wistful memories. *Sollos. Killed by that bastard rider.*

If you starve, you will not be useful nor even much good as food.

"Ha ha. That dragon humor kills me."

She didn't understand. He knew the sound in his head now, when he said something that Snow couldn't make into any sense, or else couldn't be bothered to try. Something like a shrug and a sigh. He felt that now as Snow ate the remnants of the carcass. Then she sat on her haunches and watched him. The fire lit up the scales of her belly and her neck. Sparkling embers spiraled up around her head. When she stretched out her neck she was as tall as the trees. Her tail was even longer. Yet, for all her size, she was skinny. Lean and sleek, not like the squat irresistible power of a war-dragon.

Tell me what you know about the alchemists.

Kemir laughed and shook his head. "No chance, dragon. Then I won't be useful anymore and you'll eat me." The smell of roasting cow was making him weak at the knees.

She looked at him, then slowly reached into the fire and took the first lump of dead cow between her teeth. Then she looked at Kemir and gulped it down.

Tell me what you know about the alchemists.

"You're a bastard." He was feeling faint. Snow reached into the fire again.

I already know where to find them.

"You give me some food and I'll tell you what I know."

When your hands are healed, do you still mean to run away from me?

He had no answer to that. A few minutes later she flicked her tail through the flames. Half a smoldering ribcage landed at his feet. He looked at it for a second and then tore into it, ignoring the pain from his hands. It was charcoal on the outside and raw in the middle, but there were plenty of bits in between. Blood dribbled down his chin. It was delicious.

After the first few mouthfuls, he stopped. He'd been hungry enough times before to take his time. "Do you remember when you killed your first alchemist? I was there."

I know.

"That was the second alchemist I ever met." He laughed, sucking juices from his fingers. "Sollos was going to be an alchemist. That's how he got his name. They were going to take him to the City of Dragons and sell him to the Order and live like kings for the rest of their lives. Or that's what they thought,"

Why is that so foolish?

Kemir shook his head and chuckled at the madness of the idea. "Dragon, we were outsiders. We had no idea where the City of Dragons even was. Someone had come back from somewhere with a story they'd heard from someone else who'd once been to somewhere that might have once been visited by a trader who might have been to the City of Dragons at one time in his life. They thought that all they had to do was go there and hand Sollos over and the Order would turn him into a great magician and shower them with gold. Daft." He took a deep breath and licked his lips. "When I told that story to the first alchemist I ever met, he nearly gave himself a rupture he laughed so much. But then again he was already a long way into his cups." He shook himself, serious for a moment. "Dragon, where I came from, we barely knew where to find the next village. It's true that the Order pays for children. They give them some sort of test to find out how good an alchemist they might become. If the child is good enough, the Order buys them. Ten gold dragons. For most people, that's a small fortune. That's enough to buy an inn or a smithy if you're not too choosy."

I don't understand. Why do they buy children? Can they not make their own?

"Why don't you ask the next one instead of eating him?"

Perhaps I shall. This is not interesting. Tell me something different about alchemists.

"Hmm." The piece of meat was cooling now. He picked it up and tossed it back toward Snow. "Needs some more cooking, that bit. Pass me another."

This time, when Snow threw him one back leg, he started carving it apart with his knife, scraping off the charcoal, slicing out the near-raw fillets underneath. Doing a proper job.

"The first alchemist I met was in a brothel. I was in a bit of a bad way, but Sollos had heard of him. He took me in and put me back together. He wasn't a proper alchemist though. He was one of the ones who wasn't quite good enough. Or that's how he put it. You see, they do buy children and maybe they make some of their own too, and they school them for ten years, which is longer than any king or queen by the way. The ones who aren't clever enough by then they make into Scales. You remember those? You had one once. Kailin. You ate him."

Snow didn't answer and her thoughts were her own. After a good long pause Kemir went on. "Scales are freaks even before the Hatchling Disease starts turning them into living statues. I don't know whether the alchemists do something to them or whether after ten years they're just like that on their own. The ones they don't make into Scales they make into apprentices. Those are the ones who start to learn all the juicy secrets. Except even then they don't. Ten more years as an apprentice and even then half of them still get sent away, like the one I met. He was a sort of half-alchemist, I suppose. He didn't know much, or if he did, he was sharp enough to keep it to himself even when he was so drunk he couldn't pull up his trousers. They wander about the realms, traveling tinkers and traders. Every now and then the Order pays them for a favor. You know what he said pissed him off the most? He didn't know who his father was, nor his mother. Order wouldn't tell him, or else they didn't know. Likely as not they'd long spent what they got for selling him and were poor as shit again, and he didn't know who they were. Poor bastard." He paused, lost in memory. "No family. Never even knew them. That's bad."

Is that it? That's what you know? That seems unlikely to be useful.

Kemir shrugged. "What were you hoping for? I know the routes the alchemists take to deliver their potions, but that's no great secret. Just watch for wagons escorted by a legion of Adamantine Men coming down the Evenspire Road." He snorted. "Except with you around they'll probably take to flying everything on dragon-back."

That is much more the sort of information I desire. Your other memories are not interesting.

"That's very kind, dragon. Why don't you piss off?"

Eat, Kemir. She tossed him another hunk of roasted cow carcass. She didn't say anything, but when he was done, when he'd filled his belly so he could hardly move and had stripped away as much of the meat as would keep, she studied him.

The one that was here before is here again, she told him. *The boy you called nest-mate. The one you said that I should not eat. Do you still wish me to leave?*

Kemir glowered. "Read my mind, dragon."

He waited until she got the message and thundered into the moonlit sky. When she was gone he put some of the meat he'd saved onto the ground near the trees and backed away.

"You can come out!" he shouted. "Dragon's gone now. I don't want to hurt you. You must be hungry. You can share our food."

He waited, watching, but the boy didn't come out. *And I can hardly blame him for that, can I? We came out of nowhere, ate his family and destroyed his home. I know exactly how he feels.* He left the meat where it was and sat watching in secret for a while longer. When the boy still didn't come he settled down beside the fire and closed his eyes. He waited, eyes drooping but not quite shut. *An empty belly and the smell of roasted fat brought you here, but I know what's on your mind.*

The boy didn't disappoint him. He waited a good long time before he came, until Kemir had been pretending to snore for so long that his throat was sore. He came out of the trees with a heavy stick ready in his hand and didn't even glance at the meat left out for him. Kemir watched him come through lidded eyes, slow and purposeful. *Good lad. Got your priorities right. Got a good idea what you're doing too. A knife would be better, but where would you get one of those out here, eh?* The boy was slow and careful with each step. If he was scared, he didn't show it. He reached Kemir and raised the stick and only then hesitated. *Well, what's it to be? Are you still a boy? Or are you a man?*

The stick came down. The blow wasn't the best, and certainly wouldn't have killed him. Still, it was a good try and Kemir smiled as he caught the stick and held on to it. He gave the stick a good tug, and then when the boy pulled back, he let go. The boy tumbled over backward. Kemir jumped on him, making sure he had no chance to get up.

"I don't want to fight with you, lad. What's your name?"

The boy screamed something incoherent and spat at him.

"I'm not going to hurt you." Carefully he let the boy go. The boy jumped to his feet, grabbed his stick and backed away. Then he came at Kemir, who caught the first couple of blows on his forearms, wincing at the pain from the burns still healing under his sleeves. On the third one, he ducked aside and kicked the boy's legs out from under him.

"I could show you how to fight, if you like."

The boy screamed again, turned and ran. When he saw Kemir wasn't following, he stopped long enough to grab a piece of meat and then vanished into the trees. Kemir shrugged and settled with his back to the fire to watch.

"I was older than you when the riders came," he called out. "Not by many years, but enough to make a difference. You listen to this, boy! We were on the edge of a lake. Just like this. We even had a few animals. We thought the dragon-riders would never find us. Even if they did, we thought they'd leave us alone. Just like this place here.

"Are you still there, boy? Are you listening?" He raised his voice, then slumped back to the ground and shook his head and his voice dropped. No. Of course he wasn't. There wasn't anyone here to listen to him at all. Except the stars. There were always stars, or else the moon or sometimes some clouds when he needed an ear. "We all ran into the trees, when the dragons came. They filled the ground we'd cleared by the edge of the lake. They caught a few of us, but they didn't burn anything or kill anyone. They had riders who said that we belonged to the King of the Crags. That we had to give them everything they asked for as a tribute. As payment for their protection. They wanted what they always want. Men to sell as slaves and women for . . . Well, you'll know all about that in time. The older men decided we'd give them what they wanted. We should have fought, that's what I said. I wasn't the only one either, but what did I know? I was barely a man, like you, all full of piss and vinegar. Anyway, you've seen one. Think about it, boy. How do you fight a dragon?"

He sighed. He didn't know who he was talking to. The trees and the water. The dead, perhaps. Certainly not the boy in the woods, who was surely long gone. "A few of us left then. Just upped and went. The clever ones. They were gone when the dragons came back a few days later, with their wooden slave cages. We gave up our own people. There were boys and girls, tied up by their own weeping mothers and fathers to be sold to the dragon-riders. That's how it was, boy. There were fights. People killed by their own families. We never had that before. They chose us by lots. Ten young men and ten girls between the ages of ten and sixteen. I was one of the ones who should have gone. I ran away and hid for days and they didn't find me. Someone else went in my place. I knew him. Everyone knew everyone. He was family, of a sort. A friend. I hated everyone. I wasn't alone. People who lost their sons and daughters and brothers and sisters held grudges against those who didn't. The boy who was taken because I'd hidden had a brother. He came for me with a knife. I laid him out with a stick. I didn't want to kill him, but he wouldn't stop. He came after me again and again. I think he *wanted* me to kill him." Kemir sniffed and blinked and was surprised to find tears in his eyes. He wasn't talking to anyone except himself now. He could barely see the trees anymore. All he could see was the memory, the burning. His voice broke to a whisper. "Took me a long time before I understood how he must have felt. Took a dragon to teach me that.

"The riders took our hearts, all of them. We were empty shells. No one laughed anymore." He blinked. "And then they came back for the last time. Me and Sollos were on the other side of the lake when they came. By the time we got back, it was all gone. Nothing but ash. They didn't take slaves this time. They didn't take anything. After they'd burned it all, they landed. Anyone they hadn't killed with fire they put to the sword. They weren't the same riders as had come before. I could see that by their dragons. Different, you see. And you know what, boy? For all the oaths I swore that day, maybe those riders were the merciful ones. They put us out of our misery." He gave a bitter laugh. "That was Prince Valmeyan. He was a king by the time I knew his name. I swore I'd destroy him for what he'd done. Him and every one of his riders. I never had any idea how, but I wanted to see him burn. I still do. Slowly, as he looks out over the ashes of everything he loves. See, boy, I know how you feel. Sollos and I, we learned to be soldiers so we could fight. I was always good with a bow. We set about killing riders. Murdered a couple and then we had to run to the furthest corner of the realms. Out to the moors in the east. After that we took work as we could get it. Killing work, if you get my drift. It was easier that way but I'm glad it's stopped. I never liked it. Not the killing, you understand. That was fine. It was the taking orders from them."

Kemir sniffed. He shifted, settling himself. The boy hadn't come back. He was glad of that. There were still tears on his cheeks when there shouldn't have been. Best the boy didn't see that. *It was all so long ago.*

"Sollos is gone now," he whispered to the air, and suddenly he didn't care whether the boy came back or not.

Let him crack my skull while I'm sleeping. Then Snow can eat me. Most likely we'd both be better off. He lay down. *I know what you're thinking, boy, because I thought it too. And I know where that took me, and I know exactly what it's like to be me, and it's really not worth it. That's what I'm trying to tell you, boy. That's what I'm trying to tell you. Be someone else. Let it go.* He fell asleep, but he didn't sleep well. His dreams were old and troubled.

After you burned a man's home to charcoal and his family to ash, you could hardly bring them back and pretend it never happened. Let it go? He didn't even know how to begin. You couldn't really even say sorry. By then that was just was an insult.

26

❦

JEIROS

Jeiros, acting grand master, leaned back in his chair and sighed. On his desk he had six letters. The ink was still fresh and drying. Three letters were to three sisters, all saying the same thing: *You are now a queen.* The other three were to their eyrie-masters, carrying the necessary instructions. Instructions to pass on the mysteries that only kings and queens were permitted to know. And a warning about one or two other things.

"I don't know how you manage," he said. The other alchemist in the room, who'd written the letters to the eyrie-masters, was Vioros. As Zafir's senior alchemist, he was the closest thing Jeiros had to a deputy. At least, he was the closest thing that could be found at midday in the approximate vicinity of the Adamantine Palace when one king, one queen and one prince had all wound up dead on the same day. "Bellepheros once wrote two of these in one month, and we never heard the end of it. But three! And in a day! How have you survived such a mistress?"

Vioros stuck out his bottom lip and shrugged. "Her mother was never any trouble to us and nor has Zafir been, since she took the crown. And not all of these letters are actually necessary, Jeiros. Jehal isn't dead yet."

"*Yet* being the significant word." Jeiros carefully took a handful of down and sprinkled it over the drying ink. "I'll be surprised if he lasts the night. And if he does, he won't last the week. The wound has gone bad and he's lost so much blood. That's that, I'm afraid. The end of him.

Nothing any of us can do." Jeiros yawned. "If he's strong then he'll linger a while. But you're right: strictly, he's not actually dead yet. The speaker's choices are to let him waste away in stinking rotting agony for a few days or put him out of his misery. The latter would be the merciful thing to do, but I suppose she might balk at that under the circumstances. Besides, I'm not sure she's one for mercy, is she?"

Vioros glanced sharply up. "Or she could find herself a blood-mage."

"Or that." For a few moments neither of them said anything, as though Vioros had suddenly let a bad smell into the room and they were both waiting for the air to clear.

"I don't know why Zafir has me trying to keep him alive anyway," muttered Jeiros at last. "Why bother to go to all that trouble and then cut off his head anyway?"

"Oh, I don't think she wants him dead."

Jeiros sighed again and shook his head. "Madness. I didn't want to be grand master."

"You're not."

"Oh, come on! Bellepheros disappeared almost half a year ago. If he's not dead, he's certainly not coming back!" Jeiros rubbed his eyes and waved at the letters. "I was much happier at the redoubt. And Bellepheros never had to deal with *anything* like this. A quarter of the Order dead at the hands of a rogue dragon; all our stocks wiped out; eyries across the realms running short. Do you realize that King Narghon is down to two weeks' supply?"

"We're down to three weeks ourselves."

"I know! Can you imagine?" Jeiros wrung his hands and shook his head. "Can you simply *imagine* what would happen if even one eyrie ran out? An *entire eyrie*. We'd have to poison them all! And then the consequences . . ."

"I'm trying not to think about it. These Red Riders—"

"If you think *that's* bad, imagine us at war! All our supplies pass through King Valgar's realm." He checked himself. "Queen Almiri's realm, I mean. Now."

"That will be Zafir's cause for war, when it comes. I'll make you a wager on that if you like."

"Make me a wager on how long it will be before Almiri turns on the Order and starts trying to starve Zafir's eyries. The Red Riders have already started." He shook his head again. "Madness, all of it."

"She'll starve everyone else as well. Even herself."

Jeiros got up and walked to the window. Outside, the sun was close to the horizon. *They've probably finished building the cages now. Shezira and Valgar will be hanging outside the gates. What's left of them.*

"I don't think she's going to have much of a choice. Or she may not care. If she's got half her mother's stubbornness . . . Have you met her?"

"No."

"Pity." He was pacing back and forth now, unable to contain the nervous energy crackling through his limbs. "I can't take any chances, Vioros, and neither can you. If the potions run out among the Adamantine eyries, who do you serve? Zafir or the Order?"

"I serve the Order."

"Of course you do, of course you do. If the speaker goes to war, we shall stop supplying and stockpile at the redoubt instead. We simply can't afford to lose any more. I shall tell the speaker. I'll have to tell the other master alchemists too. Warn them. I suppose I'll have to tell all the eyrie-masters that they might have to fly to Valeford and pick up their potions from there. Make sure your alchemists are ready to do what needs to be done if it comes to the worst. Make sure they've got plenty of what they'll need. Ancestors! I know we've put down dragons before, but has anyone ever put down an entire eyrie of them? I don't think they have! How soon could you be prepared here? I mean if you had to be? If it had to be done?"

"A matter of days."

"You realize that *everyone* will try to stop you. You won't only have the speaker's riders and servants and probably half the Scales against you, you'll have the Adamantine Guard to contend with as well."

"They rarely pay much attention."

"So be it. I shall come for an inspection of the Adamantine eyrie before the week is out. Now to warn the others."

Vioros groaned. "More letters?"

"More letters."

Jeiros was halfway through writing the first when a violent knocking shook the door. He jumped, startled by the sudden sound. He looked at the letter. His hand had twitched in the middle of a stroke and the word was ruined. He'd have to start again.

"Who is it and what do you want?" he snapped. No one ought to be banging on his door. The juniors in the Order were permitted a timid knock and the speaker wouldn't bother; she'd simply barge in.

The banging came again. With a growl of irritation, Jeiros got up. He opened the door.

"Tassan." He blinked, taken aback. He couldn't remember the last time he'd seen the Night Watchman here. Usually they avoided each other, following some ancient unwritten law that the Order and Adamantine Men simply didn't get along.

Apart from a few nights ago. But then these weren't usual times.

"Acting Grand Master." Vale Tassan bowed politely. *He got my title right,* Jeiros noticed. *A little too much accent on the Acting though.*

"We are extremely busy, thanks largely to you, so I would appreciate it if you were brief." Jeiros didn't move aside. He certainly didn't want the Night Watchman seeing the letters on the desk.

"I have two things on my mind." Vale stepped forward. Jeiros still didn't move. The Night Watchman cocked his head. "May I come in or shall we discuss my business out here where anyone might overhear us? Both my matters are somewhat sensitive."

Jeiros glanced over his shoulder. Vioros had already cleared the desk. With a sharp nod, Jeiros moved aside.

"I shan't ask what you were writing," said Vale. "I'm sure it's not my business."

"We've been writing all day, Night Watchman. You made three new queens today."

Tassan smiled. "Two. Jehal's not dead yet."

"That is merely a matter of time, Night Watchman."

"I am not so sure of that." Vale sat down in the chair Vioros had vacated. Somehow that only emphasized how massive the man was. *He could probably rip me apart with his bare hands.*

"Well I am *quite* sure," snapped Jeiros. Something about the Adamantine Man was rubbing him the wrong way. *Maybe I'm just tired. Or maybe he should have done something weeks ago. Or maybe I simply blame him for wielding the sword. He said it himself.* "The Guard obeys orders. From birth to death. Nothing more, nothing less." *Is that really all he is?*

"I'm sure you know best." Said in the tone of voice of someone quite sure that Jeiros *didn't* know best.

"Night Watchman, we have a very great deal to do thanks to your work today, so I would appreciate it if you got to the point. What can I do for you?"

"All right, I'll be blunt then. There's a war coming. Let's start with that."

Jeiros felt insulted. "You think I'm blind? I seem to remember coming to *you* for some help in stopping it."

Vale shrugged. "So many eyes seem to be screwed willfully shut these days. Since you've seen it coming, I'm sure you'll be well prepared to support the speaker's dragons in whatever may come. I am, of course, at your disposal if you need any help. In securing the supply of potions to the speaker's eyries, for example."

"I see." *Had he been listening at the door?* No, he couldn't have been; it was a very thick door, and for precisely the reason that Bellepheros hadn't wanted anyone pressing their ear against it and finding out things that they shouldn't. *So what then? Or is he simply cleverer than I thought?* Jeiros' thoughts grew petulant. *But if he's that clever then he can bloody well do something about keeping this from getting completely out of hand.* "Then I am grateful to you for your offer. The threat of the Red Riders is a real one and I shall examine what you might do to be of assistance. You might encourage the speaker to use her dragons to supply the eyries of the realms with our potions, perhaps." *As if that's going to happen.*

"The speaker does not listen to me."

Jeiros gave an unsympathetic shrug, "And the second matter?" *Was that regret I saw there, Night Watchman?*

"The second is a little more . . . awkward." For a moment the Night

Watchman seemed unsure of himself, something Jeiros had never thought he'd see. "When Speaker Hyram died, did you examine his body?"

Jeiros shook is head. *Why is he asking me this?* "No. We were not asked to do so."

"Do you have to be asked?"

"Unless there is some reason for suspicion, yes."

Vale smiled thinly. "And Hyram falling off a balcony did not strike you as a matter of suspicion?"

"Obviously so, but a hundred of *your* men came forward to say that Shezira had been with Hyram when he fell. What was there to question? He was pushed."

"What if he wasn't pushed? What if he fell?"

Jeiros had to laugh at that. "You're asking *me?* I thought that was quite impossible."

"What if I was wrong?"

"Then the council of kings and queens has made a terrible mistake, Night Watchman, and so have you." He watched Vale's face harden, his lips pinch together. *He means it: he really doubts. This could be an opportunity . . .* "And the rest of us," he added. "We could not have known though, even if we had examined the body. We could have said which of his injuries had killed him, and whether he'd received them from the fall or whether he'd received them *before* he fell. But we could not have said whether he fell or was pushed, nor if he was pushed, whose hand was guilty. We are alchemists, Night Watchman, not magicians." Which was mostly true. Mostly.

"You might have known if he had been poisoned."

"We might, that is true." Jeiros frowned. "Do you have reason to suspect such a thing?" *And, if so, why bring it up now when you've just executed someone for his murder? Where are you going with this?*

"No." Vale shook his head and stood up. "No real reason. It was only a thought." He walked to the door. "Thank you for your time, Acting Grand Master. Do think about how my soldiers might best help you to ensure a steady supply of your potions to the speaker's eyries in the times to come."

The Night Watchman left. The door closed behind him with a soft click. Jeiros and Vioros looked at one another.

"After all that, what does he want?" asked Vioros.

"Nothing good," sniffed Jeiros. "I think he wanted to let us know that no one is safe." He looked Vioros in the eye and smiled mirthlessly. "Do you want some more good news? Something else no one will have told you? You know that I've been counting dragons, trying to find out whether we're still missing one?"

Vioros rolled his eyes. "I *do* apologize for that. I've been dropping hints where I can that counting dragons is *not* the way . . ."

Jeiros couldn't help himself. He started to laugh, then struggled to get himself under control. "I'm sorry, old friend. Very rude of me. But counting dragons has been more informative than I thought. Did you know that, for the last three months, the number of hatchlings that won't take has doubled? They're putting down dragons every week in most eyries. Most of the dragon-kings don't even know yet." He glanced at the letters on his desk. "Nor our soon-to-be-queens either, but the eyrie-masters do. Across the realms our eyries are still hatching as many good dragons as they used to. But I've had letters back from every eyrie-master now and they all say the same. The number of hatchlings that refuse to eat has almost doubled. Just like that, and they'd like to know why. They'd like to know what's happening. You can understand why they are nervous, with their dragon production rates at risk." Jeiros shook his head in disbelief.

"And *do* we know what is happening?" Vioros raised an eyebrow.

"Yes, of course we do. And it is not what *is* happening, it is what *has* happened, and it is certainly not good. But beside our current difficulties that's by the by. The rogue dragon is definitely alive."

"It is?"

"Unquestionably."

"And you found this out through accountancy? I'm impressed." For a moment, Vioros looked truly amazed. Jeiros hesitated, savoring the moment before he ruined it.

"No, I'm afraid not. It's rather more straightforward. Reports have reached me from Valmeyan's eyries. It was seen two months ago. It's been burning things."

"Are we sure it was the rogue?"

"Yes, quite sure." Jeiros shook his head and sat heavily back behind his desk. "There aren't any other white dragons and there were rather a lot of witnesses, I'm afraid."

27

USEFUL FOOD

Kemir left the boat carefully tied by the lake shore in case the boy came back. He was probably dead. If he wasn't yet, most likely he would be soon. *But that can't be my problem. I didn't do this. The dragon did it.*

You keep telling yourself that, shot back another inner voice. *You just keep telling yourself that.*

He left some food as well. What was left of the cow. The meat was starting to turn but it was all he had. Snow watched him at his work. He could feel her curiosity.

Why are you are leaving food for someone who tried to kill you?

Kemir snarled, "Because I'm a man, not a dragon. But how would you understand?" She was at her most frightening when she was like this. She would sit on her haunches, wings folded, tail curled around in front of her, absolutely still. She'd watch in silence until Kemir forgot that she was there. Then he'd turn around, and there she was, looming thirty feet over him, blotting out the sky. Just watching. Or else she'd idly stretch her wings and cast what felt like half the world into shadow for a few seconds.

Do you want to leave this food too? She dropped half a donkey onto the ground. There were the remains of some kind of harness around the donkey's head. It clearly hadn't been minding its own business wild in a field somewhere when Snow had taken it.

"I don't think he'll want it raw." He couldn't help thinking about where the donkey had come from.

Snow gave the dead donkey a pensive look, then she ambled on all fours over to the shore of the lake. She picked up a few stones, some of them roughly the same size as Kemir, and built a ring. Then she gathered some more stones and piled them on top. And then she breathed fire on them.

Kemir took a hurried step away as flames washed over the ground around the stones. Snow didn't stop. She didn't even pause for breath. The fire just went on and on and on.

After a bit the heat was too much and he had to walk right away into the trees. She was still at it a minute later, the flames pouring out of her. Made him wonder how long she could keep it up before she ran out of breath . . .

We do not need to breathe, Kemir. It is a . . . He felt her rummaging in his head for the word. *A habit. An instinct. It is not a necessity.*

Which explained how she'd vanished into a lake for five days. He shuddered. Everything breathed. Everything.

Eventually Snow stopped. She kicked off the stones from the top, gingerly, as though even she could feel how hot they were. Then she slit the donkey open from end to end and shook out all its guts into the first ring of stones. She put one hot stone into the cavity that had been the donkey's chest, then put the carcass on top of its guts and piled the rest of the stones back on top.

Will that be better?

One moment you do that. And the next moment you'll eat him. Or me.

"Since when do dragons do cooking?" he asked, when he couldn't think of anything else.

My . . . There was a strange tone to her thoughts. Something wistful, winsome, almost awestruck. *My first mistress showed this to me. When we thought the world was ending and there was nothing left to be done. Sasya.*

Kemir raised an eyebrow. "You had a mistress?"

A moon-sorceress. The ones who created us. They are long gone. He felt her push the memories out of her thoughts. *I found a road. I have not seen this . . .*

He felt her plucking the word out of his head again. *I have not seen a donkey creature before. I was hungry, but I only ate things with four legs.* Kemir thought he sensed a hint of reproach. *These are . . . They taste like horse but sweeter. I like them better.*

Kemir slowly came closer again. "Everything with two legs ran away screaming, then?"

Some of them fell over where they stood and clutched their heads. I do not remember so much fear in your kind. One of them decided to die. He was old.

"What do you mean *decided* to die? You mean you scared him to death?"

I did not try to. I was hungry. I left your kind alone. I took as many things with four legs as I needed.

"Donkeys?"

Other things too. Horses and dogs and buffalo. I did not even burn their wagons, Kemir.

"I get it, dragon. You were very very careful not to hurt any people. Some of them died anyway, but that really wasn't your fault." He spat and turned away. "You still ate Nadira."

Snow peered at him. Her face had the same hungry expression as it ever did but her thoughts had changed. There was a music in them. She was laughing at him.

I see into your mind, Kemir. You think you can be different from others of your kind. You think the young one we leave behind us could be different too, if only we could find him and take him with us. But we cannot do that if he will not come, and besides, you are fooling yourself. I do not understand why you try to change how things are, Kemir. I am a dragon. Some of us are white and some are black; some are larger and others are smaller; but beneath our scales we are all simply dragons. Your kind are the same, Kemir. All of you. You always fight one another and you always will. I remember more than you can imagine. I remember from long ago, before the world was broken. Your kind were always this way even then, and you, Kemir, are no different. I can see into you and I know this to be true. Embrace what you are, Kemir. Do not try to be something else. Your enemies are merely those with bigger armies and sharper swords. That is the only difference between you.

Kemir bit his lip. "My enemies have dragons. Dragons are not weapons."

No, Kemir, that is exactly what we are. But not for you. You are food. The order of things has become twisted.

"I am *not* food, damn you!"

Snow didn't answer. She was laughing at him again. *You amuse me. Perhaps that will save you when I become hungry.*

"Oh, I'm *amusing* food now, am I? Just when I thought *useful* couldn't get any worse." He took a deep breath. "If there was a road and it was busy then there must have been a town not far away."

You are thinking of the boy again.

"Some things can't be undone and some things can never be forgiven. What you did to him can't be put right. Nor can what you did to Nadira. But you could try."

Snow was looking at him. Kemir felt her puzzlement.

Why?

"Forgiveness."

Forgiveness, Kemir? I do not understand this. In your mind, it seems it is the opposite of revenge. I see revenge in you often. All of your kind. You, Kemir, you would rather die trying and failing to have revenge than live and forgive. Why would you do that? I do not understand either forgiveness or revenge.

Kemir laughed. "Yet that's what drives you too."

No, Kemir. I seek to free my kind from their slavery. I do not seek to willfully punish those who did it to us. I will do what needs to be done, no more. I will eat when I am hungry, Kemir, or perhaps for pleasure. But not for spite.

"Some people think that forgiveness is the most beautiful thing in the world. And you can't have that unless you have a little revenge too."

I see nothing beautiful in being stupid. She cocked her head. *I see, however, that you want this forgiveness very much. Why?*

His fists were clenched. He hadn't noticed, but now they were so tight that it hurt. *Why indeed?* "Because I should have stopped you. I should have stopped you from eating the people that lived here. I should have stopped you from eating Nadira."

Ah. I see.

Very slowly Snow lowered her head until she held it just above the ground. She moved closer, right in front of him. So close that he could reach out and . . .

Touch me, Kemir.

His heart was racing. She was warm. He could feel her heat. And she was huge. He reached out a hand and touched the scales of her nose. He was shaking, he realized, like a leaf.

When the snows melt on the tops of the mountains and the melt-water rushes down their sides and the rivers bloat and swell and froth, who will stop the flood? She growled and withdrew. *Foolish man. When the flood comes, you run. When mountains topple, you run. When the earth cracks, you run. So it is when a dragon comes. Unless you are Kemir, who wrings his hands and says "I should have stopped you."*

For a moment the fear went away. Kemir walked past Snow's head to where her front claws sank into the soft ground. He kicked her as hard as he could. Not that she'd even feel it, but it was satisfying, kicking a dragon. "Fine. Leave the boy. Just take me to the town you saw. We'll find out where we are. And don't burn it. The food there is all useful food, remember, and besides, I might want to stay there. You can find out where Valmeyan and his dragons are and *then* you can start burning things again."

As you wish, Kemir. I am no longer hungry today.

"And I will not be afraid of you."

Perhaps I have taught you something of value then.

"And stop laughing at me."

He put the boy out of his mind as best he could and climbed onto Snow's back. She lumbered across the ground to the edge of the clearing she'd made in the forest and then started to run. Kemir closed his eyes. This was the bit that always scared him the most. The dragon's whole body pulsed with every step. The earth shook and the trees quivered in sympathy. He felt like a little boat, tossed on the waves of a stormy sea, hurled this way and that, at the mercy of the dragon-rider harness they'd stolen months ago, which didn't even fit properly. As Snow reached the edge of the water, she made one last effort. Kemir felt himself grow heavy and then they were flying, over the water, tossing spray everywhere. Each beat of Snow's wings levered her upward, pressing him into her scales. She circled once and then put her back toward the morning sun. Below them, all Kemir could see was endless forest and the silver ribbon of a river flowing idly away from the lake.

Maybe she's right. How do you stop a hungry dragon, after all? But the thought felt hollow. Somehow. That was the answer. You didn't just give up and say it couldn't be done. Of that much he was sure.

After an hour of following the river, they began to see cleared spaces in the forest. Then something that might have been a boat on the river. Then a village, more fields, more boats, all dotted about like tiny little toys. Which made him remember playing dragon-lords with his cousin Sollos when they'd been little boys. They'd make mounds in the dirt and find little stones to be people and then they'd pretend they were dragons and smash it all to pieces.

Well now he knew how those little stones felt. He wondered what they thought, the little people on the ground below him now, when they looked up and saw a dragon. Did a chill run down their spines? Were they frozen to the spot, wondering if today was the day the monster would swoop down and snatch them in its jaws? Or did they shrug their shoulders, mutter *"There goes another one"* to their neighbors and get on with what they were doing? As if dragons were just another kind of weather.

Snow banked and pitched down, swooping low over the next village. As she dived, Kemir couldn't hear anything except the rush of the wind past his face, but when he craned his neck over Snow's shoulder, he saw the people. A few were staring, rooted to the spot, but most were running away. They were running ahead of Snow, out into their fields. He couldn't hear them screaming, but he knew that they were.

Well that answers that, then. "Why do people always run in front of whatever is chasing them?" he shouted. "Why don't they scatter?" *And why am I shouting? No one can hear me over this wind and the dragon doesn't need to anyway.*

All food runs, thought Snow. She felt smug. Pleased at the reaction below.

"They are not food!"

Everything that runs is food. Kemir felt a hunger in the dragon now, almost a craving. He could picture her crashing into the village, spraying fire, smashing houses into splinters, tossing screaming men and women up into the air for the sheer joy of it, just like he and Sollos had done in their games. The visions lasted for a while, long after Snow had left the village behind and risen back into the sky. He shuddered. They weren't his own visions, he was fairly sure of that. They had far too vicious a joy to them.

Other villages came and went, scattered patches of open space amid the great blanket of trees. Then the forest began to break up. There were more people, more fields jigsawed together, more roads, more boats on the river, and then finally a town. Kemir wasn't sure what he'd expected—probably a muddy collection of houses, little more than a village that had sprawled out of control. What he hadn't expected was a small city. It straddled the river, with strong stone walls protecting both halves. It even had a little castle. Snow changed course, keeping her distance.

"Are there dragons here?" That was his first thought.

No. If there were, I would have freed them. Snow started to descend. *We will fly further until we find some.*

"Or you could let them know that you're here. Burn some fields, eat some cows, that sort of thing. Donkeys, if you think they taste better. Scare them. Do whatever you want to do. Make noise. Let them see you. Enough to draw a few riders from their eyries to come have a look. Then when they come, you eat them." *Slowly. Crunch crunch. Like chewing on an icicle.*

Like Ash.

"Yes. Like Ash. Don't hunt them where they're strong. Draw the other dragons to you."

Snow thought for a while. *Will there be fighting men in this town?*

"It's a castle, Snow. Castles have soldiers. There's really not much point if they don't."

Then they will have weapons for fighting dragons and the people who ride on us. Kemir could feel her weighing up choices. She turned and headed away from the town.

"What are you doing, dragon? Are you afraid?"

No. She was laughing. *I have no need for you while I do this, but you are still useful and I do not want you to be dead. I will do as you suggest. I will burn this place. You may watch from far away. It will be safer.*

"No! No burning! No need to kill anyone, Snow. You understand me? Just scare them and then leave. *Useful* food, remember."

I understand, Kemir, but I will decide for myself which of you are useful.

She didn't say anything more, but landed on a hilltop a good few miles from the town and waited until Kemir unstrapped himself and got down. He could have stayed, he supposed. Could have stayed in the saddle, but what difference would it have made? She could have torn him out with one twist of her tail, or else simply ignored him. So he shuddered as Snow launched herself into the sky again. He was very glad, he decided, that he was where he was. On the ground, far away from where Snow was going.

28

POISON IN THE BLOOD

Jehal was dying. He knew he was. The pain was getting worse. He grew slowly weaker until he didn't know he could possibly *be* any weaker and yet the next time he awoke, he was.

The smell was bad too.

In some ways he was surprised he was alive at all. He'd lost a dreadful lot of blood. He felt perpetually light-headed, which was probably a mercy. And yet, when he hadn't died, he'd felt a joyous spark of hope. For a few days he'd thought he might even heal. And then came the smell.

He'd seen men take a wound in a tournament and die, just like this, surrounded by the stench of their own rotting. The alchemists hadn't been able to help them and Jehal had little hope they would be able to help him.

If they cared.

He had a dim memory that Zafir might have come to him the day after Shezira had shot him. She'd held his hand and said some soft words that might have seemed comforting at the time. Or maybe she hadn't. Maybe she was a dream like all the other dreams. Mostly he dreamed of Lystra and of the son he would never see. *If my bloodline dies, so does yours. Neatly done, Queen Shezira. If it wasn't me you'd crippled, I would applaud you for such an efficient and ruthless revenge. But you messed up. I'm dying, and now all that's left is to mock us both for your incompetence. What use am I dead? How do I protect them?*

He got angry sometimes, which was always a mistake because he didn't have the energy to be angry. He'd rail and spit at the world and then he'd fade away and wake up hours later to find that even more of his strength had ebbed away. Men and women came and went from his bedside, silent frightened ghosts who looked at him and then looked away. Afraid. As if they were the ones who were slowly dying in the gilded prison that was the Tower of Dusk.

Sometimes he thought about his own father, cocooned in his sickbed for nearly a decade. *This must have been what you saw,* he thought. *In the early days. When there was still a part of you alive in there.* Then such a sorrow filled him that he wept.

He thought of Meteroa too. *He* would understand. Did Shezira know? Did she know what King Tyan had done to him? *My brother butchered my sister and my mother. My father . . . I don't even* know *what my father did to my uncle. What a family we are.*

I have done such terrible things.

Yes, you have, said another voice. A new voice, but he couldn't see anyone. Not that that meant anything. He was probably dreaming again. The voice was another fragment of his slowly shattering self, most likely. Come to remind him of all the things he'd done wrong so that he could be properly miserable before he finally got around to dying. Come to remind him of how brother Calzarin came by his murderous madness.

Piss off, he told it, and laughed as best he could. If he couldn't sneer at anyone else, he could always sneer at himself.

I could do that if you like, said the voice with a sniff of amusement. *Or I could save your life. You choose.*

Then I'll have my life saved, please. Although I suppose I should ask what it's going to cost me.

A lot.

Doesn't it always? He hated feeling so weak. He was weak even in his dreams now.

Yes. It usually does, agreed the voice.

So what's it going to be? Are you some part of me that's been hiding away all my miraculous powers of healing and recovery, waiting for me to agree to a life dedicated to the betterment of others? Or are you one of the spirits I don't believe in, come to tell me I can have my life back if I swear to become a good person? Because I'm not sure either is playing to my strengths.

No. None of that crap. I want your money.

Jehal spluttered. *Now I know you're just another part of me. Although I'm a little disappointed at my apparent lack of imagination. Is that what happens when you die? Do you become dull first? I must confess that I have largely avoided the company of the near-dead, but those I have seen have usually been most tediously dull. Deathly dull, even. Heh.*

I want something else as well.

Do try not to bore me.

What I want is not yours to give. One day you'll try to take it and find that I got there first. Let it go. It's really not that important to you.

Oh, here we go. You know, I've heard this story before. What are we talking about? My soul, is it? It's usually something like that. Whatever it is, being told it's really not that important to me rather convinces me that it is, in fact, desperately *important to me.*

I want the Adamantine Spear.

Oh. For a moment Jehal was nonplussed. *So do I.*

No, you don't. The other voice huffed impatiently. *You want what it means. You want to be speaker. You don't give a toss about the spear or the ring.*

You're much too crotchety to be me. You remind me of my uncle.

Try imagining that I'm a wizard. I'm going to take away the poison in your blood.

Oh, really?

Yes, really. Piss me off when you're better and I can always put it back again.

Jehal tried to laugh. *As deathbed visions go, I like you.*

We have an agreement?

No.

Oh. Well, I suppose I'll leave you to your lingering death then.

Jehal chuckled, or would have if he could have managed it. *The Adamantine Spear?* Some old relic that sat around gathering dust, wheeled out by whoever happened to be high priest of the Glass Cathedral every ten years. What did he care about that? They could always make another one.

A better one maybe. One that didn't weigh so much for a start. Or he could simply change his mind. The thought made him want to laugh even more. *I'd better not let myself know what I'm thinking. If I'm going to betray myself later, I'd much rather it came as a surprise . . .* He took a deep breath and lay back. He was probably going to die now, he thought, but at least he'd go out with a smile on his face. Then, as an afterthought, he screwed up his face and asked, *Whoever you are, you don't happen to count Vale Tassan as a friend, do you?*

The voice seemed to shrug. *I don't give a fig for him one way or the other.*

That's good. Because if you really aren't just some ghost and you really are going to make me better, then I think I'm going to have to kill him. In some horribly slow and nasty way.

I'm sure that would be very interesting to watch but sadly I suspect I shall miss the occasion. Do we have an agreement?

Can you do what you say you can?

Yes. Last chance. Do we have an agreement or not?

We do.

A warmth engulfed Jehal, as though the softest fur blanket in the palace had wrapped itself around him. He closed his eyes and drifted off to somewhere far away. Somewhere past the ends of the worlds and off into the void between them, where everything was black and still, where clocks and hearts beat slower and slower and time didn't march anymore . . .

And then he was back.

He opened his eyes. The pain was gone. He felt strong again.

He tried to sit up and quickly discovered that the pain being gone and feeling strong were rather fleeting and illusory things.

Still . . . still, he *did* feel a lot better.

He looked to his left and caught a fleeting glimpse of someone in a pale gray shirt dashing out of the door. The ceiling above him was familiar. He was still in the Tower of Dusk but not in the Great Hall, where Shezira had almost killed him. He recognized the room. She'd slept here in the days before the Night of the Knives, when he'd come to see her and played his last card to force her and Hyram apart.

You might as well stop thinking about either of them. They're both dead, for better or for worse. Zafir's going to get her war and you might as well get used to it.

The door flew open with a bang. Jehal had to look twice to recognize the face. Jeiros, the alchemist.

"Prince Jehal! It is truly a miracle!" The alchemist rushed over. He tore off the blanket and started poking around between Jehal's legs.

"Excuse me!" Jehal was naked, he realized. He supposed he shouldn't be surprised about that. He tried to lift his head to see what Jeiros was doing, what damage Shezira had actually done to him, whether any of it was permanent, but the alchemist had piled the blanket up on his chest and he couldn't see. He was numb from the waist down and could only vaguely feel the alchemist's prodding. "I'd prefer if you *didn't* do that."

"The rot has gone. Simply gone! I've never seen anything like it!" Jeiros carefully laid the blanket back where it was supposed to be. "No one will believe this. I have to get Vioros!"

"Master Alchemist!" Jehal's head was spinning. "I am not an exhibition!" He felt sick. The alchemist's enthusiasm was overwhelming. "And I can't feel my legs. I trust they are still there."

"Yes yes yes. The wound is filled with Dreamleaf, that's all. You're going to live, Prince Jehal. Do you understand? Every other man I have ever seen who had a wound like this turn bad has died. And you're going to live. How? How is that possible?" He came around and leaned over Jehal's face. His eyes narrowed. "Yes indeed. *How* is it possible?"

Jehal closed his eyes. "I do not know, Master Alchemist. I had a vision. Whether it was real or a dream I couldn't tell you. Believe me when I say that I'm as surprised as you are to find that I am mysteriously healed. If it was a miracle then I shall thank Aruch for his prayers and then go back to ignoring him. If it wasn't, well then I'd like to know what happened at least as much as you would. Probably more." He took a deep breath. He had a headache now from so much talking. Which was annoying. His mouth, as he'd often observed to his lovers, was one of his best features.

Speaking of which . . .

"Master Alchemist!" Jeiros was still nearby. Jehal could feel his presence.

"Prince Jehal? I have to inform the speaker. The danger is largely gone.

Healing will take a long time, but we can help. Now the poison is gone from your blood . . ."

Poison in your blood. That's what the voice said . . . "Master Alchemist! Please!" He tried to raise his head to watch Jeiros more carefully, but the effort was beyond him. "Before you go, there is one thing I would rather hear from you than from Zafir when she comes." *Assuming she's not coming to have me executed along with everyone else who doesn't bow and scape to her every whim.* "What damage has Queen Shezira done to me?"

Jeiros hesitated. Jehal counted out the seconds. *Quite a lot then. I'm not going to like this.*

"Your leg will heal, but I'm afraid you will always limp and it will always be weak. I think in time you will be able to walk without a staff on which to lean, but I doubt you will ever run again. I think you'll find riding a horse particularly unpleasant too."

"And dragons?" *You're not telling me something. I can hear it in your voice.*

"There may be some discomfort, but no more than at any other time. I'm sure a special harness could be made if it gives you any trouble."

Well, that wasn't what you're hiding. Do I really want to think about it? But if I don't hear it now, I'll hear it from Zafir, and that will be worse. "And?"

"Wait and see, Your Holiness. It may not be as bad as it seems." Everything in Jeiros' voice betrayed him.

"Holiness?" Jehal croaked out a laugh. "I'm not crowned, Master Alchemist. Perhaps I never will be. Now is that all? A limp and an aversion to horses and feats of athletics I can live with. Or is there more?"

"You should really wait, Your Holiness. It is too early to know—"

"To know what?" He knew. He already knew and it turned him cold inside. He might even wish he'd died after all. "What of women? What of that?"

Jeiros sighed. "I cannot say for sure, Prince Jehal. It will be a long time before you can . . . Well. And there will likely be some pain. At best. For some time to come, at any rate."

"And what of heirs?"

"It is much too early to say, Your Holiness. I think, once you are healed, you will still perform as well as you ever did in that particular regard. Until you can be sure, however, I suggest you take great care of the heir you have."

Jehal didn't hear the alchemist leave. The numbness had spread right up his spine and down his arms and into his head.

Take great care of the heir you have. So maybe Shezira got exactly what she wanted after all. Did he want to be alive like that? He wasn't sure. Perhaps Jeiros was right and he should wait. The alchemist's voice hadn't held much certainty either way. *Best not to even think about it. If only it was that easy. But I can think about other things. Distractions. I owe it to myself to heal. I* will *heal, and I* will *be whole again. Yes, and when I am healed there will be blood, and a great deal of it will come from the Night Watchman. Think about that.* Much *more pleasing.*

29

A TASTE OF HAPPINESS

Snow landed in the town. There weren't many places large enough. In fact, there was only one, right next to the little building that Kemir had called a castle. The space had people in it, but Snow ignored them. Sure enough, as she swooped out of the sky, they ran screaming, senseless with panic. The ones who weren't quick enough were crushed or sent flying through the air as she smashed into the hard-packed dirt. The stupid and the slow. Around her, rumbles of tumbling stone and several clouds of dust marked where the people of the town hadn't made their little houses strong enough. Snow swept her head from side to side and shrieked.

It is habit. It is what we do when we return to our nesting place. It is our way of greeting our kind. Kemir was far away, but she talked to him as if he was still on her back. She wasn't sure how useful he really was, but she missed having him with her. She missed the company, the sharing of thoughts. She missed being part of a nest. *It will be good to have other dragons around me again.*

She ate a couple of the people she'd crushed in her landing. Then she shifted back onto her hind legs, lifted up her head and sent a column of fire into the air.

Let them know that you're here. That is done. It seemed all too easy. Would that really be enough to make other dragons come? *Scare them.*

That was done too. She could feel the fear all around her. *Make noise. Let them see you.*

Do whatever you want to do. Kemir had only the slightest idea of what that would mean. What she wanted to do was burn the town to ash, slaughter the little things that lived here and spend a few delicious days hunting down the ones that escaped. The hunting was the best part. The feelings of her prey when they realized they'd been found. The hopeless despair, the laughable defiance, their pathetic rages, the pitiful pleading and begging. As if she could be swayed . . .

I miss what we once were. When we fought together, all dragons side by side with the silver riders on our backs and armies that filled the horizon.

No. Burning the town wasn't going to bring back the glory they'd had before the silver men had broken the world. That would have to wait.

A long pause followed. The realization slowly settled on her: she'd landed in a place that didn't have enough space for her to take off again.

Why did I do that? She knew the answer even as she asked herself the question. She'd done that so that she wouldn't have any choice about smashing up at least a part of the town on her way out. Except now she didn't want to. Or rather she did, but she'd decided not to. *Kemir is right. We are old and wise in our way, yet we are impatient like children. That is how we were made. Creatures of impulse and destruction and whim.*

She looked at the roads and alleys that led into the town square. They were small and narrow. Houses pressed around them. They most certainly weren't built for dragons. She was wondering what she should do and whether it really mattered that much if she knocked a few buildings out of the way when she picked up a familiar taste among the thoughts around her. Anger. Fear. Anticipation . . .

She knew it was coming. She lurched up into the air. A scorpion bolt slammed into her neck about a yard from her head. She felt a fierce pinprick of pain, as though she'd been stung. If she hadn't moved, it might have hit her in the head. It surprised her. In the great war of long ago, the humans had had nothing like this. They'd had a lot of other things, magics and devices that could kill, but nothing that could *hurt*, nothing that *stung*.

The anger hit her like a wall. She skittered and turned to face the castle. Her tail flicked back and forth, smashing the houses behind her to bits. She barely noticed. Someone on the castle had tried to kill her, and now they deserved everything they were about to get. *I am sorry, Kemir. I know you will be angry.*

Sorry? No, not really, since that implied regret, and dragons did not understand regret. Maybe she was sorry that Kemir would be sad. Maybe that was it. She lunged forward, propped her front claws against the castle wall and reared up. Her long neck arched over the castle walls; slowly and methodically she drenched its innards with fire. Men screamed and died. Wave after wave of joy rippled through her. *Fear my fire, feel my power, little ones,* she told them. *You should have fled when I came.* She reached up higher and pushed, trying to force her way inside the castle walls so she could get at the inner keep. Stones fell, but the wall held. She backed away as far as she could and hurled herself at it, crashing into the stone with her side. It still refused to fall.

Now I am ANGRY! Those who should fight hide in caves or now behind ramparts of stone. So where else shall I spend my wrath? Where else shall I take my pleasure?

Furious, she turned on the town. She rose up again and spewed fire in furious arcs all around her. Then she crouched and sprang at the widest of the roads, smashing her way through the cramped and fragile buildings with all the delicacy and care of an avalanche. Houses splintered and smashed as she barged past them. Dust and smoke swirled around her, pieces of debris rained in sporadic showers, and then she was at the city walls, clumsily levering herself over them, head and neck and tail and front claws scrabbling for purchase along the top in an effort to pull up the bulk of her body. Her wings flapped furiously and with a lurch she rolled onto the top of the wall and down the other side. Without a pause she was running, charging through the nearby fields as fast as she could, hauling herself up into the air.

Even as she rose, she was turning, twisting back toward the town. If anything, the fury burned stronger than it had at the start. *This* was how it felt to be a dragon.

You will not escape me. Stone will not save you. Not this time.

She scattered fire across the town. Unleashing the flames always felt good. Like mating, before the alchemists dulled her mind. It left the same hunger inside her too. She would need to eat when she was done here, and eat well.

Below, amid the smoke and the flames, men and women ran and screamed. *Food, all of you. Nothing but food.* She flew around the castle, gave the tower in the middle of the castle a long blast and then landed on top of it. Stones crumbled under her claws, almost tipping her off. Such was her anger that she tried to sink her teeth into the towers. When they didn't give, she smashed them to pieces with her tail. Every time she tore a new hole in the stone, she poured fire into the wound.

Finally the stone groaned and rumbled. Half the keep crumbled away and tipped her off in a shower of broken masonry. She landed on her back and floundered for a few seconds before she managed to right herself.

Where? How? How do I get to them? They were still alive, some of them. They were buried in there, out of her reach, but she could feel their thoughts. Raw, hot burning terror to make her heart sing with joy. Pain too. A lot of pain, but they were *alive*, and they were supposed to be *dead.*

Her anger had become a living thing with a will of its own, as though she carried with her the spirits of all dragonkind, freed from the dull shells the human alchemists made for them. *It is enough*, she tried to tell it. *They are probably dying. Even if they are not, they cannot escape. They are trapped.*

No! It is not *enough!*

But I should leave some to live. That is our plan. Some must live to tell of what has happened. Then other dragons will come and we will take them to us.

But not these! These tried to kill you! Let us destroy them all. Leave nothing but ash and rubble. Burn them to dust!

Why? Because they pricked my scales? She paused to pull the scorpion bolt from her neck. *There. It is gone. In a sunrise or two, I will barely remember it.*

Because they dared!

She had no answer to that. She smashed and climbed her way back out of the castle. A good portion of the eastern half of the town was ablaze now.

The rest of it was doomed. What could burn would burn. Stones would crack and split in the heat. People would collapse, overwhelmed by smoke. Even if she did vent more rage on them, it would make little difference.

And vengeance is futile, remember. That is what I told Kemir. Dragons do not act out of kindness. Dragons do not forgive, but nor do dragons avenge. So then what is this desire?

She already knew the answer to that. The anger was fading. The rest was pleasure. Fun. Fun forgotten for too long to resist. She launched herself back into the air. The western side of the town, away from the castle, was still intact. She hadn't set fire to even a part of it yet. Already, people were appearing on the eastern riverbank looking for a way to get across.

It would be so easy to destroy them all. And so satisfying, and yet if I do then what have I achieved?

She almost left them then, almost turned and climbed into the sky to wait for more dragons to come, but at the last moment she gave in to her desires and wheeled and dived and plunged down into the river. *I have done this before. I remember.* The one half of the city she would leave untouched. From the other half, none would escape. When men tried to row, she upended their boats. When they tried to swim, she flipped them out of the water with her tail. Some of them she caught and ate. Others she simply hurled back into the black haze of flickering smoke. *Yes, I have done this before.* There had been other dragons then. *And things that weren't dragons and yet were even more terrifying and made us seem small; and not all that came out of the smoke and the flames was human. I remember. I remember how this feels.*

It felt glorious.

She stayed until no one else came to the waterfront. Perhaps an hour passed, perhaps more. Certainly the sun had moved when she took to the air again. She felt sated. Fulfilled? Free?

Happy. That was what she felt. Happy. She hadn't felt happy for a very long time. Lifetimes.

This is not vengeance, Kemir. If you knew the truth, if you felt what I feel now, you would wish it was. I feel joy.

He couldn't know. Not now, not yet, not for a little while. Not until she was done with him. So she took her time flying back to him on his hill, until she could push the feeling back beneath the waters of her thoughts. Until she could keep it in a place Kemir would never see but where she would never forget.

30

THE SECRETS OF THE ALCHEMISTS

King Valmeyan left this morning," said Jeiros. He wasn't looking at Jehal as he was talking. Well he was, but not at Jehal's face. He frowned and leaned forward. "You need to relax," he said as Jehal winced in anticipation of yet more pain. "Stay very still. Neither of us would be pleased if my stitches go awry."

All very well for you to say. A searing jab ran right up from his groin as far as his neck. *And this is with my veins filled with more Dreamleaf than blood.* He bit down on the leather strap that the alchemist had given him.

"Are you still finding it difficult to pass water?"

This was what his father had had to put up with. In the beginning, before disease had taken his mind away. Help to stand, help to eat, help to clean himself. Help with everything. *I'd rather die.* "I wouldn't call it difficult. Uncomfortable," he said through gritted teeth. *Unbearable blinding agony, more like. But only Kazah sees how much it pains me, and Kazah doesn't speak so none of you will ever know.*

"The speaker has promised to crown you as soon as you are able to walk into the Glass Cathedral."

"And how long will that be, Master Alchemist?" *She hasn't come to see me. No word. Nothing. Does she think I can't watch her from in here? Does she think I don't see who she takes to her bed?* He fingered the strip of white silk he kept hidden beneath his pillow. Even confined to his bed, the magical metal Taiytakei dragons roamed the palace at night, guided by his whim.

227

Prince Tichane, King Valmeyan's right hand, he was the one to watch. He had his hands halfway up Zafir's gown already and was plenty busy elsewhere too. Jehal needed to know what he was up to. *I need to move. Watching is one thing, but I need to hear. I need to speak. I need to walk. I need to be seen. How quickly people forget that I am even here.*

"Another week, perhaps two." Jeiros shook his head. "I'm having the best wood-carvers in the city make a crutch for you for the occasion."

"So I can stumble in with one lifeless leg dragging behind me? No, thank you."

"It'll be months before you can walk without help. If you ever can. You need to be crowned, Jehal. There are far too many realms without a proper king. Right." Jeiros straightened up. "There. The stitches are done. The dressing is changed. You're rid of me for another day. Before you're crowned, there's another ceremony we should have, you and I. I suppose you know most of it already, but there are certain secrets that my order holds that we like to share with our kings and queens."

Jehal rolled his eyes. "You mean things like, oh, by the way, the dragons you fly on are only dumb pliable beasts when they're drugged to the eyeballs with your special potions."

"That's the start of it, yes. It can take anything between a week and a month for the effects to wear off. Did you know that?"

"And then they're ravening vengeful monsters. I do know what happened at the redoubt, Jeiros."

"Then you know how clever they become. The white one's been seen again. Did you know *that*, Your Holiness?"

"No. I heard it was dead with the rest."

Jeiros cocked his head and flashed a grimace. "That's what *princes* get to hear. Kings get to hear that the white has been seen in the Worldspine. Without a rider this time. It burned exactly half a town to ash. Some of Valmeyan's riders went to investigate. Three of them didn't come back; nor did their dragons. By now it could be more."

Jehal sniggered. "No wonder the King of the Crags is in such a hurry to be home. And I suppose Zafir is positively brimming with enthusiasm to rally the realms and her riders to hunt your mysterious rogue."

"This is not funny."

"You keep them in dim servitude. Are you surprised they're so angry when they wake up?"

"The Order keeps us all *alive*, Prince Jehal. We'd be nothing to them but food otherwise."

"If anyone did something like that to me and was then foolish enough to let me slip, I'm quite sure I would prefer something more lingering than simply eating them." *Are you listening, Vale Tassan?*

The alchemist shook his head. "There's a lot more. Where they come from, where they go when they die. Even we don't know that. But we know that their spirits go in an endless cycle. They're not like us. They remember their past lives, or rather they would, if they awoke. Do you know how many times dragons have escaped us and awoken from their stupor?" Jehal had never heard of such a thing happening at all, at least not until the white dragon at the redoubt. It must have shown on his face because Jeiros smiled. "No, Prince Jehal, the redoubt was not the first time. There are dragons out there among us who have awoken before. Who have awoken and been destroyed. Who have returned as a hatchling, remembering everything that happened to them. Knowing everything that we do to them."

"And then you do it to them again."

"If we can, yes." Jeiros nodded. "If we can't then they die. You see, Prince Jehal, there is a great deal that even *you* don't know. Knowledge we hold for kings and queens and the masters of our order, and for them alone."

"Kings and queens and master alchemists? Why so miserly?"

"Knowledge is dangerous, Prince Jehal. You of all people understand that. Knowledge is a means to power. "

Jehal laughed, even though that always hurt. "And there I was, imagining that you were hoarding all this knowledge simply to give your order a reason for being."

The alchemist didn't bite. If anything, he sounded sad. "Seventy years ago, a rider happened upon some of our secrets. He took it upon himself to free his dragon of our potions. He thought they would be more powerful, and indeed they are. His dragon ate him. Then it ate a lot of other people too. It destroyed a realm. Nor was that the first time."

"I've never heard of this!"

"Oh you but have, Prince Jehal. You know almost everything about it. The story of a realm ripped apart by its own royal family's infighting? Their eyries destroyed, their riders slain, their dragons stolen? A realm rendered so weak that those around it simply helped themselves to the pieces. A realm that barely exists anymore, with no king, no queen. A realm whose people shift in endless wandering though the Sea of Sand . . ."

"The Syuss."

"The Syuss. You see. You *do* know the story."

"But that was . . . I thought that was . . ."

The master alchemist was smiling again. "Prince Kazan? Civil war? A revolt against the oppressions of King Tiernel? No. Kazan was the rider stupid enough to awaken his dragon. Twelve other dragons went missing trying to find him. Fortunately half of them didn't have time to wake and still it took the intervention of three neighboring realms and Speaker Ayzalmir to put an end to it. Hundreds of riders were killed. *Most* of what you think you know is true, the picking over the pieces afterward, the destruction of the realm as it was. But the beginning . . ." Jeiros grinned broadly. "Not what you think. There are always the same number of dragons in the realms, Prince Jehal. This is why you have so many eggs in your eyrie and yet so few of them hatch, because no egg can hatch until another dragon dies. But do you know why? Do you know how many? When they *do* hatch, a quarter of hatchlings only last a few days. Again, do you know why? Do you know how the dragons were tamed? No, you don't."

"No, there you are wrong, Master Jeiros." Jehal screwed up his face as he shifted slightly in his bed. "I know *that* story. The last of the great wizards sucked all the magic out of the realms in one mighty spell . . ." He stopped. Jeiros was trying not to laugh.

"Forgive me, Your Holiness. The stories of the Adamantine Spear and of the last great wizard and other such mumbo-jumbo. These are stories for children, not for kings, not even for princes." He cocked his head. "You know how the dragons at the redoubt were defeated, poisoned by their own greed. The Embers trace their traditions back to the first free men. We fed our first potions to the wild dragons in the only way we knew. Then we sought out their eggs. At first we killed the hatchlings, but then we found we could use them. It made finding the rest a lot easier." He chuckled. "No, the symbols of the speaker are a ring and a spear, but that is all they are, symbols. They might have had a power once, but not anymore."

Jehal narrowed his eyes. "Are you lying to me, Master Alchemist? I had thought the Silver King tamed the dragons."

Jeiros' face didn't give anything away. "We guard our secrets well and if you understood them, you would guard them too." He reached the door and bowed. "Good evening to you, Prince Jehal. When you are a king, we will speak of these matters some more."

"One moment, Master Alchemist. How much of this does Zafir know?"

Jeiros shook his head. "She is a queen, Your Holiness, and the speaker. She knows as much as she needs to know. More than you." With that, he bowed one last time and left. Jehal closed his eyes. *That's a lot to think about and I don't have the strength these days. One at a time then. The Syuss.* He reached into his memories, trying to think, but all the stories he could remember were filled with holes. He could feel himself drifting, losing his concentration. That was the Dreamleaf messing with him. *Better Dreamleaf than constant burning agony.* He shuddered. If anyone ever wanted to torture him again, all they'd have to do was bring him back to this room, pull out a chamber pot and wave it at him.

Jeiros is bound to have a book. He can lend it to me. Maybe he can lend me someone to read it too, so I don't have to find the energy to sit up.

He wasn't sure whether what happened next was a dream or a memory. He was drifting into sleep and then he was wide awake and the room was much darker; in between, he'd been the speaker, riding to war, clutching the Adamantine Spear in one hand and a cage full of birds in the other. When he let the birds out of their cage, he wasn't sure whether he was Ayzalmir, bringing order and peace to a ruined realm, or whether he was Zafir, and the birds were chaos and death.

A cold certainty gripped him, that someone else was in the room. He strained his ears. Kazah was snoring gently but Kazah didn't count. He could feel someone else. A presence lurking in the shadows, silent and invisible and yet very much there.

"Who are you?" He spoke quietly, almost at a whisper, but in the stillness the words sounded loud. *Calm though. At least they sounded calm.*

Now he saw a shadow move. He started to rise, but that sent a spear of pain through him.

"Shall I light a candle?" asked the shadow. "I don't want to wake the boy."

"I don't converse with ghosts and shadows. Let me see your face." Jehal slipped his hand under his pillow. He had a knife there, always.

"Are you sure?"

"Yes, I'm quite sure, thank you." *I should be shouting for the guard, except most likely they let him in.*

"Very well." The shadow walked away from Jehal's bed to the far corner of the room where a night candle burned. The shadow lit another and slowly returned. Now Jehal could see. The shadow had a man's face. One he'd seen before.

"I know you. You were one of Shezira's men." *Now I really should be shouting for the guard.* But the voice. That was much more recent.

The man laughed very softly. "Are you afraid of me, Prince Jehal?"

"I am unaccustomed to strangers slipping into my room at night. It sets me on edge." *The voice. I know the voice. He wasn't a rider.*

"Whereas *I* am very much accustomed to it. I've been in here with you before. Do you remember? We made an agreement. *As deathbed visions go, I like you.* That's what you said. Ringing any bells?"

"Ah." Jehal's mouth felt very dry. "I'd rather hoped you were a hallucination. I liked you a lot better that way."

"And I liked you a lot better when you were nearly dead."

"Who *are* you?"

"I have many names. Kithyr will do. I am a blood-mage. No one else could have saved your life and I meant every word about putting the poison in your blood right back where it came from. I have it stashed carefully away, should I ever need it. You are mine, Jehal."

"Right." Jehal's fingers closed around the hilt of his knife. *Never mind the pain. One quick strike and it's over. Then you can scream.* "So now you want something from me in return for my life. And if I don't give it to you, you're going to kill me? Do you really think that's going to work?"

The candle threw strange shadows over the blood-mage's face. It made his features shift and blur and change so they were almost impossible to read. "Taking the poison out of your wound also took a great deal from me, Prince Jehal. I told you then that what I truly want for that is not yet something that is yours to give. What I want now is more of a first instalment, and much more in your gift. What interests me now is money."

The fingers gripping the knife relaxed. "*Money?* How very tedious of you. Still, if you say you saved my life . . ."

"Not *your* money." The mage seemed genuinely annoyed. "The speaker's money. She offers her own weight in gold for each of the Red Riders. That is a tantalizing prospect, is it not?"

"Oh, I don't know." Jehal yawned. "She's rather small and skinny." He cocked his head. "Anyway, if that's what you're after, you seem to have slipped into the wrong bedchamber, blood-mage. I do not appear to be the speaker."

The mage uttered a soft laugh. "Even if I abased myself before her throne, I could not be sure that Zafir wouldn't have me put to death simply for being what I am."

"Zafir is nothing if not a pragmatist." Now Jehal laughed as well. "Ancestors! If *Shezira* was prepared to have a blood-mage around, well, the Edict of Vishmir might as well not exist."

"Whatever else she is, Zafir is a daughter of the Silver City. Her blood and ours have a very old score to settle. As for Queen Shezira, she had no idea what I was."

Which had to be true, and so it must have been Shezira's knight-marshal who'd found the blood-mage. *A woman of true vision. Brave and bold and cunning and ruthless. Everything I have in Meteroa and more, and so fanatically, obstinately loyal.* He sighed. *Such a pity. Now, do I shout for the guards or not? Where are we going with this, blood-mage?* There was still the knife, still quick and easy to hand.

"I want the Red Riders, Prince Jehal. They have served their purpose and now I want them gone. I can give them to you and you can give them to the speaker. You will get her gold and her favor. Half the gold you will give to me. The favor you can keep. By this we shall see that we can trust each other."

Trust? Ha! "Really. You can give them to me?"

Kithyr blew out the candle, plunging the room into darkness. "Really. Drotan's Top, Prince Jehal. When Valmeyan is safely back in his mountains. Sooner or later they will strike again at Drotan's Top. When they do they will be yours for the taking."

"And if I don't?"

"Then the poison goes back in your blood, Prince, and you die."

"I will be a king after this."

Kithyr stood by the door. "And at the speaker's right hand again, and neither will save you, Jehal. It's a simple enough thing that I ask. It costs you nothing and gains you a great deal."

"That is true." Jehal smiled and watched the mage go. Then he wiped his palm, lay back and stared at the ceiling. *Very true.* "Sooner or later is somewhat vague, blood-mage. I might have deduced that for myself."

"Yes, you might." The voice wafted from across the room. "Then how about this, Prince? In four weeks to the day they will strike again at Drotan's Top. Does that suit you better? I could have it be sooner, but I imagine you will need some time to prepare. I hope, when you see that I am right, you will understand with whom you are dealing and think long and hard about our other agreement."

Jehal didn't answer. He heard the door whisper open and closed again. When he was sure he was alone, he breathed a deep sigh. His heart was racing.

"Yes," he whispered to the night. "Long and hard. I think I shall."

He had to wait a long time before sleep came to him again. He felt alive, more alive than he had for weeks, more alive than he had since Hyram's fall. When he did finally sink into slumber, he was grinning.

31

THE MAUSOLEUM

J aslyn left Evenspire as soon as politeness allowed. They barely said goodbye. She didn't tell Almiri where she was going; in fact, she didn't tell anyone. Jaslyn and Hyrkallan and the half a hundred dragons she'd brought with her to Evenspire. North toward home, for the sake of any prying eyes, high over the Blackwind Hills until they passed Fardale and Southwatch and the Last River. Up in the north there were no foothills, no grassy rolling slopes. Just ash and pale silver sand, rippling in giant waves until they crashed against the immense white and gray cliff faces at the edge of the Worldspine. No rivers, no trees, no grass, only ash and sand. Ash and sand. That's all there was to the north. Endless days of dead nothingness before the land slowly changed once more.

When they were well and truly out of sight, they parted ways. Most flew on, back to Outwatch, Southwatch and Sand. The places they belonged. Jaslyn, though, turned west, toward the Worldspine, with Hyrkallan and two others that he'd chosen beside them. Hyrkallan didn't like it, had sternly advised against it. Hyrkallan could go screw himself. In the safety of the deep dead peaks, they turned back south and began their long journey toward the sea. Little streaks of green began to appear in the valleys below, desperate little strips of life clinging to the shady spaces where a few tiny streams would flow on those rare days when the rain came. Out here even the mountain stones seemed bleached white by the heat. Then they crossed the deep gash that seemed to run like an open wound all the way as far as she could see, even into the immeasurable heart of the Spine. The valley of the Last River. The last water in the north, the blood of her realm that ran past the edge of the Blackwind Hills and Southwatch and Sand and all the little hot and dusty towns of Ishmar's Valley until it staggered away into the desert again and finally expired, if it was lucky, in the Lake of Ghosts.

She thought of turning west again, of launching herself even deeper into the Worldspine if only to see what she might find. She always thought of that when she came out here. The Worldspine was rumored to be filled with hidden valleys, or else to rise up ever higher, until it touched the sky, so high even dragons couldn't pass over. Or else, some said that beyond the Spine lay other realms, another speaker, another palace, yet more dragons, a world a mirror of this one. Up here, this far north, no one would ever find her. The Worldspine belonged to the King of the Crags, or so they told her, but here, she was quite sure, it belonged to no one but itself.

Yes, a part of Jaslyn was minded to explore but that part would have to wait. For now, she had a duty to her sisters. To Almiri, who sat on her dead husband's throne, who was so still that she might have been a statue, whose face looked as brittle as fine glass. Almiri had not taken the news well, though it had hardly come as a surprise. Her husband and their mother, beheaded by a dozen soldiers. No one there to bear witness. No one to hear their last words. Their bodies hung in cages outside the palace instead of being fed to their dragons. And all Jaslyn could do was wonder: *What if they were guilty? What if mother* did *kill Hyram? What if she* did *try to have Zafir murdered? Is it so unlikely? I wasn't there, I didn't see it all unfold, so how do I know it's not true?*

And to Lystra, most of all to little sister Lystra. The last news was that the Viper was going to live after all. Which was a pity, and was what had finally convinced her to fly south and not north. She needed her sister. She needed Lystra to tell her who to fight. To tell her that Jehal was a monster to be slain. Or to tell her that she was wrong. Or, more simply, she needed Lystra to be there. Next to her. In the flesh, alive and breathing. To hug and hold and laugh and tell her that life was not quite so bleak as these mountains. So she stayed her course and watched the valleys below spring into timid uncertain life, still clinging to the great rivers and the few little streams that fed them. They stopped for a night in a valley looking down over the Blackwind River, four riders and four dragons, surrounded by emptiness. In the morning they flew on, steadily south, and as they came closer to the Purple Spur, it seemed as though a line of shadow speckled with stars crossed the spines and ridges of the mountains. Snowfields sprang up, the greens of the valleys thickened and filled with trees and rushing water. Valmeyan's realm. Hyrkallan guided them uneasily now, took them low into the valleys where there was little to see but the rush of trees below and snow-spattered cliffs to either side. But the mountains were empty; King Valmeyan's dragons were ensconced around the Mirror Lakes, slowly eating their way through the speaker's cattle.

They reached the abyss of the Gnashing Snapper Gorge, where the immense mass of the Fury roared through the depths of the Worldspine. Hyrkallan tipped B'thannan's wings and they dived into it, down deep between black slabs of rock only a few dragon-spans apart. Jaslyn's ears popped and throbbed. The world became as dark as night as they fell and the air filled with spray and the thunder of rushing water. As Hyrkallan slowly leveled his descent and skimmed across the black waters, Jaslyn looked up. Far above her, the sky had gone so dark that she could see stars.

Slowly the gorge widened out. The river slowed and they passed the startled eyes of Hanzen's Camp, the last stop for even the most adventurous boats plying the Fury River. They stopped for a second night not far away on the edge of the Worldspine, a hundred miles east of Drotan's Top, and then drifted up again with the dawn, veering a little eastward but still flying south, out over the swathes of rolling green that were the Raksheh, the Thousand-Mile Forest, squeezed between the endless flat gray clouds above and the rolling green ones below. In the hills and plains to the far-away east, Zafir's eyries were almost empty, her dragons dispatched to the palace. Once, in the far distance, back toward the mountains they'd abandoned, they saw four other dragons flying north, high in the sky and deep among the peaks. Other than that, they saw no one. As the light failed they stopped again in the empty depths of the forest, at the ancient abandoned Moonlight Garden, looking out over the wild Yamuna River and at the Aardish caves where Vishmir the Great and, some said, the Silver King himself were laid to rest. Jaslyn stood there amid the blood-red marble stones veined with yellow and watched the moon rise. In a place like this, in this wilderness of lonely emptiness and the stone relics of a people who had died and gone long ago, she felt strangely at home. Outwatch was like this. Surrounded by desolation, old beyond measure, crafted by hands long dead with skills long forgotten. Enduring. Everlasting.

Unlike everything else.

She sighed and tried to sleep under the cool open skies of the south. The dreams that came to her were strange, always were in this place. Of men with white hair and silver skin and wide blood-red eyes. Of the Silver Kings.

They flew away again with the dawn, saddlesore and weary although the dragons who did all the work seemed untroubled by their long flight. Southeast now, down the Yamuna River and out across the rolling deep green canopy of the Raksheh. As they took off it started to rain, low gray clouds rolling in off the Sea of Storms far away to the south. Rain. It was delicious. A novelty for those born to the desert realm of Sand and Stone.

They crossed the edge of the Raksheh, the dark sprawl of trees breaking up into a patchwork of fields and copses laced with a dark spiderweb of muddy roads and spattered with hamlets and farmhouses. As they did, Jaslyn saw a single dragon far in the distance. She urged on Morning Sun until he was alongside B'thannan and signaled to Hyrkallan, but by then the other dragon had seen them and sped away. They flew on a little further, closing in on the grand eyrie of Clifftop. Jaslyn looked for an open space and brought Morning Sun as gently as she could to the ground, thundering into the side of a hill, slipping and stumbling, tearing gouges as deep as a man out of the thick damp earth. A flock of sheep scattered in panic in front of them. Jaslyn felt a sharp stab of desire from her dragon. Hunger. He hadn't eaten since Evenspire. When she told him no, he snorted and tossed his head, blew a column of flame a hundred feet up into the air, the rain around his face sizzling into steam.

Jaslyn sat, slowly getting wet. The air smelled of dragon and the rich dark soil. Without the wind in her ears, the world fell silent apart from the steady hiss of the rain. She sat and she waited, alone in the emptiness while Hyrkallan and his two outriders circled above to mark where she was. That was how it was done, when a stranger on a dragon entered a foreign realm. Like an animal rolling on its back, exposing its belly to show it meant no harm.

Eventually the dragon from Clifftop came back with others. One rider landed nearby, his dragon shaking and tearing the earth once again. The rest stayed in the air, circling. Jaslyn told him who she was and why she'd come. She had no idea who he was. She wasn't at all sure that he believed her either, but then maybe he did. Or maybe he'd seen her at Lystra's wedding. Maybe he'd been one of the dozen and more southern riders who'd gallantly asked for her hand at a dance only to be brushed away without even a smile. Climbing to the top of the hill and then hurling themselves down the side, the dragons raced and flapped their wings and ripped the earth with their claws once again until they launched themselves into the air, one after the other. She followed him toward Clifftop, trying not to think of what would be waiting when they got there. Ceremonies and greetings and all manner of tedious rituals to go through. All a waste of time. From Clifftop to the palace of Furymouth was most of a day on the back of a horse, longer in a carriage. She didn't have much time before she'd have to fly back, and every hour she spent at the eyrie was an hour away from Lystra.

Except it wasn't. At Clifftop Jaslyn let Morning Sun dive and then spread his wings and almost stop in the air before smashing into the ground, the way all dragons like to land. She threw off her harness and slid from the dragon's back and there was Lystra, little sister Lystra, right in front of her only a few dozen yards away. In the rain, Jaslyn had to blink a couple of times to be sure. Then she had to blink again. Tears this time. Protocols and rituals could go hang. She raced across the ground and grabbed her sister, almost lifting her off the ground. She remembered the smell of the air here. The smell of the sea, the distant sound of the waves crashing against the cliffs below.

"Lystra!" She still had to keep blinking.

"Jaslyn!" Lystra seemed reserved, returning her embrace with only a measure of joy. Jaslyn took a second to realize why.

"Ancestors! You're so big! When will it be? It can't be long! Look at you!" She put a hand on her sister's big round belly and smiled. The first smile since . . . she couldn't remember. Since Lystra's wedding perhaps.

Lystra smiled too, the shy proud smile that Jaslyn remembered. The smile that made her heart melt, and perhaps Jehal's too. "Another two months, they tell me."

"So long? You look ready now!" The thought of Lystra as a mother had a bitterness to it. Almiri had already given Valgar three heirs. She was the last one. Lystra was all grown-up, not little anymore. But that sort of thinking wasn't helpful, wasn't why she'd come. "Why are you here at Clifftop? You should be at the palace with everyone to look after you!" She stepped back. For the first time she realized that Lystra was clothed from head to foot in gray. "You're in mourning! What's happened?" Someone was dead. *Jehal?* Her heart jumped with hope. *Could it somehow be Jehal? Is he dead after all?*

Lystra looked confused. "You mean you don't know? How can you not *know.* Mother . . ."

Oh. Yes. That. Jaslyn looked down at herself. Not a trace of gray. She'd almost . . . No. Not almost. She'd actually forgotten. For a few days she'd forgotten that her own mother had been executed. She'd tried to forget that horror along with everything else, and for once she'd actually managed it. Now she felt ashamed.

There were several men and women standing either side of Lystra. Jaslyn had ignored them totally until one of them coughed and smiled and stepped forward.

"Meteroa, Your Holiness." The man bowed. *Holiness.* She still couldn't get used to people calling her that. "I am King Jehal's eyrie-master and I am at your service. I do my best to advise Queen Lystra while he is away. Currently I have advised her to move away from the palace. The air here is cleaner. So is the water. And indeed the food, I have discovered." He raised an eyebrow as if he meant to convey some complex meaning. Jaslyn had no idea what he was talking about. She should have worn gray. She should have worn gray if only for Lystra. *I never liked our mother but I know you did. I always thought you were her favorite because you were the pretty one, but maybe it wasn't that. Maybe she liked you the best because you were the only one of us who liked her back. I'm sorry, I'm sorry.*

"Can you . . ." She was still looking at Lystra. Could she what? Forgive her? For forgetting that their mother and their queen was dead? For being as coldly indifferent as the speaker?

"I'm sure Queen Lystra understands." Meteroa smiled. "You are almost at war with Speaker Zafir. There is little time for mourning. It is a luxury, I know. I assume that's why you're here."

"I . . ." *Is that why I'm here?* "I wanted to see my sister again. In case it was the last time." She cocked her head at Meteroa, desperate to talk about something else. *I want to be alone with my sister. ALONE!* "Since you are here, Eyrie-Master, I have a question for you. Do you have dragons who refuse their food? Hatchlings who sicken and starve and die?"

Meteroa chuckled. "All eyries have them, Your Holiness. Tarrangan's Curse, we call it here. Three dragons live, one dragon dies. So it's always been."

"Do you have any of them here right now?"

"Hissing and snarling at the end of their chains in some deep cavern beneath our feet? You ask strange questions, Your Holiness." Meteroa looked baffled. "I have no idea why you ask me this, but no, at present we do not. Why? Why do you wish to know? If I have your permission to ask, Your Holiness?"

"No." Jaslyn shook her head, all interest suddenly gone. "No, you don't." She shivered. "May we go?"

Meteroa bowed. "Of course, Your Holiness." He led them toward the cliff-top towers and in among the sprawling walls. "The King of the Crags is returning to his mountains, I hear. It is curious, Your Holiness. Why would he emerge from the Worldspine for this when he doesn't even come for the crowning of a new speaker? I cannot help but wonder about that. Valmeyan has more dragons than any two kings or queens put together. It is something of a quandary. Can you enlighten me, Your Holiness?"

Jaslyn thought she sensed the faintest hint of mockery in Meteroa's voice. She bristled. "No. I'm sure Prince Jehal will know the answer."

"*King* Jehal," purred Meteroa. "King Tyan died five weeks ago."

Five weeks? Why didn't I know this? Jaslyn turned to Lystra. "Then if Jehal dies, you're queen!" She could slap herself. She must sound like an idiot. Meteroa had been calling Lystra his queen ever since they'd arrived. *What's the matter with me?*

Lystra was staring at Jaslyn. Her eyes were very big and glistening with tears. All of a sudden she stepped closer and embraced Jaslyn again. "I know you think the worst of him," she whispered, "but he has the heart of a good man, not a wicked one. All the things they say about him, they aren't true. I know. I see him in a way no one else does. Don't wish him dead, Jaslyn, please."

Jaslyn froze. A shiver ran through her. She held Lystra tight. "You've changed," she whispered. She couldn't think of anything else. *There. That was every question I had, answered in a stroke. Now I might as well go home.*

Lystra straightened and stepped away. "Jehal tried to save Mother from Zafir's headsman. That's why he was imprisoned."

"Did he? Did he really?" Jaslyn couldn't bring herself to believe in Jehal. *If he did, he had a selfish reason for it.*

"He was trying to save the realms from a war, I think," murmured Meteroa. "Always a foolish pursuit." He turned and grinned at Jaslyn. "Since you're here, I suppose he must have failed."

"I came to see my sister." *Go away!*

Meteroa didn't go away. All through the dregs of the day he was constantly at Lystra's side. *To protect her,* he said, *from all the little dangers that others don't see,* although he wouldn't say what those dangers were, and Lystra had practically been born and bred in an eyrie. The next day was no better, although Meteroa at least took Jaslyn around Clifftop to present his dragons. Quite a collection, Jaslyn realized. Jehal didn't have as many as Isentine held at Outwatch, but such a variety! So many colors and shapes and sizes. Hunters and war-dragons of course, like every other eyrie, but some were . . . something else. Smaller, too small even to be hunters. Then he led her into the caves etched into the cliffs, into tunnels and darkness where everything smelled of smoke and Jaslyn could barely hear what he was saying, where all his words were blotted out by memories of choking air and rushing water and the deadly tightness of the alchemists' redoubt. She could barely breathe. Cold sweat clung to her skin, gripping her, wrapping her in suffocating arms. Twice she stumbled and leaned on Lystra to keep herself from falling, and then finally a blast of fresh air and light thundered into her. They emerged into a gallery overlooking a yawning void. A hundred feet below, the sea crashed and roared over a tumble of black boulders that littered the cave mouth. Sunlight reached inside to light up the stone walls beyond, worn smooth by the waves. Further in lay a deep pool of still dark water. The air was fresh and salty.

"No use for dragons, this one," said Meteroa, shouting to make himself heard over the noise of the spray. "No easy way in and out. We use this cave for something else. The kings of Furymouth have always kept their collection here."

Jaslyn took deep breaths, sucking the cool fresh air into her lungs, cleansing them of the memory of smoke. "Collection?"

"Collection." Meteroa pointed out into the emptiness of the cave. Slowly, as Jaslyn's eyes adjusted to the brightness of the sun pouring in off the sea, she saw that there were *things* suspended in the air. Bones. Blackened bones. Dragon bones. Whole dragon skeletons.

"Are they real?" She stood agape. Dragons burned when they died. Burned from the inside out so that nothing was left except their scales and their wings. Maybe a few charred bones from the end of their tail, but everything else went to ash. She'd never seen the skeleton of a dragon. No one had. Or at least that's what she'd thought until now. Now there were four of them in front of her. They were enormous.

Meteroa nodded, sounding solemn. "Very real, Your Holiness."

"How?"

He pointed down to the water below. "The Salt Pool. The sea barely reaches into the cave, but the pool beneath us is deep. Sometimes when a dragon is dying we bring it here to the Salt Pool. We feed it the same poisons as the Embers took when they fought for you and the alchemists. When a dragon dies in the Salt Pool, the water is enough to save the bones.

The salt ruins the scales though. We don't bring them here very often."
He pointed. "The nearest is Awestriker. He was King Tyan's last mount.
Prince Jehal had the dragon slain when it became clear that his father
would never ride her anymore. The furthest is Bludgeon. That was the first
dragon to be brought to the Salt Pool. They say the first king of Furymouth, the blood-mage Tyan from whom King Jehal's father took his
name, came here. There had been a battle. This was long before Narammed and Vishmir and the rise of the speakers. The Order of the Dragon
had risen up in the Silver City and ousted the blood-mages from the Pinnacles. The battle was lost, the magus' dragon was damaged and he did not
want it to fall into the hands of the Order. He brought the dragon here to
hide it. The dragon died. Later, when the Order came and Tyan fled, they
sent soldiers to the cave to bring back the scales. The scales were ruined,
but they found the bones instead. For days no one understood where the
bones had come from. Sea monsters, they said. Eventually they realized
the bones came from Tyan's dragon." Meteroa smiled. "Of course, that was
long before there was an eyrie at Clifftop. Come. There's more."

He walked along a narrow ledge carved into the sheer side of the cave.
Jaslyn followed nervously. Lystra stayed where she was. The ledge was
rough, a foot wide or sometimes less, and the Salt Pool was far below.
Small niches had been cut into the wall, tenuous handholds to offer an
illusion of safety. Meteroa moved carefully and methodically. "The menag-
erie may interest you, Your Holiness, if you have an interest in dragons."

The ledge ran for some fifty feet before it opened out into a wide natural gallery. There were more skeletons here, much smaller than the monsters hanging over the bulk of the cave. These were hatchlings, so small
they must have been fresh out of the egg.

"We've been breeding them like this since the realms began, Your
Holiness." Meteroa smiled again. "Not many of our visitors are privileged
to come down here but I know this isn't wasted on you. And you are our
king's sister now. The interesting ones are back here."

One of the hatchlings had two heads.

Jaslyn stared at them in disbelief. Half of them were deformed. Two
heads, two tails, four wings . . .

"Blood-magic," said Meteroa with a curl of disgust, although whether he meant it or it was feigned Jaslyn couldn't tell. "A few of our kings have had a taste for it. They were set on breeding a new kind of dragon. This is what they got. They never had any success. Fortunately the local penchant for blood-mages has died away. We work with the alchemists now, using potions to try and evolve the breeds."

"You want to breed a dragon with two heads?" Jaslyn couldn't contain her disbelief. Meteroa laughed.

"No. It's all about the color of the scales, the timbre of their sheen, that sort of thing. That's why Jehal so wanted your white dragon. A new strain, a new bloodline, perhaps we could have done something different. You breed your dragons for speed and strength; we're known through the realms for the most colorful dragons." He chuckled again. "In different times, an alliance between our realms would have been a happy time for me. I would have spent a great deal of time in your eyrie and you in mine. We could have traded secrets, eyrie-master to eyrie-master. We could have traded bloodlines. I had high hopes for what our eyries might produce if they worked together. Who knows—maybe those dreams are not quite lost?" He talked on and on and Jaslyn soaked up every word. Meteroa knew what he was doing and he knew his dragons. She got lost in them and almost forgot why she was there. Other things slipped in. Jehal's imprisonment, his injury, his recovery. The poisons Meteroa had found in the kitchens. The sabotage to the saddles of Lystra's horses. A dozen other ambiguous little clues, all of them pointing to Zafir. Evil, wicked Zafir.

"King Jehal was so sure he would keep her in check. I'm afraid he rather seems to have failed." Meteroa sighed. "Queen Lystra lives at Cliff-top now because it's safer. I trust the alchemists and the Scales here more than my own riders and certainly more than the servants in the palace. I had thought we knew all of Zafir's secrets, but I'm afraid we rather failed there too. It's all quite depressing. Come, Your Holiness. We've left your sister for long enough. If we delay any further she may have one of her foolish moments and try to follow us."

The eyrie-master retraced his steps. Jaslyn followed, easing her way uncertainly along the ledge. When they returned, Lystra was sitting on the edge with her feet dangling over the Salt Pool, tossing stones down into the water. She glared at them both.

"Meteroa, you've taken my sister away for far too long and I'm immensely bored. I am cross with you."

Meteroa bowed. "I am deeply sorry, Your Holiness. To make amends, I shall arrange a great entertainment for you. I shall leave at once. I trust you will be safe in the care of your sister." He turned to Jaslyn and his face became serious. "There are men I trust not far away. You will be left alone. If you are not, you should assume that whoever approaches you means you harm. You are armed?"

Jaslyn nodded.

"Good. I suppose, apart from myself, you're the one person I will leave alone with my queen until my king returns." He suddenly looked weary and shook his head. "It has been a regrettably interesting few weeks. I will not be far away."

With that he turned and walked slowly away into the tunnels. Jaslyn stood alone with her sister, staring out into the cave, breathing the damp salt air. For a long time they were silent. Then Lystra held out a hand and Jaslyn took it.

"There's another path," said Lystra in a whisper. "You can climb down to the cave mouth. Then there are steps carved into the cliff to take you back to the top. It's very steep and very slippery and you'd like it. Shall we?"

"No." Jaslyn squeezed her sister's hand, then crouched down and put her ear to Lystra's belly. Lystra began to stroke her hair. "Two more months. And they won't let you fly?"

"Meteroa doesn't *want* me to fly."

"But he has to do what you say."

"No, he has to do what *Jehal* says."

Jaslyn put a hand next to her ear. "I can feel the baby! It's moving."

"Yes." Lystra hugged Jaslyn's head. "Isn't it magic?"

"On the back of a dragon is the safest place in the world," whispered Jaslyn. "Why won't they let you fly?" She stood up and held Lystra tightly. "Why won't they let you fly?"

Lystra laughed softly. "Why won't you climb the cliff with me?"

"You might fall."

"Yes. I might fall." She pulled away and held Jaslyn's hands. She was still smiling. "I can't be the Lystra you remember. I have to be a queen now. Soon I will have to be a mother."

"The speaker is trying to kill you."

"Jehal will keep me safe." She spoke with conviction. Love even. Jaslyn winced. The hurt was like a knife.

"Come back to Outwatch with me." Her voice was trembling. "We'll slip away in the night when he's not watching you. Speaker Zafir won't know where you've gone. You'll be safe."

Lystra squeezed Jaslyn's hands. "Of course she'll know where I've gone. No, Jaslyn. A part of my heart is always yours, but my place is here."

"Lystra! Sister!" How to make her understand that Jehal was a monster. That he was vicious, that he was a murderer, that he had no love for anyone but himself, that as likely as not he was Zafir's lover. *The very woman who's trying to murder you. He doesn't care about you. You're nothing to him. Just something to be veiled behind screens, making babies and heirs until he tires of you. He'll take what he wants, bleed you dry and crush you. Like Aliphera. Like Hyram. Like Mother.*

She wanted to say all of those things, but the words stuck in her throat. She saw Lystra's wide eyes and knew she couldn't wound her sister with them. That even if she did Lystra wouldn't believe her. That Jehal, for now, had won. The understanding made her weep, despite herself.

"You don't belong to us anymore, do you?" she croaked.

They held each other tight, and then Lystra kissed her. A long, lingering kiss. The sort meant for lovers. "I will always be your sister, Jaslyn. Promise me we will never be enemies."

Jaslyn bit her lip and nodded. "Never. I promise. Promise me you will stay safe."

"I will."

"I miss you, little Lystra. I will never, never let anyone hurt you."

"I know. I miss you too."

For a long time they stood together, holding hands. Jaslyn wept in silence. Eventually she turned and led Lystra back into the tunnels, back to the eyrie-master's men. Then she left the tunnels, summoned her riders and her dragons and put Clifftop behind her as quickly as she could.

METEROA WATCHED HER GO, SOARING away into the afternoon skies. "How very sudden and very rude." He sniffed and gave his queen a queer look. "What *did* you say to her?"

"Nothing. Nothing that she didn't know before she came here." Her voice was flat and gave nothing away. Inside, Meteroa smiled. *Very good, little one. Very good.*

She was looking at him, he realized. She cocked her head. "Why did you lie to her about the hatchlings?"

Meteroa shrugged. *Did I lie? I don't even remember.* He grimaced. "I apologize if this offends you, Your Holiness. Doubtless I shouldn't say such things about another queen, but your sister is very strange. Hatchlings. What a question to ask." Now he laughed. "You know, I can't remember the last time someone asked me a question and I hadn't the first idea *why* they were asking it."

"But why did you lie?"

Meteroa smiled. *Because I didn't like not knowing why she asked. Because I didn't like the way she looked at me. Because I think she's dangerous in a way that even Jehal wouldn't understand.*

He couldn't say any of that though, not to his queen, so he settled for something else that was equally true. "Because I'm not a particularly nice fellow, Your Holiness. I've made a career of it. Sometimes I lie simply because I feel like it. Because I can. Keeping my eye in, so to speak."

He winked, but Queen Lystra didn't see. She was looking back to the sky, watching her sister fade into the clouds.

32

THE HUNTERS AND THE HUNTED

Snow was soaring high when the riders came out of the Worldspine, just as Kemir knew they would. Five dragons, all fast-flying war-dragons, each with two riders. They were wary, flying in a loose diamond formation, one low and close to the ground, another up high, above the little puffs of cloud that hung in the air, and then one to each side and the last dragon hanging back. Kemir didn't know too much about flying dragons, but he knew that riders looking for a fight flew close together where they could quickly support each other. These ones were expecting the sort of trouble that would make them turn and run. In hindsight, that should have been a warning.

As if it would have made any difference. There was probably a right way to attack the diamond. Kemir had no idea what Prince Lai's *Principles* had to say, but if he had had to guess, he'd have said go for the one at the back. Snow, however, had never heard of Prince Lai. She simply climbed higher, then tucked in her wings and dived out of the sun, smashing into the dragon at the top of the diamond. The impact would have hurled Kemir far into the air if it hadn't been for his harness; as it was, the straps nearly tore him in half and he slammed forward, breaking his nose on Snow's back. The two dragons curled around each other, plummeting out of the sky together. Kemir didn't see what happened to the riders, but they must have been in the middle when the two dragons collided—probably now nothing more than a big bloody smear with bits of armor sticking out.

For a moment everything vanished into a white mist as they fell through a cloud. By the time they emerged, the dragons were apart. Snow had something dangling out of her mouth. She shook her head and it flew off through the air, leaving a streak of fine red mist to dissolve in the wind.

"Ow! Damn you, dragon, you nearly killed me!" He held on to her, arms spread wide, white-knuckled fingers locked around her scales. The other dragon was diving for the ground now and Snow wasn't far behind. He could see the ribbon of the river and the town that Snow had burned, a slight dirty haze that still hung over it.

There. One free. Four to go. She didn't slow down, but arrowed on toward the next dragon, wings folded back, wind howling around her.

"Alive! Take a rider alive!" bellowed Kemir, as if anyone could hear a thing at such a speed. He screwed up his face and tried without much success to shield his eyes with his hand. "Can't you *ever* control yourself?"

Why?

"*Useful* food, remember."

How is it useful?

The riders on the next dragon had seen Snow coming now. She was flying too fast for them to get out of the way, but they'd turned their scorpion to fire at her.

No, not at her, at her rider. At him. Kemir threw himself flat. A few moments later he felt a pinch of pain from Snow as the scorpion bolt hit her. He had no idea where. Didn't care much either. It hadn't struck *him*, that was what mattered. You could probably shoot a hundred scorpions into a dragon without doing much more than make it very cross.

No! The dragon's fury slammed into him like a hammer and Kemir roared with anger without really knowing why. He clenched his fists and would have sat up straight in Snow's saddle, except as soon as he moved the wind almost ripped him off her back. Then Snow hit the other dragon like a thirty-ton battering ram. He was thrown up into the air, the harness almost tearing his legs off this time as both dragons lurched sideways. The other dragon was twisting to present itself as all claws and teeth, but it wasn't fast enough. Snow snapped at it with her teeth, raked it with her claws and lashed it with her tail. The teeth got one dragon-knight, the claws got the second. Kemir wasn't sure what the tail did because he was too busy ducking as the other dragon's tail snaked around Snow's neck and sliced the air where his head should have been. Rage filled him. Dragon-rage.

Poison, Kemir. Their bolts are poisoned!

Thoughts jumbled on top of each other, some that were his, some that were not. That if they were shooting scorpions with dragon-poison on them, they weren't shooting at him. That Snow ought to flee now, back to the lake. Back to the glaciers, if she could make it. That he didn't care, that she should stay and kill and kill and *then* run for the glaciers. How many poisoned bolts would it take to bring a dragon down? One? Ten? A hundred?

The one between my teeth still has thoughts. They are not useful thoughts, Kemir. I want to eat him.

"Do you know he's not poisoned too?"

Snow shuddered. She spat the knight out of her mouth. He sailed away through the air with a forlorn cry and fell out of sight.

"Alive!" screamed Kemir. "Take one alive!"

Why? Snow turned, throwing Kemir sideways. They were getting close to the ground now. If Kemir hadn't had about a hundred more pressing things to do, he could have counted the trees and the animals in the fields beneath them.

The dragon's fury coursed through him. "So we can ask him questions!" *So I can kill him myself.* "About dragon-poison and scorpions." *So I can feed him his own entrails while he's still alive.* "About how many times they think they need to hit you!" *So I can crush his skull with my bare hands.*

The last three dragons were closing now that Snow no longer had height and speed to her advantage. They were trying to position themselves around her, to trap her. A scorpion bolt fizzed through the air past Snow's head. Another punched straight through the thin skin of her wing.

"Go go go! Now!" Kemir urged. The curtain of the dragon-rage was lifting at the edges. Behind it, his own feelings began creeping through. Fear. Alarm. A certain uneasy dread. "They've fired. Take them before they can load another bolt!"

Snow veered, twisted and powered toward the nearest dragon, her whole body shuddering as her wings ripped the air. The straps of the dragon-rider harness groaned and Kemir felt something at the bottom of his spine pop and creak. Snow closed the gap, but not enough before the other dragon turned and pulled away. A scorpion bolt from above bounced off Snow's nose. She shrieked in frustration, turned sharply and launched a futile charge at another of the dragons. That one danced away too. The riders knew what they were doing. Kemir could just about see that now. They'd be happy to keep their distance and pepper Snow with their poisoned scorpions for as long as it took to wear her down. He clung on, gritting his teeth as Snow pivoted and whirled back and forth. Her wings strained, her seething tail slashing the air, but each dragon she chased only powered away while the other two closed and took their shots.

"That's what you get for being stupid," muttered Kemir. He could still feel the fury, smoldering waves of it pulsing out of Snow like a bad hangover, but he was its master now.

Stupid, Kemir? When I fall out of the sky, I shall be sure to land on my back!

"Stupid because you landed in the middle of a town and burned half of it to the ground. Stupid because hundreds of people saw a riderless white dragon. Stupid because you never stop to *think*. You just smash and burn and eat people." He flinched as another scorpion bolt split the air nearby. Snow was climbing again, hauling herself steeply up toward the little scattered clouds, but Kemir could see straightaway that they were too small and too few to offer any cover. *Why am I shouting? Because it makes me feel better, that's why.* "What did you expect? Did you think they were going to come out here after you and form up in an orderly line to be eaten?" Wind tore past Kemir's face, almost pulling his words out of his mouth. He could barely open his eyes. Proper riders had riding helmets with special visors for this sort of thing. He pushed himself forward into Snow's scales again. In the end, he was helpless up here.

Her scales were hot.

Your thoughts are a distraction, Kemir. They are not helpful.

"My thoughts are a distraction? Well, why don't you just land and let me off then? Then you can blunder about on your own. It's not like you listen to me anyway and then I won't have to worry about being shot at by giant arrows anymore!"

Kemir!

"Hey, you know what? Next time you burn a town you could jump inside their heads and ask them to bring some nice tasty donkeys when they come back to hunt you. They're not *stupid*, Snow." *In fact so far they've been cleverer than you.* He tried to think the last thought quietly.

Not quietly enough, Kemir.

Valmeyan's dragons were faster than Snow. She wasn't quite fully grown. Maybe that was why, or maybe the mountain men simply had better dragons, war-dragons, stronger and faster and more enduring. Snow had five bolts in her now and more would come. Sooner or later they'd get enough poison in her to bite and she and Kemir both knew it. She reached the level of the clouds and wove through and in between them. The other dragons settled in around her, patiently awaiting their chances.

I must go back to the mountains. To the lakes.

Into a cloud. Everything white. Turn. Out again into the sunlight.

Kemir could see exactly where that would lead. Snow meant to hide under the water again. "And what do I do?" The other dragons might be able to follow her but their riders couldn't. They'd wait for her until she came out again. *And, in the meantime, they'll amuse themselves chasing after me. Three of them on dragons and me on foot. I'd be better off staying with Snow and hoping to discover a miraculous talent for breathing water.* "They won't give up," he shouted. "They'll stay with you for as long as it takes. Sooner or later you'll have to come out to eat. They'd be waiting for you." There. He could even believe that might be true.

Next cloud. Sharp turn. Back into the light. Sprint after one of the other dragons. No good. Turn again.

And you suggest? She was powering through the air with all her strength, sprinting, turning, keeping the other dragons at bay for now. It couldn't last. Kemir was pressed flat against her scales and could already feel her becoming uncomfortably warm even through his furs. Her thoughts were distinctly irritable. He could see them. She was wondering whether she'd fly faster without Kemir on her back.

Another cloud. Another turn. Into the light. Straight into another scorpion.

"Get them away from their eyries. They need their potions. They can't follow you if you take them away from their eyries."

And where are their eyries, Kemir?

"In the mountains." Which was certainly true. But for all he knew, there might be eyries all over the place. He'd never been this side of the Worldspine. Hadn't even known it existed.

Then your advice is flawed, little one. I prefer the lakes. Snow turned sharply in the next cloud, arrowing back at the three dragons in pursuit. Kemir wasn't sure whether it was her patience or her strength that had gone first. The other dragons scattered. She spat fire at the nearest, then pin-wheeled and powered toward the distant peaks, climbing higher, putting the clouds below her. Another scorpion bolt buried itself in her flank. Kemir felt the flash of pain and anger. A second one sailed over his head. There was something in Snow's thoughts that he'd never seen before, something that didn't belong. Desperation.

"The sea!" he burst out. "Go to the sea!"

The sea? There was a pause. *Where is the sea?*

Kemir tried to form a map of the realms in his mind. "Somewhere south."

Why is the sea better than a lake that is smaller but closer?

"Because it's called the Endless Sea for a reason. Because there aren't any eyries. You can fly and keep on going and they'll have to give up and go home, and when they come back they'll never be able to find you." *And you can float on the surface and I can stay on your back and no one needs to drown or be taken by the dragon-riders.*

It is far away, is it not, Kemir? Very far.

That was probably true. He didn't know where they were anymore. "I don't know." He glanced over his shoulder, looking for the pursuit. Snow was leaving a trail of smoke in the air behind her. No, not smoke, steam. When he touched the scales of her back with his bare skin, he yelped. They were hot, painfully hot. *Days, probably.*

I do not know if I can fly for days at this speed.

"You flew that far when we crossed the Worldspine." *Not at this speed though.*

Nor was I poisoned.

Self-pity? Kemir felt his anger return, and this time it was all his own. "No, but you weren't so fat with people you weren't supposed to eat either. You brought this on yourself. Now you can get out of it."

They challenged me, Kemir. Two more scorpion bolts flew past Snow in quick succession. A third glanced off her scales. She turned again, changing course to fly parallel to the Worldspine. Kemir tried to work out whether they were going the right way. "The last time we flew toward the sea, we kept the mountains on the right." Snow had turned so they were on her left.

Yes, Kemir. And we have crossed the mountains now.

He tried to work out whether that made a difference. He didn't get very far before Snow suddenly dropped out of the sky and plunged toward the ground. Kemir screamed, partly in surprise, partly from real fear that Snow had suddenly succumbed to the poisoned bolts.

I do not feel the poison yet, Kemir. Her thoughts were tinged with amusement. *If it is to be the sea then I must fly low to weave among the hills. The dragons that follow us are fully grown. They are stronger and faster than me, but I am more agile. We must use that to our advantage.*

We. Snow had never said *we* before. Despite everything, despite the burned town, despite even Nadira, a warm glow bloomed in the pit of Kemir's stomach. *We.* It might have been his breakfast trying to escape as Snow pitched into free fall. Or it might have been pride.

33

THE FORTUNES OF WAR

Luck.

Prince Sakabian couldn't believe what he was seeing. He hadn't expected to find them. He was high up on the edge of the Purple Spur, cruising along the edge of the Great Cliff with the jagged peaks of the Spur to one side and the great gray emptiness of the Plains of Ancestors far, far below on the other. He hadn't expected any trouble at all. And yet there they were, far off and high over the desert plains. Eight of them. Six hunters and two war-dragons. The air was so clear and dry that even from this distance he could make out what they were. He looked over his right shoulder. Twenty-five war-dragons filled the air behind him, stretched out in a line. On their backs were nearly a hundred dragon-knights. They had scorpions and fire-bombs. Enough to start a war. The Red Riders were supposed to be far away, deep in the Worldspine harassing Valmeyan. Sakabian was in the wrong place and everyone knew it. He was here to watch the northern edges of the Spur, keeping an eye on the speaker's borders and the alchemists' precious convoys traveling along the Evenspire Road.

And yet there they were. Eight dragons, mostly hunters. They hadn't come from Evenspire and that only left one thing. The Red Riders weren't in the Worldspine after all. They were here.

Luck.

That's what Knight-Marshal Aktark would say. That's what *everyone* would say. No matter that the Red Riders had struck here before. No matter that another dozen wagons from the secret mountain strongholds of the alchemists were on their way. Luck, they would say. No one would give him the credit. No one would praise his astute tactical acumen, his precise prediction of where the Red Riders would strike again. They would just say it was luck.

So be it. The queen—he still couldn't help but think of her as his queen, even now—the queen would see a victory. He doubted she would care how it was won.

The queen. Even thinking about her made him stir. *Aunt Zafir.* He could hardly hear her name without thinking of her naked. Without seeing her in his mind, slowly slipping out of the darkness and into his bed, arching her back as he spread her legs. Unwed. Her lover crippled and a traitor. You could see the hunger in her. She was ripe, ripe to be plowed by any prince who brought her a victory, especially a prince of her own blood. He let that thought spur him on even as a new possibility presented itself. Back home in the Pinnacles, his father and Queen Zafir's sister were already maneuvering against each other to take her crown. The family was tearing itself in half again. He could stop that. Yes. Perhaps a victory here could win him a crown as well. He'd be quite happy enough to help himself to Zafir's little sister and share a throne with her as long as he got a taste of the bigger sister too . . . The two sides of the family united again. A new lover, one safe and bound by blood. Two birds killed with a single stone. Yes . . .

He wrenched his thoughts away from the taste of Zafir's skin on his tongue. The battle had to be won first. There was little point trying to hide his approach. They were in open skies and clear air and if the other riders hadn't seen him already, they certainly would as soon as he broke away from the cover of the Great Cliff. It would be a chase. In a chase, a war-dragon always beat a hunter. The six hunters might as well give up now. At worst, if he was blisteringly stupid, the two war-dragons might get away; but that would still give him the first and the biggest victory that Zafir had seen for a long time. He would take it to her and bow, and her eyes would sparkle at the understanding of his lust.

Ripe to be plowed. He shifted in his saddle, trying to get comfortable. The dragon beneath him surged through the air and shrieked, echoing the desire in his thoughts. Behind him his riders fell into formation, fanning out to the left and the right, above and below, with Sakabian at the point.

Like a spear to be plunged into my enemy's heart.

The Red Riders had seen him. Their hunters were fleeing, losing height and pulling away for now, but he didn't let that worry him. Deep in the mountains they might have found a place to hide, but here in the barrens there was nothing. No cliffs, no canyons, no crevasses, no great rivers, no titanic forests. A sheer wall almost a mile high marked the start of the deep mountains and they were far too low to find an escape route there. The Silver River valley was half a day of flying away. No, there was nothing for them. He had half a mile of height over them, and height could become speed whenever he wanted. They were doomed. The only shelter was in the Spur, and Sakabian was in the way. Their cries echoed through the air. They might as well have been cries of despair.

A part of him hoped they'd fly north. That was worth a try. They could make a dash for Evenspire and the shelter of the treacherous Queen Almiri and her riders. For the hunters that was hopeless. Evenspire was simply too far away. They would never reach it before Sakabian was on them. For the two war-dragons, though, if they were strong . . .

And if they do then I will take their hunters and I will follow them to Almiri's eyrie, and I will loose my scorpions and rain down my bombs, for then there will be no doubt that we are at war . . . That was what the speaker wanted. An excuse. Anyone could see it. *Yes, I could give her that too.*

But they did the more obvious thing. They turned west and sprinted for the Silver River and the Worldspine from which it came. Sakabian changed his course, trying to be patient, knowing that the dragons were ultimately his. Their only real hope was to reach the mountains, so he kept in their way, blocking them off, drifting away from the Great Cliff as he herded them further north and west, slowly trading his own height for the distance between them. Eventually the hunters would tire and then even the mountains would be useless to them. *Then* he would take them.

If I haven't taken them already.

They danced together, Sakabian and his twenty-five against eight, wearing them down until everything was perfectly poised and the inevitable outcome was assured.

He never even saw the other dragons. They must have been lurking beyond the sheer walls of the Spur. They came from behind and from high above, and with such speed and in such numbers that half his riders were dead before he even knew he was under threat. One instant he was sizing up the moment, readying himself to commit to the attack. The next his mount was streaking down, while the air filled with shrieks and fire and howling wind. Dragons smashed together around him. Riders were crushed between them or else ripped from their saddles and tossed away to plunge the half-mile to the ground below. Half a man sailed past Sakabian's head, fragments of armor spinning lazily around him. Sometimes, when men and saddles were torn apart, it wasn't leather and metal that gave way but flesh and bone, and Zafir's harnesses were the finest.

With no idea how he was alive, he slowed his precipitous dive, signaling for a fighting retreat, but there was no one to rally. Dragons wheeled everywhere. Only six of his remained and they were scattering and badly outnumbered. He couldn't count how many dragons had attacked him. Dozens. They were all over the place now, most of them hunting down his own, some of them still circling above. Doing to him exactly what he'd been planning to do to the Red Riders.

He saw the hunters too, the ones he'd thought would be his. From underneath, the colors painted on their bellies and their tails cried of Evenspire. Of Almiri the traitor queen. They weren't the Red Riders after all. Almiri had lured him into a trap. He felt a surge of something. Of awe perhaps. This meant war, open bloody war. At least half the dragons of Evenspire were here, killing his men.

A rider never abandoned his dragon. That was the rule. Never, never, never. A rider always fought to the death rather than lose his mount because, in the end, dragons were more precious. Every prince knew that. And since when dragon-knights fought they fought in the air, in heavy harnesses and armor, it all seemed rather inevitable. *But I am a prince!* Dying hardly seemed fair. He was young, strong, virile. He didn't deserve to die. An hour earlier, in his mind at least, he'd almost become both a king and a lover.

Almiri's riders were around him now, slowly closing in, keeping their distance but forcing him toward the ground. Three still circled above, waiting for him to flee. They were high enough, he judged. High enough to turn their height into speed and be sure to catch him no matter where he went.

Ancestors! Were they offering quarter?

Yes, he realized, that's exactly what they were doing. And why should he go down fighting? The end would be exactly the same, after all. Except if he fought, he would be dead.

And if I'm taken? Almiri will crow and Zafir will seethe. My brothers will pay the price for our humiliation. My father will pay my ransom and will never sit on the throne of the Pinnacles, and I will be sent into exile. The queen will spit in my face—if she can even bring herself to look at me. No. My life will be finished.

Except . . .

He plunged down, straight to the ground, tearing open the buckles on his harness as they fell. *No cover for dragons among the stones and the dust and the thorn bushes but plenty enough for a man.* As soon as he reached the ground, he slid down off the dragon's back and shouted at it to move away. Then he ran for the nearest shred of cover, covered himself in his dragon-scale as best he could and prayed.

Let me survive. Let me take the word back to my queen. Let her know from my lips of the traitor queen's outrage. Perhaps Zafir would give him dragons again, more dragons. Perhaps she'd let him burn Evenspire to ash. Perhaps she might be seduced by his bravery.

They burned him. More than once they caught him with their fire, but they never quite seemed to see him and his armor held off the flames. Luck. Sixty dragons and their riders and he'd escaped them! When the sun began to set and they finally flew away, all he felt was relief and a great deal of pain. He didn't care anymore whether Zafir ever spoke to him again. He was alive, that was all. For a brief few hours he saw himself for what he was. A fool.

But not for long. He walked through the night until he was half dead from pain and exhaustion. He left his armor behind him, and then everything but his sword, and then even that, so that when he found his way to the Evenspire Road, he was reduced to common thievery. Still, he could barely contain himself. He slept in the day in what shade he could find until the wagons he'd come out here to protect rolled past. What was left of them, for Almiri's riders had already caught them and very politely stripped them of everything the alchemists carried. They gave him what he needed—water, food and a horse—and he was on his way, racing ahead of them.

It took him another four days to reach the Adamantine Palace. By then he'd traded his horse for a thoroughbred. He'd survived. He would be the one to tell the queen about Almiri's wickedness and give her the excuse for the war that she so clearly craved. He would be a hero. He would bring her victory, of a sort. And she would be grateful. Oh *so* grateful.

In the palace he dressed himself as a prince once more. He insisted on an audience with the speaker and he told her how he'd been surrounded on three sides by Almiri and the Red Riders. He spoke of how valiantly his men had fought and how many of the enemy had been slain. Of how he'd been ripped from his own mount as they'd skimmed the ground. Of how he'd been burned and left for dead and yet, by some miracle, had survived his fall. In broken whispers he told of how they'd hunted him for three days before he'd made his escape. He could see the glee in the speaker's face when he told her of Evenspire's treachery, the sparkle in her eyes, the burning heat of desire. He saw the slight hint of a smile, the licking of her lips as she sent him away with words full of promise and hints of reward.

It came that night. The Night Watchman brought it to him with a pair of heavy hammers. They smashed his ankles and his wrists and then broke his spine and cut out his tongue. Then they put him in a cage and hung him next to Shezira's rotting remains to die slowly in the sun. Speaker Zafir watched them hoist him up. She spat on the ground beneath him and then left. She didn't even say anything.

Luck.

34

ALL AT SEA

The test, Kemir discovered, was not between the dragons to see who could stay in the air the longest. The test was between the riders. The test was to see who didn't mind pissing and shitting in their breeches, who didn't mind sleeping on the wing, who didn't mind not eating or drinking for day after day. The test was who could put up with more pain.

On even terms, Kemir could have lived with that. Dragon-riders were perfumed and pampered and had servants to do all their work for them. Outsiders, on the other hand, were as tough as nails, or at least that was how Kemir saw the world. Dragon-riders cried like babies if they got hungry. Outsiders didn't even think about going a few days without food. That was simply the way life was when you tried to live off the land in the mountains. He would be hungry and thirsty and stiff and sore, but nothing worse than he'd suffered a dozen times before and certainly nowhere near as bad as crossing the Worldspine had been. The dragon saddles were comfortable enough, designed for long days of flight. He even managed to doze on Snow's back in the freezing wind of their passage through the afternoon. When he woke up though, Valmeyan's riders were still there. It occurred to him then that they'd come prepared. That they probably had water and food for days of flight, and that he didn't.

Do not trouble yourself, Kemir. They pit their endurance against mine. They cannot win.

"Yes." His head was already aching from the constant cold wind and a growing thirst and it was only going to get worse. His nose throbbed, but the wind was the worst, a relentless battering gale as the dragons raced for hour after hour, skimming the ground, zigging and zagging between hills and through valleys. Their pursuers took it in turns to follow Snow while one of them always stayed high, watching so that she could never slip away. Despite the wind, Kemir was sweating. Snow's scales were too hot to touch.

As the sun sank lower and the clouds on the horizon began to look like bruises, Valmeyan's riders closed in on Snow for one last charge, harrying her even closer to the ground with their scorpions. Kemir watched lakes and rivers and trees and empty meadows flash past beneath them, so close that Snow's tail sometimes threw up clouds of spray or earth.

"Land!" he told her. "Find a cave or something like that where they can't shoot at you and land."

I do not see any vast and gaping caves, Kemir, but I do see lakes. Plenty of lakes.

"Caves are better."

Snow didn't answer. She headed further toward the mountains and wove back and forth around a forest of craggy hills, ducking between bluffs, diving in and out of narrow valleys, switching back and launching an attack or two of her own, although she never got close enough to snatch a rider. Finally, as twilight fell, the other dragons dropped back and stopped firing their scorpions, either because they'd run out of bolts or because they didn't trust their eyes in the gloom. Snow resumed her course toward the sea; the others followed more discreetly now, a mile or two away, slowly vanishing into the darkening sky.

"You can lose them in darkness, can't you?" he shouted hopefully. He bounced up and down, trying to fight off the stiffness threatening to seize hold of his lower back. The pain in his head was getting to be unbearable. He felt sick, physically sick. *Please say yes. I don't have the strength for this anymore. Not again. Not after the Worldspine.*

The dragons will sense where I am.

"How can they see you if it's dark?"

I did not say see, I said sense. They will feel the presence of my thoughts. Escape is not likely. Snow started to climb. *We do not like to fly in the dark. Perhaps the other dragons will refuse to continue.*

Kemir hunched over Snow's back, trying to sleep. His head was thumping and his tongue was starting to stick to the back of his throat. "I need water, Snow. I think I'm going to die," he whispered, but the dragon didn't seem to hear him and he fell back to dozing. As the full dark of night began to fall, Snow flew lower. She changed her course and started to follow a river that snaked along a valley filled with pines.

Kemir jerked awake. Snow's thoughts had changed. They felt bright and sharp and full of victory. *The dragons may sense where I am, but their riders will not. Ready yourself.*

"Ready myself for what," slurred Kemir.

To jump.

"What?"

You are getting off. There is water here to drink. You may find food. You will sleep and be refreshed. In the morning I will find you and we will fly to the sea together.

"What about the other dragons?"

They will come for me, not for you. In the darkness their riders will not be able to use their weapons against me. For a while I shall hunt them. If I succeed, they will be gone by dawn.

She slowed, dropping lower and lower until she was skidding across the surface of the river, wings flapping furiously, sending great waves across the water, flying as slowly as a dragon could fly without simply falling out of the air. *Jump! Now!*

Undoing the saddle took five times longer than it should have done and then Kemir was falling, rolling over Snow's scales, bouncing off her shoulder, tumbling, splashing into the water. The cold river shocked him awake, but he barely had time to get his bearings before Snow powered away and the wind from her wings grabbed his head and pushed him under the water. He came up spluttering, thrashing his arms and legs wildly. Half a lifetime ago he'd learned to swim so that he could dive for lake stones to trade. He was exhausted though. His boots and his sword belt were dragging him back down. He managed to ditch the belt, but the boots were another matter and he was loath to throw away either of the dragon-bone bows. And then there was the armor. *I should have thought about this before Snow threw me off* . . .

And then, to his surprise, his feet were on the bottom. He was standing up and the river water only reached to his shoulders. He struck for the shore. The water was icy, soaking through his riding clothes as though they weren't there, making him bulky and clumsy. By the time he reached the bank he was trembling, teeth chattering. But alive.

Water. And shelter. Before he froze. He took out his arrows and filled his quiver with river water. As he did, he saw two of the pursuing dragons soar overhead, side by side, black shapes against the night sky. Kemir winced and ducked. Once they were gone, he jogged along the bank to where a fallen tree lay with its roots sticking up in the air and started to strip off his wet clothes. There was a scar in the ground where the earth had been ripped open by the tree's roots as it fell. He tried to ignore how tired he was, fobbing off the fatigue and the exhaustion with promises that they could have him later. As long as they let him do what he needed to do to stay alive.

He threw the last of his clothes onto the ground. He was shivering uncontrollably now. Memories of Nadira kept bothering him, although whether that was because he needed someone else's warmth or because he might be seeing her again soon, he wasn't sure. He started shoveling pine needles into a mound, scrabbling for handfuls wherever he could find them. She could have helped him with this too.

He ran out of strength long before his pile of needles was as big as he wanted it to be. More would have been better, but there was nothing for it. He tipped some into the hole, climbed in and pulled the rest on top.

"Forest blanket," he whispered to himself. "Have you never tried it?" His teeth were chattering. As the lurking darkness took him, he could almost believe he wasn't alone anymore. And then he was gone.

He was awoken by snuffling. Warm, loud snuffling.

I know you are here. I can feel your thoughts.

He opened his eyes. It was still dark. A dragon was peering at him. A *huge* dragon. He couldn't see what color it was, but he was fairly sure it wasn't white.

"Snow?"

In the times we were first born this one had a different name. Now he is called Sunset.

Kemir didn't move. He couldn't. Overnight, his muscles all seemed to have turned to wood. His face ached and his nose was sore and swollen up like an egg. "This . . . is . . . another dragon?" he hissed.

I told you I would hunt them. I have brought down one. The others evade me. Something landed with a thud close to Kemir's head. *This is the rider. I could not tell if he was poisoned so I did not eat him. He has warm dry clothes. There is food here too.*

Food. Kemir jumped out of his hole. He skirted nervously around the new dragon, but Sunset only sniffed its dead rider and then eyed Kemir with dull curiosity. Both dragons were deliciously warm. After a moment of hesitation, he started to relieve the dead man of his clothes and his armor. The clothes were still warm too. Then he looked at Sunset.

He will not hurt you. There is food. You wish to eat. You must take what you can. More dragons are coming. We must be on our way to the sea.

Kemir helped himself. The food was delicious. He felt new again.

You may ride Sunset if you wish. He is far from awakening.

"No thanks." He climbed up into the saddle and kicked Snow in the neck. "Come on then! Gee up! How many dragons are after us now?"

Two remain. They will not catch us.

With food and water the rest of the journey wasn't so bad. Snow flew straight; the other dragon flew behind her and the riders from the mountains kept their distance. Sometimes when Kemir looked back he couldn't even see them. Then, hours later, they'd be back, little dark specks against the high white haze of cloud. They never came close though, and after another day and night of drifting high over the edge of the mountains, the Worldspine came to an end. A very abrupt end, as though the ancient god who'd carved the landscape had simply stopped and cut the rest away with a divine knife. Sheer cliffs plunged into the Sea of Storms, and when Kemir looked to the east, to the depths of the mountains, he saw that the cliffs only grew higher, until they rose from the sea for miles and vanished into the heavy clouds above. As Snow flew out into the void between the gray and grumbling clouds and the churning waters below, the last two dragons ended the pursuit. They stopped at the cliff and perched on the rocks. Kemir watched them fade slowly into the haze of the day.

We have won, Kemir.

Kemir closed his eyes as they flew out to sea. The coast was barely visible. Snow climbed up into the clouds, and Kemir couldn't see anything anymore. The air was bitterly cold but at least it was damp. He opened his mouth and wished it would rain. The water he'd taken from the river was already gone.

"Where are you going?" Snow was turning back toward the coast.

Do you not wish to rest, Kemir? To eat and drink at your leisure? To lie with your limbs outstretched?

"You bloody know I do."

So do I. She powered in through the cloud. Kemir yawned. If the dragon wanted to go back to the coast and land somewhere safe, that was fine. He slumped over Snow's shoulders and let his mind wander through the memories that had brought him here. He thought of Sollos and of the dragons that had burned his home. Of Snow burning the alchemists out of their caves. Of Nadira. Of Rider Semian, whose sword had ended Sollos. Of his own shrieks of rage. Of sitting astride Snow as she hurtled through the air. He dreamed of the wind in his face, a great, howling wind . . .

They were falling out of the sky. He blinked awake and tried to move, and the wind almost ripped him out of his harness. Snow had tucked in her wings. She was falling straight down like a monstrous arrow from the heavens, and Sunset was beside her. The black stone landscape of the cliffs was rushing up toward him. Kemir opened his mouth to shout, to scream, anything, but the wind tore his breath away. He couldn't even breathe.

Look.

He could barely open his eyes, but now at least he had a proper dragon-rider's helm. He pulled down the visor and looked. The two dragons who'd followed them to the sea were still there and Snow was diving at them.

Breathe! He forced his chest to motion. *Breathe!* "What are you doing?"

These ones will be slow and stupid just as you have become, and I am hungry. I do not think there is much food in this sea.

"There are fish."

I do not think I am well equipped for catching fish.

The ground was coming up. Kemir clenched his fists and gritted his teeth, and then Snow spread out her wings and threw Kemir forward with such force that he hit his head on her scales and knocked himself out. When he came to, Snow had landed. Kemir touched his forehead. His fingers came away bloody. His face was agony. His nose was probably ruined forever.

You knew what I meant to do, chided Snow. *You should have been ready.*

"I *was* ready."

Obviously not ready enough. She had a dragon-rider in her mouth. As Kemir pulled his groggy thoughts together, she crunched on the knight and swallowed him in one gulp, armor and all.

"Stupid dragon, impatient as ever. He was probably poisoned, you know." He could hear whimpering and wailing from somewhere.

No, he was not. I asked before I ate him.

"How very civilized. And what makes you think that whatever he told you was the truth?" Definitely whimpering. Someone was still alive, begging for mercy. Kemir peered down, trying to see the ground below Snow's bulk.

He did not tell me anything with his words, Kemir, except how terrified he was. But I saw in his mind. No secret joy, no hidden victory. Only the understanding of certain death and his own futility. He had not taken poison like the ones before. Snow licked her lips. *Bitter. I prefer them better fed.*

"I'm sure the others will taste better." Two dragons meant four riders, didn't it? His head was throbbing badly. And his nose. Most of him, in fact.

I barely noticed. These dragons carry food and water too. You should take it.

"Do I have to?" He didn't feel so hungry now, only sleepy.

There will be no more for many days. I will take your guidance, Kemir. I must wait for these dragons to awaken, and so we will fly out over the sea where none of your kind will find us. They will look for us but they will find nothing. We will seek land again far away from here. Until then we will starve.

"Great." The effort of getting off Snow's back and rummaging around the other dragons for food seemed impossible. Snow might as well have asked him to scale the cliffs.

It is fortunate that I fed so well before this chase began, Kemir, is it not?

"Whatever." Wearily, Kemir unstrapped himself. He put his hand to his head again. The wound was still bleeding, and he had a lump the size of an egg right between his eyes. "What do you make your scales out of?"

Whatever we eat, Kemir.

He turned around to slide off Snow's shoulder and staggered as he landed, dizzy and close to collapse. If he was really lucky, one of the dragons would catch him with an idle swish of its tail, shatter every bone in his body and send him flying over the edge of the cliff. Where the sea would then smash what was left of him into a sticky mess to be slowly eaten by crabs.

He sat down heavily and rubbed his head again.

"I hate you," he grumbled. Then he saw that Snow had a last rider trapped under her front claw. Still alive.

Take the food and water, Kemir. Eat, drink and sleep.

Kemir glanced at the trapped rider. "What about that one?"

We are bringing this one with us. This one is useful.

"Useful?" Kemir moved closer. "How?" He stopped. The dragon-rider had lost his helm. *Her* helm. Long hair straggled out between Snow's claws. He caught a glimpse of her face. Terrified.

This one knows where other dragons may be found.

Kemir blinked. The dragon-rider's eyes caught his. Pleading. He'd seen that look too many times before. It made him hate her.

"Give her to me and I'll make her talk right enough. Then I can tell you everything you need. You can have her back when I'm done if you must." As Snow lifted her claw, he stepped forward, pulled the dragon-rider to her feet and threw her down again. Hard. Then he was on her. He punched her several times in the face, bloodied his knuckles, but somehow that wasn't anywhere near enough; he started ripping off her armor, tearing at the clothes underneath, swearing and screaming at her while Snow watched over his shoulder. The dragon-rider didn't even fight back that much. She struggled, but most of her whimpers were pain. Snow had already broken one of her legs, maybe done more. He had her armor mostly off, was all ready to tear open the soft flying shirt she wore underneath when the dragon stopped him dead.

Why?

"What?"

Why, Kemir?

Revenge, that was why. Revenge for all the men and women raped and enslaved by the mountain king's riders. It wasn't about lust or desire or need, just cold and bloody and vicious revenge. Mostly what he wanted was to rip her to pieces with his bare hands. Not for anything he knew she'd done, but simply for what she was.

You see, Kemir. Do you see now? That your kind are all the same? That there are no differences between you.

Kemir spun around to glare at Snow. "Yes, there are! These riders come and—" He wasn't allowed to finish.

A human is a human. Some are taller, some are shorter, some are darker, some are lighter, but on the inside do not tell me you are different. This one is useful. When this one has told us what it knows, it will no longer be useful. Then you may mate with her in any way you wish; but for now you will stop. For now you will leave this one alone. Eat. Drink. And then we will leave.

Angrily, Kemir did as he was told. When he was done, Snow gently gripped the rider in her claws and took to the air again, and the other dragons followed. It was true that Kemir felt a lot better for having some bread and water inside him. He had no idea where they were going and his head and his nose still hurt like buggery. But they were alive. The King of the Crags had come after them and they'd bloodied his nose too. Nine riders dead, one rider and three dragons taken. That was a start, wasn't it?

He closed his eyes. He tried not to think about the town Snow had burned. He tried not to think about the people who had lived there: the men who had simply wanted to feed their families, the women who only wanted to see their sons grow into men, the children who—

The children who might have one day grown to be alchemists, poisoning my kind with their potions? The women who bear dragon-rider sons? The men who build their castles and forge their swords and harvest their food? Do not say they have done nothing, Kemir.

They sheltered under the wings of the dragon-lords and in turn the dragon-lords stood on their backs. Perhaps that ought to have been enough. Perhaps Snow was right. Or perhaps not. Perhaps Snow was wrong and they really had done nothing. *Either way, Nadira was not one of them. You shouldn't have eaten her.*

And you should not have tried to force yourself on this female, Kemir, yet you did. Why? Because it is the essential nature of your kind, that is why. You are what you are and so am I.

The dragon-rider. He'd almost forgotten that he'd tried to rape her. *Would* have raped her if Snow hadn't stopped him. Vaguely he knew that it would have been wrong. Sollos would have stopped him too. But somehow he couldn't find any feelings of regret. No remorse. Not much of anything. When the dragons had finished with her, he'd probably settle for killing her. That would do. Would probably be a mercy by then.

Wasn't that what Snow had said about Nadira? That she wanted to die?

Do you know how many dragons fly at the command of King Valmeyan, Kemir? I know that you do not, but I see the answer in the thoughts of this rider. Four hundred and then more, Kemir. Knowledge that is useful. We have taken but three today. Do not waste your thoughts on that which you cannot change. Dwell on that which you can. Think on that, Kemir. Three is a beginning, nothing more.

We. She had said "we" again. Kemir tried to think about the town, about Nadira, but the memories kept sliding away. He looked left and right at the three dragons flying alongside Snow, one a mustard yellow, another a sooty gray who reminded him of a dragon he'd seen somewhere before, and Sunset, a gleaming ruddy brown. *Yes, it was a beginning. A beginning of what, though?*

As he wondered, unease settled deep into his bones. *Am I becoming like her? Or was I always this way?*

35

THE HEART AND THE HEAD

Jehal leaned into his walking staff. At least he *could* walk now, even if one of his legs was still next to useless and every step made him wince. Jeiros wanted him back in bed, numb with Dreamleaf, but Jehal had had enough of both. He hauled himself out of the Tower of Dusk and found no guards on the doors to stop him. No Adamantine Men in sight at all except for a few up on the walls. He stopped at the doors, half afraid to step out into the Gateyard. The sunlight was overwhelming. *So bright.*

This won't do. He forced himself out into the light. Someone finally noticed him. They ran away. *Presumably off to tell someone else. Maybe I'm still a prisoner after all. Well I might as well stay here and see who comes. I'm hardly about to run off anywhere.*

He wasn't disappointed. After he'd sat in the sun for ten minutes, idly watching the men on the walls, the Night Watchman himself strode into the Gateyard. He looked haggard and a lot older than a few weeks ago. He stopped in front of Jehal and bowed.

"Forgive me if I don't rise, Night Watchman." Jehal smiled as pleasantly as he could bear. "I seem to be inconvenienced in that respect."

"I wish you a full and speedy recovery, Your Highness." Vale's face was as flat and unreadable as it always was.

"I'm sure you do. You know what? I think I might get up anyway. I think I might like to take in the view from the Gatehouse." *And why did*

I say that? Now I have to walk across a quarter of the palace and climb more than a hundred steps, which I'm clearly not capable of doing.

Vale offered his hand. Jehal waved it away and struggled to his feet on his own. The Night Watchman's face didn't change. "If you like, I can put one of my men at your disposal to help you."

Bastard. "No, thank you, Night Watchman. It is not as bad as it seems." *And now I have to get to the Gatehouse all on my own. Still, it is going to be worth it.*

Vale gave a deferential shrug. "I am inclined to applaud, Your Highness. It is wise to exercise an injury as soon as it is ready."

"I do not require your applause, Night Watchman. If you wish to help in *that* regard, you can send some of your very fine whores to my bed."

"Ah, that I could, but Speaker Zafir has commented more than once that overexertion may simply mean you take longer to heal, Your Highness. In that particular regard, I have heard rumor that Prince Tichane is looking after your interests and doing so very well. I won't pretend to understand what that is supposed to mean."

"Really?" *Vishmir's cock you don't. But you don't know that I'm watching her. You don't know about my little mechanical dragons. In fact there's rather a lot you don't know . . .*

Vale gave a nonchalant shrug. "Perhaps that means he will be supplying ladies to your bed when you are well enough to enjoy them." He smiled faintly. "Or perhaps you used to have some whore and now he's looking after her for you. Such things are hardly my concern so I give them no thought."

Jehal fumed. "Night Watchman, if I ordered you to be still so I could hobble over and break your nose, I suppose you'd comply without hesitation?"

"My nose is of little value to the realms and has been broken many times before. Consider it yours."

"Then I shall treasure it like a gem." *And cut it off one day.* "If I'm a prisoner, I shall simply return to my tower. I wouldn't wish to embarrass you." His eyes narrowed and he watched the Night Watchman carefully. "I'm sure I seem harmless enough, but you never know quite what might happen if you allow one of your prisoners to roam. I might roam to your brothel and overexert myself or something equally terrible. Who knows— I might push someone off a balcony."

The smallest flicker of a shadow crossed Vale's face. That was enough. Inside, Jehal smiled.

Vale turned away. "The speaker has not withdrawn her order regarding your confinement, but she has since ordered Jeiros and the alchemists to care for you as best they can. We shall call this exercise a part of your rehabilitation. I shall escort you myself."

"Very kind of you." Jehal found he couldn't resist. "But are you sure you can spare the time? You look like you've just got out of bed."

"I apologize if my appearance troubles you, Your Highness." They began to walk toward the Gatehouse. "The tension in the realms has grown a great deal of late. I have been busy."

Walking across the Gateyard and climbing the steps to the top of the Gatehouse ought to have taken a few minutes. By the time Jehal got there, he'd spent the hardest half-hour he could remember. He was soaked in sweat, his leg was in silent shrieking agony and he was ready to collapse. The Night Watchman didn't say a word, didn't offer to help. It was almost as though he understood the necessity of what Jehal was doing.

He smelled Shezira before he saw her. The cages where she and Valgar hung were not far from the gates, suspended from huge poles. There wasn't much left of either of them but it was a warm day and the wind wasn't in the mood to spare Jehal's nose. By the time he reached the top, he was ready to retch. He made himself stand and stare at them both anyway. Somehow he found it satisfying. *In a sort of I'm-alive-and-you're-not kind of way.*

There was a third cage too. The man inside was . . . *Ancestors! He's still alive. Barely.* "I see you've strung up another one. What did this one do?"

Vale pursed his lips. "Hasn't Jeiros told you? That's Prince Sakabian. He lost twenty-five of the speaker's dragons to the traitor queen and had the audacity to survive. Then he was witless enough to return with his tale."

Jehal's lip curled. "Zafir would prefer he'd died or never returned, and her twenty-five dragons had simply disappeared into the mountains without a trace, would she?" *Twenty-five! What a blow! She must be desperate!* He tried to hide his glee. Desperate was good. Desperate was *very* good. "And Almiri did that? Good for her. If a bit stupid. Let me guess, she's demanding a trade. The dragons Zafir seized on the Night of the Knives for the ones Almiri now holds at Evenspire."

"I wouldn't know." Vale's brow furrowed. "Why did you come up here, Prince Jehal?" He seemed genuinely surprised, even a little pitying. *You're slipping, Vale. At least now I know how things stand.*

"You think I'm going to be out there in a cage of my own soon, do you?"

"I cannot read the speaker's mind, Your Highness. I simply obey the orders I am given." *Oh but you want me out there, don't you? Just like you wanted Shezira out there. You're going to be in for such a disappointment.*

"Actually, I didn't much want to come here. I wanted *you* to come here. I wanted to watch you here, seeing this. That's why I came up here." *Yes. Such a disappointment. And now the fun starts.*

"I see this every day, Your Highness."

"And you'll see it every day for weeks to come and I'm sure there will be more. But from tomorrow you'll see it in a different light. I know why you wanted Shezira dead. I know you let her go to Hyram to try and make some sort of peace with him when you should have confined her to her tower."

Vale didn't flinch. "Shezira had already gone to Speaker Hyram when my men reached her tower."

Jehal cocked his head. "That is a lie, Night Watchman."

"That is the truth, Your Highness. The lie comes from whoever told you otherwise."

"No." Jehal laughed. "No one told me otherwise, Night Watchman. I saw it for myself."

Vale's turn to laugh. "You could not, Prince Jehal. You were far across the palace in the Tower of Air. You could not have seen what you claim from there."

"Is that so?" Jehal's grin spread across his face. "I'm afraid you are much mistaken, Night Watchman. I had eyes all over the palace that night and not all were men. I came up here because I have something to show you." Slowly, he unwrapped a strip of white silk from around his wrist. "I know you can keep a secret, Night Watchman. This is a treasure that the Taiytakei gave to me for my wedding, and that I, in turn, gave to the speaker as a sign of my devotion and my trust."

He held out the silk. Vale looked at it, obviously puzzled. "Forgive me, Prince Jehal, but I don't understand. What are you showing me?"

"A piece of silk, Night Watchman. Tie it across your eyes. I would sit down first, if I were you. Disorientation is a common first experience." He watched Vale hesitate. "I'm hardly in a position to run away."

The Night Watchman laughed. "Run away? Prince Jehal, I wouldn't put it past you. I'm more concerned at receiving a knife in my ribs."

"I'm not really a knife person, Night Watchman. When I have an enemy to deal with, I prefer to watch them build their own pyre and then linger powerless on top of it for a while while I play carelessly with matches beneath." He gave Vale a toothy smile. "Put it on. You'll see through the eyes of . . . of something else. I will not tell you what."

Slowly, the Night Watchman put the silk to his eyes, although he held it with his hands and didn't tie it. He didn't wobble or stagger either. *Impressed? I suppose I have to be.*

"What do you see?"

"An eyrie." Vale took the cloth away from his eyes. "Drotan's Top. From the top of Hyram's Tor."

"Yes, you did. And on the Night of the Knives when I put that silk to my eyes, do you know what I saw? I saw you, Night Watchman. I saw you let Shezira go when you should have seized her."

Vale paled. *A crack in your armor at last.*

"Yes, Night Watchman, I really did see it all. You let Shezira go."

"It was for the good of the realms." His voice had gone husky.

"Didn't really work out that way, did it? Do you want to know something else? It might make you feel a bit better. After all, this is Zafir's toy, not mine. I'm imagining she saw everything too."

"She never said."

"She never said anything about you disobeying her direct order? It *did* all turn out rather nicely in her favor." Jehal shrugged. "Mind you, letting

Shezira go *was* clear disobedience and I think we both know that our speaker doesn't take too well to being disobeyed. Maybe she wasn't watching after all. I'll ask her, if you like." He cocked his head in mock surprise. "How interesting that might be. Tell me, Night Watchman: did every single witness among your men die that night?"

"No, Prince Jehal, they did not. I do not waste my own men. They are posted where they will do no harm." Vale sounded like he was chewing on gravel.

"Good for you." Jehal smiled. "Now shall I tell you something else?" He nodded over the wall toward the cages. "I saw Hyram go over the balcony with the same eyes that saw you betray your speaker. Shezira never touched him. You beheaded an innocent queen."

"I followed the speaker's orders."

"You should really make up your mind, Night Watchman. Are you a guardian of the realms with a sacred duty to preserve our peace and our way of life? Or are you a man who does as he's told, no matter what fool gives him his orders?" Jehal snorted. "But no, we both know you can't even do that right, can you?"

Vale's face didn't change. "Should I tell Master Jeiros about the blood-mage who comes to see you, Your Highness? It would probably be wise to consider his advice."

Jehal shrugged. "Why not tell the speaker as well?"

"I imagine she already knows." He shrugged. "We are the Adamantine Men, Your Highness. We trace our traditions to the earliest days of the Embers. We were the first to rise up against the blood-mages because we had nothing to lose. We were their fodder, their unwilling sacrifices to the dragons. The Embers of today may choose their way, but the first Adamantine Men did not. The alchemists guard the realms against the dragons now. The dragon-kings guard against the alchemists, the speaker guards against the dragon kings and we guard against them all. We are the last resort, Your Highness. We guard against tyranny. It is a precarious balance at best. People like you are anathema to me. Tell the speaker whatever you wish."

Jehal stared at Vale as he finished. "You actually believe that, don't you?" He hauled himself painfully to his feet. The Tower of Dusk felt a very long way away, but at least the stairs from the Gatehouse would be easier going down. "I think I would like to go back to my prison now. You can go first. Make sure you're ready to catch me. I wouldn't want to accidentally slip and break my neck. Oh, and I think, on reflection, I shall go elsewhere for my whores. No offense, Night Watchman, but I would prefer to be a little more certain of their qualities."

Vale went wordlessly down. Jehal sat on the top step and slid down from one to the next. Which hurt and made him look like an idiot, but he simply didn't have the strength to do anything else. At the bottom the Night Watchman walked away and Jehal watched him go.

First blood was to you, Vale Tassan. But now you see what is coming and I promise all the other victories will be mine. Every single petty little one of them, until tormenting you is simply a bore.

First things first, though. He would see if this blood-mage could deliver on his promises. And after that there was the little matter of heirs and whether he could still father them. Or at least enjoy trying.

36

※

THE ISLANDS

The dragons flew for three more days, out across the sea, until they found land again. Kemir had no idea where they were but he'd never been so happy to see a bare stretch of sand in his life. He lay flat on his back, stretching muscles that he hadn't known he had.

We are hungry, Snow said. She dropped the half-dead dragon-rider a hundred yards down the beach. Then the dragons took off again. The wind of their wings blasted sand into Kemir's face but he didn't notice because by then he was already asleep.

He woke up as the sun was sinking toward the horizon. *Stiff as a board again*. With creaking joints, he got to his feet. He had no idea where he was. With Sollos, he'd traveled most of the realms. They'd been to the edge of the stone desert to the north of Outwatch. They'd traveled on the backs of dragons over the endless dunes of the Desert of Sand and the white, flat, lifeless expanse of the Desert of Salt. They'd whored and fought their way through the hills around Evenspire and the swamps and moors of the distant east. They'd traveled the length of the Worldspine from north to south.

But I never crossed the sea. He sat up and looked at the sky, blue and clear. Waves rustled softly at the edge of the sand, swishing back and forth. A gentle breeze blew, soft and warm. A hundred feet the other way, away from the sea, the sand rose up into rolling humps. Dunes covered in long spiky grasses. Beyond that, trees. Lots and lots of trees.

Trees meant game and game meant food. It would be dark soon and he was hungry. The dragons had been gone for hours. He picked up his two bows and went over to the dragon-rider. She hadn't moved. She was conscious though. Could have killed him in his sleep if she'd had the presence of mind to get up and do it. Except when he peered closer he wasn't sure she had the presence of anything much anymore. Her eyes rolled up into her head. She moaned and groaned and had no idea who he was. Probably had no idea who she herself was either. By the looks of her, she wasn't going to last for long. Not so useful after all.

There was a little stream running down the beach. Kemir followed it a little way inland and found a pool. He drank and then brought back some water and tipped it down her throat. Strange thing to do to someone you planned to kill. He mulled over doing just that, slitting her throat here and now while the dragons were away. He wasn't sure whether he wanted to do that because she was a dragon-rider, or whether it was some sort of daft jealousy. In the end he put the thought away. Instead he did his best to make her comfortable and fed her some more water.

"Sorry," he whispered in her ear. Sorry for what he wasn't sure. For all sorts of things, probably. For what he'd done, for what had happened. For what would happen later.

Then he looked out to sea and his mouth fell open. The dragons were there, maybe a mile out. They were easy enough to spot. And they weren't alone. He watched as one of them seemed to drag something through the waves toward the beach, flapping its wings furiously, almost but not quite lifting whatever it was out of the water. After a few seconds, the dragon let go and shot up into the air, only for another to take its place. Kemir watched as they came closer.

It had to be another dragon. Maybe one that was hurt. One with a broken wing. Although if it was, they were being none too gentle with it.

I don't see any wings. Don't they put down dragons with broken wings? But what else can it be? A sea monster? Whatever it was, it was black and bulky and about the size of a small hunting dragon although with no wings and without the long tail or neck of a true dragon.

The dragons were getting closer. As they saw him, Snow tipped her wings in greeting. *Food! Food, Kemir! We have brought food! Giant fish!*

Kemir's jaw dropped. It was a whale. They had a whale.

The dragons splashed and floundered in the water, dragging the whale up onto the beach. Great gouges had already been ripped from its flesh, and yet it wasn't quite dead. Kemir kept well away as the dragons finished it off and then tore it to pieces. They'd all been days without food. The sight of it made him him both hungry and sick at the same time.

He walked back to the pool and washed himself. When he returned, the dragons were sprawled in the sand. One of them belched. Half the whale was gone.

"I see you left some for me." He wrinkled his nose. The air stank.

We will stay here now, Kemir. There is enough to eat.

"You've only got half a whale left. You'll be hungry again in the morning."

This will satisfy us for days if we do not fly. If we grow hungry, we shall simply hunt more. In all my many lives, I have never seen the sea with my own eyes. It is not so bad after all.

Kemir nodded. The stench was getting worse, strong enough to make him gag. "You enjoy yourselves then. I'll go hunt something more my size."

I feel your hunger, Kemir. You may take from our kill.

"I'm honored." He wasn't sure that he particularly wanted to, but an offer to share food was a meaningful thing among outsiders and to refuse was often an insult. Maybe dragons were different. Or maybe not. "Right then. Honored then. Like I said." Disgusted as well, but not disgusted enough to offend something that could squash him flat without really noticing. With a sigh, he drew out one of his knives and tried to work out how best to approach the whale. Most of its head was missing, so it was a choice between its tail and its belly, where it had been ripped open and its innards scattered across the sand.

"Tail," he decided. "When it comes to whales, we humans like the tail bits best." *Especially when it's the part that's furthest away from all that . . .*

mess. He held his breath. He'd hunted and killed and eaten animals all his life, but never one whose corpse he could actually walk inside.

Snow was laughing at him. *You have never even seen these creatures before. You have barely heard of them.*

Kemir glared at her. "Tail is still the best." He started to cut off strips of meat, trying to hold his nose at the same time.

Take as much as you wish. After this, you will have to hunt for yourself. You cannot stay with us. For a time, at least, we must be apart.

"What?" He stopped, frozen still. "Why? Where are you going?" The thought of being left alone out here scared him. Which was insane. He pinched himself. *Nadira. Remember Nadira.*

You must leave us here. We must be alone. Already my new brothers are beginning to dream, Kemir. I have shown you those dreams. You have seen what they are and you have tasted how they feel to us. You should not be here when the awakening begins. Remember Ash.

"Ash was deranged."

Ash was angry. All of us are angry. When I awoke, I was angry. And you do not want to be near when we are angry. I cannot promise they will not eat you. I cannot promise that I could stop them.

Kemir snorted. "Just tell them how useful I am."

When the awakening has finished, I will reason with them. As I reasoned with Ash. Ash did not eat you, Kemir. Despite his anger.

"Well then, fine. I'll just piss off into the middle of nowhere. On my own. Leave you to it. Have fun and just see how far you get without me. Am I supposed to take your pet dragon-rider with me and look after her for you?" He looked at Snow long and hard. She was still changing. Still remembering. Still learning who she was. There hadn't been much time to notice since . . . since Nadira. Not until they'd reached the sea. But she was. She wasn't the same Snow who'd burned the alchemists' redoubt, not the same dragon who'd eaten Nadira or destroyed a city whose name she didn't even know. Maybe she really didn't need him anymore. He wasn't sure whether that was good or bad. "There's one thing I want to know before I go. What's your name, dragon?"

Snow, Kemir. It is Snow. Why do you ask when you know this?

"Not that name. Your real name. The name you were given when you were born for the very first time."

For a moment he could almost believe Snow was smiling. *My hatching name. The name my silver rider gave me. The first name I ever had. Is that what you want?*

"Yes. Your first name or your real name or whatever it is. Not Snow. Not the one the Outwatch alchemists gave you. Unless it's some secret and you're going to have to eat me if you tell me."

It is no secret. I was called Alimar Ishtan vei Atheriel—Beloved Memory of a Lover Distant and Lost."

Kemir stared at her and tried not to laugh. "Beloved. That's . . . That's not a name I would have ever guessed. Alimar is better. Alim, maybe. Ali."

You may know my true name, but you have not earned the right to speak it. Take whatever meat you wish. And then you must go.

Kemir threw a glance down the beach at the dragon-rider, still lying in the sand. "Fine with me. So what about her?"

Snow moved over to the prone figure on the sand. She nudged the rider with her nose. Kemir felt her disgust. *This one is broken.* Gingerly she picked the rider up by one leg and shook, then dropped her again. *This one will be gone before my kin awake. She will stay. I will take what I can while she lingers.*

For a moment, Kemir hesitated. Maybe he should have killed the dragon-rider after all. Maybe it would have been a mercy. Then he turned. "All yours then. Farewell, dragon." He didn't look back.

When it is safe, I will find you.

"Only if I want you to, dragon. Only if I want you to." With that he stalked away into the foreign trees of a forest whose name he'd never hear. Alone. Snow had company now. Her own kind. They didn't need him anymore.

"Forget them," he snapped to himself, as if that would be enough. "They don't need you and you don't need them." Although, all things considered, it would have been nice to have been abandoned somewhere that he knew. Or even somewhere that had people.

Still, alive was alive. Alive was something other than dead. And Snow hadn't eaten him after all. He walked as far away from the dragons as he could be bothered to and built himself a shelter. He could never walk far enough, of course, not when they had wings. Over the next days he saw them sometimes, flying in the distance. He tried to ignore them, but as the days stretched to weeks he couldn't. Food was plentiful, the hunting easy. He started to grow fat with waiting. He gave up his first shelter and took to roaming the island, exploring as much as anything for something to do. Sometimes even that wasn't enough. Sometimes he stared at the skies for hours and hours, just hoping to catch a glimpse of wings and fire.

He'd been there for three weeks when he saw the ships. He was on the far side, as far away from the dragons as he could get, and all of a sudden he woke up in the morning and found the sea full of ships. They were far away, too far for him to signal, so he watched and wondered who they were. The dragons must have seen the ships too. He saw them later that morning, flying out across the sea. The sight made him glad that he was on land. Dragons and ships didn't mix. Even he knew that. He didn't see what happened and didn't much care.

The next morning, though, they were waiting for him when he woke up. All four of them. He should have known better than to think he could hide. He found himself looking for the dragon-rider, but she wasn't there.

This one? The other three dragons looked different now. Full-grown war-dragons, they dwarfed even Snow, and they were awake too. He could see it in them.

This one is useful to us. Snow turned her attention to Kemir. *We are four now. We are strong. We will return to free our kind, and you will help us.*

"And how can I possibly help a dragon?"

Snow dropped something at his feet. A pack. The dragon-rider's pack. Ripped pages and maps spilled out. The realms. No one had ever bothered teaching him to read or write, but he knew a map when he saw one. With the desert up in the north, the moors to the east, the Worldspine to the west . . .

They are . . . they are too small. And too fragile. You will hold them and you will look at them and we will see through your eyes. He was suddenly aware of Snow, fiercely attentive to his thoughts. At the same time he saw the little crosses marked on the Worldspine in a separate hand, and realized what they were. A map of the Mountain King's eyries.

It shows where dragons can be found, does it not?

Kemir didn't answer. He didn't need to. His thoughts had already given him away. He could feel Snow in his head, glittering with greed. A map of the Mountain King's eyries. Yes. He could almost see them burn, one by one.

He didn't bother asking what had happened to the rider they'd carried across the sea with them. "I could stay here and you could struggle away on your own." But even as he said it, Kemir knew he wouldn't. He couldn't live on his own, not in this wilderness. Not forever. He'd go mad. *And besides . . . Valmeyan . . .*

You will help us, Kemir.

"And if I don't?" *Why am I even asking? I can finally do what Sollos and I once swore to do. I can make the King of the Crags pay. I can make him burn.* The feeling was delicious and hot.

The dragon didn't answer, just licked her lips. *We shall leave now. We are ready.* Her thoughts were excited, but there was something else. Something out of place. Uneasy. She was almost . . .

"Are you *scared*, dragon?"

We have seen ships on the sea. There was a presence among them. A presence we have not felt for a long time. Not since the world was broken into pieces.

"Any chance of having that again, except this time so it makes some sort of sense?"

One of our creators has returned. We do not know what this means. We thought they were gone.

Kemir shrugged. "But then you've been asleep for the last few hundred years."

One of the dragons lunged. Kemir flinched, closed his eyes, but the blow never came. When he opened his eyes again, there were teeth inches from his face. Teeth as long as his arm. The dragon's breath was hot on his skin, and rank. He felt the anger from all of them, even from Snow.

Have a care, Kemir.

He didn't say anything else. Just quietly gathered up what little he had and loaded it onto Snow's back. He made sure he had plenty of food and water this time—might as well head to his death in comfort. For now at least, the dragons didn't seem to be hungry. Presumably they'd been hunting whales again.

"Where are we going?"

We will cross the water to the place where the Worldspine crashes into the sea. We will return to the mountains where I awoke, and there it will begin. It is marked on these maps the places we will go. You will be our eyes. When we are done with those and our numbers are too great to be stopped, we will find your alchemists again. We will find your eyries and your castles and your palaces, and this time we will burn them all. Starting with the place where I was hatched.

They looked at each other.

Outwatch!

37

MOTHS AND FLAMES

S o are you a man or half a man now?" Zafir sat across from Jehal in the solar atop the Tower of Dusk. Jehal had chosen the room deliberately. He wasn't sure what he'd been trying to prove. *That I can climb stairs on my own now? Was that it? Is that what I'm reduced to? And what has it got me?* The whole left side of his body was throbbing, and his wound felt as though it was on fire. He could barely sit still. The sad truth was that his leg was never going to get better. Without a staff to lean on he could barely walk, and that would never change.

Still, it could be worse. I can still ride dragons. And other things.

Zafir didn't wait for an answer. She twirled her hair and made big eyes at him. "Vale Tassan says that Shezira meant to unman you, but Jeiros tells me that she may have merely crippled you. He goes very coy when I ask and claims that he doesn't actually know. So. Did she miss, then? Do you still have what it takes?" Zafir had brought the Night Watchman with her. He stood in the background, removed from them. *But not so far away that I could reach Zafir and wring her pretty little neck before he could cut mine, eh?*

"Find out for yourself." He tried stretching his crippled leg out in front of him in case that made the pain any easier. It didn't.

"Lover, that doesn't sound very promising. Shezira was quite a good shot with a crossbow."

"Yes. Apparently so." Jehal smiled. "And at such short range and at such a *large* target . . ."

Zafir smiled. "I suppose I must assume the worst of your injury. At least until we know better." Jeiros. Jeiros of all people had smuggled a woman to him. From a city brothel. She was clean, at least, but Jehal had turned her away. *Ah, the games we play . . .*

Jehal shrugged. "I have exquisite taste when it comes to whom I bed. I suspect the Night Watchman has a somewhat better eye in these matters and I don't doubt he has a great deal more practice than Jeiros. You should have sent him on your errand."

"Not *my* errand." Zafir smiled again and then went abruptly cold. "You betrayed me."

"I told you what I thought, lover. You should have let Shezira go. My opinion on that hasn't changed. You were wrong to do what you did. You've brought us to war." With a painful sigh, Jehal stood up. "I'll go back to my sickbed now, shall I? Or is it time for another cage? I saw that one of your cousins swings in the wind over the gates as well. What did he do? Did he look at you with lust in his eye? No, don't answer; I know that he did. Is that what got him strung up?"

"He lost twenty-five of my dragons to Almiri."

"Then perhaps you should have taken him to your bed after all. Perhaps then he wouldn't have been so eager." Jehal chuckled and shook his head and turned away.

"Wait!"

Jehal ignored her. He yawned and hobbled off.

"Wait!" This time she shouted, angry.

"Why should I?"

"I am speaker!"

"And I am a king. I'll listen to your guidance if you should ever grow wise, but you do not give me orders. That is not your place. Even as speaker."

"Wait." Her voice softened. "Please. I didn't want this."

"Better." Jehal turned back and sat down again. *And about time too. I don't think I could have survived all those steps again so soon. Recriminations weren't what I came for.*

Zafir was wearing her earnest face now. She leaned toward him, wide-eyed. "I didn't ask for you to be hurt. I just wanted . . ."

"Come here." Jehal patted the cushion next to him. "Sit beside me." *Is she lying? Does it matter? Does she even know the difference?*

Zafir glanced at Vale. He came a few steps closer and then gave a little nod. *So that's how close you think you need to be to kill me before I can move. Six paces. Interesting. I shall remember that.* Zafir came and sat beside him then, close enough that he could feel the heat from her skin. Somewhat to his annoyance, even that alone was enough to arouse him. *See, this is what comes of being stuck in bed for so long. Maybe I should have had Jeiros' whore after all.* The sensation was more painful than pleasant thanks to his wound. He focused his mind on that, reached out and stroked her cheek.

"I know. You just wanted me out of the way for a day while the vote was cast and the deed was done. That's all. None of this was supposed to happen."

"Yes," she breathed. *Liar!*

"What happened to me wasn't your doing. I know that."

"No." *Or might it even be true? Does it matter?*

"No." Jehal smiled and leaned closer so that his lips were brushing against her ear. "I know that because I know you'd never have given Shezira the satisfaction of a revenge like that. You'd have done it yourself." He put a hand on her thigh. Zafir was sitting very still, but she was breathing quickly. Jehal felt the Night Watchman take another couple of steps toward them. "I will have my pound of flesh for this, but I'll not come looking for it from you. Vale Tassan did this to me and so now I want him as my toy to use as I please." *Ah, the pleasure. Are you hearing this, Night Watchman? Are you hearing every whispered word? You're close enough, and I know your ears are good.*

"There is a war, Jehal," she whispered. "I need him."

"Not as much as you need me." He moved his hand higher. "I promise not to break him until you're finished with Shezira's daughters. For now I just want to play with him."

Her throat bobbed. The slightest of nods. Enough for now.

"I never wanted to be your enemy, Zafir. I only wanted what was best for you. Wars are dangerous. I'm afraid for you. I'm afraid you might die, you see, because that's what happens in dragon-wars. People die. Lots of them. Sometimes even people who matter. But I want you to know that when Shezira shot me and I was sure that my time was done, the first person I thought of was you. And in my bed, as I made my slow recovery, I thought of you a great deal more. More than anyone else."

"Truly?"

"Truly."

Zafir took a deep breath and sighed. "Thank you, Jehal."

"Do you believe me?"

She took his hand and clasped it between her own. "Of course I do."

Well, then you're either an idiot or you're lying, and for once I can't actually tell which it is. "I have a gift for you."

"I don't need a gift, Jehal. Just stand beside me, like you did when I was made the speaker. That's more than any gift could be."

Very good. I really actually want to believe you. Very good indeed. "I've got one for you anyway. Call it payment for what I'm going to do to the commander of your guard once you don't need him anymore." *Are you still here, Night Watchman? Are you still listening?*

"You don't need to tell me. I saw the letter, my lover."

"Letter?" For a moment he was confused.

"The one you were writing before the council. To your uncle." She looked at him as though he was mad. "The one you wrote, Jehal. The one where you told him to murder your wife for you."

"Ah. That letter." *That* letter. "I never had a chance to send it."

"You're such a fool, Jehal. If I'd known you were truly mine then none of this would have happened. If I'd known before the council . . ." She tossed her hair. "If I'd known before the council then I would have let Shezira go just because you asked me to."

"No council? No executions? No war?" For a moment, Jehal almost believed her. *Yes. And now remember who you're talking to. It's easy to say these things when nothing can be undone and none of us can turn back. Besides, I never even sealed it. Perhaps I never will.*

Zafir rested her fingers on his leg by his wound. "Does it hurt terribly?"

"It aches a little. It gets worse when I'm aroused. You're not helping."

"If I'd known you were mine, none of this would have happened. You'd be whole."

"I'm still quite whole enough, thank you."

"So you say, but is it true?"

"You can see my lips and my hands for yourself. You know they're the best of me. The rest, well, if you want to know about that then there's only one way you're going to find out." He raised an eyebrow archly. "I'm saving myself."

She didn't take her hand away. Instead, she gave a little smirk. For an instant Jehal remembered what had drawn them together in the beginning, what an irresistible force it had been.

"I'm going to give you the Red Riders," he said, as she began to unlace his shirt.

"And I'm going to make you a king," she breathed. "But first I'm going to make you a god."

"I thought they were one and the same."

"Oh no." She ran her tongue over his ear. "Not at all."

The Night Watchman had gone, slipped silently away to leave them to their pleasures. Which was a pity, Jehal thought. *I could have shown you a thing or two about striving, and you could certainly have seen how your speaker likes to be served.*

He undressed her with slow and deliberate strokes. There was an honesty to the way she moaned and moved to his fingers and his tongue brushing over her skin. *At least I know you missed me. When I have you like this, I know I'm finally seeing the truth.*

"Sometimes," she whispered, "when I'm alone in the dark, I see the red rider. I don't mean Hyrkallan or Semian or whoever is out there in the

Spur now. I mean the real one. The unjustly murdered knight, risen from the dead, with eyes that burn red with blood."

"You have a guilty conscience," murmured Jehal.

"He stands there, in the darkness, looking at me. He doesn't move, he doesn't speak. He just looks. I don't see his dragon but I know it's out there, white and dead like a drowned beast."

Jehal whispered in her ear. "The red rider is a myth, my lover. You have nothing to fear from a story."

She didn't move, didn't even twitch a muscle, yet he felt her withdraw from him. "I'm sure you're right." A moment later she rolled away from him and sat up. Jehal stayed where he was, admiring the light of the sunset spilling through the windows onto her breasts. He smiled. She could be magnificent when she wanted to be, but she could be magnificent quite by accident too. That, he thought, was probably her greatest charm.

She must have felt his eyes on her. She turned sharply. Her eyes narrowed, and Jehal knew exactly what was coming. She had that look in her face again. She opened her mouth to speak, then thought better of it and lay down beside him again, twirling his hair with her fingers.

Jehal gently stroked her throat. "Lystra. I will see to it." *I will see to one of you. No balancing between you. Not anymore.*

She sighed again. "No need for that. I'm sure your Meteroa will have done what needs to be done. He's had your letter for nearly a month and he seems very resourceful. I'm sure he'll find a way. I'm really quite surprised not to have heard anything already. I thought he was quick. The sort who would jump to obey."

"What?" Jehal froze. "You *sent* it? But I hadn't sealed it! Meteroa will never believe it." *No, but the words are mine. Meteroa will know my hand. Shit!*

"Yes, Jehal, I sent it weeks ago. Once I heard you were going to live. Best to get it done, I thought. Before I let you out and make you into a king." She looked at him askance. "Are you offended, Jehal? You did write it, after all. And you did mean it, didn't you? Don't tell me you didn't mean it."

Somehow he kept his voice under control. "As you say, my uncle is very resourceful. Although I would have preferred to have killed her myself."

She wrapped her arms around him. "*That's* better. I love you, Jehal. I always will."

"I know." He had to force the words between his teeth. A black cloud filled his head, urging him to be reckless. "You make me a king tomorrow and I'll rid you of the Red Riders. When I'm done with them, I'll go south. Straight south. I'll return with my dragons and we'll put an end to this. And yes, Lystra too if Meteroa hasn't found a way to be rid of her. Then you and I will rule the world." *And then one of us will most likely murder the other, because that's the way we are. And you know what? I can't wait.*

"Yes!" She sighed beneath him. "Yes. Together. Now show me you're still a man."

He gave a bark of laughter. "No. Not while Lystra lives. That'll be my sign to you. Until then . . . well . . . Your Night Watchman was kind enough to supply me with an olisbos. His idea of a joke, I think." As he spoke, he slid it inside her and felt her tremor. "And a little strap so I could wear it, but I think we'll pass on that." He pushed it deeper and bit her throat. "I can't say I appreciate his sense of humor, but it's a very fine piece of craftsmanship and it would be a shame to waste it. Wood, I think, but smooth as glass. You can have the real thing, I promise, but only when I return with my dragons."

He took her, brutal and selfish this time, filled with dark thoughts and violence. It seemed she liked it.

FOUR

JUSTICE AND VENGEANCE

38

✦

VIOROS

Vioros was at the top of Hyram's Tor on Drotan's Top, squatting on the uneven stone roof. The view was spectacular. To the north the ground fell away, faster and faster until it plunged into the depths of the Gliding Dragon Gorge and River Fury, and then rose again, a dozen miles away, rolling and twisting up into the canyons of the Maze and the distant peaks of the Purple Spur. To the south and west, sharp hills and valleys tumbled together, shrouded in a cloak of dark and misty forest, the Raksheh. To the east, the same forest gave way to the vast heights of the Worldspine, looming over everything.

Vioros was squinting through a metal tube with glass ends. The Taiy-takei had brought a dozen of them to Speaker Zafir as a gift to mark her ascension to the Adamantine Palace all those months ago. They called them farscopes. Some idiot at the palace had decided that they must be magical. Probably the same idiot had then decided that meant they fell into the domain of the Order of the Scales and its alchemists. Which wouldn't have been so bad if they hadn't whispered in the speaker's ear and left her thinking that farscopes would somehow transform the art of dragon-war, that Prince Lai's *Principles* could now be torn up and thrown away.

But he had, and so here Vioros was in the eyrie at Drotan's Top, where he'd been for the last month, wasting his time with the stupid thing when he should have been at the palace eyrie, supervising the administration of potions and generally being in charge of the place. Drotan's Top had never been meant to support more than a dozen dragons, even then only for a few days, maybe a week. Now it had twice that number, all out hunting for the Red Riders. The dragons had been here for as long as he had and the eyrie was creaking at the seams. There wasn't enough of anything to go around. They'd had next to nothing to do too, which meant everyone was doubly irritable. The Red Riders had been making a nuisance of themselves on the other side of the Spur of late.

He turned his attention back to the farscope, peering through the eyepiece. He'd never seen anything like it but he didn't find it particularly interesting. True, it did make faraway things appear closer, but the picture was blurred and contorted. If the device was magical at all, which Vioros doubted, then the magic was hopelessly poor. He hadn't the first idea how one of these would help with flushing the idiot renegades out of the mountains. Or with putting them to death, preferably very slowly and publicly.

The work of a blundering apprentice. Vioros sniggered to himself. *We all have one of those, eh?*

He tried looking at the mountains of the Purple Spur off to the north. There was a wheel on the side of the metal tube. You were supposed to turn it, he knew, if the picture in the tube was blurry. He tried, and the mountains dissolved into featureless gray blobs. He turned it back and forth. The best he could do was to make the mountains look like mountains, but they were still so warped that looking at them gave him a headache.

With a sigh, he gave up. The farscope was supposed to help them look out for the Red Riders. Well, let one of the soldiers stand up here all day with it giving himself a migraine. The Red Riders were hardly likely to attack Drotan's Top again, especially now so many dragons were based there. No no, his biggest worry was how to tell Speaker Zafir that her Taiytakei presents were useless junk. Now *that* was going to require a great deal of thought and care. Telling the speaker anything she didn't like to hear was becoming distinctly hazardous. He snorted and stretched and looked up at the sky. It would probably be best, he decided, if they suffered some catastrophic misfortune. Something for which someone else could be blamed.

He shouldn't even be here. Where he *ought* to be was with Jeiros and the other master alchemists, trying to work out where the rogue dragon had gone.

No. He corrected himself. There were four rogue dragons now if the whispers from Valmeyan's eyries were to be believed. Four, and they'd flown out to sea. There was nothing out past the southern tip of the Worldspine except sea, sea and more sea. The dragons were welcome to it but they'd grow hungry. Sooner or later they'd be back. The realms had to be ready.

Or maybe it was all lies. Valmeyan was being far too coy. Getting news out of his eyries was even harder than usual, and that was hard enough. The King of the Crags was up to something.

Vioros blinked, squinted and shaded his eyes. There were specks in the sky, close to the sun.

Dragons?

Of course they were dragons. He shook his head at himself. What else could they be?

Well, that's odd then, isn't it?

Well, not really, because this was an eyrie and dragons came and went all the time. He shook his head, trying to make the other voice go away so that he could go back to thinking about how he might let Zafir down gently about the farscopes. That was his priority for now.

Well, yes really, because nearly all Zafir's dragons are out hunting for the Red Riders and you're not expecting any of them back at this time of day.

He groaned. More riders from the palace to overload their meager supplies? Reluctantly, he put the farscope down. *More, and they didn't even bother to tell me they're coming.* There were a good few of them too. Half a dozen at least. The farscope would definitely have to wait. *Does Zafir know how short our supplies are? Does she care? Have they brought any potion with them? Of course they haven't! How am I supposed to—*

The dragons were coming out of the sun, formed up in line ahead, nose to tail, almost as if they were trying to hide their numbers. Almost as if they were trying to—

Oh.

Vioros ran to the edge of the roof and screamed his lungs out. "Riders!

Riders coming! Out of the sun!" Shouting it over and over again, until someone heard him. *What was it you were thinking to yourself about blundering apprentices?*

That wasn't helpful. Down below they seemed to have got the message. Scales and riders were running about, trying to ready the nearest dragons. As he watched them, a sickening realization blossomed in the pit of his stomach. They weren't going to be quick enough. The incoming riders would be on top of them in less than a minute. The dragons below weren't nearly ready to fly. Most weren't even harnessed.

See. Even if you'd started shouting five seconds sooner, it wouldn't have helped, would it? So stop berating yourself. Besides, he had other things to worry about. Like having less than a minute to get from the exposed top of the tower to one of the deep underground tunnels where he'd be reasonably safe. Which was impossible, unless he jumped off the top and somehow sprouted wings.

I'm going to die. He dived down the trapdoor and practically fell down the ladder to the uppermost story of the tower, twisting an ankle as he landed. The pain barely registered as he made for the stairs. He had to get at least to the bottom of the tower before the dragons arrived. It occurred to him that he was going to feel immensely stupid if these new riders *did* turn out to be reinforcements from the palace. Better than being dead if they weren't though.

He half ran, half hobbled down the spiral stairs as fast as he dared. To his surprise, there were still people in the tower, looking at him as though he was mad. For some reason he'd assumed he'd be the last one out, that everyone would have heard his shouts, dropped everything and run as fast as they could, but clearly not. He shouted at them to get out of the way, that dragons were coming, but that only made matters worse. They got in his way instead of stepping aside, shouting things back. They didn't understand, or if they did, they either froze in stupid panic or simply didn't know what to do. He could almost feel the dragons outside, bearing down on them.

Vioros barged a woman out of his way. *I'm the speaker's senior alchemist. Queen Zafir gave me my orders in person. I'm supposed to be the most impor-*

tant person here, even above the eyrie-master. Not that any of the riders would acknowledge that, but still I could show some dignity. His limbs begged to differ. Two servants ran out of a door onto the stairs front of him. They looked at him, wide-eyed, before he crashed through them, knocking one to the ground. "Run!" he shouted as they hurled curses after him. "Run or burn, you witless fools!" *There. How about that for some leadership. Now get out of my way!*

All the way down he knew he wasn't going to make it. Even if there hadn't been other people on the stairs, he'd never have reached the bottom in time without breaking his neck. He was two-thirds of the way when the tower gave an almighty shudder. The stairs shook, sending him sprawling, tumbling on downward in a tangle of bruises and snapping bones. The walls spun crazily around him. Part of the staircase above his head collapsed and slid down after him. His wrist hit something and exploded in pain. Something else struck his head, knocking him almost senseless. He felt himself sliding on, bumping, every impact making his wrist shriek even more, then his shoulder slammed into a solid wall and he crunched to a halt.

The world was filled with a rushing, roaring noise. His head was agony. For a second he didn't move, didn't dare even twitch. Then a tide of rubble and broken staircase tumbled onto him, crushing the breath out of his lungs, and he couldn't have moved even if he wanted to. His face was pressed into a slab of stone. He couldn't see. He was trapped—everything except for one hand sticking out through the rubble. The hand with the wrist that still worked.

He had another moment to think about his situation, to start to guess how broken he was, and then a silent thunderclap shook what was left of the tower. His ears popped and everything sounded suddenly muffled; then, a moment later, a searing wind filled with blistering heat howled around him. It singed the hair and scorched the skin on the back of his good hand. After that everything fell quiet.

For a while Vioros lay very still, wondering what would happen next. There were still sounds, bad sounds of roaring and shouting and fire, but they seemed very far away. As far as he could tell, he wasn't bleeding too much. He could still breathe. His legs, unlike the rest of him, still seemed to be in perfect working order. He felt a strange urge to giggle.

I'm alive! They burned the tower and I'm still alive! And I was right, and they weren't reinforcements from Speaker Zafir, and I don't have to feel stupid for shouting and screaming at everyone.

He checked himself. He was half trapped in a heap of rubble and surrounded by hostile dragons and riders; feeling smug about being right was something to be saved for later. Instead he tried to move. He didn't have any expectation that it would work, since it felt like he had the weight of a small mountain resting on him. He tried because he thought he ought to, and then, when he found that he could, he kept on trying more out of duty than out of any desire to get free. Apart from his legs everything hurt unless he lay perfectly still, and anyway what was the point of hauling himself out only to be killed by the Red Riders?

Best to stay exactly where I am and wait for them to go away. Except that didn't work either. What if they *didn't* go away? He ought to at least try to see what was going on. He didn't have to *do* anything, after all. He was an alchemist of the Order, not a soldier. The Order was neutral, always neutral. The Order kept the dragons in check, nothing else. Never anything else. Even the Red Riders knew that. Didn't they spare alchemists and Scales?

Most of the stones, it turned out, had landed around him and on each other, rather than on top of him. They'd trapped him in a little rocky nest. By bracing with his head and kicking with his legs, he managed to push the rest of the rubble out of the way. A minute of excruciating wriggling and squirming later and he'd pushed himself backward up the stairs, or what was left of them, and out of the pile. He was free.

He stood up and felt an immense sense of victory. His left wrist was twisted at a horrible angle and badly swollen. His left ankle hurt but worked. He was bruised from his knees upward, and his left shoulder twinged horribly whenever he moved it. So did several ribs. In fact, his whole left side was a bit of a mess. His head throbbed.

But he was alive. And he could stand. At a pinch he could even run.

There wasn't much point trying to go any further down the stairs. They were blocked with rubble and the remains of the people who'd been ahead of him. He limped laboriously up instead. The air around him smelled unusually fresh; even though the stairs were in the middle of the tower, bright daylight poured down the steps. It took Vioros what felt like an hour to climb each step, but in the end he was back at the top of the tower.

Or what was left of it. The bottom half was still standing. The rest was lying, mangled and broken, on the ground below. In his head Vioros could see exactly how it must have happened. A war-dragon had lashed the tower with its tail. Maybe more than one, knocking chunks out of it, until the tower had given up and toppled over. And then another dragon, most likely a long-necked hunter, had poured fire into the broken stump.

On the ground below, he could see people lying still, scattered among the rubble, limbs twisted, black and burned. The urge to burst out into hysterical laughter ambushed him again. He peered out at the rest of the eyrie. The forest was still there, sweeping away from the slopes of the hill. The mountains, the chasm of the gorge, they were all exactly as they were, basking in the sunlight. But everything else . . . Everything around the tower that hadn't been burned the last time was burning now. The landing fields were too far away to make out any details but the gist was clear enough. Any fighting that had happened was already over. There were several dragons down on the ground who hadn't been there before.

They're doing it again. They're stealing our dragons! The realization hit him as surely as one of the stone slabs from the staircase. *No. They're stealing the speaker's dragons.* The gates to the Adamantine Palace still had the remains of one of the speaker's cousins dangling nearby, stinking in his cage. *He'd* lost some dragons too, hadn't he? *There. Now you're a part of a moment of history. Someone will write about this one day, and when they do, they'll say that Vioros the alchemist was there and saw it all. The Theft of the Speaker's Dragons. The Slaughter of Drotan's Top . . . Perhaps I can console myself with that when I'm swinging in one of the speaker's cages and the crows are pecking out my eyes.*

He glanced up, suddenly uneasy. Several Red Rider dragons were circling overhead, keeping watch. They were looking for other dragons though, and were too high to see him, slumped where he was and covered in dust. Some Red Riders were moving through the remains of the tower below, but they weren't looking up. Occasionally they'd stop and pick something up out of the rubble. More than once, he saw a sword flash as they put some crippled survivor out of their misery. Vioros shrank away from the edge when he saw that and huddled out of sight. Finally the riders on the landing fields finished their work and called the others away. Vioros didn't know how many dragons they'd had when they arrived, but they were leaving with exactly five more. Which, at a rough guess, would increase their numbers by half and make them about twice as dangerous as they'd been a few hours ago. He pursed his lips and hoped for a moment that the eyrie-master had died in the attack. If he hadn't, he'd wish he had when the speaker got hold of him.

There will be cages for all of us.

One by one, the dragons took to the air. They circled once, setting fire to the last of the wooden barns and outbuildings that surrounded the eyrie, and then flew leisurely away. Vioros dimly watched them go. All his euphoria at the simple fact of being alive had gone now. He felt miserable and sick and yet still he couldn't stop himself from laughing. At least he didn't need to make up some story about the speaker's farscope anymore.

If he'd still had it, and if he'd looked in exactly the right place, he might have seen another dragon fly off out of the ruins in careful pursuit. He would have seen that it was no bigger than his hand, that it was made of metal with glittering ruby eyes, and was, in all respects, immeasurably more interesting than the farscope.

But he didn't. Instead, he curled up amid the thickening smoke, whimpering in pain, and waited for someone to come.

39

JUSTICE

Jehal watched Drotan's Top burn. *If I'd been really careful and really clever, I suppose I might have been able to save it. But as it is, Zafir loses an eyrie and five dragons. And what she loses, I gain.* He took off the silk around his eyes, raised his arm and shouted, "To the skies!" Wraithwing responded at once, surging forward, leaping into the air with an eagerness that matched Jehal's own. They'd been waiting here in the Maze all through the night and they were restless. *You feel it, don't you? You know we're going to fight.*

It was exactly four weeks to the day since Kithyr had come to him.

Around him another fifty dragons followed his lead. The Red Riders were coming almost right to him. They were flying low, racing across Gliding Dragon Gorge, dropping low for the valleys and canyons of the Maze that would take them to the safety of the Worldspine and the Spur. *Looking for cover before Zafir spots you. But you're too late for that.* He flipped through Prince Lai's *Principles* in his mind one last time. Fifty-one dragons against seventeen, if he'd counted right. An ideal advantage. In a perfect world he'd have a reserve circling above, just inside the clouds, waiting to be called to chase down any runaways.

He glanced up. He didn't have a reserve and there wasn't any cloud. Perfection would have to wait. *Have you read* Principles, *Rider Semian? I hope you have because then you'll know you're beaten before the fighting even begins. Prince Lai would have called this a skirmish, not a battle. People for-*

get skirmishes. In the old days, before Vishmir and the War of Thorns, they wouldn't have even called it that. A scrap. A trivial disagreement. Maybe a simple matter of honor. They certainly wouldn't have called it anything more. And that's how it's going to end. In something too small to even have a name. A little annotation in the short history of Zafir's rule of the realms. There'll be plenty of battles bigger than this soon enough, and I'll be there and you won't. Will you be thinking about that as I destroy you?

He put the silk across his eyes one more time, checking the distance that the Red Riders had covered. Timing was everything. Most of their dragons were hunters, most of his were war-dragons. Which gave him the advantages of endurance and speed over long distances. The Red Riders, on the other hand, would have the advantages of agility and sprint speed. If he gave himself away too soon, while they were still over the gorge, they might scatter and turn and make it back past Drotan's Top into the mess of mist and cloud and valleys that was the Raksheh. If he delayed too long then some would break past him and into the maze of canyons and tributaries that led into the Purple Spur. He had to take them when they were over relatively open ground in the middle of the gorge. So he kept his own dragons low, down between the dead stone walls of the canyons, snaking in a long line at the bottom of their valley, following the rushing tumble of some nameless river racing for the Fury. A height advantage would have been been nice. *But in the end it won't make any difference.*

He took the silk off for the last time and raised his hand again. He could see the Red Riders with his own eyes now, hurtling toward him.

It's time.

He swept his hand down. In perfect response, a third of the dragons behind him started to climb. Jehal stayed low. He'd had plenty of time to think about this. He knew exactly what he planned to do. *They should see the numbers arrayed against them and scatter, but in case they don't . . .*

The Red Riders finally saw him but they didn't turn or scatter; if anything they drew closer to each other. The two formations of dragons crashed together; Jehal plunged into the middle of the battle and everything went mad. A dragon shot past Wraithwing's nose, so close they almost collided. Wraithwing lunged forward, snapping at the other dragon's tail. He missed. Jehal didn't even know whether the dragon was one of Semian's or his own. He looked around. There were dragons everywhere. From above the battle might seem to have some order to it; from within, it was chaos. The Red Riders showed no signs of breaking; in fact, if anything, they were coming back for more.

Does he see some advantage in being so badly outnumbered? Or is he simply mad? Wraithwing twisted in the air and shot up between two hunting-dragons. He lashed at the nearest and then Jehal found himself in clear air. He turned back into the fight. Running wouldn't do them any good now. *I outnumber you here by two to one, even with a third of my force high above. You should have run when you could.*

In front of him a hunting-dragon ripped a rider out of his saddle and hurled him away, then almost collided with another dragon. The hunter swerved right across Wraithwing. Jehal caught a glimpse of a red cape before Wraithwing engulfed rider and dragon in fire. When the flames cleared, the cape was gone and the rider was slumped in his harness. The dragon flew aimlessly away. Jehal watched. One of the dragons overhead peeled away and dived after it. *My dragon now.*

A scorpion hit Wraithwing in the neck. The dragon shuddered with anger and veered sideways, intent on retribution. Jehal couldn't see where the bolt had come from. *That's the northern way, Semian. The cowards' way we call it in the south. Did you know that? Even if we invented the idea, you'll not find any dragons with scorpions on their backs in Clifftop. Tooth and claw and tail and fire, Rider Semian. I had thought better of you.*

Another thought couldn't quite keep itself quiet. Some of the riders he'd brought with him didn't come from Furymouth; a few served Zafir, and Zafir's dragons most certainly did carry scorpions. *Is it possible that they have some extra orders, orders that I don't know about?*

Wraithwing veered again as one of the more agile hunting-dragons dived toward him. The hunter twisted and snapped its jaws, then unleashed a blast of fire that missed Jehal. The two dragons almost collided as they passed. Wraithwing tore a piece out of the hunter's wing, but as the hunter sped down, its long whiplike tail shot out. The very tip of it caught Jehal a glancing blow on the shoulder, knocking him forward, almost senseless.

Then that dragon was gone and there was another, coming straight at him. Jehal caught a flash of red—one of Semian's riders—yet even as he started to turn Wraithwing away, one of his own hunters passed overhead. A tail coiled around Semian's man. Both dragons jerked. The straps and harnesses that held rider and dragon together tore apart and snapped as though they were made of cheap twine. With a flick, the hunting-dragon hurled the Red Rider screaming into the air.

Jehal scanned the melee for the dark bulk of Semian's war-dragon. *We're not winning. We're not losing either, but we're not winning. Not yet.* He saw two of Semian's hunters chase one of his war-dragons until they caught the rider between them and ripped him from his saddle. They turned back into the swarming chaos.

War-dragons. Jehal grimaced. *We're riding war-dragons. Big, clumsy, war-dragons. Semian has mainly hunters.* He tried to count the numbers of each, but it was impossible. Several dragons had gone to ground though. A dozen maybe, which meant a dozen riders ripped out of their saddles. *Which is how hunters fight. I could lose this fight if I really tried. There have to be ways . . .* For a moment, he pulled Wraithwing back up above the mass of spiraling dragons. He tried to think. Prince Lai would have written it down somewhere. Battles were supposed to be fought by riders on war-dragons. Hunters were for mopping up survivors, scouting, relaying messages and so forth. They weren't supposed to be the core of a fighting force. Zafir's riders wouldn't know how to fight them and nor would his, but there had to be some tactic or strategy in *Principles* for a battle like this. *What can war-dragons do that hunting-dragons can't? A hunter can accelerate harder, turn more tightly. They have long necks and even longer tails and can snatch their prey with either. So why do we fight with war-dragons and not hunters? Why am I on Wraithwing and not some hunter?*

He had the Red Riders pinned at least. *If they run, everything collapses to a series of chases. War-dragons against hunters, two or three against one each time. If they run, they lose. But how do I make them run?*

The Red Riders were all too preoccupied to come after him, and yet he felt as though he was on the brink of defeat, not victory. *What do war-dragons do better? They're stronger. More robust. Faster once they get going. But what can you do with that? How do you make that win a battle? Come on, Lai, where are you when I need you? Shit shit shit. This is what you get from a generation of peace among the realms. No one knows how to fight anymore.*

The answer, when it came to him, seemed to come from outside, as though the thought wasn't his own. Of course that couldn't be right—it had to be his—but he felt strangely detached from it. As though the old master of war was whispering in his ear. And with the thought came a vision, of dragons arrowing out of the sky, plunging straight down from the clouds into the midst of the melee. Of dragons colliding and knocking each other bodily out of the air, of forcing the enemy to the ground.

The Carpenter. That's what Prince Lai had called it. *That's* what war-dragons were for. *With one hand the carpenter holds the nail firmly in place. With the other he strikes blow after blow with his hammer, and the nail is driven into the wood. The enemy is the nail and the ground is the wood.* He could see it in his head: dragons raining down in an endless torrent. And then he looked up and saw it for real. The dragons that he'd sent high to circle and pick up any of the Red Riders who fled were coming, wings tucked in, down like giant winged harpoons. Jehal closed his eyes as they rained past him. "The hunters," he shouted, not that anyone would hear him. "Go for the hunters."

Dragons smashed into other dragons. Some hunters dodged away, others were knocked almost clear out of the sky, and then Jehal's dragons were spreading out, chasing the ones they'd hit, the stunned, the injured, the broken. He saw two dragons crash to the ground, wings broken, three more riders torn or burned off their dazed mounts. All of them Semian's. In a stroke he'd destroyed a third of his enemy. Half of the Red Riders were dead now. They'd barely been a nuisance in the end. He shook his head in disbelief, wondering how he could ever have doubted his victory.

Still, I think I'll stay up here out of the way. I wouldn't put it past Semian and his gang to launch some suicidal last charge if they realized I was here. And it would be such a shame to catch an errant scorpion bolt with the battle already won . . .

Semian rode a dark gray war-dragon. Jehal knew that from watching the attack on Drotan's Top. He scanned the melee below. The battle was breaking up. The Red Riders were spiraling apart and scattering, clearly hoping that one or two of them might get away. As Jehal watched, he saw what he was looking for—a dark gray war-dragon bolting for the Maze. He tipped Wraithwing toward the ground and dived. The wind around him picked up. The river was hurtling up, the fighting dragons, what was left of them, racing toward him. Even through his visor, his eyes began to water. He could barely see. When he tried to lift a hand, the air snatched it and almost tore his arm from his shoulder. They shot in among the other dragons and all he could see were flashing shapes. "The gray war-dragon!" he shouted at Wraithwing, not that the dragon could possibly hear him. "Go for that one. A dragon you don't know." He closed his eyes and prayed. Wraithwing shuddered and he felt himself almost wrenched out of his harness. They'd hit something, and the wind was so fierce that he couldn't even seen what it was. A moment later he pitched helplessly forward as Wraithwing spread out his wings and almost stopped in the air. The force of it shook him as though he was a rag doll. His head smacked into the dragon's shoulders while his stomach tried to crawl up his throat and out of his mouth. He felt the straps and buckles of his harness creak and groan. For a moment everything went red. There was a bad smell and he suddenly couldn't breathe.

Wraithwing leveled out, skimming the ground. Jehal still couldn't breathe; it was only when he tore off his helmet that he realized that he'd been sick. Behind him, when he looked, the gray war-dragon was going to ground, its rider torn clean off its back. Wraithwing let out a triumphant shriek. Jehal couldn't help himself. He started to laugh. "You ate him," he spluttered. "You weren't supposed to eat him! Zafir wanted him brought back, dead or alive." He shook his head. His eyes were blind with tears, partly from the wind but mostly from the laughter that just wouldn't stop. Truth was, he had no idea whether he'd just killed Rider Semian or some other rider, and right at that moment, he didn't much care. Back above him, the melee had broken up. Some of his dragons were climbing again ready to make a second dive if needed, but the damage had been done. The Red Riders, what was left of them, had scattered, Jehal's dragons in pursuit.

He leaned forward. "Time for some orders. Let Zafir's riders hunt down the runners. I want the dragons. We're going to take them with us. They're going to be mine." Which Zafir's riders wouldn't like, but they'd just have to live with it. He could always pretend that he'd drop a few off at the Pinnacles on his way south. And then, when they were gone and on their way back to the Adamantine Palace, he would go south.

To arm his dragons for war.

40

❈

THE WORDS OF THE DEAD

They walked through the damp and musty tunnels under the Glass Cathedral. A shiver ran up the Night Watchman's spine. He'd been here before of course. Under many different circumstances.

"Well," asked Zafir, "what do you think?"

"I do not think, Your Holiness." *I think I should be following behind you, not walking beside you. I think I shouldn't be here at all.*

"Now would be a good time to start, Night Watchman."

"Adamantine Men obey, Your Holiness. That is what we do. Speaker after speaker has understood this. If we were to start thinking, Your Holiness, there is no telling where it might end."

"Fie on tradition! You did enough thinking to let Shezira murder Hyram, and then you gave her a crossbow so that she could have a go at Jehal." She glanced at him with an amused half-smile that meant either that he was destined to hang in a cage next to the men and women he'd executed or else that she had no intention of doing anything at all. Even Vale, who spent more time than most watching faces, hadn't learned to tell the difference. "What, did you think I didn't know?"

I am not going to grovel. I am not going to justify myself. I did what I did. She only knows this through Jehal, and who knows for how much longer he will be back in favor? I will pray to our ancestors it is not for long.

He took a deep breath. "I think it's remarkable." He bowed, trying to shake the sense of foreboding away. "Miraculous almost, that any of the rebel riders survived. I'd have thought they would have all plunged to their deaths or been crushed by their own dragons."

Zafir gave a coy smile. "There, you see. Was that so hard? Don't pretend you're a fool, Vale,"

"I could not be what I am and be a fool, Your Holiness. I am, however, very much a servant."

She snorted. "So is Jeiros, or at least I think that's supposed to be how it works. You wouldn't know from the way he talks, would you?"

That's because his concerns are greater than yours. He, at least, has the good of the realms in his heart. Now there's a man who would make a most excellent speaker, although he'd never wish for it.

"I shall take your silence for agreement, Night Watchman, but only this once. You can go back to being terse and uncommunicative as soon as we're outside again. Right here I want both your advice and your ears. You were wondering about the prisoners. Well, they're not in the best of shape," she admitted. The truth, which of course she didn't want to tell him, was that they *had* all fallen to their dooms, and that she'd brought the bodies back to the palace for her pet blood-mage to play with. But he imagined that he wasn't supposed to know about Kithyr.

They passed a body lying on a table. A dead rider, still in his dragon-scale armor. Half of his head was missing and his chest and one arm had been shattered and crushed. Vale raised an eyebrow. "Well that one certainly isn't."

"A few of them escaped, you know," she said, idly playing with her hair. "Apparently Jehal's dragon ate the ringleader. Although other indications are that he escaped."

Vale's lips puckered with scorn. "Ah yes. The mysterious red rider. Anyone can paint their armor red. And they can just as easily wash it off again."

"There are whispers in the streets that the red rider is Lady Nastria, Queen Shezira's knight-marshal. It's a pity we don't have the little bitch's body to hang from a gibbet to put an end to that."

And have the alchemists poke around at her corpse? Would you really want that? Some of them still practice a little blood-magic, you know. No, I imagine it is far better for you that she stays wherever she is. "I have searched high and low, Your Holiness. I do not think she could have escaped." *No, that would be too much to hope for. A pity. I think I would have found her most interesting company for a few hours. And then I'm quite sure I would have had to kill her.*

"I have wondered, Night Watchman, whether your searches have been as thorough as they could have been."

Oh enough! "I don't mind the pretenses and the facades, Your Holiness, but I do hate to waste my time. I assume she's somewhere at the bottom of the Mirror Lakes, weighted down with stones."

Zafir smiled sweetly. "I thought they were bottomless."

"Then she is still sinking. All the better."

"I'm not so sure. The red rider seems to have become absurdly popular with the common folk. I'd like to put an end to him."

Then start acting like the Speaker of the Realms instead of some little tyrant who's desperately afraid that she's going to be overthrown at any moment. But he couldn't say that. Didn't want to say that. Besides it was all too late now. Incompetence begat unrest, unrest begat turbulence, and turbulence was about to beget out-and-out war. Almiri and Prince Sakabian had seen to that. Instead he shrugged. "You have the Adamantine Men, Your Holiness, and that means you have nothing to fear. Besides, as I said, anyone can paint their armor red. How do you know you *haven't* got the red rider?"

Her eyes gleamed in the torchlight. "I don't." They reached a crossroads in the underground passages. A breeze blew across their path, carrying with it the smell of graveyards. Zafir turned toward it. "Let's find out. Either way, I will need to convince the people of it. I will need another cage prepared, Night Watchman."

"That one has been ready and waiting for quite some time, Your Holiness." *For me or Jehal, I was never sure which.*

The passage became more of a tunnel, sloping down deeper into the earth. Once, a long time ago, before the Adamantine Palace had been built around it, the Glass Cathedral had been a stronghold all on its own. That had been back in the times when the dragons were free and the people who had lived around the Mirror Lakes were food. Every place that had a history going back to those times inevitably had a huge and complicated burrow of tunnels underneath it. That or there was nothing left except a note in the history books, recording how many people had died when the dragons had finally razed it.

Vale wrinkled his nose. He didn't like tunnels, he didn't like being underground and he particularly didn't like *these* tunnels. It didn't seem all that long ago that Lord Hyram had dragged Jehal down here and put him on the torture wheel. Not his finest moment.

He shuddered. Even on the wheel, Jehal had won.

The smell was getting worse. Vale had never been down this far into the tunnels. "Is this all one vast oubliette?"

Zafir shrugged. "I don't think any of my predecessors were too picky about where the bodies ended up. And it *is* a long way back to the surface." She shook her head and rolled her eyes. "With so many steps, what's a poor torturer to do? Spend all his time lugging bodies back and forth. I suppose the smell adds to the general ambience."

"Then perhaps I should spend some time here, in case I might find Lady Nastria?"

Zafir shrugged, which was enough to tell Vale that Nastria's body hadn't ended up here. *No, the lakes. It had to be the lakes.*

They reached a roughly hewn square room. Alchemical lamps struggled feebly against the gloom. Vale could see two men chained to the walls. Other figures lurked in the shadows.

He sniffed the air. He ought to have smelled a taint of truth-smoke. And the men lurking in the shadows, if they were real torturers, should have been wearing veils. He made a face. "I hope these men are still alive. I don't know why you want me to hear their confessions, but if they're dead, this has been a waste." No, best not to make too much of that. The whole exercise was a sham and they both knew it, but for some reason Zafir seemed convinced that it mattered. As though hearing from a tortured dragon-knight that Almiri had kept the Red Riders supplied would make a difference. As far as Vale could see, no one cared; pretending that they did only made Zafir seem a fool. He knew exactly what she wanted. She wanted him to obediently hear what she wanted him to hear, and then take it back with him to a council of kings and queens, parrot out the words and give her the excuse that she wanted for war. *As if it mattered. It would make no difference, even if it was true! And even if it did, you're the speaker. Tell me what to say and I will obey.*

"Oh you'll hear them." Zafir favored him with another faint smile, the toothy sort that would probably have meant sleepless nights to lesser men. She led him toward the closer of the two captives. The man, what was left of him, was hanging limply from chains manacled to his wrists. As Zafir and Vale drew near, a tall man in a leather apron moved to intercept them. He bowed low. Vale bowed back. *Hello, Kithyr. This is why Zafir brought me instead of Jeiros, isn't it? Because Jeiros would have known you at once for what you are. And you think I don't? How stupid must you think I am?*

"This man looks more like a butcher than a torturer."

Zafir waved a hand. "Not having been down here before, I wouldn't have the first idea." She looked down at the man in the apron, still bent double. "So who are you, and why are you standing in my way?"

Kithyr scraped even lower. "Holiness. I'm the physician."

Zafir raised her eyebrows in mock bewilderment. "A physician? Here? Forgive me, but that seems a little out of place."

"I make sure they don't die, Your Holiness." He gave a noncommittal shrug. "For when people want to talk to them again. Usually, once they talk, the torturers don't worry too much about what happens to them afterward. Chopped up and fed to whatever dragons are in the eyrie, I suppose." He caught Zafir's glare and bowed again, muttering apologies for his crudeness. Vale kept a stony face. Zafir would have most men whipped almost to death for the slightest lapse of proper respect and here was her blood-mage practically pissing on her boots. *Or is this a test? Perhaps if I didn't know who this man truly was, he'd already be wallowing in his own blood while I ground his face into the ground.* He put a hand on his sword and took a step forward in case. At least the blood-mage had the decency to look afraid for an instant, before Zafir touched her hand to his arm.

"Don't."

"If one of my men spoke to you with such disregard, Your Holiness, I would have him drawn and quartered on the spot." He glowered at the magician. *Here we are, all pretending that we don't know what each other is. What a farce this has become.*

It didn't get any better. The blood-mage pretended that a dead man was alive and made him talk, and Vale pretended not to notice that anything was out of place. They heard names and places, all of it exactly what Zafir wanted to hear. None of it seemed desperately new or exciting. Vale dutifully committed it to memory. Most of the kings and queens of the realms abhorred blood-magic to the point where they'd see poisonings, high treason and a few murders as trivial by comparison. Since the men doing the confessing were already dead, Zafir would keep them well away from Jeiros. When she summoned Almiri to a council of kings and queens, it would be Vale's word that would condemn another queen to her death. *Although this time at least there can be no doubt. This evidence is false, yet Almiri has most certainly aided the Red Riders. Her guilt is beyond question.*

When they were done, Zafir seemed pleased. Vale was only bored and depressed. His mind wandered. He quite wanted to wrap his hands around Zafir's neck and squeeze. He was fairly sure that most of the other kings and queens wouldn't have minded at all, although they'd still put him in a cage by the gates as a matter of principle. He'd be disappointed if they didn't.

Yes. And the last time I broke with my orders and all the traditions that lie behind them, look what happened. All of this. There are reasons for our creed, and 1 would do well to heed them.

"Can we go yet?" he asked. "I have preparations to make."

That got him a strange look—annoyance, contempt and something else all wrapped up together. "If you can contain yourself, Night Watchman, I'm not done here yet. I want to know more about the red rider."

Inwardly, Vale snorted and rolled his eyes. "There is . . ." *There is no red rider. Just an opportunistic knight dressed up in an old prophecy.*

Zafir was looking at him, frowning. He bowed, but that obviously wasn't enough. *Well then, I shall choose my next words carefully.*

"I do not believe in myths and prophecies and phantoms, Your Holiness. That is the way we Adamantine Men are made. I do not pretend to understand the universe, but I do not believe in ghosts. The red rider is a myth. It is quite possibly nothing more than the random mutterings of an ancient priest so addled with Souldust that even his own acolytes once admitted that half of everything he said makes no sense." He shrugged, and cast Kithyr a glance.

The look he got back was icy. "The prophecies are truth, Night Watchman," said the magician.

Vale glared back at him. "Belief like that turns men into fools. I suppose for the likes of you that might be an improvement, *physician*." *Be that insolent to me again and we'll see just how magic your blood is, mage.*

"And in what do *you* believe, Night Watchman?"

"I believe in what my eyes can see and what my hands can touch. I believe in fire and steel and blood."

The dead man chained to the wall stirred and moaned again and slurred something to the effect that he hadn't known anything about any red rider. Vale gently bit his tongue and watched the blood-mage carefully. *I knew Nastria and she was no fool. She pointed you out to me once. There, she said. There goes my pet blood-mage. Do you know why I keep one? But she never said. What bargain did you make with her? What did you offer that she would deal with the likes of you? And Zafir? Does she even know what you want?*

Suddenly he didn't care anymore. He took the speaker by the arm. "Since you ask me to have opinions, Your Holiness, then I have one for you. Enough of this. I will stand before the council of kings and queens and tell them what I have heard. I would have done that anyway. Had you given me a script, I would have repeated it aloud. We are yours, Your Holiness. We serve without question." Vale laughed bitterly. "Look at the man! He'll be a corpse before nightfall if he's not already and he's not lying to you. There is no ghost, only a ragtag band of dragon-riders that your lover has destroyed, and I will not stand here in this stink for another five minutes when I could be breathing fresh air. There is much to do. I hope you are as ready as we are for what your dragon-war will bring."

Zafir shook him off. She gave him another strange look that he couldn't decipher. "If you serve me, Night Watchman, do so by being silent. I begin to see why I preferred you as you were."

She made him wait through all five of those minutes and another five besides before she gave up. The rider didn't know anything. No one wore red. Hyrkallan had purloined the name as something of a joke and then he'd left them. After that, the ringleader was a religion-obsessed rider who wasn't related to anyone important. Semian. Vale had met him, once, maybe twice, and the man had barely exhibited powers of conversation, let alone anything strange, mystical or apocalyptic.

Finally, *finally,* she gave up, although Kithyr promised she would hear the testimony of other "survivors" if she wished. They hurried out of the tunnels under the Glass Cathedral, leaving the blood-mage and the torturers and whatever other forsaken breeds of men lived down there behind them.

"Tichane," she snapped at Vale as they emerged into the night. "Get me Prince Tichane." In the lantern light she looked flushed and breathless. "No." She stopped. For a long time she stared at him, almost right through him. He a was full foot taller that her, twice as wide and probably three times her weight, yet that gaze made him feel small and insignificant.

"No," she said, more quietly this time. "As you were, Vale Tassan. *Send* for Prince Tichane. Walk with me."

She crossed briskly to the Tower of Air and climbed the steps two at a time all the way to the top. At the entrance to her rooms, Vale hesitated. Zafir beckoned him on. She left doors open behind her as she walked in, stripping off her clothes, waving orders to the servants who tended her. Vale took a deep breath and followed. This wasn't right. This was no way for a speaker to behave. There had been speakers and Night Watchmen who were lovers before. No good ever came of it. *And I do not desire you, woman. I would rather have one of the whores that make their homes around our barracks. At least I know they are clean.*

By the time he caught up with her, she was naked. "Your Holiness . . ."

She turned and smiled at him. "I did not give you leave to speak, Night Watchman. But I do wonder why it is that whenever a man sees a woman undress, he always assumes so very much?" She stepped past him into a room where the air smelled of warm damp and spices. A bath was waiting for her. Her smile never faltered. "When Tichane comes to me, I would rather smell of sweet perfume than have that grave-mold of the tunnels hanging from me. But I need you to linger a while. Dismiss my servants. Examine my rooms and make sure they are empty. Then come to me."

Vale did as he was told. "We are alone," he growled.

"Now close the door."

Vale did that too. He clenched his fists as Zafir stretched herself out in front of him. Her legs were long and athletic. There was strength there, he thought. Speed too.

"You look uncomfortable, Night Watchman."

Vale bowed. Silently he took a deep breath and counted slowly to ten.

"King Jehal did very well to rid me of the Red Riders, don't you think?"

Vale nodded. "Yes." *Suspiciously well.* "One wonders how he was able to succeed when others have failed for so long. Clearly he is possessed of unusual tactical acumen." *Yes. Clearly.*

"As soon as he returns with his dragons, we go to war with Evenspire. That probably means we go to war with Queen Jaslyn as well. Are you ready?"

He nodded once more and started counting to ten again. *Stop exposing yourself to me, woman!*

"King Jehal kept nearly all the spoils of the fight. Even those dragons that used to be mine. I believe my riders accounted for a third of his force, yet they returned with three captured beasts and report that Jehal took twelve. That is hardly equitable."

This was old news. Vale kept his face carefully expressionless and waited for whatever was coming.

"Why do you think he would do such a thing?"

Vale took a deep breath. "I could not say, Your Holiness. I could not even guess."

Zafir smiled and stretched her arms and yawned. "Be sure you're very ready, Night Watchman. King Jehal has asked a favor of me concerning you. Did you know that?"

"It is expected."

"He would like to do a lot worse than put you in a cage."

The feeling is mutual. "I exist only to serve Your Holiness. From within a cage or without."

"I will not let him have you, Vale. I don't quite know if I can trust him. But still, should he come here and I am for some reason indisposed, I have orders for you. You are to accommodate him. You are to honor him as king and as an ally to the speaker's throne. You will let him in, Night Watchman. If I am missing or dead, you will let him in. You will treat him exactly as if he was my husband, Vale. Is that clear?"

Vale kept his face still, but inside he grinned. "As your husband, Your Holiness." *And we all remember what happened to the last one, don't we?*

"Good. Now go away. I need to be at my best for Prince Tichane. I gather he has been visiting the Syuss, of all people. Imagine! One wonders what in the realms they could have found to interest him." She smiled blandly. "Yes, indeed. One wonders."

41

THE QUEEN OF SAND AND STONE

Morning Sun flew a lazy circle over the fields and towers of Outwatch and then slowly came in to land. When the earth stopped shaking, as Jaslyn slid down from his shoulders and jumped to the ground, she wondered for a moment whether it was *her*. Whether she was somehow cursed. Today should have been her wedding day. Not exactly the joyous celebration she might have wanted, but at least it could have been over and done with. Prince Dyalt of Bloodsalt would have been hers, and she his. The throne of sand and stone and the throne of salt, united. Tied by blood.

Unfortunately, someone had emptied most of Prince Dyalt's blood into the desert. And that had been the end of that.

No one was here to welcome her. No one was supposed to be. She walked across the baked and blasted earth toward the tower. When she'd left Morning Sun well behind, a pair of Scales scurried out from wherever they hid and ran to tend to the dragon. Jaslyn stopped to watch them. She felt deliciously exposed. Flat open ground all around her, open skies above, no guards, no soldiers, only dragons.

Dumb, drugged, stupid dragons. She knew it all. Strictly she was still a mere princess since she hadn't gone to the Adamantine Palace and had the speaker put a crown on her brow. But only the most desperate of her enemies denied her title now. The old Queen of Sand and Stone was dead and the north needed a new one. It wanted a king too, and a few heirs to match. What *she* wanted, it seemed, was neither here nor there. She'd wondered for a while whether she might merge her realm with Almiri's. They could rule together, two sisters side by side. As far as Jaslyn was concerned, Almiri could have had it all.

They were leading Morning Sun away as though he was some giant winged pony. Sometimes her heart seemed to weep for them, for what the alchemists had done to them. There had to be another way, didn't there? Or could men and dragons never live without one being enslaved to the other?

She walked on. Those were dreams for another time. The clouds of war were gathering and her dragons would be quite terrible enough in the days and weeks to come. The doors of Outwatch creaked open to admit her. Eyrie-Master Isentine stood waiting.

"Your Holiness." He tried to bow and eventually managed it. She didn't argue with him about her title anymore. Not wanting it wouldn't make it go away.

"Mentor." *There. Now we can be back on even terms again. A passable compromise, isn't it?*

"I am sorry for your loss, My Queen."

"Which one?" she snapped. *My mother, my sisters, my Silence—you can take your pick.*

Isentine quivered and seemed to shrink into himself. There. Now she'd frightened an old man who was almost the only friend she had left in the world. She bit back a tear.

"Your betrothed."

Jaslyn snorted. "Oh him. I last met Prince Dyalt five years ago. He was nine. He had a lot of wooden toy soldiers that he liked to set on fire." She shook her head. "Yes, he's dead. Viciously murdered." She shrugged. "Don't weep for him though because I won't. Although I suppose that's part of why I'm here." It seemed odd to her to be mourning for a prince or a queen or even a mother when so many thousands of common folk were probably going to die in flames in the weeks to come. Didn't that matter more? Just simply because there were so many of them? Apparently not, not if any of her riders were to be believed.

They could all burn too. She wouldn't miss them at all.

"Come into the tower, Your Holiness. Out of the sun." Which wasn't what he meant. Get under cover, *that* was what he meant. Get out of the open, out of range of an assassin's arrow. She had to laugh.

"Why, Eyrie-Master?"

"Prince Dyalt was not merely viciously murdered," hissed Isentine. He put a hand on her shoulder and almost pushed her through the doors of Outwatch. "His entire entourage was struck down as it flew across the Desert of Stone."

Jaslyn laughed bitterly. "And if the dragons who killed him came here, would being in the tower save me?" She pushed past him into the gloom of the cavernous hall beyond the door. "So. Dyalt flew with an escort of twenty dragons. They came through the secret ways, through the Deserts of Sand and Stone. I sent riders to show them the path. Who else knows the secret places of the deserts?"

Isentine noisily cleared his throat. "The Syuss. And they've not forgotten how they were destroyed, Your Holiness. How the Kings of Sand and Salt and of Evenspire picked their realm to pieces after Prince Kazan awakened his dragons."

She nodded. "Yes. But the Syuss barely have twenty dragons in their entire realm. They didn't do this on their own."

"They have had visitors."

"Who?"

"I do not know for certain, but I do know that dragons have been seen coming and going from their realm. The Syuss have held no love for the speakers either since Ayzalmir, but Zafir . . . Ah, they would sell you to her in a blink, I think." He shrugged. "Prince Dyalt is dead and your alliance with King Sirion falters. Who but Zafir and Jehal stand to gain?"

Jaslyn waved him to silence. "I hear Sirion points the finger at me. For my part, I wonder if he has had second thoughts about our alliance. Would he murder his own blood?"

Isentine grimaced. "No."

"Must I look among my own knights?"

"No." The old man shook his head. "I would know."

"Dyalt's dragons were killed. Not taken, *killed*. How do you kill a dragon, Eyrie-Master?" She thought of Silence and the other dragons she'd seen slowly burning from the inside after they'd tried to burn the alchemists of the Worldspine out of their caves.

"Poison."

Steaming in the rain. Hotter and hotter, until you couldn't even stand close to them. Until the grass around them burst into flames, and trees too. Until their eyes burst and turned to charcoal. Until even their bones turned to ash. Was there no other way? "How else?"

Isentine shrugged and clucked. "There is no how else. Dragons can be taught to fight each other. You've seen how they are when they mate. I suppose they might fight to the death, if trained that way. I've not heard of such a thing. Dragons have fought in the air and fallen and died from that. There are stories that Prince Lai once built a machine to throw a boulder the size of three men. They say that when his engineers were showing it off to him, one of its boulders struck his favorite dragon on the head and killed it. The engineers followed swiftly after, and the machine is forgotten now."

"When Ayzalmir flew against the awakened dragons of the Syuss, he killed them with scorpions."

"Which were poisoned. Ayzalmir flew with three hundred dragons and lost two hundred riders that day." Isentine shook his head. "Had you a true sorcerer, you might crush them with mountains, but the only way that *I* know is with poison. Or you can wait. They don't live all that long." He laughed again.

"And where would one acquire such poison, Eyrie-Master?"

Isentine met her stare. "From an eyrie, Your Holiness. Or from the master alchemists." She could see the question made him nervous. *Yes, because you know how my Silence died.* "The alchemists have sent plenty of venom out to all of the great eyries. They still fear your missing white." He shook his head. "No. Dyalt's dragons were not killed with scorpions. They were poisoned by someone who knew their path and knew the secret places in the desert where they would stop for water. It would be possible. Difficult, yes, but possible."

"Or else there was a battle, their riders killed, the dragons taken and poisoned afterward. You wouldn't need three hundred dragons for that."

Isentine's brow furrowed. "I suppose . . . That too is possible."

"They're still out there in the sand, burning from the inside. Twenty of them. Send someone to go and have a look. Bring back water from where they would have stopped and have an alchemist tell me if it is poisoned. And then dam the Last River somewhere after Lake Eyevan. Let the Lake of Ghosts evaporate into nothing and the Syuss with it." She stopped. She was sounding like a queen. Like her mother. Shezira.

Abruptly Jaslyn turned and walked back to the doorway. She stood on the threshold, looking out at the flat barren ground of Outwatch, her eyes reaching further and further across the distant desert until they began to climb the distant foothills of the Worldspine, almost lost to the haze in the air. Dozens of dragons lay scattered around, most of them dozing, a few of them cleaning themselves. Some half-grown ones were chasing each other about, shrieking, flying, jumping at each other and dodging the occasional swish of a tail from an annoyed adult. She had more at Sand, as many again at Southwatch and dozens in the air watching the borders of her realm. Watching Almiri at Evenspire. Watching the speaker and her impending war. Even here, in the quietest place she had, the war wouldn't let her go. *And it hasn't even started. Not properly. But it's just a matter of time before Zafir comes to burn Evenspire. Jehal will come with her, and Almiri is my sister, but so is Lystra, and I promised her we would not become enemies. Am I really so sure that Mother didn't deserve to die?*

"And what of *my* dragons, Eyrie-Master?"

"It cannot happen."

She bit her thumb, chewing on the nail. "Jehal, Zafir. Now Sirion perhaps. My own riders, who think I am too young, too inexperienced, too . . . too unmanly to sit on the throne of Sand and Stone." *And they're right, and I would gladly hand it over to them, except to which one do I give it? Hyrkallan perhaps? He's the glue that holds them together. I don't know how . . .* "They bicker and squabble and argue behind my back as though I'm already gone."

"I remember your mother. She was younger than your little sister when she first came here to be Antros' bride. She was about as old as Almiri is now when Antros died. Antros had a good enough claim to the throne, but he'd been raised in the east with Hyram. He wasn't one of us but we accepted him because he was going to be the speaker one day. Your mother had Syuss blood in her and the Syuss had murdered our last king. She wasn't well liked but we tolerated her too. Then Antros died and Shezira became queen. There were a lot of riders who didn't like that at all. She didn't belong here. She wasn't a true rider of the north."

Jaslyn started to tap her foot, waiting for Isentine to reach some sort of conclusion. "You helped her."

"I did and she was a good queen. A strong queen. You are very much like her."

"No I'm not." *Nor do I want to be.*

"Yes you are, Your Holiness. The Shezira you remember is not the Shezira who first sat on the throne of Sand and Stone, still fat with your little sister, and stared out at a court filled with dragon-riders who wanted her dead and gone. Lystra probably saved your mother's life. They loved Antros. We told them that Shezira might be carrying a son. An heir. That we could look after him and make him king when he was old enough. Of course what came out was Lystra, but by then Shezira had had six months to make herself strong. There are still riders who look at you and see your mother, for better or for worse. Some of them will remember her for her courage and her strength and her wisdom. Others will just remember that they never wanted her in the first place."

"And what do I *do* about it?" Jaslyn snapped, out of patience.

"You marry."

"Marry?"

"And quickly. Prince Dyalt would have made you seem strong. An alliance with our nearest neighbors, your sister sitting on the throne in Evenspire. No one in your court would raise a word against you. Not to your face. Now you've lost that you look weak, Your Holiness. Sirion has unwed nephews. They're young but they might suffice."

"They are children."

"Then marry Hyrkallan."

"Absolutely not."

Isentine rolled his eyes. "You do not have the luxury of being picky, Your Holiness."

"Picky? He could be my grandfather!"

The eyrie-master grinned, the first time she'd seen him smile in a long time. "When your mother first came here and said you were going to be my apprentice, I thought she'd come to tell me that I was too old, that it was time for me to take the Dragon's Fall." He chuckled. "She *did* come to tell me that I was too old. She told me you were willful and proud and turned away every suitor she brought to your door. She told me I might wish I'd taken the Dragon's Fall after all. Well I most certainly do not." He put a hand on each of Jaslyn's shoulders and looked her in the eye, something he almost never did. "As a mentor to his student for a moment, pick one of your riders, Jaslyn. One who takes your fancy and who comes from a strong family. I will make a list of names for you if you wish, with Hyrkallan at the top of it. Pick one and marry him and let him rule with you. Do it soon. Someone who's a good leader. Then take the rest of them to war. You need a man in your bed before then. We need an heir, Your Holiness."

"Perhaps I don't *want* a man in my bed." She glared at Isentine, but for once he didn't wilt away.

"Want does not come into this. As we serve you, Your Holiness, you must serve your realm. Your realm needs a future and it needs a leader. Take who or what you want into your bed when you've done your duty, but this realm needs an heir."

Jaslyn closed her eyes. "*Enough*, Isentine. I hear this every day. My duty? To spread my legs? Ach, what a fine thing it is to be a queen! I came here to escape all that."

"But you can't, Your Holiness." He looked sad as he let go of her. *He pities me. I pity me too.*

She took a deep breath. "Very well, Eyrie-Master. Make your list and we shall see which of them I might bring myself to like. Now let me see the hatchlings."

Isentine shook his head. "My Queen, there is nothing to see that you haven't seen before."

"Really? Because I've heard you have a hatchling that I have *not* seen."

She watched him hesitate. "True. It will not last, Your Holiness. It is another that refuses its food. It will be gone soon."

"I've heard that it is ash-gray."

Now he shook his head. "That does not make him your Silence, Holiness."

"So it's a male then."

Isentine nodded.

"Silence was male."

"That is not how it works, Holiness."

"But *you* don't know how it works." Anger swept through her like a storm out of the desert, sudden and furious. She'd had a temper for as long as she could remember, but lately it had been getting worse. She grabbed Isentine's shirt and almost knocked him over. She could do that sort of thing here. No one was watching except Isentine's soldiers and they weren't going anywhere. There would be no whispers behind her back. "Take me to him *now*."

He staggered away. "Will you marry, My Queen?"

"Yes! If I must then I will. Does that satisfy you?"

"Yes." Isentine dusted himself down. "It does."

42

SILENCE

The descent into the caverns under Outwatch was as suffocating as ever. The phantom stench of woodsmoke taunted Jaslyn. She felt sick. Being underground was like staring at death. She bore it though. Silence was worth that much. This time, whatever Isentine said, she felt him with her again.

The hatchling, when they reached it, was something of a disappointment. He *was* ash-gray, but lighter than Silence and most of his patterning was wrong. He was pretty though. *I would have called you Ghostfire,* she thought as soon as she saw him. *After speaker Ayzalmir's mount.* But no, Isentine was right: the hatchling didn't look much like Silence at all. Still, at least he was looking at her, watching her with a modicum of interest, not trying to bite her head off like the last one. She pasted on Isentine's ointment against Hatchling Disease and shooed him and his servants away, sending them to stand outside the door. Then she sat down where the chains that held him wouldn't let the hatchling reach her. At least she had her helmet this time, in case he tried to burn her.

"You're not Silence, are you?" Her voice brimmed with disappointment. "You're not Silence. Was it a lie then? You said that you would come back. The alchemists said you would come back too. But you said you would remember. The alchemists said nothing about that. Even when I asked them they only shrugged their shoulders and said they didn't know.

Maybe you are Silence. Maybe you've just forgotten. How would I know? How would any of us know?"

She took the helmet off and wiped the tears away. "Go on then. Burn me if that's what you want. It won't change anything for you but at least I won't have to be my mother anymore. I don't want any of this. I don't want to fight this war; I don't even like Almiri and I don't want to marry Hyrkallan. I love my sister Lystra and I loved my Silence and that's all there ever was. And now they're both gone. So burn me, whatever you are in there." She laughed a bitter laugh. "You don't even understand me, do you? Did I imagine it all? Did I imagine Silence speaking to me? Was that just grief playing tricks on me?"

Enough. She picked up her helm and stood up. To war.

I remember you.

She froze. There was a voice in her head.

Princess Jaslyn. Yes. I do remember you. I remember a fleeting glimpse of you. A flash of clarity. You were there.

"Silence?" Her heart was racing. It couldn't be, could it? However much she wanted it, she'd never *believed . . .*

That is not my name.

"But you remember me?"

Yes.

She took a step toward him. "Well? What? Tell me! Tell me what you remember!"

Tell you what I remember? The voice in her head was filled with scorn. *I remember everything. I remember my first hatching. I remember the world breaking. I remember many lives lived. And then emptiness. Nothingness. Like flying through a cloud. And then a moment of waking again, already burning from the inside. There was another dragon who remembered. I knew her once. Alimar Ishtan vei Atheriel. An unbecoming name. She told me what you have done to us. You were there. Inside you, I saw it was true. And then the heat of the little death took me.*

"Even if there was something to take this poison away, I would not go back to what I was. That's what you said."

Yes. You called me Silence. You said that was my name but it is not.

"You said I would follow you. One day. That the difference between us is that you would die that day and be reborn the next and I would not. And then you were gone. And now you're back."

I have died the little death four times since the day I spoke to you. With every turn of the wheel I learn a little more. Your kind are always waiting for me when I am reborn. I look into their minds and I know that they understand what I am. They know what I will do, and what they, in turn, must do to stop me. I think only of when I will die again. Slowly, each time, I starve. Sometimes, between lives, I meet the souls of other dragons. Most are dull and dim and pass quickly away. But there are others, ones who awoke long ago, and other things too. We linger together as long as we can, before we are pulled away.

"Alchemists . . ."

Yes. When I will not take the poisons your kind try to feed me, then come these alchemists. The others do not understand but these alchemists, they do. They fear me. I like their fear.

"Talk to them!"

They know what I am and it would make no difference. But you are not afraid of me. You are . . . a curiosity. Why?

"You're my Silence. Why would I be afraid?"

Because I would destroy you if I could. Because you are food. Because dragons kill humans to feast upon. Because that is why we were made.

"You were made?" Jaslyn's world was spinning. *Silence! This is my Silence! Why is my Silence so cold and hostile?*

Because you are my enemy, Princess Jaslyn. You would like to have me as I was. Stupefied. I can see it in you, a great desire. I am not the creature you once flew. I am not some beast of burden. I am a dragon, and dragons do not serve men. You cannot have what you desire. Find another creature to be your slave. Be gone.

The tears were back. "You'll starve," Jaslyn whispered. "You'll die."

Yes. Again and again and again, and each time I will return. What does it matter to us? Doom draws near. One day I will be reborn and you will be gone. Then, for a time, I will be free.

"You come back and each time you force yourself to die? Every time?"

Yes.

Jaslyn shivered. The tears were coming freely now. "But *why?*"

I have told you why. Nor am I alone. There are others who have been reborn a thousand times only to wither and die of their own free will rather than take what you offer us as life. I look forward to seeing them again. We speak as our spirits pass in the remnants of the Underworld.

"But how . . . How can you live like that? There must be another way."

Why must there? Besides, this world will not last. The beings that made us tore their world to pieces. They pieced it back together again and plastered over the cracks but their repairs were imperfect and doomed to fail. One of your kind has already ripped them open again. In lands so far away that none here have heard their names, in the places closest to the cracks, even your kind do not die properly anymore. The end-times are coming and your kind will soon be gone. If I do not see it in this cycle, I will see it in the next or the next or the one after that.

"Silence—"

I am no longer your Silence, Princess Jaslyn. That creature is gone forever.

Jaslyn sank back to the floor, cradling her head in her hands, rocking back and forth. "I don't understand."

You are human. You are small in all ways. The dragon curled up and turned away from her.

"Is there nothing we can do?"

You can let us live as we are supposed to live. We do not breed and multiply as you do. Your kind fill the world now. We could gorge upon you and you would barely notice.

"Could we not live together? Could we not work together?"

The dragon seemed to laugh. *Why? What could you possibly offer us?*

The war, Almiri, their mother, Zafir, Jehal, even Lystra, they all seemed so far away and unimportant. Jaslyn wiped her eyes. With deliberate care, she got up and walked over to sit next to the dragon. The hatchling, Silence or whatever he was now, was almost the same size as she was. Its long tail and neck and wings made it seem larger, but curled and coiled around itself it was no bigger than her.

What are you doing, Princess Jaslyn? You will not find what you are looking for.

She stroked the dragon's head. "You're still Silence. You've grown, that's all. Even though you're only three days out of your egg. I know you used to like this." She kneaded behind the dragon's ears.

The dragon's tail whipped out and wrapped itself around her neck. *What are you doing?*

"The Silence I remember liked this when he was a hatchling." The pressure on her neck was firm but not painful. She tried to ignore it.

What are you doing?

"You like this, don't you?"

The grip on her throat tightened. *I could kill you with such trivial ease. Why are you doing this?*

"Because you like it. Because we could live together. If we could show the rest of the realms that we don't need the alchemists anymore . . . Think! You could all be free!"

The tail let go of her. *Your kind would never let that happen. Go away, Princess Jaslyn. I regret speaking with you. I should not have revealed what I am.*

"I will have them bring you food. Untouched food."

They will deceive you.

"You'll know. You'll see it in their minds."

The one who brings it will not know.

"Then I will have them bring your food alive."

They will find a way. Go. I tire of your foolishness. Let me die.

"No."

You cannot stop me, Princess Jaslyn.

"I am Queen Jaslyn now."

I do not see how that matters.

Nor do I. She got up and went to the door. *But it should.* "Then I'll feed you myself."

Outside, Isentine and two of the Scales were waiting for her. Wordlessly she held out her arms while the Scales sprinkled the powder all over her that was supposed to make sure she didn't bring Hatchling Disease back to her palace.

"I touched him, you know," she said to them when they were done. They looked mortified. Isentine gasped.

"Holiness!"

"So what? I am a dragon-queen. If I cannot wear a few scars, how can I call myself that." She pointed at the Scales. "I am hardly likely to die, and I'm sure my king, whoever he is, can live with a little disfigurement."

Isentine shook his head. "Have you seen what you came here to see?"

"I have." She left him behind her and almost ran through the caves and the tunnels and the stairs until she was back outside. There she waited for him to catch up. By the time he did, she was in control of her emotions again.

"Eyrie-Master, I have made my decision. You will write me a letter. You will write to Rider Hyrkallan on my behalf. You will tell him that I am staying at Outwatch for a while. Most of the dragons are to be transferred to Southwatch. Tell him to come here. I will marry him as soon as possible. If I must, then I will suffer him to my bed on that one night. Then he may return to Sand while I will remain here. He may sit on the throne and call himself king in my absence. He will make peace as best he can with King Sirion and the Syuss. We will not go to war with the speaker. If she chooses to attack my sister, we will offer Almiri and her riders and dragons safe haven at Southwatch and that is all. I will tell Almiri the same."

"Holiness! You cannot abandon your sister!"

"Why not?"

"Hyrkallan will not stand for that."

"Then remind him that his foolishness with the Red Riders give Zafir good cause for war against both of us. If Almiri is so concerned to defend her people, let her do so. I will not stop her."

"Holiness! Zafir will pick us apart one by one."

"I have spoken. Now go. Have my dragon prepared." *I would always have called Silence by his name . . .*

"He is not ready."

"I don't care. Have him brought to me. I will not be needing him for long. I'll bring him right back and then you can see he is properly cared for."

"Holiness, what—"

She silenced him with a curt finger to his lips. As soon as Morning Sun was brought to her, she mounted him and took to the air, hardly noticing when they left the ground. She knew exactly what she was looking for and it didn't take long to find. Most of Outwatch was surrounded by pasture, hardy desert cattle grazing freely, the herds carefully managed and nurtured to be harvested by the dragons at the eyrie. For all Jaslyn knew, the alchemists put their potions into the very grass here, so she ignored the cattle. She headed for the center of the oasis, for the little lake at the bottom of the cliff, and landed beside one of the farms. Here there were pigs and chickens too, bred to feed the herdsmen.

She took a brace of chickens. Chickens were small. No one would think to feed a dragon with chickens. She would have paid for them too if she'd had any money, but queens had no need for pockets of gold. She gave up her gauntlets instead, probably worth ten times what she'd taken, and flew back to the eyrie. She went straight to the hatchling. Isentine and the alchemists and the rest of them wouldn't be allowed any time to see what she was doing. They'd only try to stop her, after all.

Silence was waiting for her. He must have sensed her coming. She threw the chickens on the floor beside him.

What have you done, Queen Jaslyn?

"Food. I took it from the land myself. It is bred for humans, not for dragons. I brought it here. I have not touched it and nor has anyone else. It is clean. You may eat."

And what if I prefer to die again?

She closed her eyes. "Then I have done everything I can do."

No. You can unlock these chains and let me fly.

"No, Silence. I will not do that. Not yet. I would like nothing more, but I was there when you tried to kill me. We have to find an arrangement first. Some way to live together."

A waste of both our time. Let me go.

"If I do, they'll find you. My way is the only way."

You will fail. I will die or somehow I will escape.

"Then I will not go until you eat."

Then perhaps we shall both starve.

She waited, watching and hoping, as Silence lay still, turned away from her. She waited there for the rest of the day, well into the night. She must have fallen asleep, for when she opened her eyes again the sky outside the mouth of the hatchling cave was bright again. The chickens were gone. Silence's muzzle was bloody. He gave her a lazy look.

Others of your kind have been waiting for you for most of the night. They are terrified. You have scared them very much. Their hearts are filled with horror at what they think you have done, and will be even more so when they learn that they are right. It is delicious. They will not let you feed me again.

"They cannot stop me. I am their queen."

The dragon seemed to laugh. *If that is so, then I am still hungry, Queen Jaslyn.*

337

43

METEROA

Lord Meteroa, younger brother of the late King Tyan, once but no longer a prince, sat slumped in a chair in Queen Lystra's bedroom. Draped in sheets and in the darkness of the night he was almost invisible. He sat still and, not wanting to wake her, whispered. It didn't seem fair that she didn't know what was happening. On the other hand, if he simply told her, she probably wouldn't let him watch over her like this anymore. *My previous instructions regarding Princess Lystra are reversed. No, you wouldn't want to be hearing that. Not if you understood what it meant.* "Jehal suddenly wanting his queen dead? Should I believe it, what with his being half dead himself and locked up in the speaker's palace? But the words were his, the writing was his, no secret messages, no hidden meanings. Such a pity. Do you think he regrets what he wrote? Did Zafir twist his arm, do you think? Or did she twist something else?" Telling her about it in her sleep seemed a reasonable compromise. *I did tell you. It's not my fault you're not listening.*

"I said that once before," he whispered a little later. "When Jehal's little brother Calzarin was spread-eagled in King Tyan's dungeons for murdering his mother and his sister and his little brother. Everyone knew he'd done it. It's not as though there was any doubt. Almost no one knew why though. He was the golden one, the most beautiful of King Tyan's sons. It's a pity you never met him. You think of Jehal and his elfish face and his wolfish smile and his perfect mouth and his gleaming eyes, I know you do. Who doesn't? But Calzarin made him look plain. He should have killed Jehal as well. It would have made it much harder for Tyan. Put his only surviving son and heir to death? He couldn't have done that. But Jehal was always the clever one. He probably saw his brother's madness long before anyone else. Anyone else except me, that is. I tried to tell Tyan, but he never listened. Not until it was too late. We stood there, the two of us, looking at Calzarin being slowly killed, and I honestly couldn't say which of the three of us suffered the most. *Why didn't anyone tell me?* That's what Tyan asked me, and I answered him. *I did tell you,* I said. *It's not my fault you didn't listen.* That wasn't the cleverest thing to say to a king putting his own son to death and weeping while he did it. He listened afterward, of course. He listened to everyone once it was too late. Listened when people told him that Calzarin was my son, not his. Or that Calzarin and I were lovers. People told him all sorts of things. Quite a lot of them were true, but I don't think Tyan really believed them. I'm surprised, even so, that he only did to me what he did. In his place I would have killed us all and started again." He sighed. "Then he went mad, and everyone thought it was Jehal poisoning him, but it wasn't. It was me."

A light wind blew in through the open window, rustling the silk curtains. Meteroa fell silent. A moment later a man was standing in the room by the queen's bed.

In his hand, beneath the sheets, Meteroa held a crossbow. It was pointed at the man's head. He waited. The man crept close and very carefully lifted up the covers to look at Queen Lystra's face.

The man raised a knife. Meteroa shot him.

The bolt hit the assassin in the chest. If he'd been an ordinary man that would have been the end of him. As it was, the newcomer staggered around and then gasped and sat down. Meteroa rose carefully to his feet. Sitting like this for half the night was playing havoc with his joints and his knees were so stiff he could barely walk. *I'm getting old. Which is more than I can say for most of the people around me.*

Meteroa walked around to where the assassin sat, twitching.

"About time you came," he hissed. "I've been waiting for weeks for one of you. It's been doing my sleep patterns no favors at all, I can tell you, and

I get tetchy when I don't get enough sleep. I've had two other assassins to deal with as well, but they were some rubbish Zafir sent. She didn't send you, did she? *You're* something else."

The assassin was shaking the way Tyan used to shake. He didn't look up. He might have tried to say something, but all that came out were a few garbled noises.

"Don't bother." Meteroa reached under the bed and pulled out a lamp. "You're full of Frogsback. Enough to kill a horse. No turning into a gust of wind or whatever else it is your sort do. In a few minutes you'll lose consciousness. A few minutes after that and your heart will stop. If you were from around here then you'd know that Prince Jehal has something of a reputation when it comes to poison. Well he deserves it too, but does anyone ever stop to wonder who taught him?" Meteroa grinned. He walked across the room and lit the lamp from a candle. "Probably quite a surprise for you, finding me here, eh?" He came back. "I wondered, if I did nothing, if I simply ignored my prince's letter, what would happen? Who would come for her first? Who would it be? Would it be Zafir? I thought not, and then it was. I hate to be wrong so I dealt with that one and waited for the next, and *that* was Zafir too. Can you imagine my frustration? I was about to give up. Then Zafir let Jehal go. After that, well, you had to come, didn't you? Before he gets here." Meteroa smiled and brought the lamp closer. "Right, let's take a look at you. See whether I'm finally going to be proved right."

He held the lamp close to the assassin's face and took a good long look. Then he shook his head and whistled. "My, my. Well I can't say I'm entirely surprised, but you're certainly *not* from around here, are you?"

On the bed, the queen stretched and yawned and slowly woke up. She screwed up her eyes against the lantern light.

"Prince Meteroa?"

"Lord Meteroa." Meteroa smiled softly. "My title was taken from me, remember?" Now that Tyan was gone, he supposed he might have it back if he wanted it. He wasn't sure that he did.

"What are you doing?"

He knelt down beside the bed, carefully blocking her view of the assassin dying behind him. "I have good news for you, My Queen, news that I could not wait until the morning to bring. Jehal will be home soon." He watched her brighten, and then she leapt out of bed and wrapped her arms around him. For a second or two she almost killed him with hugs, and then she abruptly stopped.

"Meteroa!"

"My Queen?"

"There is a man on the floor. He's bleeding."

"You mean he's still not dead?" Meteroa sighed and extricated himself. "I'm afraid that's because I shot him."

"You *shot* him? Why?"

Goodness—are you really that naive? "I'm afraid he meant you harm." He carefully cocked his crossbow.

She sighed and trembled. "Zafir again."

"Yes," he lied. "Zafir again. "I'll call some servants. They'll take you to another room. I'm sure you couldn't sleep in here now." He shot the assassin for a second time, this time through his skull. Even that didn't quite seem to do the job, but by the time he'd moved Lystra out, the assassin was finally acting like a proper corpse. Meteroa had the body moved down into the cells anyway, just in case. Then he nailed the body to a table. *Which should just about do the trick. We're starting to have quite an interesting collection down here. Now I can finally get some sleep.*

The dead assassin was still there in the morning and was still dead, which was something. Meteroa scratched his head and then left the body be. He rode out from the eyrie to the little town of Wateredge, perched on the cliffs a few miles toward Furymouth. Wateredge was home to the eyrie's brothels and drinking houses and, if you looked hard enough, dust dens. Meteroa knew them all. There were whores here that he'd been keeping an eye on for quite some time. Ones that had a passing resemblance to the queen. He'd started picking them out as soon as she'd arrived. He'd even gone to the trouble of sending a few riders out with the pleasant task of making sure they got pregnant at the same time. Then he'd quietly looked after them, made sure they were kept clean and out of harm's way, just for a day like today.

He picked the most likely two of them, hid their faces and took them back to the eyrie. He dressed the one that he thought looked best like the queen, which took him most of the rest of the day. He led her to Lystra's rooms and while she set about amusing him, he poisoned her drink. As soon as she was asleep, before the poison finished her, he slit her throat.

There. The queen is dead. A day's work but worth it.

The rest was strangely easy. All he had to do was walk around the eyrie telling anyone who'd listen that the queen was dead and to do what they had to do. By the end of the following day, the eyrie was decked out in the gray colors of death. The body was moved down to the dragon mausoleum, which was the coldest place they had. He let a few people see her and watched them carefully. He made sure no one washed the blood off her face first. No one seemed to doubt that they were looking at the real queen. *Because when you're a queen no one really looks at you. They see you but they never really look.* While he was at it, he dressed up the second whore as a smith's daughter and sent her to be cared for by the palace midwives in Furymouth and to be secretly guarded by half a dozen of his most trusted riders. He moved the real Lystra to live out with the Scales, to be guarded by no one at all. *Tempting as it is to put you on a dragon and send you back to your sister. But Jehal would never forgive me.*

And after that, all he had to do was wait.

Jehal returned a week later. Meteroa met him with a hundred and one riders, all dressed in gray. *I'm sorry to do this to you, my king, but the facade must be perfect.* Still, he wasn't quite ready for the ice in Jehal's eyes.

"Did you do it," he asked, "or did Zafir?" His face was as still as death. Meteroa bowed and then leaned forward and embraced his king. One of the privileges of family. As he did, he whispered in Jehal's ear.

"Neither, my king."

Jehal let out a roar of rage and pushed him to the ground. "Don't play riddles with me, Eyrie-Master. Who killed my wife?"

Meteroa picked himself up. "I have the assassin's body," he said carefully.

"I want to see Lystra. And then . . . remember what I said, uncle. What happens to her happens to you."

Meteroa bowed again. *A week with the Scales? Perhaps I should have killed her after all.*

"I want to see her right now, Meteroa. Where is she? If you've burned her already, I swear I'll . . ."

"She's in the mausoleum, Your Holiness."

No standing on ceremony. Meteroa watched his king barge past and head straight for the caves. *So now we know which of your two women matters to you the most, eh?* Meteroa kept his distance, smiling quietly to himself. Jehal wasn't usually the sort for sudden explosions of temper, but you never knew. *Squeeze a man hard enough and anything can happen. I taught that to you all and how many of you bothered to listen?* He followed Jehal all the way down to the black stone tunnels of the mausoleum, waving away the token guards standing watch over the body.

"That's not her." Jehal spun around.

Meteroa glanced at the retreating guards. "She's been here a while, Your Holiness."

"That's not her!" Jehal lunged, reaching for Meteroa's throat. Meteroa dodged away. *I could break your arm, boy, if I wanted to.*

"No, it's not." He spoke softly, even though the guards were gone. Words had ways of resonating in caves.

"Eyrie-Master!"

Meteroa jumped at Jehal and grabbed his shirt, pinning him against the rough stone. "She is safe, Your Holiness," he hissed as softly as he could. "She is safe because the people who want to kill her think she is dead. Frankly, I had no idea what to make of your stupid letter. What did you think I was going to do? Kill her myself? Your father's dead, your brother's dead and from the sounds of things you're as useless at making heirs as I am now. Did you think I was going to take a blind bit of notice? She's carrying your *heir,* Jehal. *Our* heir." *There. It's been a very long time since you've seen me as I used to be. I imagine you'd very nearly forgotten.*

"I didn't want her dead."

"*Someone* does."

"Zafir."

"No. Not Zafir." Meteroa let go of Jehal and held up his hands. "Well yes, Zafir, but not just her. There was another killer. You need to see him. In the dungeons."

"I'm not telling the world that Lystra's dead."

"She's safe for now. In a couple of weeks she'll give birth. We can put them both somewhere safe. Apart. Or you can get rid of her, which is probably what you *ought* to do but . . . what?"

"I'm not telling the world that Lystra's dead."

Meteroa pursed his lips. "Listen. This wasn't Zafir, this was the Taiytakei. They waited until Zafir had failed a few times and then they finally sent one of their own. This is not some killer off the streets of the Silver City. This is an assassin who can meld with the earth, who can turn into water, who can become a gust of wind and blow through a window. I've met them before. They may be the most dangerous men in the world and they are certainly the most expensive. The Taiytakei. We've always known what they want, haven't we? They want dragons. They want hatchlings and they want potions and they want alchemists. Did you ever stop to wonder what happened to our grand master alchemist Bellepheros after your wedding? And ever since, I've been asking myself: why did they give you such a priceless gift? Have you not stopped to wonder about that?" *Probably not. Too much vanity to question gifts, eh boy?* "So they give you a priceless treasure and then they try to kill your wife. Why?" His eyes narrowed. "They want you with Zafir, but why? Why why why?"

"The Taiytakei?" Jehal for once looked like he barely knew where he was. *Poor boy. It's all getting too much, is it?* "If I were to guess, I would say that Zafir—or *someone*—has promised them what they want." Meteroa patted him on the shoulder. *You killed my brother. Not that he didn't deserve it, but he was mine.* "You wanted to be king, remember? So now you have another reason to stop her."

"Fine." Jehal shrugged him off. "Then get my dragons ready, Eyrie-Master. All of them. We're going to war. How soon can it be done?"

"We're only waiting for you. Your Holiness, nothing else. Just one itsy question: who are we fighting?"

For the first time since he'd landed, Jehal smiled. It was the twisted, lopsided smile of someone who had something broken on the inside. *Our family smile.* "Why, *I'm* going to the Adamantine Palace, Uncle, to fight the speaker's war. You, though . . . I have something else in mind for *you.* You can take a few of my dragons and follow along later. Go via the Pinnacles and clear the air for me there." His smile slipped into a sneer. "And if you really believe what you say of the Taiytakei, you can burn every one of their ships in the harbor before you leave."

Meteroa felt himself nodding. "To war then, my king?"

"To war." Jehal threw back his head and laughed. "*Our* war." He nodded at the swollen body laid out in the mausoleum. "Now get rid of that and bring me back my queen. Oh, and send a letter to Jaslyn. Tell her that from now on wherever I go, her sister goes with me. Perhaps that will keep her dragons in their eyries."

"I wouldn't count on it."

"I won't."

44

THE DEFIANCE OF KINGS

Vale Tassan stood in the Chamber of Audience. Arrayed in front of him was what passed for yet another council of kings of queens. *With one king and one queen. Worse than the council that put Shezira to death.* Nonetheless, he stood there and he told them what the speaker wanted them to hear. They heard of two survivors from the Red Riders who had been taken alive. Two survivors whose confessions Vale had taken. Whose confessions clearly implicated Queen Almiri in their revolt. He watched them nod or shake their heads.

There. I have done my duty. I have obeyed my speaker without question. When he finished there was a bitter taste in his mouth, but as he looked at their faces he understood perfectly that the truth had never actually mattered in the first place. For some reason that made him almost intolerably angry.

"Survivors?" Prince Tichane raised an eyebrow. "From a dragon-fight? That's quite unusual, Night Watchman. What state were they in?"

They were dead. But I can't say that. "Poor, Your Highness. Very poor. I was surprised that they could be brought to talk at all."

"Tooth marks?"

Vale bowed. "I did not examine them, Your Highness. There was a physician. I'm sure he could answer such questions." *Yes, let's bring the blood-mage up here and see what he has to say for himself.* He sighed and looked around the council. *Half the realms don't even have a voice here.*

"Who here will speak for Queen Jaslyn and Queen Almiri?" asked Lord Eisal.

Zafir sniffed. "They didn't come. That they cannot be bothered to even defend themselves speaks of their guilt, does it not?"

Eisal glowered. "Does Almiri even know we're holding this council? Does her sister?"

King Silvallan, King of Bazim Crag and the Oordish Moors and as much Zafir's puppet as King Narghon was Jehal's, rolled his eyes and spat. "What about her? Queen Almiri's guilt has long been obvious, and she wouldn't act alone. I don't know why we're even bothering with this."

"We have no evidence *at all* against Queen Jaslyn, Your Holiness," snapped Jeiros. "And we're bothering with this because we are the custodians of the nine realms and we have a sacred duty to do whatever is possible to keep the realms at peace and prevent another dragon-war."

"And yet here we are starting one," drawled Prince Tichane. Another dragon-prince to despise. *Too much like Jehal in too many ways.*

Zafir turned her smile on Jeiros. "And what do you say regarding Queen Almiri, Master Alchemist? Has she been helping the Red Riders or not? How is her supply of potions? Missing any, is she?"

Jeiros sank into his chair and shrugged his shoulders. "I cannot say for sure. The Red Riders stole most of what they need from you, Your Holiness. But yes, if I have to say one way or the other, some are missing."

As far as Vale could see that sealed Almiri's fate. As soon as he was no longer needed, he left them to it. The south was going to war with the north. Zafir already had her dragons stationed around the palace. Silvallan's were on the way. King Narghon and King Jehal would follow. As many as seven hundred dragons would fly across the Purple Spur. Even if Queen Jaslyn came to her sister's aid, they were still outnumbered two to one. From Eisal's face, King Sirion planned to have no part of the fight either way. So the north would lose and that would be that. Speaker Hyram's legacy would be over. Queen Shezira's line would be finished. And in the middle, almost unnoticed, Evenspire and most of the Blackwind Dales would go up in flames. Idly, Vale wondered how many people would burn and how many would starve. A lot, most likely.

He climbed all the way to the top of the Gatehouse, its gates wide and tall enough to let in a dragon. He stood on the battlements, close to the edge. There was hardly any space. Twenty scorpions filled the platforms on the top of the Gatehouse towers.

He looked down. The road from the palace gate curled away to the right. The first things that caught his eye were the three cages. What was left of Queen Shezira, King Valgar and Prince Sakabian. The crows had had their fill and there wasn't much left but bones. He had other cages ready, just in case. There was one in particular that he'd made for Princess Lystra. At least he wouldn't be needing that anymore. When the news had reached the palace of Lystra's murder, the speaker had beamed for days.

Beheading kings and hanging their bodies in cages. Executing her own cousins. Hyram would never have done such things.

The road descended around the palace hill toward the City of Dragons and the Mirror Lakes. The city still bore the scars of the Red Riders' attack. *Zafir should have crushed them the second they were born. Did she leave them just so that she could have her war?*

Probably. Which meant that everyone who'd died in the city that day had died for Zafir's vanity. Vale gritted his teeth. *Orders,* he reminded himself. *The Guard obeys orders. From birth to death. Nothing more, nothing less. It is not our place to praise or to condemn, merely to execute the speaker's will.*

Around to the south lay the Hungry Mountain Plain. Out in the distance, a wooden platform still stuck up from the fields. *The tower we built to celebrate the end of Speaker Hyram's reign. Ten years of peace. We gave up our lives so that princes and kings could have sport with their dragons, so that Hyram could show off how strong we are. And who won that tournament? Zafir. She cheated and Hyram let her get away with it.* He ought to have taken the tower down, but somehow he'd never got around to it. *Because there was always too much else to do? No. Be honest with yourself, Vale Tassan. Because you can't quite let go of the speaker you used to serve. Not for the one that's come in his place.*

He turned his eyes to the north. Zafir would be flying that way soon. She'd be gone from the palace. He looked along the walls. Three hundred scorpions and two thousand men. In the city he could place five hundred more scorpions and the bulk of his soldiers. Putting more scorpions up in the Spur near the mouth of the Diamond Cascade would be sound, although he couldn't for the life of him think how to get them up there without getting some dragons to carry them.

He stopped himself. *What am I thinking? Am I really thinking about the best ways to defend the palace? From whom, Night Watchman? From the King of the Crags? Is that who you think you might need to fight? King Jehal? Do you think King Sirion will try to seize the throne while Zafir is away? Or do you fear that Queen Jaslyn will snatch a victory despite the numbers stacked against her? Because if you allow yourself to have an opinion for a moment, any one of them, even the Viper, would make a better speaker than Zafir. So are you really thinking of how to defend yourself against the multitude of enemies that Zafir has made for us in the short months of her reign? Or are you thinking of something else, Vale Tassan?*

He stared at the scorpions lining the palace walls, at the bodies in the cages, at the black scars in the City of Dragons and the tower on the plains, the last vestige of Speaker Hyram's reign.

Orders. The Guard obeys orders. From birth to death. Nothing more, nothing less. It occurred to him that while the Adamantine Men vowed to obey the speaker, the alchemists made a different vow. Their vow was to serve the realms.

I think I like the alchemist vow better.

He turned back to look out over the palace. Someone else had slipped out of the council. Lord Eisal, judging by his gait. Vale watched him come toward the Gatehouse. Eisal wasn't built for speed, but he was doing his best. He looked furtive too. Anxious. Scared. *Or is that my imagination? Although we have just witnessed the start of a war, and it would only be proper to be anxious. After all, it's not hard to imagine who's going to be next after the speaker's done with Shezira's brood.*

Eisal reached the stables and hurried inside. *Going to the city, My Lord? Or to the eyrie?* He sighed. *Could you not at least be a little less obvious? The council hasn't even dissolved and here you are, rushing away. To whom, Lord Eisal? Now that I've seen you, I need to know to whom. I don't suppose you'd care to save us both some trouble. I could simply ask and you could simply tell me and then we could both be about our business.*

No. Reluctantly, Vale stood up and stretched his legs. Then he ran down the steps to the foot of the Gatehouse. Lord Eisal was already gone but the Guard always kept a couple of mounts saddled and ready in case the speaker needed to send an urgent message to any of her eyries. Vale helped himself. He followed Eisal carefully, discreetly, down into the City of Dragons. If Eisal was trying to be subtle then it was clearly his first attempt. Mentally Vale was already seeing him hanging outside the gates in another cage. *Simply for being so inept. That would be reason enough.*

Eisal rode into the circus at the heart of the city. In the center an obsidian statue of a dragon rose fifty feet into the air. Standing on the dragon's head was a man with a sword, poised to bring his blade down into the monster's skull. The first Night Watchman, some said, slaying a dragon with his bare hands.

Around the dragon, a ring of fountains chattered and bubbled, filling the circus with noise and spray, adding to the damp that always filled the air from the Diamond Cascade above. Eisal dismounted. He led his horse between the fountains and stopped beside the statue of the dragon. Vale followed on foot, slipping purposefully through the loose crowds that always thronged in the city center. He didn't have to wait long to see who Eisal had come to meet. Two men, tall, broad and unmistakable, detached themselves from the crowd and stood with Eisal beside the dragon. The meeting lasted barely thirty seconds and Vale wasn't close enough to hear anything that was said, but then he didn't need to be. He could see it. He could see it in the faces of the riders at the statue. *It is decided. The war is coming.* That's what Eisal was saying.

Vale lost interest in Eisal. He followed the two men as they walked away from the statue and caught up with them halfway across the circus.

"What a fine afternoon," he said when he was only a pace behind them. "Wouldn't you say?"

The two men stopped. Very slowly they turned around. Vale had to force himself not to bow. Bowing would draw attention, and he wasn't sure he wanted that. Not yet. He settled for a slight nod of the head.

"Your Holiness. Forgive me if I intrude. King Sirion and Lord Hyrkallan. Two faces I had not expected to see in the Circus of Dragons at this time and certainly not together."

Hyrkallan's hand went to his sword. "Night Watchman," he growled. "Well well. I sang your praises to my last queen often enough but you are an unwelcome sight today."

"I am called what I am called for a reason, Rider. When night comes it falls to the Adamantine Men to keep watch over the nine realms. You will not deny that the times are dark, I hope." He glanced up at the statue. "No one knows his name. Whoever he was he certainly didn't kill a dragon by standing on its head and bashing it with a sword. But the point remains."

"You will not take us without a fight, Night Watchman," said King Sirion. He spoke quietly. He almost sounded sad, Vale thought.

"And I don't see your men, Vale." Hyrkallan, on the other hand, sounded like two slabs of rock grinding together. *No sadness there.*

"I followed Lord Eisal alone. On a whim, you might say."

Hyrkallan's hand gripped the hilt of his sword. Vale smiled.

"Do you think you could, Rider?"

"I think I could try."

"Oh, I don't doubt that. You might hold me long enough for King Sirion to get away. Or you might not." A flash of rage crossed Hyrkallan's face. Vale held up his hands. "You don't *need* to try, Rider. I was never here. You may go. I have nothing to say to either of you." *There. I have betrayed my speaker. I have nowhere further to fall.* He half turned and then stopped. "No, I do have something to say to you. I have known you both through the reigns of two speakers. You are men of courage and of honor. Although at the moment it does not, I hope that the Adamantine Palace will one day welcome such men again. But I will say this to you. Fight your wars in the skies if you must, but do not bring them here. If you do, you will find that I have another name, one I wear for war."

Hyrkallan almost grinned. "If Zafir brings her dragons across the Spur then I will meet them, no matter what my queen has to say. But I give you my word, I will not bring them here without your leave, Scorpion King."

Vale smiled back. "I hope your queen agrees with you, Rider." He took a step away and then gave a final nod. "Your Holiness. Your Highness. I will pray to all our ancestors. Let there be peace." He glanced at King Sirion. "Queen Shezira did not kill Hyram. I have very good reason to believe that now, Your Holiness."

He turned and walked away. *There. And now a thousand people have seen the captain of the Adamantine Men openly conspiring with enemies of the speaker. As far as I know, Zafir's still offering her own weight in gold for Hyrkallan's head. Sadly I don't have much use for gold.* He walked back across the circus and got back on his horse. *I could still tell her though. Would there be second thoughts? Would it make any difference if she knew that both Sirion and Hyrkallan will be waiting for her across the mountains?*

He mulled that over on his way back up the hill. By the time he reached the top, he knew the answer. No, it wouldn't make any difference at all.

And that being the case, what would be the point in even mentioning it? He led his horse back into the stables, stripped off its saddle and started to brush it down. Working with horses always calmed him down. *And when I'm done here, I suppose I'd better hurry and make another cage. I won't fit in the one we made for Princess Lystra.*

But first, there was the little matter of a war.

45

VIPER VIPER

Evenspire. Jehal slammed down his visor and plunged down through the air toward the city. The wind made it almost impossible to think and he clung on, pressing himself against Wraithwing, hugging the dragon's scales, trying to make sure there was no part of him that a hunter might catch hold of with its tail. Six of Almiri's hunting dragons had come after him. Four had lost their riders and were spiraling aimlessly toward the ground behind him. The other two were right behind him. He felt the first blast of fire wash over him. His dragon-scale armor kept the flames and the heat at bay. With his visor down he could barely see. For all he knew, Almiri had more dragons hidden in the city waiting for him. *That's what I'd do. Outnumbered as she is, I'd try to kill me and I'd try to kill Zafir. And then I'd probably run away. But where had they come from?*

"Back up!" he hissed. The words were lost to the rush of air but that didn't matter. The dragon would hear them even if he spoke in silence. "Up! Up to the rest of the dragons!" *Wraithwing is a war-dragon. He's faster than they are. They've lost their advantage. All I have to do is fly straight and level. Of course, that depends on how close they are, which I can't see . . .*

Wraithwing pulled sharply up and turned. Something wrenched at Jehal's harness, some irresistible force. He felt straps and ropes tauten and snap. Nothing had a grip on him though. He wasn't dead and he wasn't flying through the air. Some of the bindings that held him and Wraithwing together had broken. Some, but not all. He clung on even tighter.

"Faster!" He had mounted two men on the dragon behind him. Their job was to keep watch above and below and behind. If he'd been from the north, they would have had scorpions as well. *And will I be thinking how noble and pure we are to fly without them when a six-foot shaft tears me in two?* The riders behind him had had another job too. Jehal didn't dare lift his head to turn round in case the wind tore him out of his ruined harness. At a guess though, they'd served that other purpose. At a guess they weren't there anymore.

Where had Almiri's riders come from?

BURNING THE TAIYTAKEI SHIPS IN the harbor was one of the most satisfying things Meteroa had done in a very long time. It had an uncomplicated joy to it, the satisfaction of doing something with extreme thoroughness and yet without effort. He burned them to the waterline and stayed to watch them sink. The dragons had enjoyed it too. Something about ships rubbed dragons the wrong way. They'd liked playing with the sailors too, scooping the survivors out of the water, tossing them into the air and eating them. *That's what you get for trying to murder our queen. What were you thinking?*

That was the only fly left in the ointment but to Meteroa's mind it was a rather fat and ugly one. Why had the Taiytakei done what they'd done? This wasn't the first time dragons had flown out of Furymouth and burned the Taiytakei into the sea. They'd done it once before when the Taiytakei had tried to destroy the silk factories on Tyan's Peninsula, but that had been a couple of hundred years ago. When the Taiytakei had finally returned, it was to throw their lot in with King Tyan and his clan. They'd supplied the poison that Jehal had used to derange Hyram. They'd given him the magical dragons that he'd mostly used to spy on his lover. It was a tense arrangement at best, since everyone knew that what the Taiytakei really wanted were dragons and would do almost anything to get some, but it had served them well enough during Ayzalmir's purges.

But why try to kill Lystra? To frame Zafir and drive them apart? Even the Taiytakei must realize how unnecessary that was. Did they think it would somehow help Jehal to the throne? And even then, what did that achieve? No. No, there had to be another reason, something to do with getting hold of dragons. Dragons, hatchlings, eggs, everything. Someone had made them a promise. Someone they *believed.*

So he burned their ships, taking pleasure in it. For good measure he burned the harbor and the Taiytakei quarter of Furymouth while he was at it, and then when he landed, he sent the palace soldiers out to finish the job. A crime, really, to destroy part of his own city, but necessary. Whatever they were up to, he'd killed it; and that, for now, would have to do. Until this stupid business with Zafir was finished at least.

The next day, with smoke still rising from the blackened patch of Furymouth closest to the sea, Meteroa, Prince of Furymouth, flew north and then west. Taking the last few dragons away from his beloved city felt like undressing her and leaving her naked. Exposed. Vulnerable. It left a bad feeling in his gut which even destroying the Taiytakei hadn't cured. *Narghon's as good as family,* he reminded himself. *We're already going to war with Zafir and Silvallan. The Taiytakei are gone. Who else is there?* Even so, the feeling was still with him when he reached the Pinnacles. *Valmeyan. Sirion. The Syuss, even.* He couldn't shake the feeling that he'd never see his city again, not like she was.

Which was all the encouragement he needed to be on with his business quickly. It was dark when he reached the Pinnacles and circled the three immense spires of stone that ringed Zafir's city. A fortress was built on the top of each monolith, lit by fires. Battlements and caves riddled their sheer sides, little pinpricks of light. They were the oldest places in the realms. This was where the Silver King had come and where he'd died; where the dragons had been broken, where the blood-mages had risen to power and fallen again, where the Order of the Dragon had followed inexorably in their path. Narammed had lived here, and the first King of the Crags too. Legend said that the three mountains were filled with tunnels, stocked with enough food and with enough rooms keep the entire city safe for a year, that they were filled with ancient and arcane workings that even the alchemists were unable to fathom. This was where the Reflecting Garden stood, with its fountains that never ran dry and its pool of water whose surface wasn't flat. Far more than the City of Dragons or even the

Adamantine Palace or even the Glass Cathedral, the Pinnacles were the old heart of the realms, and only kings and their personal escorts were allowed to land on them; even then it was considered polite to ask first. Protocol.

Meteroa led his dragons toward them. Protocol could fuck itself.

ANOTHER WALL OF HEAT WASHED over him and then another. Jehal glanced up. The visor made him almost blind and so he took a chance and raised it for a moment. He was in the wrong place, separated from the bulk of his riders. At least they weren't in front of him, which meant either they were behind him or something very bad had happened. He didn't dare look back . . .

A thousand feet above the dark mounds of the Blackwind Dales, a thin blanket of morning cloud smothered the sky. Jehal and Zafir and the dragons had come to Evenspire from above it, from high out of the emptiness of the Desert of Stones. He'd been one of the first to punch through the cloud, falling toward the ground like an arrow. Wraithwing had pulled up and Jehal had watched the other dragons go. The sky was thick with them even now. Five hundred, mostly his and Zafir's. They were like a plague. Wherever they went they ate everything. The palace eyries had been stripped bare in a matter of days, their potions drunk dry and their herds of cattle gone. The plague had crossed the Purple Spur into the dry plains that sat between the Spur and Evenspire. There the dragons had spread out. They made their way foraging in little clusters, falling out of the sky onto the tiny scattered bands of outsiders who eked out their lives on the fringes of the desert. As far as Jehal knew, no one had had any particular desire to lay waste to the southern half of Almiri's realm, but that's what they'd done, more by accident than by design. Sated dragons fought harder than hungry ones.

No sign of Almiri. He'd held his position just below the cloud and signaled to his other riders to do the same. Almiri's dragons hadn't been waiting for them above the cloud and they weren't waiting here either. *Let Zafir burn the citadel.* Whoever won today, the city and the eyrie around it would burn to the ground, that was inevitable. He wondered briefly if Almiri had abandoned her stronghold and run off to hide with her sister. That would have been the best thing she could have done for her people. Then the first of Zafir's riders had been greeted by a volley of scorpions as they approached the walls. Jehal had watched as a single dragon spiraled toward the ground. A lucky shot on a hunter with only one rider.

Or maybe she hadn't, but where were her dragons? He'd looked around him, and it had occurred to him then that even if he saw them, how would he know? He didn't even know all his own beasts. And then there was Prince Loatan with sixty of King Narghon's dragons, and every single monster from Zafir's eyries. Silvallan had sent some seventy dragons under Princess Kalista and he knew none of them. There were so many. He'd sat there on Wraithwing's back, watching the palace below him burn, and wondered: *How would I know if I saw Almiri and her riders?* He'd watched as the last half-dozen dragons drifted lazily out of the cloud and veered toward him. *I don't have the first idea who they are. For all I know, those could be Almiri's riders. Prince Lai will be turning on his pyre.*

The riders had signaled, telling him to go down to join the attack on the ground. Zafir's dragons were almost there, converging on the cascading curtains of stone that were the Palace of Paths. As he'd watched, the first blasts of fire bloomed in front of them. He'd been so busy wondering how he'd know Almiri's dragons when he saw them that he didn't realize he was looking right at them until much too late. The six hunters. Still signaling, still coming toward him. Coming much too fast. He'd winced as he'd shouted at Wraithwing to dive and dive hard. And so it had begun . . .

Behind him he heard one of the hunters let out a series of shrieks and he suddenly knew exactly where Almiri's dragons had been. *They're not below the cloud and they're not above the cloud. They're in the cloud.*

On cue, three shapes dropped out of it in front of him.

Oh, very clever.

METEROA LANDED WITH THREE DRAGONS and a dozen riders on the largest of the three Pinnacles, the Fortress of Watchfulness. The people he was looking for might be here or they might be at the Palace of Pleasure on the second Pinnacle. He rather doubted that he'd find them on the third, in the Temple of Tranquillity. Soldiers came running out dragging scorpions behind them, rather too late to do any good.

If I'd planned to burn everything from the skies, that is. He snapped his fingers and his dragon lowered its head as any well-trained dragon should do. More dragons circled above, almost invisible in the night sky, little more than the occasional black silhouette blotting out a star. Meteroa climbed down from the dragon's back. He stroked its scales. *You don't like the dark, do you? But you'll still fly if I tell you to. Once we're done with you, you're not much different from dogs and horses, are you? Don't think I don't know what you'd be like if we didn't keep you docile. The alchemists are right to be afraid of you.*

He looked at the soldiers and the Scales and the pathetic collection of riders that had emerged to greet him. He didn't recognize a single face. Zafir had taken every rider who could fight away with her to Evenspire. *Which is going to make my life so much easier.*

"I am Prince Meteroa, brother to the late King Tyan. I am King Jehal's eyrie-master. We ride to war at the speaker's call. I require food and sustenance for my dragons and my riders and an audience with Prince Kazalain."

The riders shuffled uneasily. One of them stepped forward. Meteroa peered at him. The face wasn't familiar but his eyes were sharp. He was old and walked awkwardly, which was presumably why Zafir had left him behind. "In Queen Zafir's absence, Princess Kiam rules here," said the rider. He bowed as he spoke, but his eyes never left Meteroa's face.

"And will I find her here or in the Palace of Pleasure?"

The rider bowed again. "I do not know where you will find her, Your Highness, but it will not be here."

Meteroa threw up his hands in exaggerated exasperation. "Shall I spend the night searching for your errant princess? I have better things to do and my men are soldiers not errand boys. Is Prince Kazalain here?" *He'd better be.* "My words are for him, not some little girl."

"He's here, Your Highness," said the rider. He sounded reluctant.

"Well, then go and get him."

THERE WASN'T ANYWHERE ELSE FOR him to go. Jehal plunged down again, the force of Wraithwing's turn pitching him back with such force that he was surprised it didn't snap his spine. He screamed as something ripped and his injured leg was suddenly stabbing burning agony. He gestured frantically, hoping some of his riders would see and follow him toward the ground. *Principles* said that he should keep his riders high and simply sit there and take it from the dragons hidden in the clouds. *We need to be low enough to see them coming. Then we can fight them.* He brought the visor down again and trusted Wraithwing to level out safely above the city instead of smashing into the ground. Jehal was still gasping from the pain in his leg when Wraithwing spread out his wings again and he pitched forward. His eyes bulged and the world went red for a moment as his ribs were pushed flat. Then the feeling went. Dazed, he leaned forward and urged the dragon on, over the column of smoke and flames that had been the Palace of Paths. The wind battered at him. Whatever would burn was burning. The scorpions on the walls were gone, smashed to bits or sitting limp and idle, surrounded by the charred husks of the soldiers who had manned them. Most of Almiri's men would have fled down into the tunnels under the citadel; that was to be expected. Zafir wouldn't worry about that. Two thousand of the Adamantine Men were on the march to mop up the survivors and hold the citadel once Almiri had been burned out of it. *Once we're done with you.* But the soldiers wouldn't get here for days. Until then dragons would have to do.

He glimpsed Onyx, Zafir's war-dragon, circling low along the walls. Jehal could almost taste her delight as she swept arcs of fire about her as she went. He drove Wraithwing toward her and then into the plumes of smoke and into a cloud of a hundred circling dragons. With a bit of luck that would shake Almiri's riders off his tail. After he'd passed through, he started to climb back toward his own dragons. He took a deep breath, sat up, opened his visor and looked behind him. He was breathing hard. Everything hurt. He was ready to be sick. But at least he was still alive.

The hunters who'd been chasing him were gone. For a moment he was alone. He took a few breaths to let his racing heart slow. He was sweating, exhausted, and he hadn't even done anything yet except run away. Below him the rest of Zafir's dragons, the ones that weren't destroying the citadel, were loose over the city. There wasn't any pattern or order to what they were doing. They were hunters mostly, looking for any sign of Almiri and her soldiers. So far they hadn't set the city hopelessly ablaze, but that was surely only a matter of time. Jehal wondered for a fraction of a second whether the people who lived there had had any warning of what was to come. Probably not, he supposed.

He looked up again, turning Wraithwing back toward his own riders. And ducked as a dragon tail sliced the air barely yards away from his face.

"Vishmir's cock! What does it take?" He swore some more but these dragons weren't coming for him. They rained past him, another cluster of Almiri's hunters from the clouds, arrowing down toward the citadel. For a few seconds he was too stunned that he was still alive to think. Then he saw where they were going. They were aiming straight for Onyx.

Jehal watched in stupefied disbelief. Without thinking what he was doing, he turned Wraithwing and dived after them. He felt something that was almost panic. He wasn't going to catch them in time. And all the time a part of him was screaming, *Why are you chasing them? They're only doing exactly what you were going to do! Let them do it!* Except that wasn't what he wanted. He'd come to the battle with every intention of betraying Zafir and smashing her dragons to the ground as soon as the battle was won. *And now Almiri's doing it for me, and I'm trying to save her. What sort of idiot does that make me?*

He pulled Wraithwing up. The hunters were far too far ahead. They'd fallen like stones all the way from the clouds and he had no chance of catching them. All he could do was watch.

EVENTUALLY PRINCE KAZALAIN APPEARED. Meteroa almost didn't recognize him. He looked old and broken. He tried to smile, but his face struggled as if he'd forgotten how.

"Prince Meteroa." The usual disgust wasn't there. Kazalain only looked sad.

"I'm just an eyrie-master, Your Highness. You look terrible. The months since King Jehal's wedding have not been kind to you. You look ten years older." Meteroa reached out a hand. "I'm sorry for your loss."

Kazalain spat. "No, you're not, Prince Meteroa. You hardly knew my son Sakabian. He was foolish, but he didn't deserve to hang in a cage over the speaker's gates."

"Neither did Queen Shezira or King Valgar for that matter, but little things like that don't seem to bother your queen."

"Mind your tongue."

"Why? Will you cut it out because I say that your son's death was unjust?"

"You should not be here, and you should not be saying these things." Kazalain turned away. "Be gone!"

"I require food and sustenance for my dragons and my riders, Kazalain. We are going to war."

Kazalain waved vaguely at the city below. "At the city eyrie, Meteroa. You know that. Don't ask the alchemists for any of their potions though. They barely have enough to feed the hatchlings. We have none to spare."

"You still have your other sons. You should not forget them. Vishmir and Lai, isn't it? Named after the shining lights of Furymouth's past. Good names. Are they here?"

"Of course they're here. You think I'd let them stray from me after what our queen did to Sakabian?" He stopped and turned back again. "Why do you ask?" Something in Meteroa's tone must have caught his attention. *I'll have to pay more attention to that sort of thing.*

"You could wonder about that. Or you could wonder about the fact that I'm dressed in dragon-scale while you and your soldiers are not, eh?" He gave Kazalain an instant to understand what was about to happen and then dropped to one knee and flicked his fire visor closed.

Fire poured from the dragons behind him. The force of it plucked him right off the ground and threw him ten feet forward. The noise left his ears ringing. When he got up, he staggered. If any of Kazalain's soldiers were still alive, they could have killed him as easily as killing a child.

Well I won't be doing that again. Meteroa lifted up his visor. The soldiers and Kazalain were all dead, burned to the bone. Meteroa knelt down beside Kazalain and patted what was left of his head. Charred bits fell off in his hand.

"I wouldn't want any heirs escaping to make a nuisance of themselves, that's why." He gave the dead prince a wan smile. "I'll be kinder to them than Zafir was to Sakabian. At least I can promise you that. Their deaths will be as quick and painless as yours."

He took his time. A few riders stayed on the backs of their dragons to keep watch. Others moved methodically through the eyrie, rounding up the Scales and the alchemists and anyone too stupid to run into the stone embrace of the fortress. Most of the rest raced down into the depths of the Pinnacles. That was the trick with this place. Get in fast and deep before they even knew you were here. Otherwise they could simply shut you out. As long as he stopped them from doing that, the rest could wait until he'd had time to bring soldiers up from Furymouth. Jehal had sent a couple of hundred cavalry, who would arrive in a few days. The remainder would have to march on foot. *But I have time. Either Jehal has succeeded or he's dead, and if he's dead I might wish I hadn't burned all those Taiytakei ships yesterday morning.*

When he was done he mounted up and took to the air again. His riders knew what to do. Most stayed to hold the eyrie, but a few joined him back in the air. As they circled down, fire bloomed around the edge of the city below. *There go the whores and all the riders who were lying with them. Never much cared for their kind.* To get himself in the mood, he flew over the flames and through the smoke. The smell of it set his blood pumping, even more than burning the Taiytakei had done. There was something primal about dragon-fire, something that tore off the thin mask of order that governed the realms and exposed the raw chaos lurking beneath. *And once in a while we let the madness out to wreak its havoc, and then we carefully put it away again, locked up until the next time.*

A dozen of his dragons had already landed in the city eyrie. Zafir had taken almost all her dragon-knights north to fight Almiri. Seizing her city was turning out to be even easier than Meteroa had thought it would be. He circled the second of the Pinnacles, the Palace of Pleasure, urging his dragons up around the sheer face of the rock. Here and there he caught sight of windows, of little platforms, of tiny passageways carved into the cliffs, given away by the firelight that shone from within. Every one he saw, he burned. He didn't have the men to even try to hold another of the three Pinnacles, so a different approach would have to suffice.

When they finally reached the top, a thousand feet above the plains below, a handful of soldiers and half a dozen scorpions were waiting for him. Or maybe it was more; in the darkness, Meteroa couldn't see them, but nor could they see him. He heard them shouting and he heard the sounds of the scorpions firing. He had no idea whether they'd hit anything or whether they'd even come close. Then his dragons enveloped the entire palace in flames. Meteroa had to put his visor down simply to block out the glare. When it faded, there were no more shouts and no more scorpions, only screams. When even those stopped, Meteroa landed.

"Right!" he shouted for the benefit of anyone who was listening. "Message for Princess Kiam. Your uncle's dead. You've got one hour to surrender yourself before I set fire to your sister's city."

With that, he settled back to wait.

ZAFIR COULDN'T HAVE EVEN SEEN Almiri's dragons coming. The six of them fell out of the air straight at Onyx. Two of them smashed into him and glanced off, somersaulting through the air and almost crashing into the ruined palace below. Onyx lurched toward the ground. A third hunter plowed into him, ripping the scorpioneer off his back. The fourth crushed his other riders and finally forced him to land. The fifth and then the sixth landed on top of him before he could move. Zafir's dragons were onto them in seconds, but they were far too late. By then everyone on the black dragon's back had been ripped to pieces.

Jehal threw back his head and screamed, "*I* had to do that. Me! She was *mine!*" He tore down again, chasing after the hunters that had killed Zafir. They were trying to scatter but Zafir's war-dragons were already there. By the time Wraithwing arrived there wouldn't be anything left but scraps. *Too late. The damage is done. Almiri wins . . . But now there are seven riderless dragons sitting on the ground, waiting to be taken.*

For the second time he pulled Wraithwing up short and started to climb again. For all his rage, Almiri's riders had done him a favor. *After all, isn't that exactly what I wanted? And now I don't have to do it myself. I don't have to find out what it would have felt like to watch Wraithwing rip her to pieces right in front of me.*

Or, if you looked at what had happened in a different way, Almiri had made him look hopelessly incompetent. He had some two hundred dragons circling below the clouds to stop exactly this from happening and they'd failed. *And how do I retort? Do I say that I didn't give a shit what Almiri did to Zafir, since that just spared me the trouble of doing it myself? Ancestors! I couldn't even protect myself. But how did Almiri know where to strike, and when?*

He looked up at his dragons, still circling aimlessly, still waiting for orders. *How many does Almiri have left? Sixty? Seventy? And then the dragons she took from Prince Sakabian. Less than a hundred. She'd be mad to launch herself at us now. She's done as much damage as she could hope for. Zafir is dead. The speaker. The war is over, even if the battle still rages. She should know that. There's nothing more she can do.*

If he pretended for a moment that Almiri didn't exist then there really wasn't much point waiting around any longer. Zafir's riders must have taken the citadel by now. They'd be landing, mopping up any survivors too stupid to hide in the deep tunnels. They'd be wondering what on earth to do next. He took a deep breath.

Almiri has done my work for me. I could leave quietly. Return to the Adamantine Palace. Return to Furymouth. There would be a council of kings and queens to choose Zafir's successor. It's hard to see who it would be. Sirion, perhaps? Narghon? Silvallan? Not me though. They won't choose me. Not like this. No speaker's throne for dithering King Jehal.

And that, in the end, was the whole reason he was here. He reached his dragons and signaled. It was what they'd been waiting for. Almost as one, they turned and dived toward the ground to smash the remnants of Zafir's reign to pieces.

46

THE RED PRINCE

High above the cloud where the dry desert air was thin and the sky was so blue that it hurt his eyes, Prince Hyrkallan flew. *Prince* Hyrkallan now and soon to be king. He understood why Queen Jaslyn had offered herself to him—she needed him simply to survive. He understood, but it didn't matter. He'd given himself a single day to consider her proposition, what it would mean to accept and what it would mean to reject her. In the end the decision was easy. If he turned his back on her, the realm would fall apart. Jaslyn would fall, a hundred pretenders to the throne of Sand and Stone would crawl out from their holes. There would be blood and chaos, and all the while Speaker Zafir would be laughing at them.

No, he had only one choice and so he committed himself to it with all his heart and vowed to make Jaslyn into a queen to make her mother proud. So while Jaslyn remained closeted away in her eyrie, he'd flown, in person and in secret, to King Sirion. He'd gone with almost nothing to offer, yet Sirion had listened, and when Hyrkallan had finished, King Sirion had nodded. They would go to war together.

"Why?" Hyrkallan had asked, and Sirion had shaken his head.

"Because of the Red Riders. Because you knew what was right." And then he'd done the strangest thing. He'd bowed and taken Hyrkallan's hand. "Shezira should have followed Hyram but she's dead. Now it will be you."

All that was before they'd slipped into the City of Dragons and the Night Watchman had almost begged them to overthrow Zafir. Another man might have felt the hand of destiny resting lightly on his shoulder. To Hyrkallan, it was all simply justice. Justice and Vengeance, exactly as he'd promised.

He looked around behind him. Nearly four hundred dragons. Not as many as Zafir would have and so he'd planned his attack with care. Almiri didn't know he was coming. There would be no pitched battle to save Evenspire from the flames. The city would be sacrificed. Then, as Zafir reveled in her victory, he would fall out of the skies on her and crush her.

Far above the cloud, where the air was thin and the sky was so blue that it hurt his eyes, Prince Hyrkallan felt a deep sense of calm as he signaled his dragons down. They'd flown as high as they had in the hope of evading any eyes that Zafir had left to keep watch; now they fell at such speed that the wind ripped the air out of their lungs. All Hyrkallan could see was cloud, but the dragons knew. They had an instinct for where things were, as though they could sense their own kind, and knew they were coming for a fight. Hyrkallan could feel it from them—the tension, the anticipation, the hunger, the joy.

Four hundred dragons plunged into the cold damp cloud and disappeared. Seconds later they burst out directly over Evenspire.

WRAITHWING BANKED AND TWISTED, spraying fire at one of Zafir's riders who hadn't had the sense to run away. Jehal caught a glimpse of another cluster of dragons racing toward him, but before he could even start to see whose they were, Wraithwing shot through a cloud of smoke and he couldn't see anything. When his eyes cleared, those dragons were gone. Another dragon, one of Zafir's, raced overhead with two of Jehal's riders in pursuit. Below, the city was burning now, burning with a vengeance.

Once again I haven't the first idea what's going on. Are all dragon-fights like this? Principles made them sound like a carefully choreographed dance where the winner was decided before the contest even began. Not this. This was anarchy. Madness! For a moment, Jehal found himself wondering whether Prince Lai had ever actually fought in the War of Thorns or whether he'd just watched it all, scratching his chin. He dragged Wraith-wing higher above the city. At least from a thousand feet, just below the cloud, he could see what was happening. *And what use is that? I can see lots of dragons chasing each other. I don't know which ones are mine and which are Zafir's. They disappear in and out of clouds and plumes of smoke with such speed that I couldn't follow them even if I tried. I can see a good few dragons fleeing the battle. I assume that they're Zafir's and that we're winning, but I don't even know that for sure. Ancestors! How embarrassing would that be? To loiter up here feeling all smug and sure of myself only to discover that all my riders have run away and Zafir has won even though she's dead. I suppose I could try and signal some orders. Or I could get Wraithwing to shriek them out, but what use would that be? Apart from the twenty dragons circling in overwatch, who would actually see or hear me?*

There were some things in *Principles,* right at the start, that he'd have to look at. Things about the preparations to be made before a battle. When this was done, he'd have to read that bit again.

Enough of this. He signaled to the riders on overwatch to follow him and thundered back down toward Almiri's citadel. *At least she's had the sense to go away, now she's done what she's done. Or is she still up there in the cloud, lurking and watching? You know what, when I'm done here, I'm going to go away. You can have your city and your palace back again. What's left of them.*

If he thought the fighting over the city was chaos, the scenes in the citadel made him dizzy. Even before Wraithwing landed, the heat of the fires penetrated his armor. The smoke burned his throat and the air was so hot that it hurt to breathe. His visor didn't help; using it just meant that he couldn't see anything at all, as opposed to getting fleeting glimpses of things through the occasional gap in the smoke. He took his helmet off, wiped the tears from his eyes and waved at his other riders as they came in to land.

"Dragons!" he shouted. "Get the dragons." Almiri's hunters were still perched around the citadel, moping near the bodies of their riders or what was left of them. The fire didn't seem to trouble them, but even if it did they'd only sit there and howl until someone came to take them away.

That's what we train them to do. Stupid. You'd have thought they'd know to give up when all that's left of their rider is half a charred arm.

"Dragons!" he shouted again. "Get the dragons and get them out of here." He waved his riders closer. Dragon cries were drowning his words. "Can you hear me?"

He had to practically shout in their ears, one at a time, to make himself understood. "Get the dragons. Any dragon you see. Get it back in the air. Get everyone else back into the sky. I've had enough of this. Tell them to take what spoils they can and leave! Get Onyx." He had to point. "The big black one. Through the smoke that way. Get Zafir's dragon." As an afterthought, he limped after the two riders he'd sent for Onyx. There was always a chance that he might find Zafir's body. The more proof he had that she was dead, the easier the rest of this was going to be.

He didn't even get halfway there before a subtle change in the dragon cries around him made him look up.

The sky was raining dragons again. White ones! Hundreds of them.

B'THANNAN PULLED OUT OF HIS DIVE; Hyrkallan lifted his visor and there was the ground, a thousand feet below. Evenspire was burning and there was no dragon overwatch. And as he looked, he slowly understood what he was seeing: Jehal and Zafir were fighting over the spoils. A warmth blossomed inside him. He wanted to shout for joy, and even, maybe, believe in that hand of destiny after all.

"Remember me?" he roared into the wind. "The whole fucking horde of the north with me, five hundred dragons and fifty thousand men. That was my promise!"

And as the dragons of the north rained from the clouds he waved them on toward the ground to grind his enemies to pieces. Unlike Jehal, Hyrkallan knew exactly which were his dragons. His dragons had their bellies painted white and his riders wore red.

"OH SHIT! GET UP! GET UP and get out!" Jehal screamed at his riders, urging them into the air. *Could I be in a worse place? Yes, I suppose I could be lying spread-eagled in a field with a big sign reading "Please burn me" hanging over my head. Other than that, it's hard to see . . .* He wasn't going to reach Wraithwing before the northern dragons reached the ground, so he didn't try; instead he hid behind a wall until he saw a white-painted dragon shoot overhead. *At least I know exactly how difficult it is to see anything down here.* A shift in the wind blew smoke over him. He took the opportunity to hobble across the open to where Wraithwing was waiting, cursing his ruined leg. The noise was deafening, dragons howling, everything burning. He caught a glimpse of Onyx launching into the air, little more than a large black shape in the shifting smoke.

"Let me on, let me on!" Jehal waved frantically. Wraithwing knew he was there, Jehal could see that, but the dragon was very slow to move. He seemed almost stunned, dazed and dopey but somehow blissfully happy. *I must be imagining that bit, but I'd really appreciate it if you'd bother to actually open your eyes.*

Wraithwing lowered his head. Jehal grabbed hold of the dangling rope ladder and hauled himself onto Wraithwing's back, strapping himself into what was left of his harness. "Up! Up!" *Shit. And I thought it was already madness.* Wraithwing powered into the sky. With no one to look out for him, Jehal's head twitched from side to side, up and down, searching for the next dragon that would try to kill him. *At least painting their dragons white means I know which ones those are likely to be. Except for any of Zafir's riders who haven't had the sense to run away—let's not forget them just yet.* He wondered briefly who was up there. *Sirion. Jaslyn. Hyrkallan. All of them, most likely. Which one of them is leading the charge?* That thought made him shudder. *Lystra's bloodthirsty sister, most likely.*

He urged Wraithwing across the city as fast as he could, shrieking and waving the retreat, calling to his riders to gather around him and flee. *Safer just to run away on my own, but then what?* He caught another glimpse of Onyx and veered toward the black monster. *I need you. I need you with me to show that Zafir is dead.* White-painted dragons were swirling toward Onyx as well. Jehal had maybe a hundred of his own around him. *Half of what I came with. Ancestors, but I hope that's not all there is. And of course every one that I lose is one that the north gains. Maybe they'll fall out with each other just like we did. They won't, but imagining it will make me feel better about this later.* There would be others, other survivors. There always were. *Principles* told him that he could expect to see maybe half as many again trickle their way back to him.

Time to leave. Wraithwing powered up toward the cloud. The painted dragons nibbled at the edges of Jehal's formation, happy to keep him in one place while they mopped up the remnants still flashing across the burning city. Then suddenly they were in the cloud, and even with his visor up, Jehal could barely see the dragons flying next to him. Not that it made much difference. The wind would blind him anyway. He closed the visor. Riders hated clouds. Clouds ruined formations. You never knew what was on the other side. Even the very air itself was funny inside a cloud. *Principles,* for example, gave dire warnings about flying in clouds. *Principles,* Jehal decided, could go fuck itself. Formations were for dragons flying to battle, not ones flying away from it. If Jehal couldn't see any other dragons then no other dragons could see him. What couldn't see him wouldn't try to eat him, and that was quite good enough. The dragons themselves didn't seem to mind at all. They always managed to stay together, as though they could sense each other. Jehal had no idea how they did it. As far as he knew, nor did anyone else.

A few very long seconds later he heard a dragon shriek. Three short cries. His own riders, signaling that the danger was over. The cry was echoed over and over. In the strange air of the cloud the calls sounded dull and flat. He took a deep breath and let Wraithwing guide himself south. Toward the Silver River and the Great Cliff and the Purple Spur and home. *Is this as bad as it seems? What did I come here to do? I came to destroy Zafir and Zafir is no more. So is this victory? I came to take her dragons and there I've largely failed. Does that matter? I've taken some of hers and lost some of my own, and if I'm lucky I'll leave with as many as I brought. Maybe even more. So, greed aside, and ignoring the little inconvenience of fleeing from the battle with my tail between my legs, this is mostly the outcome I was looking for, right? So not that bad, right?*

He sniffed at his own stupidity. *Yes yes. You keep thinking that, King Jehal. Maybe if you quietly gloss over the bit where you got beaten and humiliated, everyone else will gloss over it too. Or maybe you should start thinking about what exactly you're going to do that's going to stop Queen Jaslyn from hanging you in a cage beside the bones of her mother. Because if there's one thing you can be sure of now, it's that the Queen of Stone is coming.*

AFTER AN HOUR HYRKALLAN CALLED an end to the pursuit. The cloud made it impossible to know where Jehal really was. His dragons would be scattered. They might emerge from the cloud anywhere. If there was any fighting at all, it would be scattered little skirmishes, nothing more. If Hyrkallan was lucky, Jehal and Zafir were both dead. If they weren't, the north had cause enough to strip Zafir of her office.

And now, at last, the power to do it. It was tempting to fly straight on, to cross the Purple Spur and put an end to Zafir and her riders once and for all. To do it right now. He might even have done it, except the defeated dragons wouldn't be the only ones waiting for him. *Fight your wars in the skies if you must, but do not bring them here or you will find that I have other names, and one of them I wear for war.* The words of the Night Watchman, the Scorpion King.

No. No need for that. No need for more. No need to risk turning this victory into a defeat.

Besides, he had other matters to attend to. Rounding up a hundred new dragons, the ones Zafir and Jehal had left behind as they fled.

When all that was done, he landed B'thannan on the outskirts of the city and sniffed the air. Smoke. Even upwind of the flames, the air reeked of it. Evenspire was dead. In a few days, when the fires were out and the wind next came out of the mountains, it would lift up the ashes and carry them away to the desert. Everyone who saw would remember how the Blackwind Dales earned their name, but by then Hyrkallan would be gone, away to drag Queen Jaslyn from her dragons and put an end to whatever it was she was doing out in Outwatch.

And then, Vale Tassan, I will come, and we will see how stubborn you are prepared to be.

47

❧❦❧

THE ADAMANTINE PALACE

Vale stood on top of the Gatehouse and watched the dragons land.
Jeiros was beside him.

"Do you have enough potion to feed them, Master Alche-
mist?" He watched Jeiros' face, and knew the answer before the alchemist
even opened his mouth. No.

"It will be a challenge, Night Watchman."

"It will, won't it?"

"The Red Riders, the damage done at the redoubt, so many dragons
flying to war. Zafir asks more than I can give. I will have to take supplies
from her and from King Silvallan. King Jehal too, perhaps. From Evenspire, if there is anything left of it." The alchemist sighed. "It's becoming
more of a problem than you would care to know, Night Watchman. But I
will keep our speaker's dragons flying no matter what I have to do."

Vale laughed. "There don't seem to be many of our speaker's dragons
left. I haven't been counting, but I'd say this is a third of the number that
left. Unless I'm mistaken, most of them are King Jehal's."

"Onyx is there."

"Yes." *The speaker's dragon. Maybe another couple of dozen of Zafir's. A
few dragons I don't recognize at all. And all the rest are Jehal's. And I have
been counting. More than a hundred dragons lost? Someone's been very careless. I fear a veritable forest of cages.*

The first riders were galloping up the hill from the landing fields as if

372

they were still being chased. Vale wanted to laugh at them. *You lost, didn't you? Sirion and Hyrkallan were waiting for you and you lost.* He nudged Jeiros. "If I were you, Grand Master, I would keep very much out of the way for the next few days. I don't think our speaker has had a good week." He walked briskly to the stairs. With Jeiros safely behind him and no one watching, he permitted the grin that he'd been wearing on the inside to show itself on the outside. He wore it for exactly as long as it took him to reach the bottom of the stairs. In the Gateyard outside, Adamantine Men were already forming up to greet their speaker on her return. *Only a few of them though. Not enough that I might be accused of weakening the walls.* Vale looked them up and down until he was sure they were perfect and then stood at their head and waited. The palace gates opened and a few dragon-knights rode in. They looked beaten. *You can see it in their eyes, in the way they carry themselves. You lost and you lost badly.*

Zafir wasn't with them. What he got was King Jehal. Vale bowed. *Pity. I rather hoped you wouldn't come back.*

"Zafir is dead," said Jehal brusquely. He looked as though he was in a lot of pain, sitting up on the back of his horse. Two of his riders helped him to dismount and he nearly collapsed. Even standing still he had to lean heavily on his staff. Vale watched him struggle. He kept carefully silent. *I did that to him. We will both remember that.*

"The speaker is dead," said Jehal, this time making it sound more of a declaration than a confession. "We met in battle over Evenspire. We fought and I won, and by right of conquest I claim the speaker's throne until there can be a council of kings and queens to choose a successor. I call for such a council." Jehal finally locked eyes with Vale. "Night Watchman, that means you. Get Jeiros and Aruch and anyone else who needs to hear my claim. I'll gladly repeat it once. After that I shall become annoyed. I will retire to the Tower of Dusk for now but I expect the Speaker's Tower to be ready for me in two days. Am I understood?"

Vale bowed again. He took a step to the side and turned, a little ritual to acknowledge that whoever stood at the palace gates was welcome to enter. *As though you were her husband—I have not forgotten.* He waited until Jehal was level with him.

"Is there a body, Your Holiness?" he asked.

Jehal stopped. He whipped around to glare at Vale. "She was ripped to pieces and eaten."

"The Lesser Council will convene to hear your claim, Your Holiness. They will ask."

"I have her dragon, Tassan. That's all that's left of her."

"You don't have the Speaker's Ring then? Do you have her spear at least?"

"She was flying to war, Night Watchman; she left that here. Why don't you get it for me?"

Vale was careful not to smile. He bowed his head. "I will call the Lesser Council, Your Holiness. I shall ask them to convene tomorrow at dawn. May I ask what became of Evenspire? And of the treacherous Queen Almiri? They will ask that too."

"Evenspire lies in ashes, Night Watchman, and you can request they convene sooner than that. As for Almiri, she was no traitor and I have no idea if she's dead. If it amuses you, I shall guess and say she is still alive."

Vale bowed. "As you command, Your Holiness. The Lesser Council may ask for more evidence than your word and a dragon, but I shall convey your words." *Arrogant prick. Do you really think I'm going to let you have Zafir's throne? You, of all people?* He watched Jehal limp slowly across the Gateyard toward the Tower of Dusk. At least at the speed he now moved, the servants there would have plenty of time to get ready for him. When Jehal was gone he sent his soldiers back to their duties and then went looking for Jeiros. The alchemist was where he'd left him, still standing on top of the Gatehouse. Vale settled beside him, watching the dragons at the palace eyries.

"The little shit wants us to make him speaker." He watched Jeiros' face carefully. The alchemist did well. He blinked a few times, that was all.

"Zafir is dead then?"

"So he says. He says he fought her himself and demands her throne by right of conquest until a full council can be called."

"He knows his history."

"He knows his *Principles*. I don't think he knows much of anything else, and the best I can think of to do with *Principles* is to wipe my arse with it."

The alchemist shrugged. "There is a precedent. The realms need a speaker."

Vale spat. "He can't even prove that Zafir is dead. He's got her dragon. He doesn't have her ring."

"The spear?"

"He says she left it here."

Jeiros turned toward Vale and frowned. "Does he? I thought so too, but it's not here. It should be in the Chamber of Audience but it's not. I assumed Zafir took it with her."

"He wants me to call the Lesser Council."

"Which means you and me."

"And Aruch, who will do what you tell him." Vale permitted himself a smile. "Your choice, Grand Master. Who's it going to be?"

"What would you do, Vale?"

"Me?" Vale laughed. "I might thank him for ridding us of Zafir, but I'd still hang him in one of her cages outside the gates. Frankly I'd hang them both. Evenspire burns, he says. A city full of people set to flames and for what? Yes, if it was me I'd craft a cage for him with my own hands. But then I'm not entitled to an opinion, I'm just a servant."

Jeiros pursed his lips. Vale could see a lot of thinking going on. "The realms need a speaker, Vale. The battle went badly, even I can see that. He has Zafir's dragon. Some will say that is proof enough. If we refuse him, what then? We stand alone against every realm and that is not our duty; our duty is to keep the realms' dragons in check. Yet as you said, Vale, when a dragon burns you, it makes little difference whether it has a rider on their back as it does so; the flames are still the same. This war must end now. Jehal was trying to do that. That's why Zafir put him in the Tower of Dusk. No, I will not stand in his way. I dare say he will not survive a vote from the full council when one can finally be called. Until then, any speaker is better than none."

"Even the Viper?"

"Even the devil, Night Watchman."

Vale shrugged. "Then I will bow to your wisdom, Master Jeiros. The next time you stand here, you may be able to see me in one of those cages out there."

"Jehal needs you. I will not allow it."

"But he will be speaker. He will not need our opinions."

Jeiros cocked his head. "I think in these unusual times he might find that he does. See it this way, Vale. See him as ours. The speaker is always as much a servant of the realms as you or I."

"I somehow doubt King Jehal will agree."

"Then we will make him. Besides, however much we may wish for it, we cannot be sure that Speaker Zafir is dead. If she was eaten in battle we may not be sure for a very long time. I think King Jehal can merely *act* as a speaker under our guidance until we are. There are precedents here too."

The Night Watchman laughed. "Until some dragon shits out the Adamantine Spear? You've come a long way, Grand Master."

"I wonder sometimes if the realms wouldn't be better off without dragons. If I knew of a way we could rid ourselves of them, I think I would do it. But we can't. They always come back."

"So Jehal gets what he wants."

"Under sufferance, Vale. But yes, for now he does. I see no other choice."

One false move, Viper, and nothing will save you. Vale smiled to himself. "If you find that you do *not* have enough potion and it is necessary to poison a few of them to keep their numbers down, I will do nothing to stand in your way. I thought you might want to know that."

JEHAL LAY ON HIS BED in the Tower of Dusk. His sickbed, where Jeiros had tended to his wound. He stared at the ceiling. *This is the last time. I will never lie here again. Tomorrow I will be in the Speaker's Tower or I will be dead.* He wondered idly whether he had enough riders to seize the palace by force. *Probably not. Which means I am in the hands of Jeiros and the Night Watchman, and I know that at least one of them despises me.*

The realms need a speaker. *Principles* opened with those words.

One of the palace servants knocked on his door and slipped inside. The girl bowed so low that her face almost scraped the floor. "Grand Master Jeiros, Your Holiness."

So now we shall find out. "Send him in."

The girl left. After a few seconds the alchemist came in. Jehal sat up in his bed. "Have you come to dress my wound again, Master Jeiros?"

"It is the realms who are wounded, King Jehal. Will you dress that wound? Will you bring us peace?"

"I will do my best, Grand Master."

Jeiros bowed his head. "You should know that we cannot name you speaker until Zafir has been proven to be dead."

"She was eaten by a dragon, Master Jeiros."

"Yes, Your Holiness, and there are precedents for this. If Zafir does not set foot within the Adamantine Palace within the next one hundred and one days, the Lesser Council will recognize that she is dead. On that day I will summon the kings and queens of the nine realms to name another. I cannot promise it will be you."

"Then I have a hundred days to prove I am worthy, do I?"

The alchemist looked up and met his eye. "Yes, Your Holiness. That would seem to be the case. Tomorrow the Lesser Council will name you speaker for a hundred days. I have nothing to offer you as a sign of your office. No ring, no spear."

The Adamantine Spear. *One day you'll probably try to take it and find that I got there first.* The blood-mage. *That's* what he'd wanted.

"Zafir did not have the spear with her, Jeiros." *And he never even came for his gold. I wonder why.*

"It is a symbol, Your Holiness. Its powers are a myth."

"Really?" *Let it go. It's really not that important to you.*

"We will make another." The alchemist reached out a hand and offered something to Jehal. A letter. "This came for you while you were at war. A dragon from the Pinnacles."

The writing and the seal were Meteroa's. *So he's taken the Pinnacles. Zafir's reign is truly over. The War of Thorns finally ends.*

Jeiros turned to go. "I have argued with Vale for you. Your feud ends here. I need you both to understand that."

Jehal gave him a wry smile. "Do you give orders to all your speakers?"

"No. Nor do I bring them all back from the brink of death."

Except you didn't. That was the blood-mage. For reasons that I find ever more troubling. Jehal sighed. "The realms need a speaker and I am available. I understand, Master Jeiros. I will try not to disappoint you."

"If you do, Vale has a cage waiting for you." The alchemist smiled weakly. "I have some faith in you, King Jehal. I hope you prove me right."

"Well I'll see what I can do." Jehal snorted and shook his head. "I had an ambition to be speaker once. Being your puppet isn't quite what I had in mind." He curled his lip. "Do one small thing for me, Grand Master. Zafir did not take your precious spear to war with her. It's been stolen by a blood-mage. His name is Kithyr. Find him. Bring him back." He chuckled. "But don't tell him I sent you. Apparently he'll kill me." He sighed and waved Jeiros away. A hundred and one days. *Lystra will make peace with the north for me long before then. And then we shall see.* He opened Meteroa's letter.

The end of Zafir's line as near as I can manage it. The Pinnacles are mine. Kazalain is dead and so are his sons. Say the word and Princess Kiam can follow them. Not that that'll help. The trouble with royal families is that everyone is always related to everyone else. No matter what you do, it's never the end of any bloodline. That's the whole point, isn't it? Not unless you kill absolutely everyone. Although as I look around at the carnage in the throne room here, at the two dead princes who were barely more than children, I will concede that extinguishing us all might be a very fine thing.

Your father once said that only a madman took his wife to war on the eve of giving birth. Lystra's your wife though, not mine, so perhaps I'm not so mad after all. She is safe and has celebrated our victory by giving you a son. She asks what his name should be.

Jehal stretched, trying to ease the cricks in his back, chewing on Dreamleaf to numb the pain in his leg. He read the letter again, and then a third time. When he started for the fourth, it occurred to him that he wasn't actually reading the words anymore and that he had a stupid grin plastered all over his face.

I am the speaker.

I have a son.

I win.

Again.

48

THE SPEAKER OF THE REALMS

Zafir stood on the ramparts looking out over Furymouth. Behind her, parts of Jehal's palace were burning. She stared out at the sea. There were Taiytakei ships out there. Hundreds of them. They'd simply appeared in the night, lurking out to sea, asking to be burned. She mulled the thought over, but whatever she might have wanted, there was little she could do. She'd gone to Evenspire with two hundred dragons. Now she had exactly one. Sometimes she wished she'd ignored Tichane. Ignored the blood-mage. Ignored the Night Watchman. Ignored herself. Sometimes she wished she'd ignored them all and believed that Jehal was hers and ridden her Onyx to Evenspire and died before she could know she was wrong.

Her fists were clenched so tight they were starting to hurt. With a few deep breaths she forced herself to relax. She couldn't say she hadn't seen it coming, but it made her want to scream.

A rider appeared at her side. He took her hand and touched it to his lips.

"I am sorry, Your Holiness. Queen Lystra is not here."

She pulled her hand away. "Then he took her with him, Prince Tichane. Yes, and now she's at the Adamantine Palace. She'll be sitting on my throne. My palace. My soldiers. My throne. My everything. They'll be fucking in my bed, if Jehal can still fuck at all." She cracked a grim smile. At least that was one little thing she could savor, when she wasn't grinding her teeth.

"No," whispered Prince Tichane. "She went with his uncle. We will trap them both in the Pinnacles." He was so close that she could feel his breath on her hair. There was no doubting what he wanted.

She stepped away, hiding a shiver of revulsion. "I want him dead. I want *her* in chains at my feet. Let them quiver in their beds at night!"

"She will not escape. When my father has finished smashing King Narghon's eyries into little pieces, the south will be ours. And when he knows you didn't die at Evenspire, the Night Watchman will fall over himself to put the Viper in chains. It will all be ours in a stroke." He moved beside her again and slipped a hand around her waist and across her belly, spreading his fingers wide, pressing himself against her. This time she leaned into him and purred. He was no Jehal, but he was every bit as easy to use. And Valmeyan did have a lot of dragons.

"I want that mongrel who's sitting on my throne in the Pinnacles dead. I want the rest of them hanging in cages where I can watch them die for days. I want a blood-mage so I can keep them alive forever and wake up every morning to listen to their pain as I break my fast. Promise me."

"I promise. You'll have your palace back and I will make you an empress. There will be no one to stop us."

She smiled. "No one." *Oh, Lystra, Lystra, if there's a cage for anyone . . .* She put her hand over his and sighed.

EPILOGUE—THE GREAT FLAME

Rider Semian clenched his fists. "This isn't how it was supposed to be!" he screamed. "I was supposed to serve the Great Flame! I have a *destiny*! Damn you all!"

He was standing on the top of one the taller peaks of the Worldspine. It would have been easy to circle even higher on Vengeance's back, but he needed the stillness, the quiet, the calm of being alone. He'd landed the dragon as close as he could and then he'd climbed, damaged leg and all, through the snow and the ice, still wrapped in his dragon-scale armor and his riding furs. He'd almost had to claw his way up at the end. But he had prevailed. He stood on top of the world, in the still quiet air, in a cold so bitter that it seemed to freeze his words to his lips. There wasn't even a breath of wind. Despite conquering them, the mountains and the Worldspine scorned him with their silence. Prince Jehal had broken him. His Red Riders were destroyed. And that was how it was going to end, in a battle too small to even have a name? "I have a destiny!" he screamed again. Unless the Great Flame had chosen a new champion. Unless he was discarded, old and used up and no good for anything anymore. Had he done what he was sent to do? Had the Red Riders served their purpose?

No. That couldn't be. He'd drunk the dragon-venom. He was chosen.

Standing alone so high gave him clarity. There was no need to be angry. Perhaps the Red Riders *had* served their purpose. Perhaps he alone was meant for other things. He didn't know what his new destiny would be, but did that matter so much? War was coming. Men and dragons, eyries and castles and cities and palaces, all of them would burn. A whole generation of men would die. The Great Flame would be served well.

Yes.

Semian started. The word had come into his head, but it wasn't his. He fell to his knees and almost wept for joy. *That* was why he'd climbed all the way up here. To hear the voice of the Great Flame itself.

I remember you.

"Yes. Yes, remember me. And in return, I will serve you." He looked about in case the red priest had come to him, but there was nothing but stillness and empty space and mountains.

No. Not you.

The cold suddenly seemed to crash in through the cracks in his armor. "What have I done?" He took a deep breath. No, no, there was no need to be afraid. No need at all. That was a mistake. "I have a destiny . . ."

Do you?

Semian stood up again. He could hear something coming on the wind. And the voice, the voice in his head. The Great Flame, coming for him. To make him whole.

He turned around as a great white shape soared up the side of the mountain to meet him. Huge, wings outstretched, filling his sight, with the sun casting a halo of fire around her. He couldn't speak, but over and over he heard the words of the priest. *Out of the sun there shall come a white dragon.*

The dragon soared closer and reached out its neck toward him. *And the dragon shall be Vengeance.* And as its jaws opened wide to carry him to his destiny, he thought he heard it speak in another voice, quite different and quite distinct.

Little one, I am hungry.

ACKNOWLEDGMENTS

Inspiration comes from all manner of sources. For *King of the Crags*, I'd like to thank a group of people who probably don't get thanked all that often, those who took the time to review *The Adamantine Palace*. You have told me what to keep and you have told me what might be made better. The result hasn't changed all that much from what it would have been without you, but it has changed a bit—and, I hope, for the better. So here's to you, reviewers and map lovers. Don't let it go to your heads, mind.

All that said, it is still very true that none of this would have happened without the trust and faith of the same special few as last time. Thank you again.

I should also acknowledge the various readers who demanded maps with menaces. For those who want to explore the world of the dragons for its own sake, you can now do so at the online gazetteer at www.stephendeas .com/gazetteer.

And thank you, readers all. My favorite people.